Dryad Dungeon

By

John Stovall

Published by
CS BOOKS, LLC

Cover Design: Darko Paganus
Editors: Amy McNulty, Nia Quinn

IF YOU WANT TO BE NOTIFIED WHEN JOHN STOVALL'S NEXT BOOK RELEASES, PLEASE VISIT HIS FACEBOOK PAGE OR CONTACT HIM DIRECTLY AT https://john-stovall-author.com/

john.w.stovall@gmail.com

DEDICATION

First, as always, to my wife, **Shami Stovall**, who has made this career, and many other things besides, possible. You are the most amazing person I know. With—and because—of you, my life has elevated multiple times. Hopefully also my writing :P

Secondly, to **Dana Ardis**, a wonderful friend who spends a ridiculous amount of time editing my books despite an active writing career of her own, and despite (sadly) moving away from us.

Thirdly, to the other members of my writers' group. To **Mary, Emily, James, Scott**, and **Ryan** thank you for the efforts you put into this as well. You've been helping me since the inception of the series and its sub-series as well. Especially to Ryan—if this book succeeds, part of it will be due to a lot of late-night SEO skull sessions.

Fourth, to my parents, **John and Gail Stovall**. Your support throughout my life has been over the top, and you are the perfect parents everyone else wished they had. And in my "master's degree in English" mother's case, one of my editors as well.

Fifth, to my editors **Nia Quinn** and **Amy McNulty**. Thanks for doing this, I know I don't make it easy.

Sixth, I'd like to thank the giants who came before me. I have long read the old staples of Science Fiction and Fantasy, found through my father's physical library, and played *Dungeons & Dragons*—which I also found through his library. But when Shami picked up authoring, I picked up Kindle, just to see how her books were doing, and I became addicted to a whole new generation of amazing authors through Kindle Unlimited. A friend recommended the Cradle series by **Will Wight.** I loved it, and the Also Boughts led to the Chaos Seeds series by **Aleron Kong,** and I discovered LitRPG. Also Boughts of that led to The Divine Dungeon series by **Dakota Krout,** which I still consider the premiere example of Dungeon Core in this genre I've come to love so much, and which I discovered through him. Every few months, I read that series again. And the Also Boughts of The Divine Dungeon led me finally to The Hapless Dungeon Fairy series by **Jonathan Brooks,** which had many of the ideas in it that led me to dream about cool things. I dreamed of those things enough to finally write my first novel, *Corrupted Core.*

In this case specifically this book was the of me dreaming of being a Chaos Seed in Aleron Kong's world. Obviously, everything diverged wildly, and I set the magic and the world in my own 'Toth' universe from the 'Fall of a Dungeon House' series, but much of the story is from all that dreaming I did. So an extra thanks on that one.

I'd also like to thank **Chris Zinn**, who recommended I start a Patreon and has stuck by me from the beginning, when no other Patreon did.

CONTENTS

Dedication iii

Chapter One
Attempt Number Three...1

Chapter Two
Follow the Great Marble Road....................................8

Chapter Three
Small, Middle, and Very Large....................................15

Chapter Four
Do Over 23

Chapter Five
The Other Made Man...31

Chapter Six
Dungeon Lord's Handbook, Part One.........................44

Chapter Seven
Dungeon Lord's Rulebook, Interrupted......................51

Chapter Eight
Business Negotiations...61

Chapter Nine
Hot Chicks 69

Chapter Ten
The No Tank Blues 81

Chapter Eleven
A Good Morning for a Beating 89

Chapter Twelve
The Dungeon Life 96

Chapter Thirteen
Level Up! 103

Chapter Fourteen
Dinner and… 115

Chapter Fifteen
The Bro(ther) 121

Chapter Sixteen
Magic Red of Tooth and Claw 129

Chapter Seventeen
Dungeon Lord's Rulebook, Part Two 137

Chapter Eighteen
Level Two Again and Three 145

Chapter Nineteen
Just Because You're Paranoid Doesn't Mean
They're Not After You...152

Chapter Twenty
Dinner with Daddy Dearest, Part I 159

Chapter Twenty-One
Dinner with Daddy Dearest, Part II 166

Chapter Twenty-Two
Just So Much Family 174

Chapter Twenty-Three
Just One More Thing in the Longest Day Ever 183

Chapter Twenty-Four
A Week of Bliss and Power Leveling.....................................190

Chapter Twenty-Five
Thea Again 197

Chapter Twenty-Seven
Zadrid's Hallow 205

Chapter Twenty-Seven
All Leveled Up 212

Chapter Twenty-Eight
I Was an Adventurer Until I Took an
Arrow to the Knee 225

Chapter Twenty-Nine
Losses… 232

Chapter Thirty
…and Gains 239

Chapter Thirty-One
The Fallen 247

Chapter Thirty-Two
How the Dryad Got His Grove Back 254

Chapter Thirty-Three
It's Good to Be the Dungeon Lord 266

Chapter Thirty-Four
Enter Belika… and One More, Itsy-Bitsy, Tiny Thing......273

Chapter Thirty-Five
Tit for Tat and Then Tit Again 281

Chapter Thirty-Six
Planning Domestic Bliss 287

Chapter Thirty-Seven
A New Look 293

Chapter Thirty-Eight
This Is More Like It 301

Table of Contents

Chapter Thirty-Nine
A Great Spot to Raise a Family 308

Chapter Forty
A Brief Idyllic Interlude..315

Chapter Forty-One
Redemption?..320

Chapter Forty-Two
District Two (But also Five)..326

Chapter Forty-Three
The Undercity of the Ancient Ones, Part I............................333

Chapter Forty-Four
The Undercity of the Ancient Ones, Part II 340

Chapter Forty-Five
The Undercity of the Ancient Ones, Part III.........................346

Chapter Forty-Six
Summonus Interruptus 352

Chapter Forty-Seven
The Father 358

Chapter Forty-Eight
The Last Remnants..363

Chapter Forty-Nine
Déjà vu, just a bit 370

Chapter One

ATTEMPT NUMBER THREE

This was Ty's third attempt at greatness. He would be less concerned if the first two hadn't been disasters.

Ty could barely contain his excitement as he stared up at his king, Leo Stardew, who was making a speech on a small stage in the center of the Grand Plaza of Star Port. His majesty's long, metallic gold hair—a sign that the king was a *full* elf, unlike Ty—sparkled in the noon sun.

Ty liked his own copper hair, as it signaled his elf heritage. Every other feature, from his round ears to his freckles, was a sign of his half-human parentage.

He grazed his fingertips over his dungeon core where it rested in the inner pocket of his best robes, the sky-blue ones. The core was smooth and round and shining with a white light. He probably should have left it in a vault somewhere, but he couldn't stand for it to be out of his reach. It would fix everything, make everyone forget about his shameful parentage.

Ty touched the crack in his dungeon core. *If it doesn't result in its own disaster,* Ty thought. *I might fail at this, too.*

Ty stared at the great tree Ygg'drasil in the background, as the king wound down his speech about the glories that everyone had shown in the recent defense of the kingdom. The tree would, supposedly soon, open gates to other worlds. Ty's dungeon would sit square in the middle of a city that straddled worlds, and he hoped he would be *extra* famous and rich as a result.

The king turned and faced Ty where he waited at the outer edge of the crowd, near the entrance to the walkway that would lead him up to the stage. "Finally, as my last act today, I would like to call Ty Bel—excuse me, Tywyndyll il Belmoria—to come forward."

Ty strode toward the stage, up the walkway. As he did, elves clapped for him, and a few waved. But one large group gave him no accolades, simply glowering at him as he walked up.

As Ty passed the glowering crowd, he heard someone mutter, "Bastard halfie will certainly make a mess of this as well. They should have given the dungeon core to a true elven noble."

Ty glanced to the lot. Helryn ap Mosstone, the ex-duke whose title came from before the original empire of Averia had fallen, stared at him balefully. It was an extra unnerving stare, his right eye ice-blue... but his left eye had an actual glowing diamond set in the socket. Ty shuddered briefly—Helryn was known to be Level Eleven, very powerful, more even than Ty's Level Six. Although Ty would certainly fight if it came to it.

Ty faced forward and tried to stride to the stage with confidence. Helryn certainly wouldn't attack him here, in front of everyone. Around Helryn, other elves sneered at Ty. Waves of pointed ears and metallic hair over said sneers mocked Ty with what he would never be.

More than Helryn himself, however, Ty feared that his detractors were right in their assessment of Ty. That he was a failure and always would be one. His captivity at the hands of the orcs, his near-death to the dragon, his rejection at the hands of every woman he had approached in his home city of Steelport, even his father sending him to live with his mother when his parents had separated... it all haunted him.

But it also drove him to overcome. He vowed to himself again that he would make the disdain of those that hated him for his heritage the fuel to drive him to greatness.

He did see one face in the crowd of ex-nobles that wasn't mocking him, however. A beautiful elven girl, with indigo eyes and copper hair that shaded toward green patina, her face a vision of youthful beauty. She caught his eye as he walked, and subtly gave him the three-finger signal of approval the elves of Averia used.

His spirits buoyed, Ty squared his shoulders as he marched the rest of the way to the stage. He was going to be an excellent dungeon lord, no matter what. He would use the dungeon to make his mother's people, the elves of Averia, wealthy and happy. By doing so, he would also earn their accolades and respect. Ty had already become a minor minister-at-large for the king and served his new people that way—now he would become a dungeon lord, far more important, and help their civilization grow to unheard-of heights.

Ty stepped onto the stage.

The king took Ty's hand and raised it up above their heads. "Tywyndyll il Belmoria, who just recently became a citizen of Averia, will be doing us all a great honor. He has agreed to use a treasure he gained, a dungeon core, to help our small civilization regrow and rebuild! He will create a dungeon here in our reborn town. In return for his generosity, I am giving him land in this plaza, the heart of our demesne, to create the entrance to that dungeon."

There were cheers at that. Dungeons were a permanent source of leveling—and even a single level gained would unlock magic for anyone that made it to Level Two. Having a dungeon made any locale far, far richer.

The king continued, still holding Ty's hand aloft. "Ty will be leaving tomorrow morning to seek a boss monster for his dungeon. That will determine what magics, monsters, and treasure will appear in his dungeon, for our people to harvest!"

There was more cheering, and Ty steeled himself—he needed to find a boss monster and beat it into submission or convince it to join him. He had had a thought, a glorious and terrible thought, on a monster that he might acquire. One of truly unprecedented power for a dungeon. But he had no idea where his potential boss was.

He knew who he might ask, however.

***

Ty stepped into the Emerald Bee. It was the only eatery and inn operating in Star Port's central district, where the Grand Plaza was. Forli, the person he needed to talk to, didn't live in town—she had just visited for the celebration. So he figured he would find her here.

The inn was a refurbished marble building. The marble had been magically melded together and hardened to make it a viable construction material for the outside of the building. All the tables, however, were made of fresh pine, and the dishes and utensils were shaped wood of various types. To cut costs but maintain an air of upper-class mystique, the proprietor, Mirafol Blueleaf, had taken the wood-shaping power at Level Two. She was creating fine works of craftsmanship, quickly learning to be a master wood crafter. The utensils had fairies carved on the ends, and the chairs had symbols of the fifteen magics and four magic high-gods carved into their handles.

Ty saw a few human ship captains in tricorn hats at one table before his eyes alighted on Forli, sitting at an empty table by herself.

Ty walked over, pulled one of the intricately carved chairs out and sat down across from her. She glanced up with a hint of fear before sagging in relief upon seeing Ty.

Forli was a dryad. Most of the dryads disappeared fifty years ago when the original Averian kingdom fell, and only a few had come back since the new kingdom had been founded. All the dryads were descended from a single 'Mother of Dryads', known as the Crone because she had existed longer than the elves' recorded history. The Crone was a progenitor, a name for a proto-god that got its start as a spirit overseeing a class of creature. Like the dryads, in this case.

Forli was the Crone's youngest daughter, the last dryad she had ever created. Ty and Forli had once worked together to set up a trading encampment, near where her tree was. Both felt themselves outsiders, for slightly different reasons, and they had developed a friendship. They had gotten to talking over watered-down wine one night. Forli had informed Ty of the fact that convinced him he might be able to have the Crone join his dungeon—the fact that the progenitor was dying.

Forli might be the Crone's youngest daughter, but she wasn't the prettiest. Cute, but not gorgeous. Most dryads were tall, willowy-thin tree people with beauty, elegance, and a decent amount of magical power. They were born from great trees, even magical ones, by planting a special seed the Crone created into the trees.

Forli had been planted in a scraggly pine tree in a mountain pass. She was short, a mere five feet, and very curvy. She appeared halfway between a human and a halfling but for her pine board skin and spikey green pine needle hair.

She was one of the nicest people Ty had ever met, however. Cute and fun beat gorgeous and sneering at Ty any day of the week.

"Ty!" she exclaimed, a smile overtaking her face. "What brings you here? Now that the ceremony is done, I figured I'd just wait till tomorrow morning and head back to Cliff Pass, but I'm surely glad to see you again."

She stood from behind the table, leaning over to try and hug him, then settled for a shoulder pat when she couldn't reach him. Most dryads simply walked around naked—a practice that Ty secretly applauded—but Forli wore a long cornshuck dress, very simple, over her form in deference to the mortals she mostly worked with.

Forli frowned. "Wait, why are you here? Shouldn't you be making a dungeon?"

"Keep your voice down," Ty admonished, glancing around.

Forli glanced around as well, her brown eyes curious. "Who are we watching out for?"

"I think Helryn might try to kill me and take the core. I don't want him, or anyone that might report to him, to overhear my plans."

"Who's Helryn?"

Ty frowned. "Never mind. Look, I need your help with my dungeon core. What do I need to pay you to assist me?"

Forli quirked one eyebrow, which appeared to be a flexible needle itself. "Um, I mean, probably nothing, Ty, I'd love to help you. I don't even know what you're asking me though. Start at the beginning, okay? For me?"

Ty took a breath. "Every dungeon core needs three things, besides itself, to become a dungeon. It needs a person with the dungeon lord perk—that's me. It needs a magical node, one that doesn't already have a dungeon. We have the Calasti Tree node, a node of Wyld magic, right here in town. But last... last it needs a boss monster. The more powerful the monster, the more powerful the dungeon."

Ty paused.

Forli leaned in, her eyes alight with excitement. "This is fascinating. Don't make me wait, you tease."

Ty leaned closer, so close they were nearly kissing. Not that a dryad would ever kiss anyone. At least, he didn't think they did that.

"I want to ask the Crone to be my boss monster," Ty whispered.

Forli sucked her breath in. "Wow, Ty. That's crazy. I did tell you that my mom is dying though, right? I mean, it might be a few decades, but it could be a few years."

"You did... but a boss monster in a dungeon becomes immortal, able to be reborn inside the dungeon even if slain by sword and magic."

Forli leaned back, her eyes so wide they threatened to flee her face. "You can save Mom? Save a progenitor? Really, Ty? You're not tricking me, right?"

"No, really, my research says it should work. But I need to find her. I don't know where she is."

Forli smiled. "Oh! That's why you came to see me! You want to find Mom, right?"

"Yeah."

"I'd do anything to help, Ty. You do know I'm the weakest dryad ever, right? Is it still okay?"

Ty nodded.

Forli continued. "I can do even better than just telling you where Mom is. I can lead you there! If I help you save Mom, then she can probably make more dryads still, so it'll be like I saved all my sisters, too! Then my sisters will all love me, even though I'm a scrag dryad!"

Ty had a huge amount of empathy for Forli's position—it mirrored his own to a degree. But... "Even if we save the Crone, I don't think she'll be able to make more dryads. But sooner or later I would think the seeds would show up as loot, once the dungeon gets strong enough. Probably... Maybe. I think so."

Forli's face sagged, but then she perked right back up. "Well, that's better than nothing. Let's do this!"

"Alright, we'll leave tomorrow morning, okay?"

"Wait, you said you were afraid of that Hell Rune guy, right?"

"Helryn, and yes. He's a tough bastard. I mean, I'll fight if he attacks me, of course. Still, I'd really rather avoid it. I don't think my odds are great."

Forli slapped the table, a wood-on-wood sound. "Then let's just leave right now! Don't wait. Get a head start on your competition and let's go!"

Ty felt his own eyes widen. "That's brilliant. I'll run and tell Dad's assistant, Cuwylla, to have him prepare the plaza for my return, and we can be off."

"Why your dad?"

Ty sighed. "He's our king's seneschal."

Chapter Two

FOLLOW THE GREAT MARBLE ROAD

It was the third day that Ty and Forli had been heading north on the great marble road, hurrying to find his boss monster. Forli was talking to him about something, but he was having trouble paying attention. For some reason, his mind was focused on the thought that his dungeon core wouldn't work because it was cracked.

All the tests had said it was still potent, that an insane amount of magic was still present in the core. But whether it would work, no one could say.

You're a fool, Ty, he thought to himself as he hurried, clutching his backpack straps tightly. *You always come up with these wild plans, but you never see them through right. They always backfire. And now you're going to try to convince a veritable god to become your dungeon boss. With a cracked core! You're going to get in trouble again. Only this time you'll take someone with you, poor little Forli.*

Who was still talking. "So, Thea, that's Mom's oldest living daughter, she told me to..."

Ty hurried on, still barely paying attention. Forli was weak and a touch slow, but she had no real limit to her stamina it seemed, so she was able to keep up with Ty's pace—not that his pace was exceptional.

Ty heard footsteps behind him, the clear tap of wooden soles on the marble road. *By Iluvin, someone did come after me!* He wondered if it was the champion of the Havi Imperium, Chester Adamant, coming to claim the core for his kingdom. Or perhaps it really was ex-Duke Helryn Mosstone, who had made his feelings on 'half-breeds' clear even before he'd become the leading member of the 'old nobility' faction in Averia.

Ty turned to face his pursuers.

There were three of them. The first was a tall and muscular elf, but a young one. He was carrying a saber in his right hand and a small shield on his left arm. The shield had the broken-and-moss-covered rock symbol of the Mosstone family on it. He had a smug, self-assured smile, indigo eyes, and copper, shading-to-green hair.

Dalryn Mosstone, Ty thought with relief. Dalryn was Helryn Mosstone's son, and while he was still trouble, he wasn't potentially unbeatable trouble like the father.

Although with his two friends, he might still be real trouble. The first companion was Elyndira, a short, iridium-haired elf with a bow in her hands. Second was Ilkoran, a weasel-faced elf with emerald-green eyes, whose hands were weaponless but clenched into fists.

Ty glanced to the side and saw that Forli had backed away down the road. She was clutching her hands in front of her chest, her brown eyes large and fearful.

For a moment, Ty was deeply afraid. But then he felt the Air magic within himself, the lightning ready to be called at a moment's notice. It was his heritage from his mother—the old dukes of Belmoria had created a magical line of Air magic, and it had carried down to Ty even though his father was a human that had purchased his captured mother to be his bed-slave.

Ty didn't know much about his enemies, but he trusted his lightning to protect him. Once, he hadn't had it, and had failed his first adventure and been captured by orcs. But not this time. This time he would protect himself and Forli both.

The three that faced him were all part of the 'old nobility' faction in Star Port that Helryn had founded. The 'old nobility' were elves from lost Averia who had fled to the Havi Imperium but never given up their titles, even though they had no lands or subjects. And now that they were back, they blamed Averia's fall on others—others whom they hated. Orcs, humans... and half-breeds like Ty. They wanted lands, titles, and wealth given to them again, simply because of who they had been once, without doing anything to help earn it back, in Ty's opinion at least.

Ty's musings were cut short as Dalryn moved forward. "Hand it over, half-breed. If anyone deserves to become a dungeon lord for Star Port, it isn't the likes of you. Give it to me and no one gets hurt."

That's direct, painfully so. Where's the witty banter? The repartee?

"So rude!" Forli whispered from behind him.

Ty felt a few sparks between his fingers as he faced the other elf on the road. "I *earned* this, Dalryn, by saving my liege's life and helping him to complete his quest to save the dwarves of Stonehaven—who have their city back and pay us taxes now. Like the *king* told your dad when he gave me the land grant. Who are you to try to take it from me?"

Dalryn sneered at him. "A full elf and the son of a duke of Averia. Not the bastard child of an ex-scion of the human family that tried to gut our kingdom once. I hardly think you have our people's best interests at heart."

Ty saw the other two nodding along.

Dalryn continued. "Besides, you have a magic bloodline that gives you more than one magic already, Ty. One that your father stole—nay, raped—from our people, which means you inherited stolen elven magic. It's time to return some."

Is he actually trying to appeal to some bizarre, insane form of fairness here? Although he has a point about my father. But

I'm not him. I shouldn't bear his sins. I've borne them long enough.

"You have a bloodline as well, Dalryn, and it's not my fault it still only gives one magic. Plus, your dad is still—"

Dalryn raised his sword and pointed it at Ty. "Enough. Give me the core, and you can live out your half-breed life. Don't, and I'll take it from you by force. I won't try and kill you, but you might die—or end up crippled, which is no way to live."

Ty raised his hand and called on the Air magic that was the legacy of his bloodline. He forged his essence into lightning in a fraction of a second and struck the tree next to Dalryn. It left a small scorch mark... and further boosted Ty's confidence.

"I'm Level Six, Dalryn. You're Level One. Even with three of you, I promise this won't go how you want."

Whatever other personal failings could be laid at Dalryn's feet—and Ty was sure there were plenty—he wasn't a coward.

"Feh. A noble elf is way better than any traitorous half-breed, and I'll prove it." Dalryn rushed at Ty, stabbing forward with his saber. Ty called the lightning again, a quick defensive use that put a field of electricity up around him. Dalryn's weapon stabbed through it, but he was shocked, and the twitching threw his aim off—he stabbed Ty's shoulder before yelling and collapsing, then rolling away.

Ty's storm shield, rank I, damages Dalryn for 2 [1x 1.2 air affinity x1.2 Occult x1.1 Occult Lightning specialty] damage and imposes a -15% accuracy to attack.

Dalryn stabs Ty for 4 [4 unmodified] damage.

Ty took an arrow to the arm from Elyndira right below the saber wound. At the same time, Ilkoran rushed forward.

Forli yelled, "Watch out!" from behind him.

Thanks, on it, Ty thought sardonically as his arm bled.

Ty's storm shield was still active and drawing on his magical essence, so he trusted it to protect him from Ilkoran. He moved to the side and fired a lightning bolt at Elyndira. It hit her and sent her to the ground, its base three damage netting him five total after his modifications to lightning damage.

Ilkoran was brave. He gritted his teeth and attempted to punch through the storm shield but ended up tensing and missing, and then falling to the ground, lightly smoking as well.

Dalryn stood, and Ty hit him with another lightning bolt. Dalryn twitched, a grunt escaping through clenched teeth before falling to the marble road, smoking similarly to Ilkoran. Mind-blowingly, however, even after two hits from lightning, Dalryn struggled to his feet again.

Gotta hand it to him—he's tough as nails and has a ton of will. Shame he's a complete weed.

Ty hit him again, hoping he wouldn't kill the jackass. Dalryn finally collapsed, not moving but for the faint rise and fall of his chest.

"Wow," Forli said, walking up beside Ty. "That was impressive, Ty. You always kinda struck me as, um, *refined*, I guess. Not violent. But yeah—impressive."

The other two must have thought the same thing, because even though they weren't incapacitated, they didn't move against Ty. Instead, they remained on the ground—in Elyndira's case, with hands away from her weapon. Ty raised an eyebrow and nodded his head to the bushes, and Elyndira, still lying prone on the ground, kicked her bow into the underbrush.

Which Ty appreciated, as he didn't want to be forced to finish them off.

Ty did give some honest thought to the proposition of just killing them. *They attacked me—and were obviously willing to chance murdering me—in order to take the dungeon core I won. I mean, at some level, they totally deserve to die.*

Ty didn't have the heart to execute three elves, all in their late forties like him—which for an elf was about the same as seventeen in a human. He was a touch physically older from his human parentage, but not much.

And he thought Forli might disapprove. She had been kind to him, a friend whose naturally sunny disposition offset his gloomy and darker nature. Not to mention that she was helping him find the Crone. Ty didn't want to reward her kindness in helping him with trauma.

"Dalryn's daddy isn't here to save you, huh?" Ty asked, trying to ignore the pain in his arm. The two blows had taken more than half his health and hurt like crazy. Which also wasn't helping the case for sparing the miscreants. The precious blood running down his arm and dripping to splatter on the detritus-covered marble road argued for finishing them off.

Elyndira shook her head *no*. "Dalryn said that if his dad came, the duke would take it and make himself the dungeon lord, and probably kill you as well. We didn't tell his dad that we had learned where you were going, okay?"

He was worried his dad would kill me?

"How *did* you learn where I was going?"

"Dalryn didn't tell me that."

Ty hit a tree near her with a blast of his lightning.

Elyndira screamed and covered her face. "Please, Ty! Please don't kill me! I'm sorry. I don't know how he found out. I swear to Iluvin Eturia!"

Then she made a brief speech in High Averian—a beautiful, melodic language that Ty didn't understand. Her hands were held palm up, and tears leaked from her eyes. She seemed sincere.

But she could have been using the language of the upper class of his mother's people to insult him, for all he understood it. And it rankled him.

I'll never be one of them, no matter how hard I try. I won't be a slave-trading banker like my father's people, and I can't be a noble and cultured high elf like my mother's people. Hell, I can remember the last rejection from Yen, who was a slave, *back in*

13

Steelport. Yet even though she was the lowest of the low, I wasn't good enough. No one wants me to belong, and they won't let me. Dalryn and his ilk, Elyndira, all of them, won't let me. I have nowhere to belong...

He felt his essence gathering and saw fear invade Elyndira's eyes.

She held her hands out in front of her, as if she could push Ty away. *"Please!"*

Forli echoed it from beside him, her whispered "Please" joining Elyndira's.

Ty let his hands fall. He didn't have the heart to kill her anyway.

Also, if I'm a dungeon lord, I can still build somewhere for me to belong. Become strong enough to take care of my own people, rich enough to build my own family. Their disdain won't matter anymore.

"Run. Leave your weapons and Dalryn's. But take him with you. If I see you on this road again, I'll kill you. I have more important things to do than finish off weeds like you."

"I—" Elyndira began.

"Go!"

Ilkoran and Elyndira stood and then grabbed Dalryn. Then they began, with difficulty, dragging his body back down the road. Ty guessed Dalryn would wake soon and worried he might plan a rematch—especially since Ty was wounded.

If they did, however, the power of the storm that was Ty's would serve him again.

Ty turned to Forli, and nodded his head to the north.

"Let's go."

"What about your arm?"

"I have more important things to worry about."

Chapter Three

SMALL, MIDDLE, AND VERY LARGE.

It turned out, Forli hadn't actually known where the Crone was. But she had known where Thea, the Crone's eldest daughter was, and she knew that the Crone had entrusted her location—which was nearby—to Thea.

Right now, they were in a very idyllic grove around a small pond, looking at a beautiful—and absolutely gigantic—willow tree. Everything about the location was lush. Berry bushes grew, bees buzzed, the grass was perfectly green... but nothing seemed dangerous. No thorns or predators that Ty could see.

But nothing compared to the willow, which towered hundreds of feet into the air, and whose branches delicately fell to create almost a perfect curtain around the tree.

Forli stepped forward, put her hands to her mouth as a small cone, and called out, "Thea, it's me! Your sister, Forli! Come out, come out wherever you are!"

Thea stepped from the willow in the center of the Grove. She was five-foot-ten, thin and graceful, and beyond gorgeous in the dryad fashion. She had long deep green leaf hair, honey wood-colored skin, and perfectly symmetrical features.

She was also utterly naked, and Ty, after an embarrassing lapse, faced his eyes skyward, feeling his cheeks burn—although he knew dryads cared not at all if he gazed.

"What brings you here, Forli?" Thea asked, her voice almost musical. She held her hand out and a few butterflies flitted over and landed on it.

Forli nervously tapped her fingers together. "Hey Sis. So, true story. Ty here thinks he can save Mo—um, save the Crone."

"That's not possible for a mortal," Thea said, not deigning to address Ty directly, or even take her eyes from her sister.

Forli half-turned to Ty, motioning to him. "Well, he has a dungeon core. If Mom becomes his dungeon boss, then she'll be immortal. And perhaps more seeds of our future sisters will be born from the dungeon. Ty thinks it could happen, and he's super smart."

Thea thought for a moment. "Well... I was told not to admit anyone to the Heart of the Forest to see the Crone fifty years ago. But, I have to admit, sister, you tempt me to violate that rule now—a second time, I might add—as that is... potentially wonderful. I didn't even know we had any dungeon cores on this continent."

Forli nodded to Thea's words as if subconsciously trying to encourage her. "I think it'll work. Please, Thea—let's at least try, okay?"

Thea considered for a few seconds longer, then gave a firm nod. "Very well—if it doesn't work, the Crone can punish him. But the chance it does is worth the violation. I would want this as well, very much. Let's be off."

That easy? Ty thought. He hadn't even spoken! Thea must have *really* wanted some chance to save her mother.

Ty had another thought and took a chance to speak. "Actually, fair Thea, would you be willing to heal me, perhaps? I find myself... perforated."

Thea chuckled, then reached one willowy arm out, her grace somehow perfect even in that tiny movement, and touched his shoulder. A wave of Wyld magic, that felt like the essence of spring, renewal, and new growth distilled, passed through him. His wounds healed, and then the scabs fell off. An unblemished, uninjured arm was all that remained.

Thea uses regeneration, Rank V on Ty. You receive 8 health per 6 seconds.

It all happened extremely quickly, but Ty was staring at Thea, and he knew his own eyes were huge now. *She has to be at least Level Twenty to have a rank V ability! That's amazing!*

She smiled a small, smug smile at him. "It'll be about twelve hours of walking to reach the Crone," Thea said, turning, her perfect rear exposed as she walked away. Forli hurried after Thea, the shorter dryad's curves bouncing as she walked.

***

Finally, close to fourteen hours later—when Ty was exhausted far past the point of anything more than the vaguest appreciation of the naked dryad he was walking near—the three broke out from the latest path they were travelling.

They entered into the Heart of the Forest, a huge glade. It was a couple hundred feet across, with most of it shielded from the sky by a single great tree, its gnarled branches thrust into the sky. The tree was truly massive, a couple hundred feet tall and spread widely across the heavens. Dappled light came down through the thick leaf canopy, and there were patches of moss on the few stones in the glade, giving it an ancient feel. A few bees and butterflies flitted about, and the air felt tranquil.

About twenty dryads, most similar in appearance to Thea—green leaves for hair, slightly brown woodgrain skin, but still utterly beautiful and utterly naked—lounged around the grove. At the far end, near a large pond, sat the target of his expedition—the Crone herself.

She was sitting on a moss-covered rock, her feet in the water of the pond. Ty had heard she was over ten thousand years old, and she *looked* it. The dryad was probably ten feet tall standing, but she sat hunched over. Her limbs, even though wood, appeared shriveled. White moss hung down around her head and face, and the wood that was her skin was wrinkly like old human skin but cracked in places like untreated wood as well.

But Ty could feel her power. It felt ancient, primeval, and it radiated from her in waves. Ty found his attention drawn to her as the strength of her magic compelled his attention, despite the youthful-appearing beauty of the others around him.

Thea stepped in front of Ty, bowing almost double while facing the Crone. "I brought visitors, progenitor. I know you bade me not to, but please, hear them out."

"Welcome to my home," the Crone rasped out, her voice cracking branches and the speech of a very old woman mixed together. She didn't gesture much as she spoke, only shifting slightly on her rock. "And welcome to our heart, my youngest."

Ty bowed deeply, hand over heart, in the Averian fashion. "Thank you for having me, progenitor. I am deeply honored and privileged to be allowed into your home and your presence, and to be able to present my proposal that you become my dungeon boss and live forever."

Forli bowed as well next to him, but the Crone ignored her after the initial welcome.

The Crone gave a raspy chuckle. "You're smooth, aren't you, Tywyndyll? And polite. Not like the Wyld magic I represent at all, are you?"

"I...?" *What?* "Yes, I'm polite? But why does that make me unlike your magic?"

"Nature is never polite. It might be eating your face, it might be a subtle dance of tree, flower, and bee. It might be invisible, a stalking panther ready to pounce. But never polite."

"I guess I hadn't thought of it that way. Should I be rude?"

How did I get into this bizarre conversation?

The Crone shifted on her stone again, as if she were shifting a weight on her shoulder. "Where did you learn this politeness, and why do you use it?"

Ty hadn't really considered it, but, in the face of questioning by a near-god, gave it some honest thought.

"I use it because it's the most likely demeanor to get me what I want without getting me in trouble. I guess I learned it from my father, one of the very few things he taught me."

"Don't care for your father much, do you, youngling?"

"He was a slaver and a rapist," Ty said. *And human. Who gave me up after getting us tossed from his wealthy house. He's why I have no place I belong.*

"True, for as far as it goes. Does it mean nothing, then, that your father turned from the path he knew his whole life, from wealth, power, and prestige, to set your mother free? That he gave up his power and control over others, his luxury, and turned to the path of good without being forced to it?"

"How... How do you know that?"

"I hear things, youngling. Like how the new kingdom you've joined has itself a human seneschal. Your father. But enough of that—answer my question."

"Of course it means something. But his actions had consequences."

"Hmm..." the Crone said, staring at him with her nearly empty eye sockets. The silence stretched uncomfortably.

Ty was sick of discussing his father. "Wouldn't you rather talk about my proposal? To become a dungeon boss?"

She gave a sigh of long suffering. "Mayhap. But on the other branch, perhaps knowing whose garden I will plant myself in forever is a worthwhile way to pass time. If I become your dungeon boss, I have no say anymore. You choose the rooms of the dungeon—all I can do is advise you. Plus I can choose to reveal, or not reveal, the secret paths to power that are unique to the dungeon I will form. It's a very small tool with which to accomplish my goals. I'm not sure I want to take that path, and learning about you will make my decision easier."

"I understood the alternative was dying," Ty said cautiously, noting that the dryads were all slowly making their way closer to him. He was a hundred percent positive that the Crone could kill him fine without help, but still, their closing ranks felt... sinister, somehow.

Ty ignored the dryads moving closer and continued. "When your daughter Forli and I were friends in Cliff Pass together, she told me that you were almost at the end of your time on this world, and I read that a dungeon boss is immortal."

"Yes. I have very little time left. A few decades at most, a few years more likely. My power has, finally, faded from this world."

Ty spread his hands, still eyeing the dryads approaching through the glade. "Well, then."

The Crone gave a raspy laugh that turned into a cough. "Well, what, youngling? You think I'm afraid to die, to leave this world? That a chance at immortality is an unbeatable argument for me to join you and serve you?"

Ty felt his face heat. He *had* thought that.

The Crone gave another raspy laugh. "I like that the current batch of elves are a bit more honest. Or at least their cheeks are. But know, youngling, that you've got a frog's position. I took, and lost, multiple progenitor lovers before the Dark God Cyr even started his big hoorah."

Big hoorah? Ty thought wryly. *The cataclysm was a big hoorah?*

"I saw the earliest stripling high elves of Averia when they were first fumbling together a city. When I saw them, I rejoiced, you hear? I rejoiced because *I had also seen* the rise of the Ancient Ones and their depravity before the elves. I saw those blighters build the *undercity* of Calasti, the city that is now but a layer that the *current* ruins rest on."

Okay, yeah, you're super old. It's genuinely impressive, but—

The Crone wasn't done. "I have seen twenty-eight progenitors of the forest rise, nineteen whose very *names* are now lost.

And in the forest of Averia alone, I have seen six dark progenitors rise and I was involved in putting all of them down."

She paused in her tirade for a moment, and Ty politely waited. "I'm tired. Tired to my very roots. I'm ready to give up this toil and accept that I failed in my attempt to rise to the next stage. Of all the beings like me whom I've ever heard of, whether they take the name proto-god, progenitor, abomination, herald, or some other silly title, all failed or ascended in less than half the time I have managed to just stay me."

The sheer depth of time and experience that the Crone had experienced was shocking to Ty, and he just bowed again, hand over heart.

The Crone coughed, a longer series, and Ty wondered what could be stuck in *her* throat, or if this was just some metamagical representation of her failing nature.

Then she jabbed her sharp, branch-like finger in his direction again. "So it behooves you, youngling, to answer my question. Did your father redeem himself by giving up his wealth and power to set your mother free? Because if you don't answer, or if I think you lied, I will happily choose to be done with it all."

Ty really didn't want to talk about it, but the Crone had made clear that if he refused to answer, his whole plan would fall apart. He didn't have another boss monster in mind if she turned the offer down.

And the dryads had all gathered very close in the dark glade. Some merely had to reach their hands out to grab him.

Even Forli was clutching her limbs to herself, looking at her sisters with wide eyes and biting her lip.

Up close, they all appeared slightly different—different-colored wood skin or eyes, and hair that might have been vines, or moss, or hanging leaves. Ty suspected that they'd come from different trees, some magical, some mundane.

He tried not to notice their slightly different womanly parts, either. But every culture he had grown up in had possessed a nudity taboo, and seeing naked women all around him made it hard to stay focused.

Although they all had a hard cast to their features that made that a bit easier than it normally would be for Ty. He figured he better answer the Crone for his personal safety as well. "It's hard to come back from such a thing, but I'll accept that perhaps he did redeem himself. While my mother will never love him, she does feel that he is morally clean, and she was the wronged party. But it was arrogance that made him conceive the terrible plan in the first place, and it was arrogance that caused him to decide for me and my sister that we would grow up poor with my mother when she left him, and to strip from us the chance to be scions of House Orsini. He could have kept us in the divorce—he had all the power. Then we would have been heirs to seats in its ruling structure. So even if he redeemed himself of the one act, even his redemption requires redemption."

The Crone took a moment to answer. "House Orsini is a pack of jackals, run by those who deal with the Blood Tribes of the orcs and a hundred different slavers. Every member of its council is evil. And the realm your family comes from, the city Steelport, is a filthy human hive built on breaking the land as well as war against others. Would you rather have been one of them, youngling?"

"I could have reformed them, if I'd inherited a council seat, like I should have."

The Crone laughed. "I would be curious to see if you would have reformed them, or if you'd have been corrupted, youngling. Very, very few have the moral fortitude to spurn the seat they sit on. But I judge you have answered honestly, at least."

"You'll join me, then?"

"Hmm..." the Crone said, pondering. "Honest is not the same as *well*. But you're young, and you do seem to try for the good..."

Ty waited, his breath held, for her answer, praying to a whole host of gods that his own answer had been good enough.

Chapter Four

DO OVER

"Fine, I'll do it," the Crone said.

Before Ty could respond, the sky was suddenly filled with light, as if the sun had risen early. A great eagle with a forty-foot wingspan, glowing with sunlight, dropped into the clearing. With him came noon. Even the sky appeared to lighten, and vibrant colors of the glade—crystal-blue pond, deep-green leaves, and flowers in every color of the rainbow— became as clear as the noon day the sky now resembled.

As the great eagle descended, Ty felt the magic, magic of Air and Light. It felt like a summer breeze, a run on the plains, the wind beneath him as he soared.

But the bird's face was somehow... somber, and the wind stopped blowing almost immediately.

The trees around one edge of the clearing moved to the sides, and a huge wolf, ten feet at the shoulder, enormously gravid, entered the clearing, numerous small pups following behind her. But the pups didn't frolic, and the wolf walked slow, head down, tail tucked between her legs.

With her came Wyld magic, fertile and virile, but also red of tooth and claw, the sensation of hunting and being hunted through a great forest.

Ty knew of these two—the progenitors of the sun eagles and the ghost wolves, mystical beasts that were allied with the elves of the Kingdom of Averia. The other two progenitors of the forest faction, each nearly as strong as the Crone.

But why are they here? Ty thought, clutching the dungeon core tighter to his chest.

"Worry not, youngling," the Crone said. "They come to pay me respect as I make my way to be your dungeon boss and leave them to defend the forest and its allies by themselves. Unneighborly of me, I suppose, but it's my time. Leading the forest is a mantle I have carried for ages beyond count. I have led many coalitions of progenitors. One of these, my allies, can do it now. And they can act as my funeral procession as we head south. I like that. It's the least they can do after all I've done for the forest."

"It's not a funeral procession..." Ty said, lamely, still mostly thinking, *she'll do it, she'll do it!*

"Eh, it is for my involvement with the forest. Close enough, youngling," the Crone said, then stretched and slowly got to her feet. "Well, enough of your inane chatter. Let's get walking, we've got a ways to go."

***

It took five days, almost twice as long, to get back.

The Crone walked like an old woman—slowly. She made up for it to a degree with her long stride, but mostly she would have made up for it by never needing to rest. Instead, she was forced to stop because Ty couldn't handle more than about eight hours a day of walking on a consistent basis, his frail elven form not suited to long distances. The fourteen he had done to get to the Crone in the first place had left him sore and tired.

It was an easy time, however. Most of the dryads could make any plant generate its fruit even though it was winter, and Ty ate very well on a vegetarian diet. The walk back through the forest was idyllic. The occasionally moss-covered floor of the forest and the leaves of the trees that hadn't given into winter gave the place a healthy, green look. The air was filled with the scents of nature, and occasionally he saw bunnies rushing about, a touch thin but still basically healthy amid the easy winters of his new land.

And no one would bother the powerful progenitors of the forest.

As they all walked south, Ty talked to many of the dryads—Forli the most by a wide margin, but he spoke to Thea quite a bit as well. He learned a few things about 'the forest', the faction that the Crone was part of, along with the progenitors of the ghost wolves and the sun eagles that had come to pay their respects. It was a 'mortals and nature in harmony' kind of faction that Ty could get behind.

Over time, the road began to show the ruins of old Calasti, the elven capital from before the fall of the first Averian kingdom. Shattered houses of marble, smaller paths off the main road, and occasional rotted fences all signaled that they were getting close to Star Port, which was a town built in the heart of the old ruins. They would head south for another couple miles and then reach the wall that let them into the Central District of Star Port.

When they were within shouting distance of the north gate, the Crone stopped them.

"Are we close enough, Ty?" she asked.

He looked at the walls, a few minutes away. "Yes, easily."

The Crone sighed. "Then now is the time. I would merge with your dungeon here, rather than enter the city and create a spectacle. I've no interest in that sort of thing any longer."

Ty pulled the dungeon core out, staring at the handkerchief-covered crystal in his hand.

It's strange that none of my family—mother, father, sister—or my liege are here, but a bunch of random progenitors are.

Ty took out the crystal, unwrapping it from the handkerchief he carried it in, and triggered the dungeon core.

Instantly, he could sense the crystal's desire for a boss monster—and it would find something, even if only a frog or a fly, it he didn't give it one near immediately.

The Crone reached out—gingerly, for all her talk of not fearing the end—and touched the crystal with a crooked, branch-like finger, similar to how she had poked Ty in the chest.

> The Crone of Averia wishes to become a boss monster for the dungeon. She has the magic of Wyld, is a Level-88 proto-god, is sentient, and is considered a 'Tier-4 boss' for a dungeon. Once chosen, a boss monster may never change. Accept Y/N?

Yes, Ty thought at it, and without any fanfare at all beyond a 'pop' on inward-rushing air, the Crone of Averia disappeared.

The core didn't shatter, much to Ty's relief. But he felt the potential in his hands, mighty magic contained within the dungeon core, ready to explode. He was still hyper-aware of the crack in it.

The two progenitors each gave a half-bow—awkward on a bird and a wolf—before the wolf walked into the forest and the forty-foot-long sun eagle progenitor let out a mighty screech and flew into the air, heading east.

Ty hurried south along the road, reaching the huge, twenty-foot-tall, magically reinforced marble gate around the old city of Calasti, and the north gate. An elven soldier named Vyneal Iron-branch waved him through with wide eyes as Ty and a gaggle of naked dryads hurried into the city.

He found his plot in the marble plaza cleared completely, and he stood. A small crowd of about fifty had followed him as he rushed through the city, and Ty could see various people spilling from the Adventurers' Guild—the guild leader, Kadrath, a nearly six-and-a-half-foot-tall dworc—half-orc, half-dwarf—the most obvious in his massive plate armor. But he also saw the beautiful elf girl with copper hair and indigo eyes, the one that had given him the three-fingers of approval sign when he had accepted the plot of land from King Leo.

As the crowd gathered, Ty, a bit self-consciously, held his cracked dungeon core in his hand, staring balefully at the imperfection. He couldn't help but think that this was the moment of truth—and that he had failed these moments of truth before. The core hummed with the power of the Crone, vibrating in his hand, and Ty knew he only had about thirty minutes before the core established itself with or without his consent.

He was afraid, however. Afraid of what his damaged dungeon core would do.

He saw the guildmaster, the hopeful dryads, the beautiful mystery elf... all looking at him, faces excited and hopeful. But still he hesitated.

What finally drove him—beyond his own feelings of inadequacy that he hoped to quell by becoming a dungeon lord—was curiosity. He knew that his dungeon would gain three magics. Normally, all three came from the boss monster. But the Crone only had Wyld magic, the magic of nature in all its aspects—agriculture, red of tooth and claw, idyllic. She had no other types of magic.

And there were a lot of fascinating possibilities.

There were the most common elemental magics, of course, like Ty's own Air magic that gave him access to the lightning abilities he had learned. Or Earth, which would likely synergize well with Wyld magic.

Or perhaps Light or Eclipse magics—Light magic would also synergize well with Wyld, and Eclipse magic had extremely cool shadow powers—Ty had once briefly adventured with a deep elf teenager named Zir who had fought with blades lengthened with solid shadows, and slipped from location to location through magical darkness. That could be cool.

Then there were the Being magics. A mind dungeon with illusions and increased knowledge might be fascinating, although it didn't synergize with Wyld well. A Body magic dungeon focused on increased physical stats, healing, and alteration, or a Soul and Wyld combo dungeon that gave access to familiars could both also be amazing.

The rare magic of Metal, the magic of organization, civilization, and crafting, could be a good fit. It would seem that a Wyld and Metal dungeon would make for excellent agriculture.

Ty prayed to Iluvin Eturia, goddess of Wyld magic, that he wouldn't get Entropy magic. While powerful, the death magic was usually used for evil and utterly gross, with pollution effects and undead monstrosities, and Ty wanted no part of it.

There were other magics, but they weren't ever acquired by dungeons—the Ascendency magics.

At the end of the day, Ty had to *know* what his dungeon, and his own powers, would be.

Ty took the core and placed it down into the ground, selecting 'yes' from the notification window.

The world disappeared.

For a brief moment, Ty felt as if he were floating in nothingness. Then he saw the *potential* form, the patterns of the building blocks that *could* become his dungeon if he gathered the power to actualize them. Hundreds of building blocks, from the most easily accessible up to vague eldritch patterns of power untold that needed grand artifacts from the outside world to trigger their formation.

Each block could also act as the basis for others, an ever-expanding magical pattern that, despite a start dictated by the form of the forest progenitor near him, could head in thousands of different ways, becoming tens of thousands of different dungeons, from useful and idyllic resource producer to dreadful murder machine.

But this pattern was broken, much like the core that Ty had carried.

The power from the broken core spilled out, his dungeon damaged and trying to repair itself, the magic knotting in new ways. But power still escaped, and it had to go somewhere in the nothingness. Much like the lightning that Ty commanded, it flowed along the path of least resistance, down the existing magical connection to Ty.

Ty could sense that the magic should have destroyed him—it should have utterly obliterated him, in fact. But for a moment, Ty felt some presence, arcane and eldritch, in the nothingness with him. And it *guided* the magic, for just a moment, attaching it to Ty slightly differently than it had been.

Ty was shocked by the presence of the inexplicable mystery entity, but it disappeared almost immediately.

The dungeon was still incomplete, however, and neither it nor Ty could reform until it was complete. It needed three magics before it could assume its true form.

It searched for something to gather the magic from, and the power washed over Ty again. Ty knew the dungeon was evaluating him—the weakness he had before he mastered his lightning, and the strength he drew from it to overcome the most recent challenge against Dalryn. Also the fact that he had a perk called 'Line of Belmoria' that gave him advanced Air magic.

It was enough, and the dungeon became a dungeon of Air magic as well.

Air was the magic of wind and weather. Of travel and lightning and archers. Of those that traded for a living rather than built for a living. It was the magic of those that liked new things and places, and were willing to step outside the box a bit to accomplish their goals, to live outside of the strictures society placed on them.

Wyld and Air magic, Ty thought, but the dungeon needed more, a third magic.

Ty also cared about people. He had strong emotions about a great many things. He sought magical power. Ty also sought the approval of others, and the connections that could be made. He had sought a true sapient ally in the Crone, not a mere boss monster to order around.

At the same time, he caught fragments of the Crone's visions. Of a time when she had been a progenitor of the forest that had opposed all habitation by mortals. But dark powers had risen, and she had allied with a mortal champion and then become his lover. She had also allied with other progenitors like herself, to put down evil. After, she had grown ever closer to different mortals.

And he remembered how, even when she had agreed to become his boss monster, she had been surrounded by her family and her allies—the latest in a long, long line of those allies.

Ty and the Crone shared a characteristic of personality that informed the last magic the dungeon took—Soul magic. Soul magic was the magic that governed two things. First was the concepts around emotions, interactions, communication, relationship... things revealed as important to them by the experiences of both. Things that were important to a person who desperately sought a place to belong. And also important to a being who allied with others beyond her own circle to advance the needs of her people and her cause.

Second, it was also the magic of magic. And this dungeon was becoming a font of bizarre magic as the link to Ty intensified and magic poured down it, linking the two souls as part of the dungeon.

The power of the dungeon was finally complete, and poured into Ty, changing him fundamentally and forever.

Chapter Five

THE OTHER MADE MAN

Now that the dungeon had chosen, Soul, Air, and Wyld magic poured from the outside, into the dungeon and out of the damaged pattern and down the link into Ty as well. He felt the magic of the Crone, overwhelmingly powerful, flow into him, as his nature changed. He stopped being a half-elf, and instead became... something else.

Skin hardened, and magic replaced biology. He felt himself losing much of what he had become as a half-elf—his levels, his mastery of lightning magic. In his soul, he knew that he was barely mortal anymore. As he floated in nothingness, he reached down, and soft wooden fingers brushed supple wooden skin.

Dryad.

But not just any dryad.

The magic of the dungeon had changed him, making him similar to itself. He could sense hundreds of new routes to power, secret ways to change and grow that weren't available to most half-elves or dryads—they were unavailable to most mortals, really. Ty couldn't make them out in detail, but they were there.

With a thump the dungeon managed to finish, closing the slightly broken link off, and the magic stopped pouring into Ty. His form, his very *nature*, solidified, and he dropped into the new reality of the dungeon.

Ty returned to full consciousness inside a stone cavern. He managed to groan, then rolled over, his skin 'feeling' the stone ground he was on, but even when rocks jabbed him, it didn't hurt.

His status chart wasn't anywhere to be seen, and Ty pulled it up again as he lay on his back, half-conscious from whatever had happened to him. Over his status sheet was a blinking notification, telling him to pick a 'branching path perk,' but he had no idea what that meant. He dismissed it for a moment to focus on his chart.

Tywyndyll il Belmoria						
Level One	Air, Soul, Wyld					
Health	12	Stamina	12	Essence		10
Level Stats						
Strength	12	180 base pound-lifting capacity, +10% melee damage, +6% running speed.				
Agility	8	+10% enemy hit chance, -10% hit chance with all weapons, -4% running speed				
Dexterity	8	-10% base success for crafting and physical skill success rate, 20% chance to lower base weapon damage roll by one step				
Endurance	12	+2 base Stamina, +10% Stamina Recovery Rate, +10% base Health Recovery Rate				
Toughness	14	+2 base Health, +10% base Health, +10% base Stamina, +1 to resist poison, disease, and physical status effects				
Perception	10					
Connection	10	+00% Essence recovery rate (17/day)				
Capacity	10	+0 Base essence, +00% essence				
Appearance	10					

Non-Level Stats		
Intelligence	16	+60% skill acquisition rate.
Magic	14	+16% Magic Effects. +1 Maximum affinity.
Charisma	10	+00% perceived social skills
Luck	10	The Fates neither dislike nor care for you
Secondary Stats		
Air Affinity	1	-10% essence cost to all Air abilities, +10% effect for all Air abilities or +1 to the difficulty to resist
Armor	1	-1 from all physical damage
Birth Perks		
Race: Master Dryad		Unique
		+2 to Strength and Endurance. +4 to Toughness. -2 to Agility and Dexterity. +1 armor.
		+4 to Magic stat base
		Tireless (Needs only 2 hours of sleep per 24-hour period.)
		Gain an additional Wyld ability at Levels 2, 10, and every multiple of 10 thereafter.
		Immortal.
		Access to the 'branching path.' One pick per ten levels of the bonded dungeon.
		May breed with female dryads, producing dryad seeds. Female dryads will feel attraction to you.
Rank: Natural		May obtain Level 80 without ascension. Access to a significant number of rare or upgraded magical abilities.

Remnants of the Storm	The levels and power were altered and assisted by the magic that came down the dungeon to you. The Belmoria magic line, and five gained levels as a lightning mage, have been combined to this perk. Gain 1 extra Air ability at Level 5 and every 10 levels thereafter. Gain Air auras 15 levels early. Gain +1 actual and +1 maximum Air affinity.
Dungeon Lord	You may become a dungeon lord
Smart	+6 intelligence
Acquired Perks	
Bonded Dungeon Lord of the Dungeon of the Dryad's Grove	No powers of the dungeon lord are gained. Instead, powers taken through the 'branching path' may synergize with the dungeon.
Polite	Naturally inoffensive. -10% chance for someone to take offense to your position on a matter.

Skills	Level	Effect
Academics	5	Moderate understanding of history, culture, geography, and important people throughout the world Special Level 10 skill: Encyclopedia of Magical Phenomena: +5 effective skill level to recognize magical phenomena.
Architecture	3	+3% to final building quality, may build basic buildings
Administration	9	-5% to realm administration costs, -18% to business costs
Athletics	1	+3% to run speed, +1 to check to climb or avoid obstacles
Business	3	+15% to expected income, and -3% to expected costs, for operating any business
Cooking	5	+25% quality to cooking

Dodge	3	+9% to dodge incoming attacks
Farming	4	+16% to base farming output
Imbuing	7	May use advanced lesser rituals in magics possessed to create items
Leadership	2	People consider you to have 4% more status than you do, and if they are followers, are willing to accept conditions 2% worse than baseline without complaint
Natural Sciences	4	You have a solid grasp of basic concepts
Occult	9	You can sense magic that is not concealed that is connected to you, whose area of effect you are in, or that is within 9 feet of you. Your magic powers have 18% greater effect. You can sense the purpose of simple magic and vaguely discern more complicated magical purposes. +18% to accuracy with magic attacks.
Seduction	1	People find your attempts to seduce them 2% more favorable than baseline, compared to what they are looking for
Survival	1	+3% hunting and foraging
Sword	3	+12% damage with swords, +12% to hit with swords

Abilities	Effect
Air	
N/A	
Soul	
N/A	
Wyld	
N/A	

The Branching Path (1 available)	
Abilities	Effect
N/A	

Ty stared in absolute shock at all that had transpired. It was almost impossible to take it all in.

His first thought was a lament. *I lost all my levels! I was Level Six! That's way higher than the vast majority of people ever make!*

He had possessed his solid lightning abilities, the ones he had used to defeat Dalryn. That was within Air magic, of course. But he had also had some minor plant growth powers in Wyld. He'd been hoping to become a hybrid lightning and plant growth aura mage. It would make him extremely valuable to a civilization—and probably extremely well-respected—but also able to fight and adventure and stop bad things from happening to himself and those he cared for.

He supposed he could rebuild that, and perhaps even be a bit stronger, as he still got bonus Air abilities... but still, losing his levels was downright *blighted*.

But it was far more than that. He had been a half-elf—well, technically a half-high-elf—before. Now he was a 'master dryad,' and could propagate the dryad species somehow. Since the Crone had been lost, and she was the main source of new dryads, Ty supposed that was a good thing, but it was utterly alien to any thought he had ever had for his own future.

Plus, he was a 'natural' magic soul, with a maximum level of eighty. Before he had been a remarkable soul, with a maximum level of seventy and weaker special abilities.

He was also clumsy but tough compared to before. He wondered how much he would notice the difference.

He raised his hand up again, staring at it. Previously, he had pale, milky white skin, and now he had slightly brownish skin with a muted woodgrain pattern in it. But it moved and felt barely different than his old arm.

He reached up and touched it with his other hand. Perhaps a touch smoother, cooler, and just the tiniest bit harder.

Ty sighed. He couldn't decide if this was good or bad, but things had certainly gone sideways on him at some level. *It never quite works out the way I wanted. I wanted to marry a nice, cute elf girl now that I was rich and powerful, and my children would become full elves, hopefully. I'd have had a ton of kids, gotten a great mansion with a huge orchard, been a respected member of elven society, rich and important.*

Instead, I turned myself into a tree. Well, tree-person.

Ty rolled to his knees, then looked around him.

He knelt in a huge cavern. The cavern was boring, frankly. Huge, but empty, with stalagmites and stalactites occasionally placed, and a single exit out. There were glowing bioluminescent mushrooms around, but that was the extent of the décor.

As Ty glanced around the cavern, space *twisted* in the center, and the Crone appeared, writhing on the ground. Magic coursed through her as well, and she started to grow younger. Her skin smoothed, her knobby joints became normal, her white-moss hair lengthened, thickened, and turned leaf green. She de-aged before his eyes, until she appeared to be in her early to mid-twenties, wrinkle and crack free.

Her eyes were still wooden sockets, but they now had a powerful green glow coming from them, a magic aura so strong it was almost a normal eye in appearance. Her hair was a cascade of tiny leaves, giving the impression on long, wavy green hair down her back. Her skin was brown, with a straight wood grain pattern throughout it, but she moved with a sinuousness wholly animal. And she grew a bit, till she was nearer to twelve feet tall.

A scent of spring and flowers wafted from her.

The Crone's magic also felt different. Before, it had felt old, primeval. Now, he could sense a *playfulness* to it. A picnic, perhaps, in a beautiful fairy grove. Or perhaps newborn magical beasts chasing leaves that the wind blew through a forest of glowing flowers. It was *more* than it had been before, and even apart from what her body looked like, Ty could sense the renewal from her magic.

Ty had *so much* to ask, but first, he had a question, one that truly perplexed him. "Are you still... you?"

The Crone—which was an extra weird name now—smiled at him. "My power is the same no matter how I appear—but the form reflects me, and the renewal I have received. But I am not as I once was, when I was playful, whimsical, and *reckless*. I would not be that one again if I could help it. But this... this is good. I haven't felt mature in my power in hundreds of years, maybe thousands."

That makes sense, I guess, Ty thought.

Then the Crone focused on him again. "I also feel an attraction to you. An attraction I have felt to no man in thousands of years. I could always have relations with men, unlike normal dryads, but this feels different. What did you do?"

"Apparently the magic of the dungeon... altered me. I'm no longer a half-elf. I'm a 'master dryad,' a unique race. It makes me capable of siring new dryad seeds, with dryads. The, well... the usual way—for mortals. Not dryads."

"Interesting. And fortuitous at some level, since my status chart informs me that I'm unable to propagate dryads any longer. Any other changes?"

"I get something called 'The branching path' that lets me gain new perks whenever the dungeon makes ten levels. And one now I think. But I haven't looked at it yet."

"Hmm... well, shouldn't we look at it?" the Crone asked, stretching again, causing Ty to blush. She walked over to him before continuing. "I can feel a connection of sorts to you... I'd like to see it."

"Can you see my status chart?" Ty asked, trying to maintain his focus.

The Crone nodded, her new, thick green hair almost covering her face when her head was facing down. "Oh yes."

Ty shrugged and pulled his status chart up, then selected the 'branching paths' option. A list popped up in front of him.

Name	Effect
The Heart of the Forest	You are a master of familiars. You gain more familiars, and each familiar is higher level. An extraordinarily powerful build for those that want others to do the work for them.
	You gain +1 familiars, and each familiar gains +1 levels. Each familiar gains another level for every full 10 levels the dungeon gains. Absorbing a dungeon core or killing a progenitor gives you another familiar to bond to. Will provide unique leveling ability choices to further enhance familiars
	If not taken at Level 1 this path is forever lost.
The Million Trees	You are the master of dryads, who will serve you fanatically. This power is enhanced by your dungeon's power.
	You may bond with a dryad every 5 levels, gaining a small amount of power from each dryad so bonded. You gain an extra dryad per 10 levels for every 10 levels the dungeon achieves. A dryad that sleeps with you will feel an overwhelming urge to bond. A bonded dryad will serve you as a willing slave.
	This provides a collection of unique abilities able to be taken upon normal leveling specifically designed to enhance dryads.
Roots of the Dungeon Tree	Your power slowly stretches between numerous dungeons, multiplying and increasing all future powers.
	You *may* become dungeon lord for multiple dungeons. When you do this, you pick a subordinate dungeon lord, regardless of whether they have the dungeon lord perk. When a dungeon lord dies, you choose the next one, breaking the normal dungeon lord cycle. The dungeons will become a loosely interconnected, single mega-dungeon with separate segments. Each dungeon so gained will provide additional benefits for all remaining 'branching paths' abilities chosen, as well as a small static bonus. Additionally, each dungeon will provide a small bonus to your primary dungeon.
	If not taken at Level 1 this path is forever lost.

World Storm	You become an absolute master of Air Magic, a mastery you may increase by slaying proto-gods of Air magic to claim their power. This also allows you to master Air auras extremely well.
	+2 Air affinity and +2 maximum Air affinity. Every 10 levels, you gain an additional Air magic ability. Every Storm or Air or Lightning-associated progenitor that you destroy will become an additional maximum and actual +1 Air affinity. +5 magic Stat.
	Auras in Air magic may be taken thirty levels early, and exceed normal level maximums. Unique Air magic abilities may be chosen.
	If not taken at Level 1 this path is forever lost.
Primordial Font of Magic.	You become an absolute master of Soul Magic, a mastery you may increase by slaying proto-gods of Soul magic to claim their power.
	+2 Soul affinity and +2 maximum Soul affinity. Every 10 levels, you gain an additional Soul magic ability. Every Soul magic progenitor, or those associated with magic, that you destroy will become an additional maximum and actual +1 Soul affinity. +10 Magic stat.
	This path will give powerful but generalist magic-enhancing abilities to choose at level as well as its normal increases, and if the mage ever becomes Arcane in magical quality, they can learn Meta magic.
	If not taken at Level 1 this path is forever lost.
Forest Demesne	You have a realm that can act as both a haven where your power is dramatically enhanced, and as a multiplier for other branching path abilities, potentially.
	You gain a heart tree and a realm. It has a radius of a mile per ten levels of dungeon associated with the mage. Inside, the mage has halved essence cost, regenerates at 5 health and 5 essence per 6 seconds, and has +10 on all checks against any negative effect. His abilities do double damage, impose double benefits and penalties, and are at -10 to resist.

	Up to ten dryad trees may be replanted, and each dryad so relocated gains significant power but becomes permanently loyal to the master dryad. This must be a voluntary relocation.
	The Demesne enhances other Branching paths and is enhanced in turn. Additionally, unique magical abilities can be taken by the mage at all levels related to the demesne.
	If the heart tree is ever destroyed, you die as well.
Elder Treant	You become a war tree of unmatched strength.
	You gain +5 Strength, +5 Endurance, and +10 Toughness. All 'were' powers in Wyld magic add bonuses that require a single essence upkeep no matter the level. You grow to ten feet in height, and will grow more with further stat gain.

There was a long, long pause as Ty and the Crone examined the chart. After a bit, the Crone gave a long, drawn-out whistle.

"Well, those aren't mere branching paths as they claim. Youngling, these are very nearly *progenitor*-level capstone abilities that would, at your current level, define you to a very large degree. Each of these will change your build, will change *who you are* to a huge degree. That last one would give you *twenty* stats. If you did nothing but level and choose stat-enhancing abilities, nothing else, it would take almost *four levels* to equal that one ridiculous ability."

She sounded as animated as Ty had ever heard her, although perhaps that was just her new form. But he couldn't disagree. If anything, she had understated the powers of the abilities.

"It's more than that—since most of those 'were' abilities add eight to ten stats each, and a normal stat gain ability adds four, the second half of the power, in the long run, would be stronger than the first. With decent essence I could fight far, far above my level. Impossibly far, it seems. How does this not make me a magical being and restrict my level gain?"

"No idea, youngling. Magic was never really my specialty. Seems like a thing you should figure out at some point, however, as it would be amazing to be able to replicate it."

"Something was with us, when the dungeon formed," Ty said. "It *helped* me."

The Crone raised one wooden eyebrow, an odd expression over her glowing green eye. "I felt nothing, youngling, and I was there. With a far greater connection to magic than you. I would have known."

Ty didn't argue the point—perhaps she was right, although Ty didn't believe it for a second. He couldn't prove either side right now, however, so why get in a fight with his dungeon boss?

"What are you thinking, youngling?" the Crone asked. She gently touched a bioluminescent mushroom. Ty felt a burst of Wyld magic, but nothing happened with or to the mushroom.

Is she testing her powers in this new space? To see if they work the same in her new form?

Ty didn't talk about his actual thoughts and instead spoke about the chart. "Well, I almost feel as if I have to default to the ones that aren't lost if I don't take them now... would you agree?"

"It's not my build. And since it said they're branching paths, it seems to me that they would lead upward to new and better things regardless. So take what will make you the most *you* you want to be."

Somehow, the Crone's awkward statement still made total sense to Ty. He looked at it again.

He could become an extremely powerful familiar mage. Normally, familiar abilities were rare, one ability to gain them per five levels. They were also half the level of the mage using them. So a Level Twenty familiar-specialized mage might have four level-ten familiars. Nice, but not so powerful that a non-familiar level twenty couldn't compete.

But if Ty's dungeon hit level twenty, his same build would be five level-fourteen familiars. That felt way more powerful to Ty.

He could also have auras as a *level two* wielder of magic if he took the air ability, or theoretically gain one of the ascendency magics, meta-magic, if he took the soul one. These were incredible abilities.

Ty was uncomfortable with The Million Trees, even if, in his darkest mind, the idea of numerous sexy dryads serving him appealed to him greatly. But he really didn't want to go evil—he didn't want to do to some dryad what his dad had done to his own mom. He dismissed that one quickly even if he had a certain shameful temptation to take it.

"What are you going to take, youngling?" the Crone asked.

Chapter Six

DUNGEON LORD'S HANDBOOK, PART ONE.

Ty was almost paralyzed by indecision. This was such an integral, important decision that he couldn't decide. His whole future—

"Snap out of it, Ty. Whatever you pick is an incredible amount of power—just go with it. And you're hardly weak now—your base is very strong. Even if you are Level One again."

Ty paused again, then spoke. "I think I want to take the Dungeon Roots ability. I know it appears on its face to be a weak pick—since, at the moment, there are very few dungeons here—but it's potentially the most powerful. It will synergize with any other route I take. Additionally, it allows a theoretically unlimited amount of power gain, since I'm effectively immortal. Additionally, it says branching paths themselves are gained every ten dungeon levels. What if that counts for *all* dungeons?"

"In considerably over ten thousand years, youngling, I've seen but one other dungeon core in these parts. No matter how good the ability is, that's a deal breaker I would think."

"I know," Ty said. "But Star Port has Ygg'drasil. Sooner or later, it'll grow and open a way between worlds, and we can try and find new dungeon cores in those new worlds."

The Crone's eyes widened, causing their green glow to shine over the rest of her face slightly. "That's very true. I hadn't thought about that. Take whatever you want."

With half his mind on the fact that he was giving up a great deal of immediate power—power that he could use to help himself in other ways, such as defending against Helryn and his son—Ty thought at the chart. He felt a subtle change in himself, and received a single prompt.

> Roots of the Dungeon Tree chosen. For being Dungeon Lord of the Dryad's Grove, you gain +1 Capacity and +1 Magic. The Dungeon of the Dryad's Grove provides no special benefits to itself.

Ty briefly looked at the notification. *That's pretty small, but still, every bit helps. And that does focus me a bit more back towards being a mage.*

Ty closed the notification and stared around the cavern they were in.

"So what now?" Ty asked. "How do I form the dungeon now that we're done working on me? This cave can't be all of it, right?"

The Crone waved her hand, and at the far end of the cave, a wooden throne grew. She *skipped* over to the chair and sat down. As she did, flowers and vines sprouted from the chair, till she sat in a veritable tiny garden. "Despite its appearance, this cave is both my boss room and your core room now. When you want to enter the dungeon as dungeon lord, you may do so by declaring it before you enter the stairs to the dungeon. Only you will be admitted, and you'll be taken here, safe from me, to work on the dungeon together."

"Safe from you?" Ty asked. "Why would I need to be safe from you?"

"I'm the dungeon boss now. Anyone entering the dungeon to challenge it who reaches me, I will be compelled to fight. I'm sorry, but it is how it is. And since I'm a Level Eighty-Eight protogod, you'll not be able to stand against me for even seconds."

She pointed a thin, stick finger at him and gave him a quirked smile. "Don't accidentally enter my boss room through the normal dungeon, under any circumstances."

Important safety tip.

"If I enter as dungeon lord, I can work on the dungeon?"

The Crone nodded slowly.

"And I assume, since you haven't killed me, that I'm here as dungeon lord now?"

"Yes."

Ty waved around the cavern—hundreds of feet in all directions, but bare of anything but the faintly glowing bioluminescent mushrooms. "Well, then? How?"

"Calm yourself, Ty." The Crone concentrated, staring off into nothing for a moment, and then turned back to Ty. "Alright, I think I have it."

She waved her hand imperiously, and a stone tablet began to rise from the ground. Vines sprouted around it and wrapped it as it rose to chest height on Ty. The tablet was cracked and broken, but the vines were new and sprouted flowers that glowed faintly with beautiful pink bioluminescence.

Magical etchings, glowing in a bioluminescent green that clashed a bit with the flowers, formed on the tablet, becoming words of Middle Averian. Ty stared down at a table of contents, of all things, and below that, a series of other pages. But first, he looked at the basic dungeon status sheet.

The Dungeon of the Dryad's Grove		
Air, Soul, Wyld	Level One Dungeon (1 room pick remaining)	Score 11 (12-1) Dungeon
Category	Score	Effect
Monster Level	2	The dungeon has a maximum of Level Two monsters. [1/10th of Base Dungeon Score, rounded up. Monster Levels may not normally exceed dungeon Level +2]

Maximum Monsters	11	The dungeon can have 11 monsters, spread out roughly equally between its possible levels. [Base Dungeon Score]
Recovery Rate	1.1	The dungeon recovers 1.1 monsters per hour. [.1 x Base Dungeon Score] Note: Baby monsters cost .5, sub-bosses 2, bosses 4. Stronger creatures may cost more recovery.
Magic Effects	2	Two small magical effects or a slightly bigger one. [One-tenth Base Dungeon Score, rounded up]
Traps	0	
Loot Rate	1	If they find any monster that drops loot, they'll count themselves lucky. [Always 1 base]
Loot Quality	1	Oh, joy, a rusty knife! Mom can stop working the fields! [Always 1 base]
Magic Output	12	The dungeon adds to the magic of the world, and in its local area. At current level, it adds 11% to the base magic level and node effects and .011% to the rest of the world's base magic level. (Base score plus Dungeon Level and same over 1000 percent for world level.)
Special Categories		
N/A		
Rooms		
Category	Number	Effect
N/A		

Ty had learned the very basics—or at least he'd thought he had.

You got one room for every level the dungeon made. Each room altered the fundamentals of your dungeon, increasing one or more aspects of it. Each room made the whole dungeon stronger by the amount it told you on the dungeon's status chart. Easy.

And, unlike people, who didn't get their first ability till Level Two, the dungeon got a 'room' at Level One.

He also knew how his score was calculated—or he thought he did. It was three times dungeon monster level. It should have been twelve—which would also give three magics for his dungeon, which he had—any score of nine or higher would give his dungeon three magics, in fact. But why was it an eleven?

He put the question to the Crone.

"Probably because the core was cracked and some power leaked out. A shame, but it certainly seems to have paid off with a bumper crop for your personal power."

Ty nodded and got back to thinking about his dungeon.

Each dungeon room selection would be one of four types. First, there were the Basic rooms that every dungeon got offered.

Second were the advanced rooms that every dungeon could get if they had certain basic rooms in certain numbers first. Ty knew, as an example, that if you had a Nest room and a Spark room, you would be offered a floor boss room. It happened every time in every dungeon, apparently.

Third were specialty rooms. Specialty rooms were rooms that only some dungeons got, which were based on their boss monsters and magics. Like an Air Spark for a dungeon with Air magic—dungeons without Air magic never had a chance to acquire an Air Spark.

Fourth, there were eldritch rooms—rooms with basic and specialty room requirements both.

In addition to the main categories, some rooms were considered master rooms—unique, one per dungeon. Most of these required numerous basic and specialty rooms to exist first before they could be unlocked. They were technically still either advanced rooms or eldritch rooms, but they were usually vastly more powerful, giving the dungeon far more benefits.

And Ty thought he knew the numbers outlined on the chart, but he wanted to be sure.

"Okay, I think I get it, but explain to me the categories on the status page for the dungeon, please," Ty said.

The Crone nodded from her throne of flowers. "Makes sense, doesn't it? Some rooms will raise monster levels. You know that, right?"

"Of course. The literature was pretty clear."

"Then why are you asking me, youngling? Never mind. The point of it is, that will literally be what maximum levels your monsters are. With a final maximum of two more than your dungeon level. So you could have monsters with a maximum of Level Three right now."

"But my current base is Level Two, right? Because my dungeon gave that as the current?"

"Of course, and good job telling me all the stuff you know."

Ty flushed.

"But it's important to remember—even if you got a lot of rooms that added levels, it wouldn't go past three. Dungeon level plus two is the most you can get, no matter how many level rooms you buy."

Ty nodded.

"Recovery is how fast you get monsters back after someone prunes them. With no rooms at all, your dungeon has eleven monsters and a one point one recovery rate per hour, so it could refill itself entirely in ten hours from ambient magic. Got it?"

Ty nodded again.

"You look like an idiot doll, bobbing like that. Answer me when I talk to you, sheesh. Just because I have a new, young, and sexy shell doesn't mean you can sass me."

I've got a very snarky boss monster. But Ty answered anyway. "Yes. Thank you for explaining."

"Magic effects are just that—places where magic affects and alters the dungeon. Oh, like a place where Wyld magic makes vines grab adventurers. The magic is scaled to where it's placed in a dungeon, so a small effect on the first part of the first floor would be very different than a small effect on the last part of the second floor."

She gave a sigh. "And loot rate and loot quality are what attract adventurers who can't just enjoy a nice picnic. It's the rate at which precious metals and eventually magical items and such fall, and how good the stuff actually is on each level. Right now, since there is a loot rate of one, and a monster maximum of two, adventurers will count themselves lucky to get a nice oak shield or a flask of clean water."

"Is that a magic item?"

The Crone raised an eyebrow at Ty. "No, it's just water. That's why it's funny."

She paused for a moment, then continued. "Hmph. Now, what's *really* important to understand is floors. When you make a floor, it's ten levels. Every room picked normally applies its bonuses to the entire dungeon, but some will affect a floor much more strongly, giving it a unique flavor. So pay attention to that."

"What's the level limit for my dungeon?"

"There isn't one. But since it normally requires adventurers within ten levels to die in the dungeon to gain any experience, dungeons grow a lot slower as time goes on, since it's very hard for adventurers to get to high levels. Just how it is."

"Normally?" Ty asked. "Why 'normally'?"

"Well, there are other options... as you can see on the pages below."

Ty reached for the tablet, his hands hovering over the other 'pages.'

Chapter Seven

DUNGEON LORD'S RULEBOOK, INTERRUPTED

There were a few other options.

The first was 'available rooms,' the second was labeled 'Legacy of the Forest,' and the third read, 'Growth of the Grove.'

Ty knew that 'available rooms' would show all rooms he could pick at level. But he had never read about any of the others, although the material on dungeons was scarce.

"What are these?" Ty asked.

"Each of those options, both Legacy of the Forest and Growth of the Grove, are a set of ways to gain different and stronger rooms, unique to my dungeon. They'll advance the dungeon far more than any normal room pick."

These are the secret options that higher-level, rarer boss monsters earn you! And since I convinced a progenitor to join me, I bet they'll be insanely powerful. I want something to make my dungeon even better than the dungeons of others, more noteworthy. This is perfect.

Ty reached toward the small podium and the glowing green crystal lettering that outlined 'Legacy of the Forest.'

"Wait," the Crone said, raising her hand, her thin fingers a touch too long for her frame even with her new body. "How about, you instead pick your first room and then go find a nice adventuring party to do dungeon delves with? Do a run or two and get a feel for what the dungeon will be like. I want some time to mull over the stuff here. A lot of this other stuff is personal."

How could the dungeon building be personal?

"I mean... are you sure? That seems less than ideal—shouldn't I know all my options to increase the dungeon?"

"Nothing here will affect you picking your first room, youngling. Have some trust. You would need the Shrine of the Forest to be able to utilize anything else, and you shouldn't take that as your very first room."

Ty had his misgivings but decided to trust the Crone.

He was struck by a thought. "What's your actual name, by the way? Or do god-beings sometimes just have title names? I mean, I find it weird that you're just 'the Crone.' Especially now—you look nothing like a crone. If I was using the 'the something' format, you'd be more like 'the hot wench.'"

The Crone pointed at him. "Still with the sass. You know darn well I once went by the name 'Mother of Dryads.' You can call me 'the mother' if you want."

That weirded Ty out, feeling like some kind of strange fetish. "Still feels more like a title and less like a name."

The Crone hesitated, but finally spoke. "I was once known as Saelenia. Saelenia of the Ilum. But I gave that name up a long time ago. Before Averian, High or Middle, was even a language. I haven't gone by that moniker in ages."

"The Ilum?"

"Youngling, if you don't choose a room and get out of here, I'm going to try to violate the dungeon rules against giving you a thrashing when you're here as the dungeon lord."

Ty laughed and held his hands out to the ancient—but now youthful—dryad where she sat on her wooden throne. "Fine, fine. But may I please call you Saelenia?"

"Hmmph. Fine. But don't go spreading that around—I would rather people still think of me as the Crone outside of here. I earned my age and status, and people treat young women differently. A lot better in some ways, but not ways that I care about anymore. I did that part of my life and I'd rather have the perceived wisdom people assign the elderly."

"Thank you... Saelenia."

Then he turned back to the tablet and hit the 'rooms available' prompt.

The glowing runes shifted, showing him a new chart.

Room	Effect
Basic Rooms [Available to all dungeons, no specialty requirements]	
Lair	+8 Maximum Monsters. This will look like an inhabited space for monsters, and encounters in this room will seem like it is, in fact, a lair.
Nest	+1 Sub-Boss. +4 Baby Monsters. +2 Recovery. This is a breeding space for monsters.
Spark	+1 Magic Effects Level. +1% Local Magic Level. +.1 Loot Quality.
Treasure Room	+.5 Loot Rate, +1 additional Loot Rate for the floor it is on.
Advanced Rooms [Available because of combinations of Basic rooms]	
N/A	
Specialty Rooms [Available because of the Dungeon's Magics or Boss]	
Air Spark (Max 1 per floor)	+2 Magic Effects Level, shifts the magic toward Air. +3% Local Magic Level. +.2 Loot Quality.
Fae Grove (Max 1 per floor)	+2 Monster Level. +4 Max Monsters. The monsters on this floor are shifted toward Fae and Fae subtypes.
Beast Woods (Max 1 per floor)	+1 Monster Level. +6 Max Monsters. The monsters on this floor are shifted toward beasts and magical beasts.

Living Forest (Max 1 per floor)	+1 Monster Level. +4 Max Monsters. +.2 loot level. The monsters on this floor are shifted toward plant monsters.
Master Rooms [Available because of combinations of Basic rooms and advanced or specialty rooms, always number limited]	
N/A	
Eldritch Rooms [Available from fulfilling conditions of the Shrine of the Forest, or fulfilling the conditions and having prerequisite other rooms.]	
N/A	

Where is the shrine of the forest? She's hiding the room! Ty briefly considered picking a fight over it, but knew that Saelenia had near infinite patience. Ty... didn't. He decided to wait till she was ready to share, to not irritate her into holding out longer.

He focused on what he could do. "So, I could theme the floor right now? The Specialty room seems quite strong, as it will give me two additional monster levels."

He saw Saelenia's brow start to furrow and realized his mistake.

"Wait, wait," Ty said. "I can only have Level Three monsters max. Sorry."

She relaxed.

"The specialty rooms seem a lot better, however... Could I get it now and still get the benefit once we level and the max monster level is four?"

"You could," Saelenia said.

Ty was torn. "I read that to get a floor boss monster, you need a nest and a spark or specialty spark. Should I get the nest instead?"

"Talk it out," Saelenia said with a languid wave of one arm.

Ty rubbed his chin even as he talked, his eyes staring into the distance. "Well, I get a sub-boss for people to fight, and four baby monsters, but the plus two recovery is the big one. Even with the extra monsters, I would have the equivalent of sixteen monsters to recover... but I would have a three-point-two recovery, so I would recover every five hours. If I was really careful, I could run the dungeon five times a day. More if anyone messed up and didn't finish a run."

"And?"

"*And* it would allow me to help a lot of new people get their first level or two. I mean, a group of four adventurers would all make Level Two even if they only fought Level One monsters. For a while, I could run newbies through, get everyone up to the standard. I mean, if I really, really pushed it, I could run over nine thousand people through in a year. It would be a huge boon to our civilization."

"You're overly optimistic, youngling. For our dungeon to level, you need higher-level adventurers, so allowing newbie adventurers will cut into the experienced adventurers' time. Additionally, you'll lose some people to the dungeon. They'll die, remember? And a lot of people aren't as crazy as you. They'll be happy staying Level One if risking death in a dungeon is the alternative."

Ty continued to stroke his chin, absently noting how his chin felt subtly different now. Saelenia made sense. Still... "I think I want the recovery rate. And most of the literature I read indicates that Nest is the most common first pick. I know I'll have all these special options later, but I want the base to be strong. I'm going with it."

He reached out and touched the 'Nest' on the list.

A box popped across the tablet, outlined in crystal red.

You are about to pick a dungeon room. Dungeon room selection is permanent, and once selected, may not be altered. Do you wish to proceed? Yes or no?

Well, that's good to know. And it makes me want to sit here and try to work out a thousand possible paths and not do this haphazardly.

Ty looked up from the glowing plinth and at Saelenia. "Are you—"

"*Yes*, youngling. The remainder of the dungeon will require all your thinking, and you'll have to plan and all that, but this will be fine. Get the dungeon going. Every day you don't is a wasted day, for the dungeon and adventurers both."

Ty looked back down at the ominously outlined box and thought 'Yes' at it.

He felt magic shift around him, but nothing else happened for a moment.

Then a box outlined in what appeared to be green crystals popped up on the tablet.

'Nest' Room selected. No new options opened by this selection. Dungeon Chart updated.

While Saelenia indulgently looked on, Ty pulled up his dungeon chart again.

The Dungeon of the Dryad's Grove		
Air, Soul, Wyld	Level One Dungeon	Score 11 (12-1) Dungeon
Category	Score	Effect
Monster Level	2	The dungeon has a maximum of Level 2 monsters. [1/10th of Base Dungeon Score, rounded up. Monster Levels may not normally exceed dungeon Level +2]

Maximum Monsters	17	The dungeon can have 17 monsters (cost 16 recovery), spread out roughly equally between its possible levels. [Base Dungeon Score + Nest(x1)]		
		Monster	Number	Total Recovery Cost
		Special		
		Boss	0	0
		Sub-Boss	1	2
		Monster	12	12
		Baby Monster/Minion	4	2
Recovery Rate	3.2	The dungeon recovers 3.1 monsters per hour. [.1 x Base Dungeon Score + Nest(x1)		
Magic Effects	2	2 small magical effects or 1 slightly bigger one. [Base Dungeon Score, rounded up]		
Traps	0			
Loot Rate	1	If they find any monster that drops loot, they'll count themselves lucky. [Always 1 base]		
Loot Quality	1	Oh, joy, a rusty knife! Mom can stop working the fields! [Always 1 base]		
Magic Output	11	The dungeon adds to the magic of the world, and in its local area. At current level, it adds 11% to the base magic level and node effects and .011% to the rest of the world's base magic level. (Base score plus Dungeon Level and same over 1000 percent.)		
Special Categories				
N/A				
Rooms				
Category	Number	Effect		
Floor One				
Nest	1	+1 Sub-Boss. +4 Baby Monsters. +2 Recovery. This is a breeding space for monsters.		

I can work with this, Ty thought to himself, suddenly extremely excited about his future. *I can't wait to build my dungeon, make it a true wonder of the world—one more thing that attracts people to our city and gives me prestige and wealth. But mostly, I just want to see what I can make of it. Given my special abilities, perhaps someday I can have a network of dungeons throughout Averia, even!*

I wish Saelenia was ready to show me the advanced options. I want to know what we might do.

"All right, youngling, get out of here and go make an adventuring group. You should start living and working with your own people. That's part of your problem, you know—why you're always afraid. You haven't been making friends. Go find some other kids to play with. I'm tired."

Ty honestly couldn't decide if she was being condescending or if she was effectively just the oldest grandmother in the entire thousand continents of Toth. He half-expected her to offer him some food. Her body might have become that of a youngish fertility goddess, but Saelenia still had a great deal of the Crone inside her.

"All right, I'll head up." Ty glanced around and then pointed to the one tunnel out. "Just take that?"

"Obviously. And be quick about it. I tire of the company of children."

Ty frowned but headed into the tunnel. It was barely ten feet before he reached stairs heading up. As he climbed, he felt a subtle shifting of the magic, a *twisting*, as if, for a second, up was down and down was up. He grabbed his head and swayed, but as he took the next step, the feeling cleared.

Ty walked out into a beautiful garden surrounded by what could have been described as a huge, marble gazebo, if a gazebo had had a hole in most of its center. It had close-worked fencing made of tiny, marble posts hitting the railing at about three feet off the ground, and a few columns, each with bas-relief marble vines and leaves, led to a merged ceiling with pictures of famous scenes from the history of the forest of Averia done in bas-relief as well.

A single pole didn't resemble the others—it was clearly a stylized version of the Crone, in her new body as Saelenia. He wondered if anyone would figure that out, or just assume it was some random dryad decoration.

Ty also thought it a bit disrespectful that the dungeon had a naked dryad on one column, but he let it go—it wasn't like he could do anything about it.

The garden itself was filled with very small ornamental trees, flowers that glowed slightly with magic, and a tiny pond. It was about thirty feet on a side. Ty couldn't help but notice that all the flowers and the trees appeared the same—the basic oak trees around here, but far smaller, and basic wildflowers that could be found in any clearing in the forest.

He had come out of a natural-looking hole in the ground. As he did, he saw quite a few of the people who had been here to watch him still waiting. Many sat on the ground, and everyone was subdued. But when he appeared, people nudged each other and pointed, and a ragged cheer went up.

Ty was immediately inundated with praise.

"Congratulations, Ty!"

"Thanks for giving our city a dungeon!"

"Good job, dungeon lord!"

"Do you have an adventuring group yet?"

Ty smiled and gave a wave to the people around. After fifty years being the reviled half-breed, hated by the humans for being an elf 'slavey' and the elves for being a half-human, it was good to hear cheers of approval.

Kadrath, the Adventurers' Guild Leader, clanked up to him—while wearing full plate armor for some reason. He climbed the outside steps to the inner edge around the gazebo garden. He was grinning from ear to ear, his mouth threatening to declare a coup against the rest of his face.

Said face was very slightly green, with canines that were a bit pronounced, and he had bushy, black hair and a bushy, black beard. Dworcs tended to be rather striking.

Kadrath held a hand down to Ty, who accepted it with his own free hand. The dworc helped Ty onto the inner edge of the marble gazebo, even though there were stairs from the garden a mere ten feet away. Up close, Kadrath was *huge*, almost seven feet tall and broad, and his armor was sized to fit.

And he was supposedly leveled into his teens. Ty could feel a tingle of magic, heavy, solid, and somehow organized, as Kadrath clapped him on the shoulder—painfully—and turned him toward the Adventurers' Guild.

The huge guildmaster, still smiling like a loon, gently pushed him in that direction. "Come with me. There are several important things that need to be dealt with without delay since you're a dungeon lord now. Things that will influence all our futures."

Chapter Eight

BUSINESS NEGOTIATIONS

Kadrath herded Ty—who suspected he weighed less than a third of what Kadrath did—with a steel-encased arm over his shoulder, directing him down the stairs and toward the Adventurers' Guild. Like nearly everything in Star Port proper, it was a ruined, magically hardened marble building that had been refurbished. Now, the walls had been smoothed, windows had been inset, and the area behind the Guild had been cleared and turned into a huge training area.

Ty reflected that the entire city of Star Port's architectural style was only possible because the four magical abilities used to sustain it were relatively common low-level abilities. Mold stone was available to Level Two Earth wielders, shape wood to Level Two Wyld wielders, and both the general repair and the mold metal were available to Level Two Metal wielders. The elves had *very* few Metal mages, of course, even the high elves, but they had plenty of Earth and a decent number of Wyld users.

And the strengthening ability was available to both Earth wielders and Metal wielders once they'd taken their respective mold ability first, so it was quite common as well.

The Grand Plaza had been growing in other ways as well, many designed to accommodate the adventurers and higher-level elven citizens. Across the way, a workshop had just opened its doors. The Forges of Stonehaven, as it was called, was a forge and magical imbuing shop both. The shop could barely keep up with the demand for weapons—even magical weapons—created by the ever-growing number of leveled people in the city.

Two dwarves, one named Ratham and one Andul, ran the place. Ty had heard that both were fantastic crafters. They had apparently adventured to a degree with King Leo and followed him back to Star Port.

Ty's musings were cut short by Kadrath. "What happened to your skin, Ty?"

Ty shrugged awkwardly with Kadrath's arm still weighing him down. "Side effect of my dungeon." *I don't really want to give away the specifics at this moment.*

"Also, where's your dungeon mask?"

"It was a cracked core, I think it was a bit defective. I didn't get a mask. The dungeon building part seems fine however."

Kadrath nodded slowly as he ushered Ty into the Adventurers' Guild.

It somehow reminded him of the slave camp cafeteria he had been stuck in once—four walls, one with a counter on it, and row after row of long tables with benches at them. Although the whole thing was a lot spiffier.

Unlike at the Emerald Bee Inn, the floor was still marble, but it was tiled marble and very slightly unsmoothed so that walking was easy. But even in the Adventurers' Guild, elven style dominated—there were numerous potted plants, and one entire wall had an interior trellis with flowering vines on it.

The other wall had a counter set in it, with a window above to another room, and a jobs board next to it. Only a very few jobs were posted on the board, and Ty couldn't make them out anyway as Kadrath steered him past the little scraps of paper.

A gnome lady, barely four feet tall, was working the counter.

The last two walls had ornamental armor and weapons, as well as wooden doors with carvings of famous elven heroes on them, which led to other parts of the building.

The center of the room was filled with circular tables surrounded by chairs, all of lower quality. Numerous adventurers were there, about half of them elves, the rest beings of numerous different backgrounds. He saw multiple humans, most dressed in outfits from the city-states. A dwarf in chain armor argued with a giant ox-kin wearing thick furs at one table. Two rabbit-kin, both wearing ordinary clothes but carrying an implausible number of knives, talked quietly while scanning the rooms. Ty also saw two dryads walking around. One was Forli. Ty recognized the other as Adwoa, the dryad formed from the Lightbao tree in Green Apple Grove.

Forli waved to him as he came in, a smile on her face. She started toward Ty, but hesitated as the huge Guildmaster continued to push him.

Ty had a general urge to pollinate the beautiful Forli—

The half-alien thought brought Ty up short. *Pollinate?*

He looked away in sudden acute embarrassment.

As he did, he also caught a glimpse of a beautiful elven girl among the adventurers. It was the lady from earlier!

She was as gorgeous as Ty remembered, with silken, metallic-copper hair shading very slightly toward green down her back and large, indigo eyes set in a heart-shaped face. She was also lean and shapely, and Ty stared for a moment, halfheartedly trying to push back against Kadrath's arm as he was guided toward one of the doors. The mystery elf was dressed in high-quality leather armor and carried a high-quality but non-magical short sword on her hip.

As he was being pushed by Kadrath and checking out the mystery girl, he wasn't watching where he was going. Ty caught the edge of a table leg, tripped, and crashed to the ground. There was some good-natured laughter around the tables, and Ty flushed with embarrassment.

This is what you get for being a degenerate distracted by every hot elf—and now dryad, apparently—that you see, Ty! You're barely better than your father!

Kadrath reached down, grabbed him, and hauled him to his feet by the back of his ratty robe. Being reminded of how torn and dirty his robe was drove Ty's embarrassment to almost terminal levels. The beautiful elf girl smiled at him, and he tried to flee the room through the door he was obviously being guided to. He yanked on it, but it remained closed.

Ty waited, imagining everyone laughing at him or staring at his back, where his robe was gross, torn, and stained. He had a flashback to the last straw that had sent him out to the orc tribes to make levels, where he had been captured and enslaved himself, briefly. He had asked a slave elf—Yenrael, who went by Yen, a pretty elf with bronze-colored hair and green eyes—to date him, even though she wasn't free. She had laughed at him, and some of the other slave elves had as well. This was different, but every stare still burned.

Kadrath came up to the door. He pulled a key out and unlocked the door, and Ty fled through into another hallway, also marble but far plainer than the outside room.

Kadrath pointed to the nearest door, a plain, wooden one, and Ty rushed through that as well.

He entered a small room with a table on it, and a map of the ruins of Calasti spread over it. Ty's embarrassment faded as he stared at the map with interest. Calasti was the name of the old elven capital, a city that had once housed almost four million people. Now, however, it was filled with corrupted magic and monsters.

It was, however, divided by huge walls into thirty-one distinct districts. Each district could be reclaimed one at a time, and King Leo had made clear to both Ty and, in more detail, Ty's father, George, that he planned to recover the ancient capital a district at a time as they grew. And since the ruins had probably *thousands* of corrupted rituals now, each spawning corrupted magical beasts, there was a hefty amount of work for adventurers.

And none of that even counted for the *huge* undercity, which was comprised of the ruins of the capital of the Ancient Ones, who had existed here before the elves had. Technically, Star Port was kind of the third city on this spot, at least. After the Crone's speech, Ty wondered if there'd been even more.

Kadrath grabbed the map and rolled it up, sitting down. He motioned to Ty to take a chair.

"So, what kind of relationship are we going to have?" Kadrath asked.

Ty felt vaguely threatened. "What? You told me we had to come here to talk about important things for our future. This is your meeting. What are you trying to ask me?"

"Well, you have a dungeon, and you're under no obligation to make any kind of arrangement or deal with the Adventurers' Guild. We're getting a percentage, as does the king, from the people paying to go into the outer parts of the city to train. The king allows us that privilege because we train and organize the adventurers, making them more likely to survive and help the kingdom when they're higher level."

Ty had been aware of the deal and its basic outlines from his father.

"My question is: Are you seeking that kind of relationship with us as well?"

"You mean, do I want to give you a cut of the fees people give me to enter the dungeon in order to help you train and equip adventurers?" Ty asked.

"Exactly."

Ty didn't want to sound like an ingrate, but... "What do I get out of the arrangement? I mean, people going off and having great lives doesn't help me—I'm not taxing them like the king, after all."

"Well, your dungeon needs high-level people to grow, and the stronger it is, the more treasure comes from it, and the more you can charge to let people in, right? So, having well-trained and prepared adventurers is to your advantage."

I seriously doubt that's worth all that much, but I guess he has a tiny point. However, on a different issue, I did want to give back to the community to some degree. Maybe I can have this guy manage that? And he could manage fee collection—they have expertise in getting a share from adventurers, after all, and I don't need to learn a skill I can contract out.

Ty straightened. "How about this? You do two things for me, and I'll give you ten percent of everything collected—that's ten percent of fees, not ten percent of gross."

Kadrath's eyes widened.

"First, you collect the fees and keep an accurate accounting for me."

Kadrath nodded. "Fair and more than fair. We have expertise and do that after all the runs to other districts in the ruins. Policing adventuring parties into your dungeon will be far easier. That's barely asking anything, and I appreciate your generosity."

Ty held up a finger. "Well, I have a second request. I want to give back to the community that has accepted me here, and to King Leo. I figure the easiest way to do that is to allow Level One people to run my dungeon and become Level Two so they can access their magic. For the most part, I doubt they'll get very far, so hopefully soon, it'll barely even affect how often the dungeon can be run."

Kadrath nodded his head inside his armor and leaned back in his chair, which creaked ominously under the weight of his massive armor. Ty was honestly surprised it had survived being sat on by the dworc at all.

"Makes sense, in theory, although I have little actual experience with dungeons—we only know of one, and while I have delved it, I haven't ever talked to the dungeon lord there. But sorry, continue."

"So, I want you to equip and train anyone who comes and asks for it. Train enough people that the first run each day can be made by Level One citizens."

Kadrath narrowed his eyes. "That would be a hundred and fifty people a month, even if I only gave them a month's training.

Properly equipping that many people would be prohibitively expensive. I don't think ten percent will come close to that cost."

"Yet," Ty said with conviction.

"Hmm?"

"It won't come close to that *yet*. But imagine that I have a Level Twenty dungeon with a decent loot rating. Just a small percentage of one run's loot would pay for the whole month. The rest is just wealth for your guild. And the same argument you made to me applies to you triply—high-level adventurers will only benefit you. And training half the population here can only benefit you as well."

Ty waved his arm, palm out, in a wide circle. "Kadrath—Mentor to the city."

Kadrath smiled and nodded. "That's true—although it'll be taxing early. But I think I can handle it. But just to make sure you don't go back on this once it's benefitting us, would you sign a ten-year deal on it? I doubt, very seriously, that your dungeon will be Level Twenty by then—but I think it'll be high enough that we're making money."

Ty held up a finger. "Totally fair. I'll even do twenty years to make sure you get a fair deal, but we need to add a clause about general gear quality as well, in case a successor to you tries to play games and alter the agreement."

Kadrath smiled. "You've got a deal!"

He held his hand out in the position for the dwarven clasp, but Ty held his own up.

"Not yet. One more thing. I want it named the Ty Belmoria Training Program, or something close to that. I've spent most of my life as a pariah, and I want some recognition now."

Kadrath shrugged and pushed his hand out farther across the table. "Sure, sure, that's fine. Anything else?"

Ty reached out and took the offered hand. Kadrath's wrist clasp was strong and sure to the point of being slightly painful on Ty's own thin wrist.

Ty had a sudden dark thought. "Yes, one more thing. I don't want Helryn Mosstone, Dalryn Mosstone, or his two lackeys—Elyndira and Ilkoran—admitted to the dungeon."

"Pissed you off, did they?" Kadrath asked, a broad grin stretching across his rugged face.

"Tried to murder me," Ty responded with a deeply furrowed brow.

"That would piss a person off," Kadrath said. "It's a good reason to exclude them, not that you need a reason to exclude someone from your own dungeon."

"Thanks," Ty said.

"Is there anything else, Ty?"

Chapter Nine

HOT CHICKS

"No, thank you, Guildmaster. I appreciate the arrangements we came to. I'm going to go and see about getting a few other members for my adventuring party as well. Unless there's anything else?"

"No, Ty—excuse me." Kadrath coughed. "That's going to take some getting used to. What I mean to say was—no, Dungeon Lord. That concludes our business for today, and I think we'll have a long and profitable relationship. I'll work hard to make sure you're not disappointed and it goes exactly as we planned."

"Thank you," Ty said, standing from the table.

Kadrath held the door open, and Ty walked back into the plain, marble hallway, and from there into the central room of the Adventurers' Guild.

He immediately noticed the beautiful indigo-eyed elf, who was facing him as he exited. She sat at a table with the two rabbit-kin guys, an elf woman with glowing green bracelets floating around her wrists, and the huge ox-kin that appeared to be a scaled-down minotaur.

"So, you want to apply, Ivy?" the green-braceleted elf asked.

Ty stopped abruptly, listening in.

The indigo-eyed girl—Ivy, Ty assumed—kept a serene smile on her face. "Yes, Ulivarae. I have Wyld and Soul as my magics."

"And what build were you looking at?" Ulivarae asked.

"Hybrid healer and pet master, perhaps with a touch of social-enhancing magic thrown in." Ivy spoke loudly, and it was easy for Ty to hear.

"Would you accept a probationary period, where you won't get any shares?"

"I don't think healers normally need to have a probationary period—we're quite in demand. Very desired."

A healer? I need a healer!

Ty hurried over to the table. "A probationary period? Are you insane, lady? I would be willing to take her in *my* adventuring company without any such nonsense."

"And who the fall are you?" Ulivarae asked, standing up from her chair and turning to face him.

When she caught sight of his face, though, she paled. "Dungeon Lord... Ah, sorry if my speech was... rough." She winced. Her eyes lingered on his face a bit long, and Ty guessed she was trying to figure out his new, slightly wooden, brownish skin tone.

The indigo-eyed girl stood, still with a broad, serene smile on her face, and then gave a bow with her hand over her heart. "I'm so pleased to meet you, Dungeon Lord. I am Ivilunae—'Ivy' for short. You have an opening in your party for a healer, I take it?"

As she straightened, Ty saw an amulet to Cerivae Nerithin, goddess of family, community, social gatherings, and kind gestures, around her neck. It hung down to a point between her not-very-ample cleavage—but in a location that called attention to it. For once, however, Ty was more interested in the meaning than the location of the necklace. *Not sure if that's a good deity for an adventurer, but at least she's probably a nice person. A person who chooses a specific deity to serve is telling the world a lot about themselves.*

Ulivarae looked as if she'd been hit in the face with a club. "But, ah, you... us..."

"Would *you* not take the offer of the dungeon lord?" Ivy asked, fiddling with her amulet and watching Ty, not Ulivarae, as she talked. "I mean, I am truly sorry, but you and I had no agreements yet. I have an excellent feeling about Ty as well. King Leo spoke so eloquently about what a good person he was last week."

Ulivarae seemed to gather her composure, to make one more sally, although Ty could see her heart wasn't in it from the cast of her features. "Do you even *have* an adventuring party, Dungeon Lord? I mean, you weren't exactly popular before."

Ty clenched his fists. *Before, when you were just the half-breed ex-slave who had to be rescued,* was what he heard, although it remained unspoken.

"I'm forming one now," he said. "The Dungeon Lord's Own. We have a ranged damage dealer—me, and I'm a Dungeon Lord to boot. Now we have a healer. Shouldn't be too hard to find a guardian and one to two others."

Ulivarae smirked. "In this city of elves? I think you'll find a guardian far harder to locate than you think."

Ty raised an eyebrow.

Ulivarae grimaced. "Although I suppose that the Dungeon Lord will have as easy a time as anyone would."

"Thank you. I appreciate your vote of confidence."

Ty decided not to make enemies, even if he felt Ulivarae had been looking down on him. "As thanks for your advice, would you care to have the first run? It's pretty-low level, two maximum on the monsters, so you should be all right to adventure even without a healer—maybe buy a potion or two first."

Ulivarae's smile returned. "Thank you, Dungeon Lord! I truly appreciate that. I can't afford a potion, but I'll make sure that we're careful. We're all Level Two, from adventures in the ruins of Calasti—I think the Ready Blades will be fine."

Ready Blades, huh? Ty thought. *Not a bad name for an adventuring party, but hardly inspired.*

"If you could see fit to let Kadrath know what monsters you encounter," he told her, "I would also take it as a favor."

Ulivarae bowed, her hand over heart. "It shall be as you say. When is it time for the first run?"

"Now—but check with Kadrath first. There're still rules on fees to the Adventurers' Guild and such. But let him know I'll waive my portion for you this time, which should be most of the fee."

She nodded and motioned to her people. "Let's go, boys! We can try to recruit another healer later. Ivy can't be the only elf with Wyld or Body magic who would want to adventure enough to fill the role. For now, we have a dungeon to delve!"

They rushed the few feet over to Kadrath and mobbed him.

Ivy smiled up at him. "Too nice for your own good, although I think you did yourself a favor here—word of you being careful of her honor, when you won me from her, will spread."

Ty was taken back. *'Won me from her'? That's weird phrasing... It feels flirtatious, somehow. In fact, it feels a bit like she's coming on strong in general. I wonder why?*

"So, whom will we recruit to be our guardian?" Ivy asked, still playing with the amulet on her chest.

It took Ty a second to switch gears to thinking of his adventuring party again. "Not sure, truly. Do you know any guardians?"

"No one with magical abilities that lend themselves to being a guardian, but my brother would make a decent one if he leveled a few times. He's got the perks for it. He's kind of a colossal weed, though, even if he does always try to stick up for me. If there are better options, or even any decent ones, we should take them."

"The gods don't smile on us, then," Ty commented. "And Ulivarae may get the last laugh. Because I have no idea where we'll get a guardian now."

Ivy quirked a half-smile at him. "Speaking of Ulivarae, I guess I technically know Rathcorb there, who's already in the Ready Blades." Ivy pointed over at the ox-kin.

Ty checked the nearly eight-foot-tall, broad ox-kin out. *Yeah, he'd make a fantastic guardian. I don't want to join the Ready Blades, though—I want to run my own team. And stealing someone else from them who was already fully on the team would be a real insult. I don't want the whole Adventurers' Guild hating me...*

Ty sighed and decided not to poach Rathcorb.

Instead, he asked a different question. "So, what perks, magics, and such do you have, exactly? I mean, I heard your description, but I was curious."

Ivy's cheeks grew pink. "You could just buy me an adventurer card."

"What?" Ty said, feeling foolish. He had never heard of such a thing.

"My adventurer card. Kadrath has a device that will grab my stat sheet and transfer it to paper so people can see when making decisions about whether to recruit me. It costs ten silver, so a lot of new adventurers can't afford it, but I'm sure you could either afford it or get it for free, right? I mean, you do have a dungeon—Kadrath would order them to do it for free, right?"

"I... Probably," Ty said. "Okay, let's get the card."

"Excellent. I also wanted to have it framed, as who I was before I started making levels. It feels inspiring, somehow, right?"

I might want to do that myself, now that the dungeon made me Level One again. But I don't know if I want to discuss that yet. Ty smiled at her. "Not a bad idea. Let's go."

Before he could move, however, he was interrupted.

"Um, excuse me, Ty?" a voice asked, hesitantly.

He turned, and found Forli staring at him. Her hair was composed of a ton of green pine needles that she had now pulled into a ponytail, but otherwise, she appeared as before, basically.

Once again—out of deference to local mores, Ty guessed—she had donned a long shift that hung down around her knees. It was barely clothing, even if she was fully modest. It certainly wasn't armor. Plus, she had no other gear.

Ty was still fighting against his new feelings of sexual attraction to her as well. He hadn't felt that way about her the whole time that she had been helping him, before, but he felt it now.

As Forli talked to him, it seemed to get her as well. Ty could see her eyes half glaze, and she rubbed her inner legs together as she stood. She *definitely* hadn't acted interested in him before.

"Yes?" Ty asked, his voice just slightly husky.

Ivy stared at Forli, then at Ty with a quirked eyebrow. He couldn't explain it either. He normally preferred the elven frame, thin and almost boyish, on his women. Forli was a curvy girl with pine skin. But all his instincts were screaming at him to pursue her.

Ty cleared his throat and tried again. "Yes, Forli?"

"I, um, was wondering if I could adventure with you as well."

"Wait, what?" Ty asked. "You kinda hid when I fought Dalryn, Forli... and you haven't displayed an ounce of combat skill or desire. Do you have any dangerous abilities or skills?" Ty was trying to just be rational as they all stood in the center of the Adventurers' Guild, surrounded by numerous people, many with levels that Ty hoped would think well of him. *Don't let your past friendship or sudden feelings of attraction affect your decision.*

Forli hung her head, staring at the floor. "Um, not many. I have Air and Water magic, rather than the normal Wyld that dryads usually get, but my stats are, um, kinda low, honestly."

She kicked the marble floor, fluttered her hands for a moment, and then, when no one said anything, she spoke in a whisper. "I'm sorry, I was being stupid. I'll go now. Thanks for at least taking me on the trip to save Mom."

She started to turn, her eyes never leaving Ty.

Ty's heart went out to her. He knew how it was to be weak and helpless and powerless. "Wait, you can stay with me and join our adventuring group. We'll figure something out for you, a role you can take."

He hoped his weird new dryad attraction wasn't making terrible decisions for him. He was pretty sure it was his desire to save people, really. Although he hated himself for being a sucker, occasionally, as well.

"Okay, well, let's go get a card!" Ivy said, smiling. "Maybe Ty'll get one for you as well, Forli!"

Ty went to the counter, where the cute if older gnome woman, a mere four feet tall with thigh-length black hair, worked.

She glanced up, a somewhat bored expression on her face, as Ty came over. When she saw it was him, however, she straightened a bit and gave him a glowing smile. "What can I do for you, Dungeon Lord?"

"I wanted to purchase the status sheet service. I mean, the adventurer card service. Sorry."

"That'll be ten silver," the gnomish woman said, standing and leaning over the counter, hand out.

Ty fished it from his coin pouch and paid her. It was about half of his random money, and worth a couple of months' food for a peasant family, but he knew that he would have a lot more money soon. Plus, he admitted to himself wryly, he desperately wanted to impress Ivy and Forli both.

"This way," the gnomish woman said, sitting on her chair and then hopping to the ground. She took Ty, Ivy, and Forli around the corner and into another room, a small one, off the room behind the counter.

They went around to a large table with a strange device on it: a metal tube, about three feet long and about six inches in diameter on the interior. Medium sized—the third tier—gray crystals were all along the inside, and a flat, metal table stuck out to the side.

There was a chair right in front of the device, and a stool next to the chair.

As they approached, the woman went to a small shelf, grabbed a small sheet of vellum, and came back. She climbed up on the stool and then spread the paper onto the metal plate.

She motioned to Ty and then the chair. "All right, take your place."

Ty shook his head. "I purchased it for Ivy."

"Well, then have *her* take her place," the gnomish woman said.

"You should go first!" Ivy said suddenly. Ty saw worry in her eyes.

Maybe she's afraid of the device? Although that would be pretty odd for a Soul wielder—they tend to love magical devices. Still... I don't want to show everyone that I've lost five levels and picked up absolutely crazy abilities!

"Maybe Forli can go? Did you want an adventurer card?"

Forli nodded eagerly, a smile on her face. She sat down in the chair.

"Put your arm into the tube," the gnomish woman said.

Forli smiled and did, but she was staring at Ty as she did it.

The gnomish woman touched the side of the tube and closed her eyes. She furrowed her brow a bit, and Ty felt a surge of magic—inquisitive and probing, obviously an aspect of Mind magic.

Without any other fanfare, words appeared across the page.

Ivy leaned over and glanced at the sheet, but the gnomish woman gave her the stink eye and handed it directly to Forli. "That's confidential. She can show it to you if she likes."

Forli withdrew her hand from the device and shifted in the chair. "Let's check it together, if that's okay, dungeon lord."

"Of course, and thank you. And for all the god's sake, Forli, just call me Ty. It's weird the other way."

Forli giggled, nodded, and then spread her sheet on the table.

Almost immediately, the gnomish woman made a sort of slightly dismissive grunt and turned away.

Ty stared at the sheet. It was pretty underwhelming.

Forli of Cliff Pass				
Level One	Air, Water			
Health	12	Stamina	11	Essence	10

Level Stats		
Strength	10	150 base pound-lifting capacity, +0% melee damage, +0% running speed.
Agility	8	+10% enemy hit chance, -10% hit chance with all weapons, -4% running speed
Dexterity	8	-10% base success for crafting and physical skill success rate, 20% chance to lower base weapon damage roll by one step
Endurance	12	+2 base Stamina, +10% Stamina Recovery Rate, +10% base Health Recovery Rate
Toughness	11	+1 base Health, +5% base Health, +5% base Stamina, +0 to resist poison, disease, and physical status effects
Perception	10	
Connection	10	+00% Essence recovery rate (12/day)
Capacity	10	+0 Base essence, +00% essence
Appearance	8	Most judge you moderately unattractive.

Non-Level Stats		
Intelligence	10	+00% skill acquisition rate.
Magic	8	-8% Magic Effects. +0 Maximum affinity.
Charisma	10	+00% perceived social skills
Luck	10	The Fates neither dislike nor care for you

Secondary Stats		
N/A	1	-10% essence cost to all Air abilities, +10% effect for all Air abilities or +1 to the difficulty to resist.

Birth Perks	
Race: Scrag Dryad (Pine)	+2 Toughness, +2 Endurance, +1 Armor -2 Agility, -2 Dexterity, -2 Appearance, -2 Magic
Magical Rank: Poor	May obtain Level 40 without ascension. Loses access to most magical options except the absolute most basic, and perhaps one to two slightly unusual abilities related to nature.
Flaw: Cracked	-1 Toughness
Acquired Perks	
N/A	

Skills	Level	Effect
Academics	1	The absolute most basic understanding of history and culture from your region.
Athletics	1	+3% to run speed, +1 to check to climb or avoid obstacles
Cooking	5	+25% quality to cooking
Dodge	1	+3% to dodge incoming attacks
Farming	6	+24% to base farming output
Natural Sciences	4	You have a solid grasp of basic concepts
Occult	2	You can sense magic that is not concealed, and that is connected to you, whose area of effect you are in, or that is within 2 feet of you. Your magic powers have 4% greater effect. You can vaguely sense the purpose of simple magic. +4% to accuracy with magic attacks.
Survival	3	+9% hunting and foraging

Abilities	Effect
Air	
N/A	
Water	
N/A	
Air/Water	
N/A	

As Ty and Ivy stared, Forli shifted uncomfortably. "So, um, I can still adventure with you? If I make a few levels, I can still be useful, right?"

Ty had no idea where her build would go, but he supposed she could do something with it. "Of course, Forli. We'll take you on a run, and see what we can do about getting you some levels, see what your build looks like."

"So, are you going to go now?" Ty asked, turning to look at Ivy.

She came over and put her hand on his arm. "Perhaps later. I don't want to waste your coin, now that I think about it."

Her eyes flicked down to the page, and she furrowed her brow a tiny bit.

Ty sighed. *I know damn well there's something on her character sheet she doesn't want me to see that this reminded her of. And I'm sure I'll regret this... but I do really like her on short meeting, and I want her to feel comfortable and trusted. I can respect her privacy for now.*

But part of him found it hard to trust. *You always get yourself in trouble, Ty.*

Ty was torn, between demanding that she show him her status sheet so he could plan accordingly and would be safe, and supporting her so she would like him.

She waited, her eyes slightly wide as she stared at him, as if she knew what he was deciding between. Her lip trembled the tiniest bit.

What to do?

Chapter Ten

THE NO TANK BLUES

Ty sighed again, opened his pouch to take another ten silver out, very nearly the last of his money, and handed it to Ivy. "Well, whenever you want to get it, feel free—and we can take a gander at it whenever you feel ready to share."

Forli gave a big smile as Ty made his pronouncement.

Then he took a few copper out and passed it to Forli as well. "And get a nice frame on me as well, please."

Ivy visibly relaxed a small amount. Then she smiled, lifted onto her toes, and kissed him on the cheek. "Thank you."

And now you're happy, you idiot. Even though she's probably going to stab you at some point.

But Ty couldn't stop grinning from ear to ear regardless. Ivy was the best.

He saw the gnome roll her eyes. *Okay, fine, you old geezer. So I've only known her for thirty minutes. She's still the best.*

"What now?" Ivy asked as she lowered herself, her cheeks slightly pink again.

Ty was tempted to suggest something different—the Emerald Bee for lunch, perhaps, and then on to his home, to show her his garden—but he stuck to the plan he had. Get an adventuring team, get some experience, and get some levels. He really needed to get his abilities back.

"We need to go see about another teammate, a guardian—maybe we can get one of those dragons from Dragon Beach to join us."

Ivy's eyes widened and her hands fluttered slightly. "A dragon? Are you sure that's a good idea? I mean, it was the great dragon Chao who destroyed the first Averian Kingdom—and dragons are notoriously the enemies of elves. I mean, a lot of people hate us and are jealous of us, but dragons are some of the worst."

Ty was surprised by her reaction. "Really? I mean, I know about Chao, but the Ash Dragon destroyed the dwarves, and I know the Havi Imperium took a lot of damage during the last dragonflight, and my old home in Steelport... I think dragons just tend to be aggressive to everyone."

"That's not exactly better, but I still think that dragons tend to hate elves the most."

"Why do you think that?"

She blushed and turned away. "My dad told me."

"Well, these ones are all apparently friends of the king at some level. I wouldn't worry about it too much—like I said, they're friendly. And he pays them to defend the town. So their hoards are dependent on being nice to us."

Ivy took a deep breath. "Okay, I can do this." Then she smiled slyly again and looked up at Ty. "Going to go grab a girl dragon, maybe? Shall we call our adventuring party 'The Dungeon Lord's Harem'? Or maybe the 'Dungeon *Master's* Harem?' I mean, you've already got two women in the party."

Ty coughed explosively and felt his own cheeks flush. *This girl... She seems crazy forward. Although that was a very fast switch of topic from 'I'm afraid' to 'I'm overly flirty.'*

Ty's instincts were telling him that there was something here, some reason that he wouldn't like behind her flirtations, but he couldn't fathom what the issue was and was willing to give Ivy the benefit of the doubt that her motives weren't to screw him. *Metaphorically, at least. If literal, I hope that is, in fact, her motive.*

Ivy was watching him, her indigo eyes alight. "C'mon, let's go see if we can get a dragon to be our guardian. I'm sure I'll be safe if I'm with you."

Ty felt ten feet tall.

It was a fifteen-minute walk from the Emerald Bee to Dragon Beach. Ty walked down across the quarter-mile-long bridge from the Central District to Elgin Isle in the middle of the Blue River. Then he walked hallway across Elgin Isle—another quarter mile total—till he reached the entrance to Dragon Beach on the south side of the isle.

The whole time, he bantered with Ivy and Forli. Both laughed at all his jokes, even a few bad ones he threw in intentionally, and both smiled at him a lot, and nodded along to his words. *This must be what it's like to be important and rich. I have to admit, I like it. Women simply scorning and ignoring me before was... hard. But it does feel odd, somehow, this new reality.*

Ty also noted, casually, that his feet hurt less than they normally would—from his very slightly wooden nature, he suspected. He still felt a bit odd looking at his brownish-colored skin—he felt like a wood elf and not a half-high elf—but for the most part he was becoming content with the changes that had occurred in him.

Once he had reached his destination, he walked down the stairs cut into the fifteen-foot cliffs that marked the change from Elgin Island proper to Dragon Beach, stepping out onto the sands.

He saw two bronze-scaled dragons frolicking—no other word for it—in the shallow water, and a third one sunning itself on the beach. The one on the beach was very clearly missing its right front foreleg.

While Ty doubted, very strongly, that this *particular* dragon would be the one that joined him, he went to it first, walking across the sands. Forli and Ivy followed him, both with a bit of trepidation, staying a few feet behind him. When he got close, he called out. "Excuse me, sir dragon. I wanted to inquire about adventuring dragons. Do you have a moment?"

The dragon looked up at him. The face and body were covered in bronze scales, with a swept-back horn pattern, a plate that turned into three horns facing almost backward. They couldn't be useful in an attack, but their positioning would make it a moderate challenge for someone to bite their neck, Ty suspected.

"I doubt I can help you, but you're more than welcome to talk to me, elf. I'm Tea, storm dragon of Dragon Beach."

"Hi, I'm Ty. I was wondering if one of the other dragons here, one that..." Ty trailed off.

"One that is whole?" Tea asked, her voice reeking with sardonism.

Ty winced, moving closer to the dragon and talking more normally. "Yeah, sorry. I was wondering if one might want to go adventuring in my dungeon, to make levels and gain treasure. I need a guardian, someone that can keep monsters busy while we fight."

"I doubt you'll find what you're seeking here, elf. None of the three dragons currently here can gain experience—we're too young, our magic is completely tied into our flight and breath weapon until we're aged twenty-five years. The two dragons that could've helped you left with King Leo on his latest adventure."

"One wouldn't want to do it for the treasure?" Ty asked, hopeful, glancing at the seven-foot dragon now right in front of him.

The dragon grinned at him. "I'm sure we would. But... I'm missing a leg. Of the two remaining dragons—the ones in the surf—Cal is missing his lower jaw, and Kel, while whole, has a personal flaw that makes him weak and puny for a dragon."

Ty grimaced. "Okay, yeah, you're right. I don't think this is where I'll find a guardian for my team. Curses. I had thought I was so clever, asking a dragon to do it. Ah well."

Tea laughed at him and butted him with her head, nearly knocking him over. "Well, I hope you do find someone. And if you need something else with the dragons of Star Port, let me know."

As they walked back up the stairs from the beach, Ty wasn't sure how to proceed. "Well, I don't think we're going to be getting a guardian today. How about we break, take care of any business we have, get what gear we can, and we meet at the Emerald Bee for breakfast tomorrow before we do a dungeon run. It's Level One... hopefully we can do a successful delve and make some levels."

"Sounds good," Ivy said. "I really look forward to seeing you again soon."

**

Ty returned to his house. It required him to walk another half-mile, from the middle of Elgin Isle west across a second bridge and into Green Apple Grove.

Most of the farms in Green Apple Grove had gotten eight acres of prime land inside the Calasti Tree node, which made trees grow twice as fast, bigger, and produce twice as much. Leo had handed out the grants early, with a preference for couples, during the first wave of the resettlement of Averia. But Ty had gotten the eight acres and his sister, Val, had gotten eight as well, next to each other, thanks to contributions each had made for the kingdom. They had made a single large house they shared as well and were working on making it fancy.

They had both been very poor at one point, as well as despised for being half-breeds. Neither wanted to return to that.

As Ty stared at his house, and his burgeoning garden, he felt a sense of displeasure. It wasn't lush enough, and it wasn't big enough. Something in him called for him to own square miles of land, to have a region that was his own. He was a master dryad now, and it wanted more. Perhaps a stream through the region he would have, as well...

Ty shook the moment off.

He wished his sister, Val, were here. He had so many questions. Most of them might not be entirely appropriate for a sister—what *was* the etiquette for asking her for advice about propagating the dryad species, Ty wondered with an internal laugh—but there was no one else he trusted enough. And some questions, like whether he should trust Ivy, felt very much in the 'ask your sister' category.

As he ruminated, looking at his house in the dying sunlight, he heard his mother's voice.

"Ty? Ty, is that you?"

Ty turned around and beheld his mother.

She was commonly known as Ola the Seamstress, even now that they had returned to an elven kingdom. But once, before he had been born, his mother had been Olanalinae Turventi ap Belmoria, the Duchess Belmoria, who had ruled over a portion of the Averian Kingdom, one with millions of elves. She still looked the part in many ways. Elven lifespans were such that she appeared in her prime, perhaps late twenties by the standards of the humans that Ty had grown up with, with watery-green eyes and copper hair. Although her eyes had lines that most that age wouldn't have. She was dressed in a thick, green woolen dress, full-body length.

"Yeah, it's me," Ty said.

"What happened to your skin?" his mom asked, walking over and reaching out and touching it with one hand. In her other, she had a large basket of ripe vegetables.

Ty frowned. His mother had counseled him against his first adventure, which had resulted in his capture by orcs. He was sure he was going to get guff, and tried to spin it as much as possible.

"When I became a dungeon lord, I received a very large set of new abilities. This is a manifestation of one of them."

"It turned your skin brown? And kinda hard?" Ola asked, surprised.

Ty grimaced, but didn't enlighten her any further as to the whole 'not an elf' thing. There was an awkward pause.

"Why were you standing in the walkway, staring at your house? Is everything okay?"

Ty loved his mother, but he wanted to exit this conversation as soon as possible. "Look, Mom... what brings you here? I'm important now, okay? I have things I need to do."

His mother frowned, but didn't make a huge deal of it. "I brought some of the best vegetables from the garden—Kivryn really has a touch when it comes to farming. He was wasted as a fisherman."

Ty didn't really want gifts from his mother's new husband. Kivryn was a decent guy, but the whole thing felt... pedestrian. His mother had been a duchess, once, and settling for a fisherman-turned-farmer, no matter how nice, felt... disrespectful, somehow. She had a magic line, even. She could do better.

Maybe Ty was being unfair, but he remembered the family they had been. Destitute and despised. He could remember the one-room shack they had lived in when he was a child, and the names that had been hurled at them—his mother included.

Now, they weren't the family they had been, once. Val was a general and Ty a dungeon lord, for the good god's sake. That family they had all been a part of, poor and despised by everyone, didn't exist anymore. It was just memories now. Memories that Ty wished he didn't have.

Ty gave a sigh and took the basket. "Thank you."

"Also, your father asked—"

"No," Ty said, forcefully. "I don't want to be bothered about Dad right now, okay? I'll do whatever I do on my own time, and in my own way." "He got you your first position in the government. You could at least invite him over for dinner sometime."

"Why do you care? He was your *owner*, once. I don't understand why you keep defending him to me! You should be the angriest."

His mother sighed. "Ty... even if I was angry, it doesn't help you. Your dad is a complicated and flawed man, we both know that. But he really does mean well. Just think about it, okay?"

Ty reached out and gathered his mother into his arms, feeling a bit the heel. He embraced her, and she embraced him back.

He loved his mom, deeply. He remembered what she had gone through to keep him and his sister alive and get them educated. It wasn't her fault that Ty had a complicated relationship with his own dad.

"Love you, Mom. Sorry. I'll try and see Dad soon, promise."

"Thank you," she said. She patted him on the back, awkwardly. "You're a good boy, Ty. But you can relax sometimes."

"I'll try, Mom," Ty said, but in his heart he knew he was going to keep driving. The demons of his own past, including his relationship with his dad, drove him.

Ty made a bit more small talk with his mom before she headed back, returning to her house before darkness fell completely. Ty went to bed thinking about his father.

But soon, his thoughts turned to other things. To Ivy, Forli, and adventure.

Chapter Eleven

A GOOD MORNING FOR
A BEATING

The Emerald Bee was a touch different in the morning. They didn't serve wine that early. Instead, they had fruit juice. They also made pancakes with emerald-pollen-infused honey and butter melted on it, as well as oranges, grapefruit, and melons—although the melons were sad little gourds, as compared to the epic, tree-grown fruits, thanks to the Calasti Tree Node.

The decorative utensils were still just as fine, and the food was still extraordinarily tasty.

The proprietor, Mirafol Blueleaf, walked up to the table Ty was seated at, carrying a tiny, ornate pitcher in one hand. She was very typically elven, thin and slightly boyish, with pointed ears and long, straight hair the color of spun silver. She wore an apron today over a plain, white dress that only reached her knees, as opposed to the fancy dress she had entertained guests with the last time Ty had been here.

She pulled a chair out and sat down across from him, holding herself with poise, and set the tiny pitcher on the table.

"The pancakes are excellent," Ty said, giving her a raised eyebrow, "if you came to check on the food."

"I came to congratulate you, Dungeon Lord. And to make an offer."

Ty forked a small piece of pancake into his mouth, liberally slathered in spiced but non-magical butter—he couldn't afford the emerald bee honey at the moment—and motioned for her to continue with his other hand.

She obliged. "I would ask for a permanent spot for me and a team of my choosing in your dungeon, one run a month. In return, I would hold a table always open for you, with breakfast, lunch, and dinner for you and up to five people free from the normal menu. And once per month, from the magical menu—emerald bee products, as well as anything else we happen upon."

Ty thought about it as he chewed. Even without the magical components, it was a cursed fine pancake. *In the long run, I think I can charge more for a run... but at the moment, this would be a good deal for me. If I really do have five dungeon runs per day, she's asking for two-thirds of a percent of my dungeon time. I can handle that. But...*

Ty swallowed. "That sounds like an excellent idea, subject to two provisos. One, it'll start as a five-year deal, subject to mutual agreement to continue."

She smiled. "Five years is fair and more than fair."

"Additionally," Ty continued, "your run owes me nothing, but you must pay the percentage of treasure to the guild they normally take as their portion. I already made a deal with Kadrath, and I can't just alter it. It'll be ten percent of the normal fee—so really, what you're getting from me is a ninety percent discount on the entrance fee and a guaranteed spot."

I don't actually know what the normal fee is, Ty thought to himself.

"So two percent total? Not a problem at all. Again, fair and more than fair."

Okay, cool, that means that the normal fee is twenty percent.

Ty nodded. "Perfect. In that case, although they're late, I'd like to order breakfast food for two others. Hopefully, they'll be here soon."

Mirafol smiled, took the pitcher, reached across the table, and slowly poured pink-tinted honey on Ty's pancakes. "Well, as a celebration of the deal, this time, the magic honey is free. For you and your guests. I'll bring breakfast out—hopefully they show up soon."

Life is good, Ty thought.

Then he frowned. *Although where are they? Did they somehow both get cold feet?*

Some time—and a delicious pancake—later, the door was pushed open by Forli. Ty breathed a sigh of relief, although he couldn't deny he would much rather it had been Ivy. No matter how much sudden desire for Forli he had.

A couple of the other patrons watched with interest as the dryad paused in the doorway. Star Port had two dryads now, in a population of over a thousand, so while they weren't super rare, they were unusual enough to attract notice. And only Adwoa was a native—Forli's tree was located in Cliff Pass, a hundred miles away.

"Over here, Forli," Ty called out.

Forli's face split into a huge grin, and she walked her curvy frame up to the table. As she got close, her eyes fixated on Ty, and her gaze ran up and down his body. She licked her lips. She was still wearing a normal if short dress, and one hand fell down to the hem, gripping it tight.

There was a brief pause. Ty saw some of the merchants and ship captains at tables around them nudging each other and subtly pointing at Forli. There were only two elves, and one was wearing the traditional daisy garland of someone who had accepted a new proposal to be a significant other and go to the Impending Flowers Dance at the upcoming winter solstice celebrations.

Dirty old men, Ty thought, half amused.

"So, how's it going?" he asked, saccharine sweet.

Forli sat in the chair. "I feel... really odd. Like I always imagined a mortal woman felt when she saw an ideal male mate. Only more so, and more like an animal, I guess. But it only happens when I'm near you. Why?"

Ty was torn. He didn't really want to explain his status to anyone, but the fact that he was having a direct, magical effect on Forli made him feel obligated.

He leaned in close and spoke very softly. "Don't talk about what I'm about to tell you, okay?"

Forli nodded, her eyes still slightly glazed as she looked at him. *This does seem like far more than normal attraction.*

"What you're feeling isn't real. When I was in the dungeon, something... went wrong. Some of Saelen—the Crone's power transferred to me. I am apparently part dryad now, and can make dryad seeds like the Crone could, only differently, I guess. Like a man makes a normal child."

"You can make more dryads? Like, right now?" Forli asked, her eyes wide.

"I think so?" Ty said, still not sure.

"And you just have to fornicate with me like a mortal animal to do it?" Forli asked.

"Again, I think so. This is new to me as well."

"You need to take me right now, Ty!" Forli exclaimed. "And you need to tell Thea. We wanted this, all of us!"

Ty glanced around, feeling his cheeks heat and wondering how visible a blush would be through his darker skin. Six pairs of eyes were staring at him, bemused, and after a moment a couple of them started chuckling.

"Ssshh!" Ty said to Forli. "Explain, please, but do it *quietly.*"

"We, the dryads, all wanted your plan to work. The dungeon plan, I mean. Part of it was to save our mother, the Crone, but part was because we hoped the dungeon would hand out loot in the form of dryad seeds. No more dryads will come into existence unless that happens. Or unless you make more, now! Wait, is it *we* making more? Or just you?"

"I don't know. I'm sorry. I feel like you weren't really paying attention the first time when I said this, but to repeat myself—this is all new to me as well."

Forli nodded. "Well, um, okay, but we need to try as soon as possible."

Is this real? Is some woman, even if she isn't the most beautiful, really just demanding I take her as soon as possible?

Ty pinched himself, but everything remained the same.

I better not be having a wet dream right now.

"Well, we'll see. I'm not saying no. But we should go adventuring first, no matter what—even though it's my dungeon, Kadrath has a schedule now, and I don't want to mess it up for everyone who paid for a spot."

"Speaking about the dungeon run, where's Ivy?" Forli asked.

Ty sighed. "I'm not sure what happened with her—she may have decided this wasn't the life for her. Which is unfortunate—we need a healer. And I liked her, personally."

As if speaking about her summoned her, Ivy walked through the door.

She appeared... terrible. Her metallic-copper hair was an absolute mess, and while she had leather armor on, one forearm bracer was completely missing. But her short sword was strapped to the belt at her hip, at least.

But the thing Ty worried about most was the massive bruise around her left eye.

She caught Ty staring and pushed her hair across half her face with a grimace, then walked over to Ty's table and sat down.

"What—" Ty began.

Ivy's eyes watered. "Please, Ty. I don't want to talk about it, okay?"

"Did... Did someone, um, take you against your will?"

Ivy stared up at him and answered in a sardonic voice, "You needn't worry yourself about my purity, my good lord. I remain an unravished virgin. And someone who *still* doesn't want to talk about it."

She picked up the knife and fork and began cutting away at the pancake in front of her. "Thanks for breakfast."

"Well, we could get a healing—"

Ivy slammed the fork and knife down flat on the table. Although her thin, noodle arms didn't really 'slam' well.

Forli reared back, obviously frightened by Ivy's outburst.

Ivy's eyes were watering again as she glared at him. "*Please*, Ty. I. Don't. Want. To. Talk. About it. Besides, we're going on a dungeon run. One level, and I'll have access to healing magic. So I can take care of it myself then. Let's not parade my weakness and dishonor any further than it has been, hmm? Can you please do that for me? Please?"

Ty nodded mutely.

Ivy picked her fork up again and violently shoved a piece of pancake in her mouth. Her eyes got wide and dried a bit. She slumped in her chair. "By Cerivae Nerithin, Ty, did you spring for the magic honey here? God, you treat me so right. I could get used to this. It's *so* good. Mmm..."

Ty was still concerned—very concerned—about the bruise on her face but couldn't bring himself to push her further. She had made her wishes clear. He was at least glad that his status as a dungeon lord had allowed him to acquire food good enough to take her mind off everything. Whatever 'everything' was. He hoped.

Ivy swallowed and then went still, not moving.

After a moment, she glanced up at Ty, and tears spilled down her cheek. Her hands shook. "Hey, I'm really, *really* sorry I yelled at you, especially when you went and did all this for me. You won't kick me out, right? And you still like me? Right, Ty? You still like me? I didn't screw everything up?"

Ty's heart went out to her. She was obviously suffering through some trauma. He reached across the table, pushing the dishes aside, and gripped her forearm. "No. You have a spot in our party forever. It's okay. We're fine."

Ivy wiped the tears away. "You're sure? Really sure?"

"Of course."

"Thanks, Ty. So much. And… sorry again."

"I'm here for you as well, Ivy," Forli said, reaching out and putting her hand on the elf's shoulder. "We'll go make a bunch of levels, and then you won't have to worry anymore."

Ivy gave a hiccupping laugh but didn't respond.

For a bit, no one said anything, except for occasional quiet grunts of pleasure from Ivy as she ate. She did throw him a smile more than once. Ty was a decent cook himself and made a promise to keep his small house stocked up on all the finest ingredients, magical included, for when—if—he was able to convince Ivy to come over.

Although he felt like a heel for thinking that in this moment of her distress, but he was who he was. His thoughts were his own—he could only be blamed for his actions. He just needed to make sure his actions were always worthy of an Averian noble. Even if he wasn't one.

Forli spoke up. "So, what's the plan? I'm really weak, and Ivy is a proto-healer. How are we handling the adventuring?"

"Well, again, the dungeon has a maximum of Level Two monsters. So I think that we can handle it even without a guardian," Ty said confidently.

Forli hesitantly nodded and bit her lip.

Ivy hung her head.

Ty gripped her shoulder. "The dungeon is only Level One. I also have really solid perks. We can probably handle it."

Almost as if planned, all three of them shifted their eyes in the direction of the dungeon.

I really hope I'm right, and none of us dies.

Chapter Twelve

THE DUNGEON LIFE

Ty and Forli geared themselves from the Adventurers' Guild stores. Forli owned an extra-long shift, basically a cheap dress, as her entire life earnings. Ty hadn't ever expected to need a weapon again once he had mastered lightning. He had lost his first sword—a sad cast-off training piece made by a forge apprentice named Vito back in Steelport—to the orcs, and hadn't replaced it once he had made a level and gotten his first weak lightning attack.

So Ty had gotten himself a stout wooden staff with a built-in lightning enchantment—a topaz tip that crackled with electricity—and three healing potions. They were purchased against proceeds from the dungeon, and he had fronted the money for Forli to get a short sword as well. It was a low-quality match for the sword that Ivy carried. He had also gotten Forli some leather armor, but hadn't gathered any for himself.

Once geared, they left the Adventurers' Guild and walked the couple hundred feet to his dungeon entrance.

There was an elf whom Ty didn't recognize waiting at the edge of the interior stairway downward, with long platinum—the metal, not gray—hair. A hasty wooden podium had been erected, and on it, Ty saw a ledger and an inkwell and quill.

He waved as they entered, then inked a note in the ledger.

"What's your name, my good man?" Ty asked the elf that was obviously running the dungeon for them.

"Liwynsiel ap Latan," the man replied with a smile. "Call me 'Li.'"

"Ap Latan?" Ty asked.

The man nodded.

Ty remembered his studies on dungeons. A huge number of them were based on one thing only... "As in, you're from the other family that has a dungeon around here?"

"Yup. Well, if by 'around here,' you mean three hundred miles south and a touch east. I'm dungeon born and everything. That's how I came to work for the guild, actually. Had a falling out with my family, but I got along well with Kadrath before he was a guildmaster. When he got appointed here, I came up."

Forli walked down the interior stairs past Li. "What does 'dungeon born' mean, exactly?"

"I have the dungeon born perk—it starts me with the dungeon's magics, and I got the mask when I was a baby. Mask of the Undrashi Chimera dungeon."

"What's 'Undrashi' mean?"

"No one knows—but that's the name carved over the entrance."

Li reached into the folds of his cloak and withdrew a mask—it was a carnival-style mask, with the left half a dragon's head and the right a goat's head. A snake's mouth was at the top junction of the mask. "See? Chimera."

Ty could feel faint magic coming from it, but it was too complicated to easily identify.

"How do you become Dungeon Born?" Ivy asked as she descended into the interior of the gazebo-style dungeon entrance room.

"You are literally born to a dungeon lord, or, so long as that dungeon lord lives, born to one born of him, and so on. So an immortal dungeon lord would spread the line to all his descendants. But as soon as the dungeon lord title passes, only those descended from the new dungeon lord get the perk. If you already had it, you keep it, but none of your children will get it thereafter."

"What does the mask do?" Ty asked.

The elf wiped his brow. "Full of questions today, aren't you, dungeon lord? Well, it's a free magic item that usually gives a few stats, but not much else. But you should always wear it while adventuring, since it literally doesn't count against the maximum magic items you can wear. The stats are almost always baby versions of what the dungeon lord gets. But it stacks, so you'll be in great shape."

I didn't get a mask. I wonder if I will at some point? I wonder if my children will?

"Appreciate the advice," Ty said. "Should I just go down the stairs to enter the dungeon?"

"Yup, it's that simple. Once you enter, whatever new configuration the dungeon has chosen will stabilize, and it'll stay the same till everyone leaves—but it also won't start recovery till you're out. I'll monitor here to make sure no one goes in after you, until you've left and we're ready for the next team."

Ty nodded to the man, hand over heart. "Thanks, I really appreciate it."

"Of course, dungeon lord. Now, please, the monsters await you." Li motioned to the stairs. Ty went down, followed by Ivy and then Forli.

The stairs never went completely dark. Light from the lower stair exit always provided enough illumination to at least make out the steps, though barely.

When Ty had finally reached the lowest landing, he exited into a bland cave. Nothing interesting at all—it was about a hundred feet on a side, with stalactites and stalagmites, one ambitious pair of which had turned into a column. A couple of bioluminescent mushrooms that provided light. And that was it.

"So... this is the dungeon?" Ivy asked, and Ty heard the disappointment in her voice.

He felt it himself. It was… underwhelming. He felt the need to defend his dungeon. "Well, it's a Level One dungeon. It'll get better."

Forli walked out of the stairway as well. "So, um, are we going to fight things? To get better?"

"That is the plan. I think I have the most health, so I'll go first," Ty said aloud. "Ivy, Forli… If I get jumped, save me, okay?"

Ivy pulled her sword out from its sheath and held it in a practiced grip, but Ty could already see that she wouldn't be able to hold it long. Forli took hers out as well. Her hold was extremely awkward.

The group stalked forward slowly, their eyes darting from shadow to shadow.

An eyeless rat creature with giant incisors crawled out from behind a stone column where a stalactite met a stalagmite. Two more quickly joined it. Each was about three feet long, and a good six inches of them appeared to be the mouth and crazy incisors.

"Okay, so it generated some defective rats. I'll try to shock them with the staff when they charge. I doubt I'll get all three, so please be prepared to defend yourselves."

Ivy held her sword ready, and Forli at least held hers out.

The three rats charged.

Two of the rats charged at him, and one ran past at Forli. He poked one in the face, doing a single point of physical damage, but his lightning sparked around the topaz tip and coursed through the rat. Said rodent failed its Toughness check, taking additional damage and collapsing to its side.

The second rat bit his leg. His magically wooden skin resisted the bite, but not completely, and the creature's teeth sank into his thigh.

Ty grunted, half-screamed, and collapsed to the ground. "Stab it, Ivy, stab it!"

Ivy, her face all scrunched up and afraid, stabbed the rat that had collapsed a couple of feet from Ty.

Son of a...!

"The one on my leg. My leg!" Ty screamed out as the rat started yanking. Ty tried to punch it but was so weak that he couldn't really do enough of a sit-up to get leverage. He ended up lightly batting at the rat's head.

Ivy came forward and stabbed at the rat on Ty's leg... and missed entirely. "Sorry!"

At least she didn't stab me. Thank Eturia for small favors.

Ty gave up on competent assistance, and started slamming the rat with his staff.

Ty spasmed, jerking, as he shocked himself for another two damage through the rat. The rat sizzled and spasmed, however. According to the notification Ty got in his head, it died on the third blow.

I just lost six health to a freaking Level One rat! This was barely better than my fight with Dalryn and his damnable cronies, and I was alone then.

Although I was Level Six.

"Help!" Forli cried, and Ty glanced over from the ground and saw that she was running from the last rat, managing to barely keep ahead of it.

Joy.

Ty turned over, braced one leg, and pushed off the ground, standing awkwardly as he glanced up at Ivy.

She was completely white and shaking, barely able to hold her sword. Her lip trembled and her eyes watered.

Before she could burst into tears and start apologizing, Ty gave her a smile. More of a rictus of teeth, really, given the pain, but he hoped she would think it a smile in the dim light.

"It's okay—this is why we're learning in a low-level dungeon. And you'll be a healer soon. Now we need to go save Forli!"

Ty limped over to the rat chasing Forli and poked it with the staff, shocking it.

"Stab it, Forli!" he cried.

She turned, ran over, took the sword in an extremely awkward two-handed grip, and stabbed downward. For a wonder, she hit, poking into its belly.

"Again!" Ty cried out.

She grimaced in disgust as she pulled the sword out and viscera and blood poured across the floor, but she stabbed it again. This time, the rodent died.

The rat, and its blood, disappeared in a puff of dissipating magical energy. It left behind a small pile of well-made oaken boards.

"Well, we can retire from this life of adventuring now," Ty quipped.

Ivy stared at the ground. "Was I that bad?"

"What? No! I just meant it as a joke about the quality of the loot, sorry."

"Oh, thank goodness, I also thought you meant we were so bad we had to quit," Forli replied.

Ivy pulled herself together a bit but still stared at the ground as she answered. "I'm sorry about that—I've never really been in a real fight. Also that only gave me thirty-four experience. I need a hundred to level."

"I got fifty-one, and I'd be willing to bet that Forli got seventeen, right?"

Forli nodded and cracked a smile.

"You need three on-level creatures killed by yourself to level until you are past Level Ten. So each one gives thirty-four experience, but it's divided by the number of participants. If we fight as a team, it'll usually divide by group. But since Forli just ran and we fought that rat separately from you, Ivy, I think the gods, or whomever created the status charts and such, treated it as two separate fights."

"I'll try and stay with the main fight in the future." Forli pointed at Ty's leg. "But are you going to be okay, Ty? I mean, that looks pretty bad."

Ivy came over and gave the wound, through his breeches—which were a total loss—a thorough look. "That does seem pretty bad."

Ty pulled a potion out of his belt, holding it up. "Yeah, it hurts something fierce. But, I have this as well. And two more. Just to get us through until Ivy can make enough experience to become a healer."

Ty pulled the stopper out and threw back the contents of the tiny potion.

> Ty is healed by Least Healing Potion for 6 points of damage. All status negatives are removed.

The effect was almost instantaneous, with the flesh healing over extremely rapidly. He could also feel his burns and subtler internal damage heal. In six seconds, he went from heavily damaged to completely hale.

Ty smiled up at everyone. "If we stick together as a group and fight those again, we should all gain a level in two more groups. Then, we'll all have abilities, and it should get easier."

If, of course, I can avoid getting bit by rats each and every time. Because these two aren't going to stop it from happening, for sure.

Chapter Thirteen

LEVEL UP!

Ty didn't, in fact, manage to keep himself from getting bitten again. In fact, he was bitten quite a bit. He was out of potions. But, two groups of three rats later—handled with the same lack of aplomb as the first—Ivy called out "Ding!"

"Ding?" Ty asked, bemused, staring around the cavern at the various plain rock formations, wondering if more rats were concealed.

"Yeah, ding. After the chiming sound it makes when you level."

"That makes sense I suppose," Ty said. "And I'm glad you leveled."

"Thank Nerithin, yes. I can become a healer now, which I always wanted to be, and fix the hurt things of the world."

"Which is me," Ty said. "I'm the hurt thing. In our little world. Right now."

Ivy giggled, her hand in front of her mouth.

Forli laughed so hard she snorted. The laugh had a vaguely hysterical edge to it, but it was better than weeping—which she had done after one rat bite. Ty was honestly concerned about her long-term mental fitness to be an adventurer.

Ivy walked over and touched Ty. He felt a sense of renewal, young growth, springtime, and being healthy in his prime as the magic of Wyld entered his body. A translucent box appeared over his vision.

> Ivy uses regenerate, rank I. Ty is recovering 1 health per 6 seconds for 90 seconds.

Ty didn't need the box to tell him that he was getting better and dismissed it with a thought. His pain disappeared, and he watched as the burns on his leg disappeared, and the bite mark closed. In a mere thirty seconds, he was at maximum health.

Although the robe was a total loss again, in addition to his breeches. *I need to find some cheaper stuff to wear. I also need to get magic items beyond this staff, really. Adventuring in my social robes, no matter how fine, is a bit ridiculous.*

Ty stopped watching his leg. "What was your other ability? The one you get for being a high elf."

Ivy glanced to the side then stared at the ground. "I took familiar, rank I. I can get a familiar now."

"Nice! It's cool that you're getting a rare build going right out the door. Few people qualify to be familiar mages."

Ivy glanced up. "You do—you have Wyld and Soul as well, right?"

"I do—but that's only because of the dungeon. I didn't before."

"Hmm."

"Maybe we can get you a familiar when we leave the dungeon—I understand the forest is rife with them, if you're quiet and have someone that has an open familiar ability. Apparently, familiars can almost smell that."

Ivy smiled at him. "That sounds fun. I would like that. Although it might be better if we wait."

"Why?" Ty asked.

"Well, your dungeon is also Wyld and Soul, as you said, and that means that it will almost certainly create familiars as loot. I think I might be well served just waiting for the improved-quality familiars I'm assuming the dungeon will put out."

"You got an ability you just intend to sit on?" Forli asked incredulously. "Really? Why would you do that?"

Ivy shrugged. "I can heal, that should be enough for a bit. I can get the familiars later, like I said."

Then she gave Forli the eye. "What did you get?"

"I had mostly boring powers, all the basic stuff you read about if you study builds—which I did last night before going to bed. But I did start with a combination option out the door— Ice blast, an Air and Water magic ability. It's weak, but a touch stronger as a combo power than things like the basic lightning attack I could get. It has a slowing effect as well as some small damage, and it hits things in a larger area. I took it. No more having to get up and personal to stab things." She shuddered dramatically.

Ty idly enjoyed her dramatic flair.

"What did you take?" Forli asked, her face alight as she watched Ty.

He hadn't picked any abilities yet. The truth was, he didn't know what path he wanted. When he was Ty with the Belmoria line, it had made sense—just take lightning. Now though? He wasn't sure if it still made sense. He pulled up his options.

Leveling Options, Level Two [pick two, one must be Wyld]	
Air	
Airborne Reflexes, Rank I	+4 Agility
Strike of the Wind, Rank I	Spend 2 essence. You move with blinding speed, gaining +50% accuracy and a 50% chance to land an extra blow against an equal speed target every 6 seconds
Wind Parry	Spend 1 essence, +50% to dodge incoming ranged physical attacks and +20% to dodge all normal attacks

Master Parry, rank I	+20% dodge as a static buff
Sky Archer	+50% to rate of fire and damage with archery weapons
Lightning, Rank I	1 essence. Do 1-3 base lightning damage, with +100% to accuracy, as a ranged occult attack
Whispered Words	1 essence. You can speak and have it carried by the wind to only your chosen target, up to 200 feet away
Wind-Boosted Leap	Jump +10 feet, modified by all air-magic-modifying abilities
Shocking Shield, Rank I	1 essence per 6 seconds. Anyone attacking takes 1 base lightning damage and must make a Toughness check at +2, -1 per Air Affinity, to resist shock (lose 6 seconds of actions and take -40% to dodge)
Air Affinity, Rank I	+1 Air Affinity
Soul	
Soul of Magic, Rank I	+2 Magic
Natural Leader, Rank I	+2 Charisma
Improved Connection, Rank I	+4 Connection
Improved Capacity, Rank I	+4 Capacity
Shield, Rank I	May spend 1 essence and gain a 4-hit-point shield that lasts for 6 seconds.
Barrier, Rank I	May spend 1 essence and gain a 2-hit-point shield that lasts for 1 minute. Damage is taken off from the barrier before any critical multiplier is applied.

Talk Down	The wielder may spend 2 essence and make a contested Charisma check against the target's highest Intelligence, Magic, or Charisma score, with the defender getting any bonuses against mind-affecting powers. Success will calm the target so that they won't initiate or continue aggression, unless harmed or witnessing others they care for being harmed.
Soul Affinity, Rank I	+1 Soul affinity
*Eldritch Power, rank I	+10% damage to all energy attacks, as well as all shields and barriers.
*Magic Wellspring, rank I	+10% to Capacity and Connection Score
+Dungeon Passage, rank I	+100% magic benefit to region and world from all dungeons tied directly or indirectly (through sub-dungeon lords) to the Dungeon Lord
Wyld	
Bestial Strength, Rank I	+4 Strength
Bestial Agility, Rank I	+4 Agility
Bestial Endurance, Rank I	+4 Endurance
Bestial Toughness, Rank I	+4 Toughness
Bestial Senses, Rank I	+4 Perception
Were Form, Rank I	May spend 1 essence, and 1 essence per every 6 seconds, to assume a partial were form. Gain +4 to Strength, Agility, Endurance, and Toughness for the duration of the ability.

Resilient, Rank I	Gain back 1 Health per ten minutes at no cost.
Regeneration, Rank I	Spend 2 essence. Gain 1 health till max per 6 seconds for 1 minute.
True Grit	Wound penalties to accuracy, dodge, and Stamina recovery are halved
Wyld Affinity, Rank I	+1 Wyld affinity
Animal Companion, Rank I	Gain an animal companion. That animal gains +2 to all physical stats. "Animals" includes any magical beast less than Level 6 for this power.
+Thicken Root to the Dryad's Grove	The Dungeon Lord enhances his connection to the Dryad Grove Dungeon. His stat gain becomes +3 Magic and +3 Toughness, and the dungeon gains +1 magic effect and +.1 loot rating.
Soul/Wyld	
Familiar, Rank I	May bond a single familiar. This familiar gains half the level of its master and is a sapient magical beast.

Ty stared, fascinated, at his new powers. Although he was clearly stronger at both Wyld and Air magic, he had some fascinating abilities in Soul. A build began to take shape in his mind—he could take lightning abilities, shocking shields, and barriers, as well as the Capacity increaser and damage-increasing abilities in Soul. He could become a veritable god of storm magic and shielding both.

He would need at least one Wyld ability every ten levels, however.

As he looked at the chart, though, two things stood out. The Dungeon Passage ability and the Thicken Root to the Dryad's Grove ability. He focused on them, expanding their descriptions.

Dungeon Passage: Ability is rare, gained from the combination of Soul Magic, Natural Magic quality, and the Branching Paths Perk.

The Dungeon Lord is a conduit, effectively allowing magic to travel from the dungeon, in its personal dimensional space near the source of magic, the Sea of Chaos, out into the world more effectively. It travels through the Dungeon Lord due to his close connection to the dungeon.

The Dungeon Lord adds +100% to the magic sent to the world from the dungeon.

This power *will* lead to advanced versions of itself, and *may* lead to advanced combination powers with other specific abilities.

Thicken Root of the Dryad's Grove: Ability is rare, gained from the combination of Wyld Magic, Natural Magic quality, the Branching Paths ability Root of a Thousand Dungeons, and Dungeon Lordship over the Dungeon of the Dryad's Grove.

The Dungeon Lord has a deep connection to his dungeon, along the paths specifically built in its formation. The Dungeon Lord gains power from the dungeon. With this ability, he enhances the magical connection, weaving in deeply into his magical soul, gaining a far stronger benefit and providing a small benefit in return.

The Dungeon Lord changes his benefit from the Dryad Grove dungeon on the branching path from +1 Toughness and +1 Magic to +3 Toughness and +3 Magic, as well as giving the Dungeon +1 magic effect and +.1 loot quality as the magic of the dungeon lord flows back as well, enhancing the dungeon.

This *may* lead to advanced combination powers taken in the right combinations.

Ty barely noticed as Ivy shifted on her feet, and Forli did the same, glancing at each other as Ty studied his charts.

I must take a Wyld ability as a Master Dryad—my racial modifier requires it. The 'thicken root' ability gives me as much Magic stat as the normal Soul Magic stat gain ability. Plus, it makes me tougher and gives my dungeon a slight boost as well. It feels like a no brainer, unless I want to specifically be a familiar build. Which I don't, really. I would have taken the branching path focused on it if I did.

Beyond that, however, I get one ability at this level—and I'll get an average of twelve abilities every ten levels instead of the normal ten going forward.

If I start my lightning build again, I'll also get bonus Air abilities at level five...

Ty selected lightning, rank I and Thicken Root to the Dryad's Grove.

His new chart was a bit more impressive. He hovered his focus over his lightning, rank I ability.

Lightning, Rank I	Spend 1 essence. Does 2-5 total (1-3 x1.28 magic stat of 17, x1.18 occult score of 9, x1.1 Air affinity of 1) damage with +100% accuracy. Damage can pass through things to hurt those touching them.

Before becoming a dryad, Ty's Magic stat had been limited to ten, and he had possessed no way to increase it. He previously had the second level of lightning, which did 3-5 base damage. His previous rank two version was barely stronger than the enhanced rank one version now.

He could work with this. In fact, he was pretty damned excited by it.

He looked up at the others. "I took increased Magic stat, survivability, and my basic lightning attack again."

Ivy gave him a glowing smile. "That's great, Ty. So you're recreating your lightning build?"

"Among other things."

Ty stared down the far hall. "Shall we go see about a boss?"

They both nodded, a bit more enthusiastically than they had been before gaining their abilities.

Ty banished thoughts of his eventual build and what it might encompass, and refocused on the delve. "Alright, we've gone through ten Level One beast monsters, which seems to be what this dungeon defaults to. We've got three and the nest left, based on how many monsters the dungeon chart told me we have. I'd be willing to bet that they're all Level Two now. So, now that we have a healer, we can keep moving, and we'll still make a decent amount of experience. But that means the boss will almost certainly be Level Two as well."

Ivy and Forli both nodded.

There was only one way out of the cavern they were in, besides where they had come from. A single tunnel, as boring as the main cavern, with stalactites and stalagmites and a few bioluminescent mushrooms, but naught else.

Ty headed down it, followed by his team, who crept very closely behind him. Neither was exactly physically brave he felt, but they were still here. That was something.

From around a bend in the tunnel, three larger rat creatures, with metallic-iron skin, charged.

Ty pushed his hand out and shot one with lightning. The armor appeared to give no protection as the creature twitched, hitting the ground. Forli threw her hand forward, and a spray of icy wind passed over it. The iron rat expired, its skin no protection against either magic.

Ty clenched as the two rats ran him down, one of which had caught some of Forli's ice blast as well. In an eerie replay of the first time he had faced rats, he poked one that was shocked enough to miss and the other got the same leg, same place—but Ty felt *bone* crack as the metallic teeth of the monster bit down hard.

He hit the ground again, not waiting for Ivy—then shot the monster with lightning, which passed into him. But the increased sturdiness from his Toughness let him weather the attack. Somehow, he was tougher and meatier where the rat was biting. It hurt less, and his penalties were smaller.

It still hurt like hell. Just a touch less.

"I need healing!"

Ivy touched him on the shoulder, pushing a regenerate into his body. Ty hit the rat on his leg again, and between the two lightning bolts it was enough, and the rat died.

As the other rat that had missed charged back, Ty rolled to the side, yelling—he knew that if the last rat got him, he was in trouble.

Fortunately, it missed as he rolled away. Unfortunately, Ivy also missed touching him for the next regenerate.

Ty kept rolling, but the rat was nearly on him. Ty hit the rat at the same time it bit his arm. But the few moments for Ivy's regenerate had replenished blood loss and some damage, and he managed to survive with a fair margin.

Ivy touched him, and a second wave of regenerate went through him. The effects stacked. He could feel his leg resetting, an experience simultaneously dearly welcomed and completely unsettling. His arm started to heal.

That's a lot of my essence, but I've still got some, Ty thought. Before he could shock the rat, however, Forli stuck her hand right in the rat's face and iced its whole head. Like the first rat, lightning and cold both added up to 'too much,' and it died.

"Yay?" Ivy asked, her lips quirked to the side.

"We *need* a guardian," Ty said. "Just, absolutely, so badly. I mean, not to be an ass to you guys, but right now we've got two frail ranged damage dealers and a healer, basically. One a lot more frail than the other, but still, we're both frail. You said your brother was kind of a jackass, Ivy, I know—but please, just bring him."

Ivy tapped her fingers from both hands together in front of her and stared at the ground. "I'm not sure that's a great idea, Ty, I think you guys will hate each other, there's—"

"I'll get over it to not get eaten by rats again," Ty said, fervently. "Trust me. Bring me a guardian, and I'll forgive his personality flaws, promise."

"I, I..." Ivy appeared very flustered. "Okay, I'll bring him, just don't be mad at me."

"I'm not going to be mad at you, you warned me fair and square that he was a jackass."

Ivy appeared very skeptical but said nothing else. "Shall we fight the boss?"

Ty looked at the last room at the end of the hall. He could faintly make out a huge mound and a much larger rat at the end.

It was bigger than any he had seen. "No, frankly. I'm sad we didn't make Level Three, but let's do that tomorrow. We really need that guardian."

As they were talking, the rats dissolved. Again, one of the rats left a few short planks of well-cut oak boards behind.

Ivy stared for a moment and then started laughing. "It's a do-it-yourself oak end table!"

Ty stared—he was pretty sure that's not what it was, just some nice oak boards. A couple coppers' worth at best.

"Be still my beating heart," Forli drawled out. "We can retire from this life of adventuring, and I can open that eatery I always dreamed of."

I made that joke earlier.

"You got sassy as an ability at Level Two, didn't you?"

Ivy was tapping her fingers together. "You know, if you give a dungeon things, they can add to their treasure drop abilities. This is a forest dungeon, but it can still give coin if we give it coin first."

She met Ty's eyes with an expectant look on her face.

He sighed, reached into his pouch, and tossed a bronze and a silver coin into the far end of the cavern. They hit and rolled, and a few seconds after they came to a stop, they dissolved into nothing as well.

"Okay, now hopefully we won't have to haul oak boards out to get paid," Ty said.

"Much," Forli said.

"Much," Ty agreed. "It's still on the treasure list I assume."

"We taking these?" Ivy asked. "I'm… not great at carrying stuff."

"Nor I," Forli said.

They both looked at Ty with large eyes.

"Fine. Care to join me for a meal afterwards?"

Forli grimaced and twiddled her fingers. "I, um, actually made an appointment with an occult trainer. I need to get a lot better at magic. I'm sorry, Ty, I really, really want to, but next time, okay?"

Ty nodded.

"I'd love to," Ivy said, staring at him with violet eyes that he felt were filled with promise.

Chapter Fourteen

DINNER AND...

"Thank you, Ty, again. For your kindness. And thank you, Cerivae Nerithin, for spreading kindness throughout the world."

After her brief thank you, Ivy dug into the meal with gusto. It was a dish of walnuts and various honeyed fruits, with a glass of cider to wash it down.

The Emerald Bee wasn't terribly busy, but Ty figured his ordering of the magical food—again—had likely made tonight profitable for the inn and eatery. Ty also noticed that a new set of decorations, wooden statues of the ghost wolf and sun eagle progenitors, had gone up on the far wall.

Ty had the same food in front of him but found himself watching Ivy eat rather than eating himself. She was quite beautiful. Her long, copper hair, with just a hint of a slight greenish tinge, was fascinating to him. While copper hair was extremely common among elves, the metallic green tint wasn't. Her face was rounder than normal for an elf, quite cute, and her ears were elven perfection.

She had gone home and changed, and now wore a somewhat sheer white dress, just on the non-scandalous side of acceptable for style in Averia. A pair of emerald earrings—extremely rare in these parts, and a sign she came from wealth, although she hadn't purchased anything or shown any coin.

Ty couldn't help thinking that Ivy liked him. All the signs were there—she had been flirting quite heavily, he felt, almost *too* forward in her advances. Ty assumed his status as a dungeon lord, and his approval from the king and job as a minister-at-large, had made him far more attractive. *I set out to do great things and make a name for myself, not the least of which was because none of the girls, not even the elf girls, would give me the slightest look back in Steelport. I guess I can't blame them. Back then I was a scrawny guy with no job that came from the freed-slave family of a seamstress. Hardly what gets the girls excited. And definitely not what gets their dads excited, either. I didn't have any angle.*

But now, Ty did—he was important and prosperous.

Ivy glanced up from her food, and her violet eyes met Ty's green ones. The tableau held for a moment, but her cheeks reddened and she went back to eating, stuffing her mouth with a slice of honeyed apple and chewing furiously.

Ty dithered, trying to reach the courage necessary to ask her on a formal date.

After a moment, without glancing up, Ivy asked, "Do you think I'm pretty, Ty?"

"Very much," Ty replied with as much fervor as he could put into his voice.

"Do you... do you think maybe after dinner you could show me your place?" Ivy asked quietly, growing redder.

Is she suggesting what I think she's suggesting? It was improper in Averia for someone to have relations before they were married. Not that it didn't happen—a lot—but still. *I had thought maybe some dates, but if this is the route she wants to take...*

"I would love to," Ty said. "It's a decent place, and I have a nice garden set up, thanks to my magic. Well, the magic I had, before. Although, normally, I share it with my sister, Val. We get along extremely well, and neither one of us wanted to remain with my mom. And since we're both—"

Ivy smiled, still staring down a bit. "We should go. I don't mind that you share with your sister. I know a dungeon lord and a kingdom's general could each have a house of their own if they wanted."

"Yeah, sorry, that makes sense."

They ate in silence for a bit longer, the atmosphere feeling electric to Ty. Everything tasted amazing, yet Ty barely noticed it as he waited.

Eventually, they finished, and stood. The proprietor, Mirafol Blueleaf, gave Ty a raised eyebrow and half a smile as he and Ivy left the Emerald Bee, as well as the three-fingers held up gesture the Averian elves used for 'good-luck,' 'approval,' or sometimes 'okay.' Its specific meaning was a bit fuzzy.

As they left the eatery into the Grand Plaza and turned to make the walk to Ty's house, he girded his loins and, breath held, reached out and took Ivy's hand. She accepted, letting him take her hand and gently squeezing back.

Her hand was tiny and frail and feminine in structure, but he could feel the calluses on her palm that reminded him that she was also a trained swordswoman, despite her obvious attempt to switch to a different build.

It was a mile and a half walk to Ty's house. A thousand feet to the East Bridge, then a mile across the bridge, through Elgin Isle, and then across the West Bridge. Once there, he entered his home neighborhood, Green Apple Grove.

Green Apple Grove was a neighborhood of orchards. The king had given each family roughly eight acres of orchards. Ty and his sister had sixteen between them. The Calasti Tree node made the trees grow fast and produce twice as much fruit as they normally would, so the orchards were prime real estate.

Each little orchard family aspired to acquire a central house of the ubiquitous hardened marble that made up Star Port's architecture, with a small artistic garden around the house, and the orchards outside that. With marble fences, of all things, the norm. Ty followed the designs so he wouldn't be an outsider, but he wondered as to why this architecture all the time.

Even the road they had built the town around was an old marble one from the empire.

The town also had a lot of nature, but *controlled* nature. Rose bushes in neat lines along fences. Flowering vines growing up marble pillars. Gazebos—so many gazebos. Ty felt that his mother's people were less of a forest-oriented people—which was how he had thought of elves once—and more of a *garden*-oriented people.

The town center was a small work of art in and of itself. It had a statue someone had made—from marble. It was of Calida, the king before King Leo, fighting a demon. Flowers had been planted, and, Ty knew from conversations with his neighbors, magically grown artfully around the place. A whole swatch of close-set red ones at the feet of the statue were clearly meant to be the splash of blood from the demon.

The store fronts were all marble, but with trellises up the fronts with vines grown in artistic patterns around them to give the store fronts color and character. There was a wrought-iron gate around the town center with a flowering vine woven all through it. Ty was pretty sure the prevalence of Wyld mages Star Port had inherited was a significant reason for the prevalence of 'plants as art' to complement the marble buildings.

Right now, as they approached Ty's home, he saw many of the elven decorations for the solstice festival coming up. Trees covered in flowers of various colors, signifying different things, most of which Ty didn't know. But he did know that white daisies were for lovers, or those you wanted to become lovers. A garland of white daisies was how you invited someone to the Impending Flowers Dance, the big event of the season for the Averian elves.

Eventually, they reached his house, on the outer edge of town before the road turned north, headed for Wheat Town. A marble cobblestone walkway led through the orchard, just wide enough to see the house with ease. It went past a small statue of Iluvin Eturia, goddess of Wyld magic, to his front yard where he had trellises prepared for spring, when they would have flowering vines everywhere.

He reached the great wooden door—currently decorated with a ghost wolf because of his sister.

"This is a very nice house," Ivy said, glancing around. "Large. It speaks well of you that you have it."

"Well, Sis and I are—were—both Level Six, and work for King Leo. Our levels mean we draw four gold, sixty silver a year each now, so even without the dungeon I'm very well off."

Although, I may need to reregister as Level Two. Let's see if I can level up enough to make a difference before the next pay period.

"I'll say," Ivy quipped, smiling. Ty made about nine times what a peasant family would, and his sister the same. They were better than 'well off,' for the most part. Although their money had only been coming in for nine months. Even with the free land grant, they had spent most of it to get the house and the grounds ready. They had both been quite poor and despised in their childhood, and neither wanted to return to that.

Ty opened the large front door, blushing as he had to openly struggle with it, and walked inside, motioning Ivy in as well.

"So, this is the foyer," Ty said, motioning around. It had almost nothing in it, and he winced slightly. "Sorry, it's still a bit plain, we're—"

"Ty," Ivy said, letting go of his hand and moving forward to put her arms around him.

"What?" Ty squeaked out, almost dying of embarrassment at the sound of his voice on the question.

She took a second staring at his chest, biting her lip, then leaned up and kissed him on his lips. He did his best to kiss back, feeling awkward. He started to stick his tongue out, having read about that, but she pulled back a bit. He could feel her trembling in his arms, as well as his own heart hammering in his chest.

She stared up at him. "I didn't come here for a tour of the house, Ty. Please, I just want to, well… see how you decorated your room."

She blushed, furiously.

Ty became completely tongue tied. He took her hand and led her to the back. His bedroom had a nice bed, large enough for two and with a fine down mattress. He had a shelf for books, and about ten of them, including his mother's old husband's journal, on it. He had a chest of drawers for his clothing, two potted plants, and his room overlooked what would become the garden. Ty stared at it, hoping Ivy found it adequate.

"Sorry my room is so bare, I just got this a few months ago and I've been busy. It'll get some art and such when I have time and have gotten paid from the dungeon."

He heard a light thud, and turned to find that Ivy had shut the door. "It's fine, Ty."

She hesitated, then reached up and unfastened the white dress, allowing it to fall to the ground. She was dressed only in silken underwear, her pale, near naked form gorgeous beyond words. Ty found it hard to breathe.

And impossible to speak.

Ivy smiled, her eyes on his, her lip trembling slightly. Then, one bare foot in front of the other, she moved toward him…

Chapter Fifteen

THE BRO(THER)

Ty woke, happier than he could ever remember being. He was floating on top of his sheets, his whole body filled with lassitude. Late morning sun flowed into the room from the window—which faced east, almost perfectly toward Ygg'drasil, easily visible a mile and a half away, the giant tree towering above the marble palace.

Ty rolled over and reached for Ivy, only to find she was gone.

His heart pounded in his chest, and it felt as if freezing lead settled into his stomach. Ty's good mood evaporated almost instantly, and he leapt to his feet, tangling himself in his sheets and then crashing to the floor. It hurt, but not as much as it would have before his switch to being a Master Dryad.

Ty cussed out loud. "By the fall!"

Then he gathered himself, and went to his door, pulling it open, naked.

Is she here? Or did she leave me? Was I that terrible?

Ty raced into the kitchen of his house, finding nothing and no one. He repeated it in the dining room and the foyer, and then returned to the kitchen.

She left me. I can't believe she abandoned me that fast. I must have been the worst.

It had been a fumbling first experience for both, but Ty had thought they had both had fun... Maybe he had been wrong.

Before Ty could formulate a plan—or fall into depression—there was a knock at his door.

He raced to it, pulling the door open. It wasn't until the chill outside air washed across his nethers that he remembered he was naked.

Standing at the door was an elf with copper-color hair shading toward a slight metallic green, with violet eyes. But he was nearly as tall as Ty himself, with lean muscle, and was dressed in a breastplate with leather armor below. Most importantly, he was a 'he.'

"You!" Ty cried, pointing out at Dalryn.

Dalryn glanced down briefly and sneered. "For Eturia's sake, get ahold of yourself, ya freaking fruit pie. Put some damn breeches on. This weather isn't doing you any favors."

Ty was suddenly conscious of how *very* chilly the morning air was.

A giggle came from behind Dalryn, and Ty noticed that Ivy was there, her eyes wide, but with her hand covering her mouth.

"What are *you* doing here, Dalryn?" Ty said, prepared to summon lightning at a moment's notice.

"What?" he barked. "I was *invited* here by my sister. To be your guardian! Which was mighty presumptuous of you, halfie, since I went to the Adventurers' Guild yesterday and was told I was specifically banned!"

Ty was shocked. "Your... your sister?"

Ivy flushed and stared at the ground, kicking at one of the marble cobblestones.

"Are you gonna stand in the door all day flashing your tackle at me like the uncultured half-human you are, or are you gonna put some breeches on—for the second time I've asked—and serve me brunch like the cultured Averian elf you pretend to be?"

Don't kill him, Ty. It's not worth it no matter how much the mouthy bastard deserves it.

"I'll get some clothes. But then I want explanations."

"Yeah, and the elves of the fall wanted dragon repellant. For the third time, *get some damn pants, man!*"

Ty nearly shook with rage, but turned and headed back into the house to go find clothes. He heard Dalryn and Ivy entering the house behind him.

***

Dressed and not at all ready to deal with the coming conversation, Ty stepped out of his room to find his "guests" still standing awkwardly in the entryway. He waved his hand toward the kitchen. His cozy kitchen table at least had a thin table and six rickety wooden chairs that could accommodate them all, even if not in style.

"Let's sit in here."

Dalryn dropped into his seat immediately, as if he lived there, and Ty sat on the opposite side. Ivy hesitated for a moment, then leaned down close enough that her warm breath brushed Ty's ear.

"Please don't be mad at me, Ty," Ivy whispered. She kissed him on the cheek afterwards, then licked his ear ever so slightly.

And just like that, Ty wasn't mad anymore. At her, anyway.

Ivy went and took a seat at the cozy kitchen table, between Ty and Dalryn, who sat at opposite ends.

Ty was completely out of sorts in this situation, he had to admit. But last night lingered in his mind, to put it mildly—honestly, he wasn't mad at Ivy at all, somehow, and hadn't really been even before the ear thing. He guessed he understood why she hadn't wanted to tell him who she was… but at the same time, he did wish she had trusted him.

They had been intimate now, after all. Trust felt like part of that package. Although, he supposed he could have explained a lot more of his unusual status than he had to her as well.

"Where's brunch?" Dalryn asked. "Do you not have a servant?"

Ty closed his eyes and whispered a third affirmation against murder.

"I'll get it!" Ivy said, popping right back up from where she had sat at the table and rushing into his kitchen. Ty had a stone fireplace set up, with a chimney outside through the second story, and a large bench with pots and pans in front of it. The inside of the fireplace had places to hang the pots and even spit meats, although few elves ate much meat. A small basin had fresh water in it, brought in yesterday from the blue river, but that was it.

A basket on the bench had some fruit, and he had various spices and root vegetables hanging above the fireplace.

As Ivy started working the fire in the kitchen, Dalryn stared the newly dressed Ty in the eyes. "So, how long have you been rutting my sister?"

"Oh for the good god's sake!" Ty yelled. "That's how this conversation is going to go?"

"Please, Ty, play nice," Ivy said.

He glanced over at her, and she was standing with hands clasped in front of her, appearing nervous.

Ty tried again. "Can we just talk about why you're here, Dalryn?"

"I told you. My sister invited me to be your guardian. I think I've got what it takes, frankly. And since I can't get in the dungeon *without* being your guardian, I guess I'm stuck with it, huh?"

"Wait, you think I—"

Dalryn interrupted. "Plus, I can't imagine you going adventuring without me and *not* getting my sister killed, so it behooves me to come along and protect her. Which I would do even if you weren't holding entry to the dungeon over my head."

Ty pinched the bridge of his nose again. "I wasn't trying to force you to be my guardian, I was punishing you for *trying to murder me*, you freaking *orc*!"

Dalryn leaned forward, his pale skin flushed, spots high on his cheek. "I didn't try and murder you, baby, I tried to take the dungeon core for more worthy hands."

"Yours?" Ty asked, giving a sneer back to Dalryn at least as good as the ones Dalryn gave.

"Well, my hands are better than some half-human's!"

Ty almost said, "*Your sister doesn't think that,*" but, since said sister was kindly making them food not but ten feet away, he checked himself.

Dalryn must have taken it as some kind of victory, leaning back in his chair and saying, "Exactly."

"So you want to be the guardian for our adventuring party then?" Ty asked.

"Well, you need me, so it's not really about what I want."

"But you obviously wanted it enough to come work for the 'halfie,' as you say."

Dalryn was heating up again. "Work *with* the halfie. And I need to protect my sister, after all."

Ty had a sudden thought. "Wait, are you the one that gave her that black eye the other day?"

Dalryn deflated completely at that, his body slouching. "No, that was our dad. When he found out she had been hanging out with you, a half-human, he flew off the handle."

Then Dalryn suddenly leaned forward again, eyes narrowed. "And when he finds out she's been *rutting* you, he's going to kill her, by Eturia! Did you think about that, huh? Did you?"

"I didn't know who her father was until you showed up!" Ty said.

"So you just bedded some lady whose last name you didn't know, huh? Is that how much you care for her? That's so much better, you onion."

Ty glanced over at Ivy, and saw that she had again paused in her food preparation activities and was staring at Ty, her eyes watering.

Ty turned so he was half-facing each sibling. "I care for Ivy *very, very* much. I knew she was hiding things from me, but I respected her privacy. Perhaps that was an error, but it was not because I found her lacking or because I just wanted to fornicate. I will find a way to fix this."

Ivy's whole face lit up. "Can I move in with you, Ty? Please? I'll be the best ever. I'll make you food, and clean, and—"

"You can't move in with Ty!" Dalryn exploded. "Are you serious?"

Ivy slapped her hands down on the table, then winced and shook one out. "I *can* move in, Dalryn. I want to. And you can't complain about Ty—maybe he is half-human, but he's also a paid minister of the king and now he's a *dungeon lord*. He's powerful and important and he's so nice to me, Dalryn. Even nicer than you are. I promise, he treats me really well."

"He just wants you to lift your dress for him!" Dalryn shouted.

"Hey—" Ty started.

Ivy was utterly livid, however. "*How dare you, Dalryn*. Can't you believe that he might truly like me? I'm pretty! My status sheet has great perks, and I'm nice, and Ty likes me."

"You can live with me," Ty said. It honestly sounded like the greatest plan to him. *I hope my sister doesn't get upset about it when she gets back.*

"C'mon, Ivy," Dalryn said, "You don't want to live with this guy! He's half-human. You know how they are."

"He seems a perfect elf to me," Ivy said, going back to cooking down some apples in a big metal pan. "I would also remind you that he helped me make a level, so I can better take care of myself as well. Plus, he treats me amazingly. All the stuff Father provides, and more. And he doesn't beat me every time I have an opinion he doesn't like, or go somewhere he doesn't like, or when he drinks and remembers stuff he doesn't like!"

Ty was warmed by the praise—however faint it might be. Also by the fire that Ivy now had going. The house had been chilly.

"Look, just because our house isn't great, doesn't mean you should shack up with a half-human! You can wait for a nice elf noble, and I can protect you—"

"Like you've been protecting me so far, Dalryn? You can't protect yourself! I had to heal *you* this morning 'cuz Dad beat you just because you didn't know where I was!"

"Well, once I make a few levels I can."

It was Ivy's turn to throw Dalryn a powerful sneer, and she was violently chopping vegetables now, cutting them with a knife in a way that suggested she wished she could go after Dalryn.

"And how will you do that, Dalryn? In a dungeon you lost the chance to delve because you're a colossal ass? Or will you go and fight in the ruins, which are far riskier for what they offer?"

Dalryn flushed, but then rallied and stared Ivy in the face. "What would Mom think?"

Ivy stopped cutting, flushing herself. Her eyes watered again. "That's not right, Dalryn. You can't keep throwing that at me. It happened, but that wasn't Ty's fault."

What are they talking about?

Dalryn slouched in the chair, scowling. "Fine. Whatever. You live here, I'll be the guardian, and I guess I'll just stay at the inn or something for a few days until Dad's gotten over it."

"Can you afford the inn?" Ivy asked.

"Well, maybe I'll shack up with Cuwylla," Dalryn said.

"I knew it!" Ty cried out.

"What, that you're a jackass?" Dalryn asked.

"That you found out from Cuwylla! That I would be leaving that night! I sent word to Dad's secretary!"

Dalryn flushed and muttered, "By the fall, I'm an idiot."

"First step to fixing something is realizing it," Ty quipped.

Dalryn's brow furrowed, but he didn't say anything till his brow smoothed out. "Can I ask you to perhaps forgive her and never mention this to your dad? Cuwylla didn't know what I was planning, I promise, and she really needs the job."

"You're actually worried about her?" Ty asked, surprised.

Dalryn glared. "Yeah, I'm not like you, just rutting some girl whose full name I don't even know! I worry about my partners. Cuwylla is hoping that this job will lead to a chance to work higher in the government, and she wants to save enough money to have people help her to make a level, so she gets the extra gold per year from the king. That'll pretty much set her up for life, and she can afford to have someone take care of her kids once she has them. Do you even know what Ivy's dreams are?"

Ty almost flew off the handle again, but he was beginning to think that maybe, just maybe, Dalryn's heart wasn't in the wrong place. He was just, as Ivy had said, a colossal weed. "She wants to be a healer and a familiar-mage."

"That's just her role. I said her dreams."

Ty pinched the bridge of his nose. "Dalryn, I'll make you a deal. I'll say nothing, *and* we can help Cuwylla through a run in my dungeon, on me. *If* you never refer to me and Ivy rutting again, or refer to me as a half-breed, or halfie, or anything like that. It'll also reduce your 'giant penis' level by no small amount."

Dalryn frowned. "Fine. Also, like I said, I'll be your guardian. But I'm still gonna call you a fruit pie. Because you are one."

Before Ty could flare up again, Ivy came around the cooking bench, and placed a bunch of glazed and spiced potatoes in front of Ty and then Dalryn, then went back and got herself a plate and sat down.

They ate quickly and in silence, stuffing their mouths. Once they were done, they glanced around at each other, as if unsure what to do now.

Ivy bit her lower lip for a second and glanced at Ty. "Did you really mean it? About me staying here? If you don't want me to, I'll understand, and we can still, you know, and adventure together."

Chapter Sixteen

MAGIC RED OF TOOTH AND CLAW

"Of course," Ty said. "I said it and I meant it—I think it would be wonderful for you to stay with me. I have a couple of spare bedrooms, and—"

"Well, I would be staying in *your* room, of course," Ivy said, smiling.

Dalryn frowned. "Really? Not even a hint of propriety?"

Ivy turned on him, her face stormy, and she held one finger out. But then she dropped it. Perhaps, like Ty, she was realizing the futility of arguing about certain things with Dalryn. "You know what? Never mind. Let's just go to the guild. We have the noon run again, right?"

"Yeah. We can meet at the Emerald Bee again as well, but we won't be able to get the good stuff."

"You just ate," Dalryn said. "Don't be a pig."

Ty sighed. He hoped Dalryn was an amazing guardian, because this was going to be... fun.

"When we get to the guild, I'm going to take a look at your adventurer card, okay? Because I need a lot from you to make up for... you."

"I have it right here," Dalryn said, proudly for some reason, as he reached into his jacket and pulled it out, rolled up. "And you'll be impressed."

He passed it over.

Ty took it and smoothed it out, staring at it.

Dalryn ap Mosstone					
Level One	Earth, Wyld				
Health	17	Stamina	17	Essence	10
Level Stats					
Strength	8(9)	135 base pound-lifting capacity, -5% melee damage, +-3% running speed.			
Agility	12(14)	-20% enemy hit chance, +20% hit chance with all weapons, +8% running speed			
Dexterity	12	+10% base success for crafting and physical skill success rate, 20% chance to raise base weapon damage roll by one step			
Endurance	12(14)	+4 base Stamina, +20% Stamina Recovery Rate, +20% base Health Recovery Rate			
Toughness	12(14)	+4 base Health, +20% base Health, +20% base Stamina, +2 to resist poison, disease, and physical status effects			
Perception	10				
Connection	10	+00% Essence recovery rate (12/day)			
Capacity	10	+0 Base essence, +00% essence			
Appearance	12	Decently attractive			
Non-Level Stats					
Intelligence	9	-10% skill acquisition rate.			
Magic	12	+8% Magic Effects, +1 Maximum affinity			
Charisma	7	-30% perceived social skills			
Luck	10	The Fates neither dislike nor care for you			

Secondary Stats		
Wyld Affinity	2	-20% essence cost to all Wyld abilities, +20% effect for all Wyld abilities or +2 to the difficulty to resist.
Birth Perks		
Race: High Elf		-2 to Strength, Endurance, and Toughness stats base
		+2 to Agility and Magic stats base
		Increased chance for Being magics and Wyld magic. Gain an additional ability at Level Two, Ten, and every ten thereafter from one of those magics if possessed.
		Lifespan average of four hundred years. Maximum of three perks positive and negative each, with standard chance of inheriting or acquiring at birth.
Rank: Quality		May obtain Level 60 without ascension.
Line of Mosstone		Always start with Wyld. +2 maximum and actual Wyld affinity. Treated as a quality rank higher for purposes of plant-based Wyld abilities. +2 Appearance.
Tough as Nails		You have +4 Endurance, +4 Toughness, and only suffer fifty percent penalties to hit and dodge from physical damage. +6 to resist incapacitating effects such as knockout.
Physical Learner		While not smart, per se, you have an instinctual grasp of athletics and fighting. You gain +60% learn rate for physical skills.
Flaw: Unreasoning		-1 Charisma, -1 Intelligence, -4 to resist mental effects
Acquired Perks		
Athletic Tier-1		The time you spend working out and training has paid off. +20% effective rank to Strength, Agility, and Endurance, round down.

Smoldering Rage	The world stole much of your happiness as a child, and your abusive family made things far worse. You are angry at everything and everyone. -2 charisma, -4 to resist rage effects.

Skills	Level	Effect
Academics	1	You know how to read and write
Administration	2	-1% to realm administration costs, -4% to business costs
Athletics	6	+18% to run speed, +3 to check to climb or avoid obstacles
Business	1	+5% to expected income, and -1% to expected costs, for operating any business
Dodge	5	+15% to dodge incoming attacks
Leadership	2	People consider you to have 4% more status than you do, and if they are followers, are willing to accept conditions 2% worse than baseline without complaint
Medium Armor	3	+9% armor rating, -6% dodge penalty
Natural Sciences	1	You are aware of basic concepts
Occult	2	You can sense magic that is not concealed that is connected to you, whose area of effect you are in, or that is within 2 feet of you. Your magic powers have 4% greater effect. You can sense the purpose of simple magic and vaguely discern more complicated magical purposes. +4% to accuracy with magic attacks.
Seduction	1	People find your attempts to seduce them 2% more favorable than baseline, compared to what they are looking for
Shield	3	+12% chance to parry with a shield
Survival	3	+9% hunting and foraging
Sword	7	+28% damage with swords, +28% to hit with swords

Abilities	Effect
Earth	
Wyld	

Ty, almost against his will, *was* a bit impressed. In at least one category. "I have to admit, Dalryn, you actually appear to have a decent guardian setup, for an elf."

"That's right!" Dalryn said. "And with Earth and Wyld magic, both of which can add to the wielder's defensive abilities, I'll be amazing."

"Well, you're no dwarf, but you'll do. Why train with medium armor and not heavy, however, if you plan on being a damage-soaking-style guardian?"

Dalryn flushed and coughed. "I didn't have the strength to use the big stuff. Truthfully, I can barely wield the breastplate, helm, and shield. I wanted to move to a tower shield and heavier armor, but I'll need some levels first."

"Ah, is wittle baby too weak to—"

Ivy put her hand on Ty's shoulder, and he subsided.

Dalryn snorted. "You and I are gonna have issues, I can tell. But if you do your job decently, I can do mine well. Fair?"

"Fair," Ty replied. "Let's go pick up Forli, and then we can do a run and make Dalryn a level so he'll be a true guardian."

"Wait, who's Forli?" Dalryn barked. "No one mentioned a Forli!"

"Our dryad?" Ty asked.

Dalryn turned to Ivy. "You didn't say anything about a dryad! First you want me to partner with a half-human, despite everything that happened, and now you want me to be on a team with a dryad?! My god, Sis, where are all the elves?"

Ivy stared at Dalryn with wide eyes, and tapped her fingers together in front of her. "... sorry?"

This is going to be a very... unique... adventuring party.

***

They found Forli back at the Adventurers' Guild.

Ty walked up to the table where Forli was sitting, chewing on a head of lettuce that was nearly rotten.

"Where'd you get that?" Ty asked as he walked up.

"I, um, used all my money on occult lessons and a place to stay, so this is all I could afford—it was free. I mean, those oak boards didn't go for much. Where were you guys?"

Ivy leaned in. "You should come stay with Ty! He has a great pantry with good food, a garden, and a whole lot of extra rooms. He's letting me stay there. I bet he would let you stay there, too."

Forli turned, eyes wide, and stared at Ty.

"Sure, you can stay with me. And as to your question, I had some family drama. However, we have a guardian, so as soon as you wolf down that chunk of lettuce that was clearly harvested around the time of the cataclysm, we can get going."

"Who's our guardian?" Forli asked, then she stared at Dalryn. "Is it you?"

"Yup," Dalryn replied.

Ty didn't feel like listening to them cover a bunch of ground he had just been through, so he cut in. "Dalryn is Ivy's brother. He's a colossal jackanapes, but a pretty solid guardian. There. We've covered the introductions. Can we go delve now? I want to explore the dungeon with someone else being eaten by the rats."

"About that—you might want to go talk to Kadrath. There's been an incident, and I think you might be needed to handle it. Or be made aware of it. I'm not sure."

Just as Forli was speaking, the door to the back offices—where Ty had just been two days ago—banged open. A female rabbit-kin, appearing to be in her late twenties or early thirties, came storming out. She had digitigrade legs covered in white fur below the thigh and a fine, white fur across her forearms. She also had rabbit ears and a cute bunny nose, but otherwise appeared human.

She was weeping almost unconsolably as she rushed from the room, but as she did so, she caught sight of Ty.

Her face twisted in hatred, an expression that it didn't wear easily. "You!"

She flew at him, hands extended, clawing for him.

Dalryn dropped his shield to his arm and swung it backward, taking the lady full in her face and chest. She slammed backward and hit the ground, out cold. There were gasps from the other adventurers around the guild.

"See, I'm a great guardian," Dalryn said with a smirk.

"You just knocked out some old lady, you jackanapes!" Ty cried out.

He heard an elf, who looked thirty or so, mutter, "Old?" as he stared at the wrinkle-free rabbit-kin.

Dalryn grimaced. "She was attacking you! You hired me to protect my team, and I did."

Ty pinched the bridge of his nose again. "Dalryn, please, just sit. And, Ivy, if you could heal her, that would be great. I'm going to go see Guildmaster Kadrath and find out what's happening."

Ivy nodded, and Ty headed to the door to the back. Fortunately, it wasn't locked this time. Ty headed in. Immediately to his right, he saw the same conference room, door open, and Kadrath—still in his implausibly huge armor, which, it occurred to Ty, he had never seen him out of—doing some paperwork.

He glanced up as Ty walked in. "Ah, Dungeon Lord Belmoria, pleased to see you. I had wanted to talk to you before you went on your delve today. It appears that on our first day in operation, we had a party wipe. A group of total newbies paid for the right to enter—a full gold, I might add—and weren't ready. We found nothing of them, of course, since the dungeon absorbed everything, but they've clearly been eliminated. Your dungeon has made a level, so you might want to go in as dungeon lord and see about increasing it."

"Wait, people died?" Ty asked. "Who?"

"Four men—two rabbit-kin, a human, and an elf. I didn't know any. They refused my request to join the training programs first. I guess the two rabbit-kin were related, distantly, to the rabbit-kin trading house master, Laurel Whitewater, so I might get a bit of official guff on this, but they knew the risks."

"That's… sad," Ty said. "I'm sorry my dungeon killed people."

"It's going to keep happening, lad. A dungeon is like most of the beasts of nature—it has to feed to grow. By the time they went in, we had a pretty good idea of what was in there, and we gave them the information, I promise. And I did try to convince them to train more. But at the end of the day, they took the risk to get the rewards, and it didn't pay off this time."

Ty nodded.

"But, their loss, however tragic, is our gain—they do one last service in death. They likely made the dungeon stronger. I would check—the stronger the dungeon, the better off we'll all be."

"I'll go see Sae—the Crone," Ty said. "And thank you."

With a heavy heart, Ty walked out. He gave a quick and quiet summary to the others and asked them to wait. Then he headed out to the marble gazebo that was his dungeon entrance. He nodded to the guard and took the stairs down, calling out, "I enter as dungeon lord" as he did so.

He wondered if the dungeon had, in fact, made a level. And whether or not the Crone would share the secret powers of the dungeon now that he had been adventuring.

Mostly, he wondered what those paths to power would be, and what they would bring him.

Chapter Seventeen

DUNGEON LORD'S RULEBOOK, PART TWO

T y walked out of the stairs down from his entrance, and into the cavern that was the Boss room and his Core room both. Saelenia was sitting against the far wall, on a rock, her head back and her eyes closed. Her twelve-foot-tall body appeared closer to its actual height with her stretched out instead of hunched over. Her green moss hair hung down around her shoulders. Still as she was, she resembled a carving of a woman more than she resembled the actual Level Eighty-Eight near-god that she had been, or the Level Eighty-Eight Dungeon boss she was.

The center of the room still had the great stone tablet with glowing, green crystals outlining words on it. Ty walked up to the tablet, expecting the Crone to say something, or even move, but she didn't.

He waited for a bit, attempting to be respectful, but still nothing.

Is she dead? She cannot be dead. Right?

He coughed. "Good morning, Saelenia. I heard the dungeon, well, ate some people last night. What was that about?"

Saelenia gave a long sigh, stirring, and sat forward. "Are you back already, youngling? I thought I told you to go live life for a while. No offense, but even in my current revived form, I enjoy a good nap."

Dryads don't sleep, and I know you know I know that.

"I did. Live life, I mean. A lot. I had an adventure here in the dungeon, made a new friend, made a few kinda friends, kinda enemies, and well, not to be indelicate, but I'm not a virgin anymore."

"Congratulations on achieving what millions, mayhap even billions, of high elves did before you," Saelenia said, her voice as dry as old twigs.

Ty flushed. "I wasn't trying to brag, just, I did what you wanted. I went out and lived life, and mostly, it was wonderful."

"I can't even recall those times, except as a vague memory that I had them," Saelenia said.

"You had sex?" Ty asked, flabbergasted into indelicacy. Then his cheeks reddened even further. "I mean, I didn't even think dryads had sex normally."

Saelenia chuckled richly. "Yes, I did. To answer your other question, most dryads don't have sex. But some can, and I've always been more than just a dryad. Surely, you know *that*, youngling."

Ty frowned. "Right, well, to circle back around, Kadrath did tell me that some people are no longer living their lives anymore. He said you probably leveled. I was hoping my accomplishments in living my life would convince you to show me the secret leveling options."

"Hmm..."

"I don't really have anything to compare to, but I can't help but imagine that a dungeon that has a progenitor for a boss probably has some great secret options."

Saelenia gave a long sigh and stood from her stone. She walked over to the tablet slowly, despite her beautiful young body, as if she'd forgotten she wasn't still an aged crone. She motioned Ty a bit closer.

"It wasn't really for you, youngling, that I asked you to wait. It was for me. I don't feel ready yet to deal with it. But I guess those four idiots last night practically threw themselves on the rats, and you're right—if the dungeon leveled, we need to deal with it."

Saelenia touched the stone plinth, and the glowing crystals shifted, flipping to 'Legacy of the Forest.'

At the top was an explanation, and below were sub-categories.

Ty read the explanation first.

"'Progenitors are one form of proto-god. When proto-gods first come into existence—either through the natural upwellings of the Sea of Chaos or when created by high gods—they are flush with power. But each starts on a timetable, trying to become a lowest-tier true god, through accumulation of powerful magic and the worship and belief of others in the concept they represent. Most last a few hundred to a few thousand years before either ascending or failing and ceasing to exist, their magic returning to the world—the second option far more common.

"'But as they try to become more, they also become different, changing slightly to fit the sources of magic and faith they have acquired.

"'The Crone, rather than lasting a few hundred to a few thousand, has lasted *tens of thousands* of years. During that time, she has been many things to multiple civilizations. She was once a *red of tooth and claw* force who sought to keep the forest free of mortals. Then she was a warrior who fought against darker magics that would harm the forest. She was perceived as the assistant to multiple gods. Mother to champions. Mother to dryads. A guide to farmers and gardeners. And finally, as you knew her, an ancient force protecting a geographic locale and the head of the loose coalition of proto-gods and beings known as 'the forest.'

"'But, like a mortal who was once a talented seaman who quit and chose to become a farmer instead for fifty years, those other aspects of the Crone have slowly faded. She isn't who or what she was—she ascended to her new existence as just one of those things, despite her new form.

"'But, as a dungeon now, she is a magical matrix who can be *all* those things. She can acquire objects, mementos, and remnants from those various time periods, to reacquire those aspects of herself and grow her power—and the power of the dungeon.

"'The objects collected must either be inherently magically powerful—remnants of a progenitor or artifacts in power minimum—or they must have a significant basis in the faith of a people to become magically relevant to the dungeon.'"

Ty looked up at Saelenia. "I... Wow. That's interesting."

"'Interesting,' he says," Saelenia dryly commented. "The dungeon grows from gathering remnants of my existence, of the '*who*'s and '*what*'s I was before. I'm sure you wouldn't find that at all invasive. Perhaps we should go gather the bill of sale for your mom that your dad signed? Or last night's stained bedsheets? Then we'll put those on display, see how you feel about it."

Ty flushed again, hating the repeated feelings of embarrassment he was having from his trips to see Saelenia. But when she put it like that... he supposed she had a point.

Saelenia gave an exaggerated and dramatic sigh. "No help for it, though. It'll add a huge amount of power to the dungeon if you do it right. So, I guess we've got to work on it."

Then she pointed down to the three categories. They were, "The Lost Siblings," "The Champions," and "The Pantheons."

"What are these? Did you have brothers and sisters?"

Saelenia gave a rich laugh. "Of course not, you stump. I was born from the Sea of Chaos directly. This refers to all the progenitors who were with me—previous allies of the forest, those whom I slew who sought to harm us, things of that nature. Many of them left... essences behind. For those who did, the more that you collect, the more power that will be added to me."

She sighed. "'Champions' are for those few people who allied with me who have objects and memories strong enough, somewhere, to matter. And 'The Pantheons' refers to the various gods with whom I have allied or been perceived to have served—it's for their temple stones and relics."

"Wait, so if I stole the temple stone from the shrine of Iluvin Eturia in Wheat Town and gave it to you, you'd have more power?"

Saelenia gave a chuckle. "Yes. But let's not do that, 'kay? I like that goddess. If we recover a lost stone, or a fresh stone and dedicate it to her, that's one thing. Stealing it is another."

"What about the progenitor parts? Do you know where any are?" Ty asked, excited. *Those can be used, along with shards and the most advanced imbuing, to make artifacts of truly exceptional power!*

She winced. "I do. Most are utterly out of your reach at your current level... but two aren't."

"Which two?" Ty felt his eyes widening. *Two?*

Saelenia sighed. "The Heart of Zadrid, the Endless Undead. Also, the Claws of Foriveltain, the Primeval Bear."

She's whiplashing between happy laughter and sighing a lot. Is it just the situation, or is she in some kind of flux between her old self and new?

Then Ty had another thought. "Wait, Zadrid, as in Zadrid's Hallow? That place where the undead form all the time?"

"Yes. Zadrid is... very hard to kill. He doesn't draw his power from faith, like most—he draws his power from fear. Fear of the undead. And he has the power to come back, given enough time and magic."

"'Is' hard to kill? Not 'was'?" Ty asked. Then he briefly shuddered, imagining a being as powerful as Saelenia but evil and destructive.

"He's still existing, in a way. Although we kicked the ev-er-loving magic out of him. We took a fourth of his heart and sealed it away from the rest of that black organ because, if you brought the pieces back together for long enough and gave it enough magic, Zadrid might reform. He's destroyed in most senses... Certainly, his power is far below that of a progenitor at this point. But he could come back."

"Who was 'we'?"

"My first lover—the Ancient One hero Zar'Kre'Rusth—and the first 'forest' triad I was a part of. I already told you about Foriveltain, the primeval bear. The other was Xilick the Emerald Fae Queen. Xilick and I were the only survivors—Zadrid was quite powerful. And Xilick passed a few hundred years after from a total lack of support, leaving me alone for the first time. This was all before the elves came. You'll be going after the parts of enemies from the first war I ever fought alongside a mortal, and the ones I lost in that war as well."

That's... fascinating, Ty thought. *Sad as well, I suppose, but still...*

"I see. Thank you. And you think I should head to Zadrid's Hallow first? Where are the other ones located?"

"Those two are located deep beneath the city, in the under-city of the Ancient Ones, at a sealed temple to the elder god Xalkri. Long story, not for now. Also, you should head to see Thea first, not go directly to Zadrid's Hallow. Ask her for the heart—tell her, 'The six and the twenty-nine have passed, but the forest perseveres.' Explain what you want it for. Then go and see about Zadrid's Hallow. Then come back here. Simple."

"Shouldn't I get that last piece of the heart on the way back? If it might combine with the other pieces."

"I...." Saelenia's eyes widened. "That *would* make more sense. But stop by and talk to her first anyway—if you can't convince her, you might need to come back here. But yeah, let her hold it."

Saelenia reached down and tapped the page. "But before all that, you should pick a room. I strongly suggest that you start with the Heart of the Grove. It's the one that'll be worth the most power in the long run, since it'll add new and more powerful room picks, and we know where two progenitor parts are."

Ty pulled up the room options. He didn't look at the basic options—and didn't have any advanced, master, or eldritch ones. He just focused on the specialty ones.

Room	Effect
Specialty Rooms [Available because of the Dungeon's Magics or Boss]	
Air Spark (Max 1 per floor)	+2 Magic Effects Level, shifts the magic toward Air. +3% Local Magic Level. +.2 Loot Quality.
Fae Grove (Max 1 per floor)	+2 Monster Level. +4 Max Monsters. The monsters are shifted toward Fae and Fae Subtypes.
Beast Woods (Max 1 per floor)	+1 Monster Level. +6 Max Monsters. The monsters are shifted toward beasts and magical beasts.
Living Forest (Max 1 per floor)	+1 Monster Level. +4 Max Monsters. +.2 loot level. The monsters on this floor are shifted toward plant monsters.
Heart of the Grove	+1 Magic Effects Level. May accept pieces of progenitors to increase power and gain new rooms. Each one adds a small direct amount of power as well as new room options.
Shrine to Lost Glory	+.1 Treasure Level. May accept the regalia of lost heroes still venerated enough to have faith. Each set adds a tiny amount of direct power and will generate a special encounter. May add more room options, but it's unlikely.
The Forest Temple	+1 Monster Level. May accept attuned Temple Stones to gods associated with the Crone. Each adds a decent amount of power and may add new room options.

"So, I should pick the Heart of the Grove, and then go collect Zadrid's heart? That's what I'm being told?"

"You got it, youngling. And since you'll be gone for a few weeks at least, it's possible that my dungeon will make another level, and you can pick the room after you bring me Zadrid's putrid remains."

"How do I find Thea?"

"Just follow whatever you did the first time. I seriously doubt she left the grove. Have Forli show you the way again."

Ty nodded and headed up to tell his adventuring party what he had planned. He wanted them to at least get a few fights in, to make Dalryn a level, before they went. And this adventure might level most of them up once or twice.

Or kill them. Kinda fifty-fifty, Ty figured.

Chapter Eighteen

LEVEL TWO AGAIN AND THREE

"So that's the plan," Ty said.

In the stunned silence that followed, he reached across, grabbed some honey—non-magical—and poured it over his apple-chunk pancakes.

Ty had been gone long enough that they had decided to have lunch at the Emerald Bee after all—he had switched his run with a local adventuring party, the High Reborn. They were five elven ex-nobles and had easily cobbled together the coin for a run, but Ty couldn't help but dislike them—they were pretty blatantly part of the faction that wanted to outlaw all non-elves from positions of authority. As a once half-elf and current dryad who held a pseudo-minister position, he took that a bit personally.

They had switched with him, though, and been relatively polite. Perhaps they could be convinced to see the error of their ways.

"By Eturia," Dalryn said, smacking one fist into the palm of his other hand. "This is how you get strong, isn't it, you tuber? You just do insane things and hope you survive. You mince around as if you're meek and proper, but it's all a lie, isn't it?"

Ty shrugged.

Dalryn wasn't finished. "Trying to recover the heart of a dark progenitor, to power up the dungeon you made with a forest

145

progenitor. I have to hand it to you, this is simultaneously the dumbest and the most legendary thing I've heard."

A bit too much truth to that, Ty thought to himself.

Forli twiddled her fingers. "It does sound... challenging. Can we really do this?"

Ty pointed his fork at Dalryn. "It should be, well, not perfectly safe, but controllable. We can get the first piece with almost no danger, and then we'll fight through to the last three."

Dalryn laughed in Ty's face at that. "Yeah, that's how you do things. Safe and controllable."

"We should be able to handle it, once we all get a couple more levels and a familiar for Ivy."

Dalryn waved his own fork at Ty. "You're a crazy fruit cake, but if you're going to be insane, I can at least try to keep you from killing my sister. And if we don't all die, some leveling will be wonderful. Maybe I can get as strong as Dad."

"Your dad? He's Level Eleven, right?" Ty asked.

Ivy hesitantly nodded. "It's more than that. He's got a crazy amount of magic and abilities, far more than when he had back in Lakusi. I think he got stronger when he got his eye. And meaner. We were only here for about a month, and he's already gotten physical, like, four times."

Ty stabbed his fork into some more pancakes but waited to stuff them in his mouth. "Where'd he get the eye?"

Ivy shrugged. "I don't know. Maybe adventuring in the undercity—he went there a few times. But wherever he got it, it did seem to make him darker."

Dalryn shrugged. "Nah. It's not the eye. I figure that escaping the Havi Imperium and all its dirty humans, thinking he would be finally free of them, and then finding George Orsini running the place here didn't sit well with him. That's why he got so mean. He certainly had a lot to say about it."

Ty frowned. "Enough about my dad, please. I don't want to hear about him. Let's just go run the dungeon."

Dalryn used his fork to point down at his plate. "Sure. As soon as this food is all gone."

***

As they walked into the cavern, Ty noticed that there were now small patches of white moss on the bottoms of some of the stalagmites, and he felt a tiny whirl of Wyld magic in the area.

This must be the result of the one magic point that the Heart of the Grove room gave me. I suppose I should be glad that we hit the magic effect here and not later. I wonder what it does?

"Watch the moss, please," Ty said.

"Teach your grandmother to suck eggs," Dalryn responded.

Forli chuckled, Ivy punched her brother in the shoulder, and Ty pinched the bridge of his nose.

"Try to act professional—if you see something, call it out. You don't have to be an ass. We might have missed it."

"And I have limited essence for healing," Ivy said, fingering her amulet.

"All right, we'll do it your way, you wet blankets," Dalryn said.

Despite his poor attitude, Ty had to admit that Dalryn cut a nice picture, fully decked out. He had a large shield, a long sword, and a breastplate and helm, as well as leather leggings and sleeves. Not the stereotypical plate-armored dwarven guardian you saw, but still—he appeared quite impressive. He moved well, albeit a touch slower than Ty would have liked.

Even as Ty was giving Dalryn's outfit a critical eye, three of the hairless, wrinkly rats popped around a stalagmite.

"'Ware. There are tiny rats ahead," Dalryn called out. Ty honestly couldn't tell if he was trying to be helpful or sarcastic.

Even as Dalryn called them out, two of the rats began gnawing on the white moss. The third charged.

"That stuff wasn't here before. The fungus got added once I put the new room with its magic rating in—it has to be a buff. Get them!"

Dalryn surged forward, and Ty hit the first rat with lightning, dropping the Level One rat in a single hit. Dalryn reached the rats and slashed one, cutting it—but it must have been buffed, as it survived. Both rats came at Dalryn simultaneously, one from one side, darting forward and back, the other from the other.

But Ty had to admit, against his own secret semi-wishes, that Dalryn was good at what he did. Ivy's brother slashed at one, holding it back, and crouched enough to drop the shield bottom onto the head of the second rat, stunning it and then putting the shield between himself and the rat.

At no point did he really try to kill a rat—but he kept himself safe and out of harm's way while keeping both rats focused on him.

Ty fried the wounded one, and then a few moments later, he and Forli hit the next one once each to finish it off.

"Easy as pie," Dalryn said, but Ty could see his huge grin. *He's glad he didn't screw it up as well.*

That feeling was the closest Ty got to connecting with Dalryn, except perhaps the jackanapes' desire to keep Ivy safe and happy. He could see eye to eye on that as well.

"So, ready for the next few rats?" Dalryn asked.

"Maybe scrape some of that moss off the walls?" Ivy asked. "I wonder if that could be a form of loot now. We should take it and see if it's worth anything."

Ty chuckled. "I like how you think, Ivy. But at the risk of swelling his delusional head, I like that your jackanapes brother knows his stuff even more. Why, you might ask? Because I didn't get gnawed on by rats. Let's fight our way through this, but now that we've tested everything, we need to alter our strategies to maximize our success. We need everyone to make a level at least while we're down here. That requires us to take damage infrequently enough that Ivy can keep us alive."

***

Ecstatic Dalryn was at least tolerable.

For the fifth time, as they climbed the stairs, their new guardian exulted. "I leveled. I mean, I always knew I would. Somehow, it still doesn't feel real though, you know? I can get the tower shield now—I have the strength for it, easily. This sword feels as light as a feather."

Dalryn swung his sword, hitting the wall of the stair. It was subtly different than hitting a normal wall—no chip, no mark, nothing to show that a guy with a newly minted fourteen strength had hit it.

I guess being the edge of an extra-dimensional space, whatever it appears to be, makes it invulnerable to normal damage.

Ty could *feel* the moment they left the dungeon and returned to normal space.

"We all leveled, Brother," Ivy said. "I took bestial toughness, rank I as my ability. I want to be able to live if we get hit by something."

Ty nodded along to her words. "We should get you your adventurer card as well, Ivy."

She smiled. "Thank you, Ty. I'm going to hang it in our room."

"Do me a favor and don't talk about the fact you guys are together, okay?" Dalryn asked. "I don't want to hear about my sister being with anyone, much less... well, I don't want to hear about her being with anyone."

"Yeah, because we're just going to not mention living together," Ty said, obviously sarcastically.

"Look here, you tuber—" Dalryn started.

Forli cut in. "Guys! It, um, kinda makes me nervous that you argue all the time. I want us to be a team that would save each other without a thought. I don't think this is how you do that. Can we please try to get along? At least a bit?"

There was a brief pause, and Ty couldn't deny the truth of her words. "I'll try."

After a moment, Ty had a sudden thought. "Wait a moment. You both have the Mosstone family line, right?"

Ivy and Dalryn nodded.

"So, I know you took regenerate and familiar, both rank I, but what was your third ability, Ivy? You had a bonus Wyld one you never told me about."

Ivy blushed, and her lower lip trembled. "Oh, well, it didn't really matter. I took the improved familiar power that gives an additional level to familiars, so my familiars will be a level higher—half my level plus one. I figured if they'll just be a touch stronger, that would be fine, right? And you didn't really need to know my familiars were a bit stronger for group planning, right? Right, Ty?"

Before Ty could even speak, Dalryn went and put his arm around his sister. "You onion, you went and made her upset already. Some paramour you are."

Ty was flabbergasted. "Everything is fine, Ivy, and for the good god's sake, Dalryn, *she's* fine as well. Silence your tongue."

Ivy smiled up at her brother. "I'm okay, Dalryn, swear."

He didn't let go of her shoulders but said, "Well, as long as you're okay."

Before anyone could say anything further, an insane, warbling laugh, far too loud for normal laughter, floated across the plaza.

Ty's blood froze, and he turned toward the sound, which he, and everyone in Star Port, knew well. *Corrupted wolves.*

But this district was cleared, and the entrances to the undercity all sealed! I organized a lot of that!

Four wolves came exploding out of a house, all of them running for Ty as fast as they could, slavering with pink-tinged spit at the mouths even as they laughed insanely. Each was slightly larger than a normal wolf, and twisted—fur rotted, muscles knotted oddly, a strange hunch in one.

The wolves passed a couple of elves, about half of whom went running, and the other half of whom pulled out knives or swords, except a few who threw weak magical attacks at the wolves. A few hit, but the wolves even ignored those, heading straight for Ty.

Ty's testicles retracted as fear invaded him, but he threw lightning at one of the wolves, scoring a hit that didn't drop it.

I need to do something! Ty thought as the four wolves closed in, blindingly fast, heading straight at him across the plaza.

Chapter Nineteen

JUST BECAUSE YOU'RE PARANOID DOESN'T MEAN THEY'RE NOT AFTER YOU

As Ty's mind raced, he remembered that he was a dungeon lord. *The Call!*

He focused and felt a twisting in space, a change in the distance between *here* and *elsewhere*. The fat mama rat from the dungeon nest formed in front of a charging wolf. The wolf slammed into it, and the mama rat screamed, pupping a baby rat, all in just a few seconds.

But Ty didn't have time to deal with it. Dalryn, earning a lot of favor back from Ty, slashed at one wolf, delaying it as it danced around the attack, and shield blocked a second. But that left a single wolf that charged Ty. He hit it with a lightning bolt, but it came on and bit his thigh—in the same place both rats had gotten it, and for the fourth time, blood gushed from his leg.

Diseased Wolf bites Ty for 4 damage. Ty has suffered a crippling wound to his leg. -40% to dodge and -20% to accuracy. Ty fails Toughness check against bleed. Ty is bleeding for 1 damage per minute until 10 damage has occurred or medical attention has been received. Ty fails his Toughness check against Thel's Rot. Bleed damage does 200% and has 200% the duration.

Ty screamed and fell, but he was becoming a bit experienced with the situation, and he shot lightning, accepting the damage to fry the insanely cackling wolf on his leg. The wolf, already hit once, gave up the ghost. But blood was still *gushing* from the wound on Ty's leg.

Ty screamed out, "Ivy! I need a regenerate. I'm dead in about thirty seconds otherwise!"

Thel's Rot wasn't to be screwed around with—a lot of people had died of the hyper bleed already, trying to clear the ruins and fix all the corrupted rituals around the Central District of Star Port.

Ivy ran over, but as she did, the second wolf made it past her brother and rushed straight at Ty, pink-tinged spittle flying from it. Ivy reached Ty, standing in front of him, and bent down and touched his leg. Ty felt the renewing Wyld magic, and his bleed effect disappeared. The last wolf, however, was still headed for him where he sat on the marble cobblestone plaza ground.

But Ivy was in the way as the wolf leapt at Ty, and she cowered low, covering her head with her arms.

There was a blur of movement, and the wolf was bisected in an absolute shower of blood, the power of the attack skewing its leap sideways. Two separate pieces of the canine blasted diagonally past Ty and Ivy.

Helryn Mosstone stood there, his one diamond eye glinting and a sword extended with an aura of black around the blade.

"Are you okay?" he asked Ivy, and she nodded, still trembling.

"Wolf's down, and I'm fine too!" Dalryn called from about ten feet away, but Helryn ignored him. He reached out and gripped Ivy's arm, hard. Ty could see the discoloration on her arm where his fingers gripped.

"You need to come—"

"Hey!" Ty said, standing. He put his hand on Helryn's shoulder, and the elf turned, staring at Ty with one blue eye and one glowing, diamond one. Ty felt magic wash across him, inquisitive and probing.

"What do you have to say to me, human?" Helryn asked through clenched teeth.

"You're hurting your daughter," Ty said calmly, staring pointedly at where Helryn gripped Ivy and then looking at the tears leaking from her eyes.

A notification that his summoned monster had defeated a 'diseased wolf' flashed across Ty's vision, and he dismissed it.

Helryn turned away from Ty and stared down at Ivy's arm. Then he released it as if the arm were fire, pulling his hand back rapidly.

He fumbled at his belt, pulling out a potion. "I'm, I'm sorry, Iv. I didn't mean to. It's just, you keep putting yourself in danger, and you won't listen to reason, and you almost died because you were near this halfie... here, take this. It'll heal you."

Helryn held the potion out to Ivy, but she shook her head. "Give it to someone else who needs it, Dad. I can heal myself now. But thank you."

She reached out tenderly and touched Ty's arm slightly before withdrawing her hand. "And thank you, Ty."

Helryn grimaced at the show of affection but cleared his face and straightened. "I won't pretend I love you, Tywyndyll, nor will I pretend I'm happy to see a bastard half-elf in charge of a dungeon—but it's obvious my daughter wishes to be with you, and I do love her, whatever flaws I may have. Given the circumstances, would you and your adventuring party care to join me, my friend, and his wife for dinner tonight?"

Ty stared at the fried wolf literally at their feet. *We're just ignoring the whole 'monsters just attacked me' thing, huh? All right, I guess it's domestic mode time.*

Ivy smiled at that, which Ty took to mean that she was in favor.

So Ty obliged her. "Of course, sir, I would enjoy closing the day by sharing a meal with you. I look forward to it."

"At first twilight, then," Helryn said, then he stuffed his blade back into its sheath and turned, walking away. Ty watched as he went to another elf, well-dressed, with metallic-black hair—a color not normally found among elves. Ty didn't know him. As Helryn reached him, the elf raised an eyebrow and nodded toward Ty. Helryn just shook his head, and the two walked away across the plaza.

Bastard's friend probably hates me as much as Helryn does, for the crime of being born not wholly elf. If only they knew I wasn't an elf at all anymore, technically. But I'm used to the disdain by now. I just need to show them I'm as good or better than they are.

"This is great, Ty!" Ivy said as Dalryn walked up. She grabbed Dalryn's arm and squealed happily, jumping up once. "You'll go and meet with Dad, we'll all have dinner, and he'll see you're a great guy, even though you're part human! Then you guys can work together and stuff. Dad knows a lot from his time as a duke before the kingdom fell, and you're friends with the new king—"

"Kinda," Ty said, frowning.

"Kinda friends with the new king, and a dungeon lord. It'll be wonderful!"

Dalryn looked over his sister's head and met Ty's eyes, and her brother shook his head ever-so-slightly. Ty knew they shared a thought—neither wanted to disappoint Ivy, who was too precious for this world—but neither believed it would go so easily.

There was a pop of displaced air, and Ty glanced over to see that his rat had disappeared.

Forli came running over. "So, what's the deal with the diseased wolves? Why did they attack you? In fact, *how* did they attack you? Aren't all the corrupted rituals supposed to be cleared from the Central District of Star Port? And the entrances to the undercity sealed?"

"That's... a very good point," Ty said. "I'd had the thought myself. Additionally, they seemed utterly and solely focused on getting to me. I wonder why."

Dalryn pointed to the building that the wolves had come from. "Don't wonder, you tuber—figure it out. That's where they came from."

"Huh," Ty said. *Do I want to go confront what will possibly be a large number of diseased wolves?*

Even as he was thinking it, Kadrath clanked up to him in his massive plate mail. The man's green face was barely visible above the lip of the armor.

"Are you all right, Dungeon Lord?"

"I'm fine, although a bit shaken up—I wasn't expecting the wolves. I was hoping that you might help me to investigate that."

He put a hand on Ty's shoulder. "Hmm... I need to figure out what happened regardless. I'll be grabbing a diviner, a Mind user specialized in divination magic—sorry, not sure if you guys use the short names up here—from inside the guild, and then I intend to investigate regardless of whether you do. But you're more than welcome to come along, Dungeon Lord."

"I would like that." With Kadrath there, Ty would feel safe—no slight to Dalryn, but Kadrath was a vastly higher-level guardian. And the guild leader, so he had to have skills.

"All right, meet me at the house they came from."

Ty, Dalryn, Ivy, and Forli wandered over to the outside of the boarded-up marble building on the south side of the Grand Plaza that the wolves had come from. It was smallish, and it fronted the plaza directly. Ty assumed someone would purchase it from the government extremely soon, since it was absolutely prime real estate in their growing kingdom. But they weren't, as a society, large enough yet to need a 'Grand Plaza,' so some of the buildings stayed unoccupied and unrepaired for the moment.

Ty hoped Star Port would soon reach a point where they had a need for a Grand Plaza. He was very attached to his adopted town. He had been before, but now that his dungeon was permanently located here, he was deeply attached. Well, his dungeon's entrance was located here, anyway. He wasn't sure exactly where his dungeon itself was located. Some kind of extra-dimensional space, he supposed.

"Where is Kadrath?" Dalryn asked after a few moments. "This is boring!"

Ivy shuffled closer to Ty and leaned on him. "It's fine. It's a nice day outside, we're all okay, Dad was kinda reasonable, I can smell the ocean... Nerithin is kind."

Dalryn frowned and pulled his sword from its sheath. "Yeah, sure."

He began swinging it around, going through some kind of repetitive training motion. Ty surreptitiously backed away a bit.

After a few minutes, Dalryn stopped swinging his sword. "I can't handle this. It's boring. I'm going to check the inside of this dump."

Ty narrowed his eyes. "I'm the party leader, and we're waiting for—"

"This isn't formal adventuring stuff. I can go where I want on my own time. And I want to go inside, oh, high-and-mighty dungeon lord!"

Dalryn turned to face the front door, his sword held in front of him, and slowly moved toward it.

"Oh, for the good god's sake," Ty said in disgust.

Ivy leaned up and whispered in his ear. "Can we follow him, please? He's my brother... I'll make it up to you, I promise."

Her hand briefly strayed across his midriff.

Ty found himself nodding and following Dalryn, his own hand out, ready to call forth the power of the storm.

Forli followed behind, her hands nervously clenched in front of her.

Dalryn reached the door. It was hanging a bit off a hinge from when the wolves had crashed out of it, and Ty peered into the house. He couldn't see anything of note inside, for the small portions he could see. Just disturbed dust on the floor and a door to the back room. But he tensed as Dalryn threw the door open.

Chapter Twenty

DINNER WITH DADDY DEAREST, PART 1

Dalryn flourished his sword at nothing, and Ty relaxed his magic. The room was empty.

It had obviously been an inn, once. There was a fireplace for cooking. There were stairs to the second level. At the back, an empty doorframe led to what most likely had been a pantry.

"They must have come from the undercity, which means it wasn't the second story. Follow me." Dalryn stalked forward, leading the group into the other rooms.

Ty followed, still ready to call his lightning.

The doorway led into a smaller room. At the back, there were stairs leading down into a basement or the undercity. An iron-grate cover had obviously been pried off. Judging by the damage to the hinges bolted into the floor, it had been done on this side, not the side below ground.

And there was also a small stone, with twisted symbols on it and a gray crystal inside—a Mind magic device of some sort. But Ty could also feel the twisted magic of the thing. It wasn't normal Mind magic, but it was clearly corrupted.

Ty heard a clanking, and Kadrath came stomping into the back room, a gnome woman in robes following.

"Just couldn't wait, huh?" Kadrath grunted out.

"Sorry, we got bored," Ty said.

"Your head," Kadrath said, shrugging.

The gnomish woman walked up to the stone and pulled a pouch from her belt. She had hair graying with age and wore robes that seemed more for lounging than adventuring, but her eyes were sharp, and as soon as she started using her powers, Ty felt strong Mind magic from her. She reached out and carefully jiggered a piece of paper until it was under the stone, then sprinkled silver dust on it. The Mosstone siblings crowded around to look, Forli looking over their shoulder.

Words appeared on the paper in Middle Averian, the language common to most of the Inner Sea.

Stone of Guided Insanity, Targeted
Least item. Corrupted Mind magic. This stone causes any creature driven insane as the result of blood abyss corruption to target a single person. Tywyndyll il Belmoria.
A simple item, really, for such a dark purpose. Any creature created by or driven insane by the corrupted powers of the blood abyss that comes within 10 feet of the item must make an Intelligence check at -10 or be overcome with bloodlust, desiring only to kill Tywyndyll il Belmoria.

"Wow," Dalryn said. "Someone really doesn't like you, Ty."

I think that's the first time he's ever used my actual name, Ty's mind gibbered at him as he tried to adjust to the reality in front of him.

Someone was still trying to kill him, most likely to free his dungeon to be taken by another.

***

Ty adjusted the collar of his formal robes, which were blue with stitching in the outline of the Belmoria family crest on it.

160

He also wore fine buckskin shoes with buckles on them. Ty had had a local seamstress sew cheap apatite into the center of the buckles. It was a style that had been popular in the very last stages of Averian elf culture, before the fall.

Just standing in front of Helryn's house made him feel inadequate. It was on only eight acres, unlike his house's sixteen—but everything else was insanely impressive in comparison. It had gardens surrounding the entire house, including magical flowers, a few of which glowed. Ty could only assume that they were magically grown as well since Helryn had shown up mere months ago. The house itself was a massive monstrosity, done in smooth, polished granite, an odd choice in the city of marble. It was three stories tall and over two hundred feet wide, as well as surrounded by a giant, granite wall with iron spikes on the top that enclosed nearly an entire acre.

It must have cost a fortune to build it all so quickly. Ty wondered how the heck Helryn had squirreled away so much coin. The elves of the Havi Imperium had been forced to give up all their goods and money to pay 'back taxes' before they had left the Imperium to come here.

"Stop fidgeting," Ivy said. "Dad won't bite."

"Ivy, honey, I adore you in all your kind and sexy glory—but your dad clearly thinks the dungeon core should have gone to him, and from the sense of what Dalryn said to me when he ambushed me, I think your dad might have been planning to kill me at one point. Plus, he apparently beats you and Dalryn regularly. I *wish* biting was the foible he had."

Ivy's lip trembled and her eyes watered. "You don't know that he was trying to kill you, Ty. You should give people more credit than that, please. For me."

I know damn well he was trying to kill me, Ty thought to himself, but he put his arms around Ivy. "Well, we're all going to get along great now, so we don't need to worry about it, right? All's well that ends in a node."

Although Ty noted that even Ivy had just made a general pronouncement—give 'people,' not 'my dad,' more credit.

Ivy smiled up at him through her lashes. "Thanks, Ty. You're the best."

Ty stepped toward the wrought-iron gate. He did think it was odd that he was presenting himself at a house that Ivy had lived and slept in not but thirty-six hours before.

And what do they think they're hiding themselves from? Or protecting themselves from? The detail was nagging at Ty, but he pushed it aside. *Whatever, it's not my problem. This is about making Ivy happy, and perhaps mending fences with an obvious political player in the nascent kingdom reborn.*

Ty's thoughts turned briefly dark. *Although I didn't break the fence in the first place.*

Ivy must have sensed his mood as she slipped her hand into his as the guard, dressed in black and white for some reason, approached.

The guard nodded stiffly to Ty, then smiled slightly as he spoke to Ivy. "Welcome home, miss. It's good to see you—and better to see you smiling."

"Thanks, Kelwyn. I really appreciate it."

The guard—Kelwyn—motioned them in with a flourish, and Ty entered a half-step behind Ivy, who was bubbling with enthusiasm. "It's gonna be great, Ty. I can't wait for Dad to understand how wonderful you are! He's sure to love you when he gets to know you."

At the end of the gray, stone path, the front door had statues of glowering dragons made from stone out front, and the door itself was nearly twelve feet high and six feet wide, with a wrought-iron door knocker done in a credible imitation of a dragon's mouth.

Ty gingerly took the bizarre knocker and smacked it sharply, twice, into the imposing but spare door. *Yeah, I'm sure the guy who wanted to live in a house looking like this will just be feeling all warm and fuzzy soon.*

The door was pulled open by Dalryn, who was in fancy doublet and breeches, a fancy sword—obviously not a weapon used for war, from the hilt structure and tiny gems—at his waist.

And he had on an honest-to-the-gods cloak. Indoors.

He gave Ty an obvious onceover, then sneered. "Well, look at you, you onion. Stylish. You here to give a presentation on your latest findings in bug magic or something?"

Ty rolled his eyes. "You're one to talk—that cloak is ridiculous. Gonna throw it over your house's numerous floor puddles for when your lady love is here?"

Ivy giggled, her hand in front of her face.

Dalryn blushed, then took it off and put it on something behind the door that Ty couldn't see. "There, all better. You gonna do the same with your robe, maybe get some more tackle action going on?"

"Can we please just go inside?" Ty asked with a roll of his eyes.

Dalryn, somehow maintaining a superior smile the whole time, stepped aside and motioned Ty in.

The front room was a huge, stone reception area, but it was bare of the usual plants and murals that most of the walls of Averian households had. Instead, the opposite side wall was a single, huge painting, stretching from the floor to the ceiling fifteen feet above, and nearly as wide.

It was an extraordinarily well-done painting of a severe-looking elf, one that was a touch thin even by elven standards. At her feet was a green-scaled wyrm, a wingless dragon, although a very small one. Her hair was the same color as Ivy's and Dalryn's, copper with a hint of green to it, and her eyes were purple. She wore an elegantly stitched green-and-gray gown, the colors of the Mosstone family crest.

Her face was just a touch sad, but firm. Somehow, from this one painting, Ty thought he could sense a great deal of her story. He also thought he would have liked her.

"Whoa."

"My mother," Ivy said sadly. "I never really knew her. She died. It happened when I was very young, and I have only a tiny number of hazy memories of her."

Dalryn's superior smile slipped, and his voice went hard. "She didn't die, Ivy. She was murdered."

Murdered?

"What happened?" Ty asked.

Before either of the siblings could respond, the door knocker hit again.

Dalryn shrugged, muttered, "Some other time," and then went to open the door.

Standing in the door was the black-haired elf from earlier. He stood almost six tall but was quite muscled for an elf. His most notable feature was, in fact, his metallic-black hair—a color that Ty had never seen on an elf before. His skin was pale white even by the standards of the high elves.

His eyes were ice blue.

Next to him was a woman, also elven, with lustrous silver hair, wearing a long, flowing black gown that hugged her slight curves tightly.

Dalryn bowed slightly to both, hand over heart in the Averian style. "Count and Countess Grayshore. You all know Dungeon Lord Ty il Belmoria by reputation, I believe."

"I do know how reputable he is," the count said, a slight smile playing on his face.

Ty felt his eyes narrowing. *What a snake. I wonder how he would look lightly toasted with lightning.*

Even Ivy wasn't meeting the count's eyes, staring at the floor and tapping her toe on it behind her.

There was another knock at the door, and Dalryn opened it to reveal Forli, standing in a green dress with floral stitching. It appeared cheap and didn't fit quite right, but it was a major step up from her previous one.

"Well, shall we head to dinner?" Ty asked.

Count Grayshore sneered again, an expression that came easily to his face. "Generous of you to volunteer your host's services, but I guess since his children were too ill-mannered to do so, someone had to."

Ty gave a small smile and turned, waiting a second before following Dalryn. But his mind was elsewhere. *Is every elf in this whole group a bag of unimaginative sneers? Did they only have servants that laughed at their insipid little digs and went along with their petty cruelty or something? Also, why gratuitously insult the children of your benefactor?*

Ty couldn't place his finger on it, but something about the whole situation felt off—more off than some racist elves who wanted their realms handed back to them on a platter would account for.

I was right that Ivy was hiding things and that worked out okay... but something tells me that this one won't go as smoothly, or as wonderfully, as she did. But I'll give it a chance. For her sake, if nothing else.

Ty could still feel his trepidation as he followed the Mosstones and their guests deeper into their lair.

Chapter Twenty-One

DINNER WITH DADDY DEAREST, PART II

Ty followed Dalryn into a massive hall, mostly empty, before coming to a giant double door. A single guard in the same black-and-white outfit as Kelwyn outside waited at the door. As they approached, he opened the door and motioned them inside.

It was a huge dining hall, very long and narrow only for its length, with gray, stone walls that were currently undecorated. A massive, wooden table—*how did they even fit that in here through the doors?*—occupied most of it.

A pair of maids waited on the inside—human maids, Ty noted with some surprise, as there were very few humans in Star Port, and most of them were in positions of power, either related to George and working in the government or related to a single human family that ran a trade house named the Seahavens. He honestly hadn't even been aware that there were any others.

Although he couldn't fault Helryn's taste, whatever else was wrong with the man. The girls, while clearly human from their non-metallic, brown hair and smaller, rounder ears, were almost elven in their thinness, very well proportioned, and in the first blush of full adulthood, probably eighteen to twenty. They were also wearing rather short uniforms, nearly scandalous by Averian standards. It felt subtly degrading to Ty, somehow, and he mentally tossed the information into his 'Helryn is a jerk' bin while still involuntarily appreciating the beauty of the two girls.

One blushed and looked away as Ty stared too long. He blushed with shame in turn, wishing he didn't share his dad's—and he would bet Helryn's—weakness for women. It was a failing he wished he could get past. Although he was pretty sure it was what drove him to try to be great, since, supposedly, the women would want him then. He remembered a great deal of rejection when he'd been a poor man in Steelport, much of it by women who'd looked very similar to these two.

He stole a furtive glance to the side and saw that Ivy was watching him. She smiled at him and rolled her indigo eyes.

I wonder why she doesn't seem angry or hurt that I was checking out another woman. She isn't super-confident in herself. It's an interesting reaction.

The guard, either missing the five-second byplay or ignoring it, motioned Ty to a spot two down from the head of the table. As Ty took his place, he noted that most of the dishes were the finest silverware from the dwarven craftsmen of Stonehaven from before the dragonflight and the collapse of both Stonehaven and Averia, and that the glasses were forged from the city-state of Kulisyn on the southern shores of the Inner Sea, one of the very few elven settlements to have survived the fall of Averia. In fact, *everything* on the table was extremely fancy and from the time when Averia had been a true kingdom... except Helryn's cup. It was made of steel and had a green-glass snake somehow worked around it, with a tiny faux-sword in the head of the snake. The design felt almost organic, and it was subtly unsettling to Ty.

Why the cup?

Ivy was seated next to Ty and also next to the head of the table, and Dalryn sat down next to Ty on his opposite side, frowning. The Grayshores sat on the opposite side, the count on the side closest to the head of the table. Forli was sat on the far side next to the countess. She scooted a tiny bit away from the woman and leaned away from both the nobles.

Then they waited, fidgeting, for a few moments, no one saying anything. He tried to focus on the abilities that might be revealed when he acquired powers in certain combinations, and it worked—his eyes glazed out and he forgot about the tension.

Then the guard opened the door and called, "Duke Helryn ap Mosstone, head of the Mosstone family."

Helryn strode into the room in a swirl of his own black cloak. His silver hair was long and straight, and his one ice-blue eye briefly focused on Ty with a slight tightening of the muscles around his thin, pressed-together lips. Ty once again felt Mind magic wash over him as Helryn's glowing diamond eye also focused on him.

That's... rude. He keeps using some Mind ability, probably analyze, on me, which we both know isn't acceptable in polite society.

At least it's clear Dalryn comes by his cloak love from somewhere.

The two maids began walking in and out with dishes of food—candied apples, various tubers, and roots covered in spices and with accompanying dipping sauces, and wine for everyone. They set them down around the huge table in places between the diners that told Ty these were shared pre-meal dishes.

He grabbed a couple of spiced asparagus and a small container of a white dipping sauce.

After a brief rustle of movement, everyone settled back with their appetizers of choice. Another brief moment of silence followed, and Ty decided to break it.

"So, I hear you've been adventuring deep in the undercity, Duke Mosstone." *It's silly to call him that, but politeness never hurt, and flattery very rarely.* "Have you found anything that would make a good story to regale us with? An adventurer of your level and power must surely have a story we could draw wisdom from."

That's right, Ty, just lay it on thick for Ivy's sake.

"I understand you've had me banned from delving your domain, dungeon lord?" Helryn asked.

Well that was an aggressive non-sequitur.

He glanced to the side, and Ivy's eyes were wide.

"An error, I'm sure," Ty said. "I'll make sure it's fixed tomorrow morning. My deepest apologies for any inconvenience."

Helryn dipped his head at Ty and raised his odd wineglass ever-so-slightly. "Well, then, enough said about that. A story, hmm? Well, the undercity is filled with the most fascinating things. The Ancient Ones were extremely powerful, and extremely wise, and built a great many things—including objects of great power."

Ty raised a wineglass to his mouth to hide his expression. *Wise, huh? Saelenia seemed to think they were a horrid society, filled with depravity—she specifically mentioned it when I first talked to her.*

"One of the most fascinating objects I've come across is my eye. I found it in a temple, a very strange temple. It had, at its front, a statue of a god that I've learned is named Xalkri—"

Ty gasped as he was drinking and sucked wine into his lungs. It burned, and he sprayed the reddish liquid across the table as he coughed and choked. Ivy stood, dabbing at the wine and patting Ty on his back.

The count sneered at him. "Can't handle your wine, boy?"

But Ty ignored the count—ex-count—whatever. *Xalkri! That's what Saelenia was telling me about earlier today.* Helryn *already knows where the temple that has the claws of Foriveltain is! Has he taken them?*

He glanced up at Helryn, whose ice-blue eye bored into him. "Did that name mean something to you?"

Ty prevaricated. "No, great duke, just trying to breathe and drink at the same time like an idiot."

He coughed again and dabbed at his mouth.

Helryn settled back. "Very well. So, the temple. Apparently, the elder ones had some strange gods. Xalkri was apparently the god of improvement. But not in the usual sense of leveling. He was the god of fusing magic to people directly to make them better. But his form was the strangest thing. The temple's central feature was a statue to the god. It was a slug—a giant slug with thirty-seven tentacles coming down to thirty-seven different, smaller statues. Each of them was carrying a magical item once, I think. Powerful and unusual things. But they were all guarded by powerful magic. I found my new eye there."

"Is there anything left?" Ty asked.

Helryn hesitated before speaking. "I'm honestly not sure. Some of the statues are... very strange. I know most, if not all, have been looted."

I know that's not the full truth.

"What does your eye do?" Forli asked.

Helryn hesitated again. "It gives me powerful divination magic, quite a few tricks. Since I lack Mind magic, and the eye sees in its own way, the trade felt worthwhile."

He really did stick an Ancient One object into his eye, right next to his brain.

There was another awkward pause.

Ivy sat tall, a smile plastered on her face. "So, what've you been up to today, Dad? Besides saving me?"

"Well, I adventured in the undercity a bit this morning, but then I spent most of the day trying to convince the Eveningtide family to support our request for reforms in the government, as well as the land requests."

"Did they?" Helryn's daughter asked her father.

Helryn's voice was bitter. "No. They're a pack of fools. They said that the king bought them from slavery and gave them land, so they'll trust him to do the right thing without intervention. As if signing a petition would get them in trouble with our weak and naïve new monarch."

Well, I'll agree with the naïve part, at least. Although honestly, I trust our king to do the right thing as well.

Some of Ty's expression must have made it to his face, because Helryn narrowed his eyes at Ty. "What do you think of the king's refusal to hand out noble titles, or land grants, at this point? Especially to the old nobility?"

"Well, technically he made an elf who was noble before into the Duke of Stonehaven."

Duke Helryn used his fork to pierce a spiced onion, fare bitterer than more elves preferred. "That elf was a deep elf, not a high elf. But do you think that he should hand out land grants now? Larger ones for nobles?"

Ty had no idea. Maybe the elves spreading out, new locales to grow, would be good. On the other hand, goblin camps still existed in the forest, monsters prowled, and the dragons still raided.

"I apologize, Duke Mosstone, I've genuinely not given it enough thought to know. I can see arguments either—"

Helryn's fork snapped in his hand, sending a half-eaten piece of onion spinning onto the floor. One of the maids went and retrieved it.

That's... a lot of strength, Ty thought, a bit shocked.

Helryn thumped the table with his fist so hard that wine spilled. "Do you agree with your father, then? That giving back the elven nobles their land and titles, if not their stipends, is foolish?"

Well, although I hate to admit it, yes.

Ty narrowed his own eyes intentionally, mimicking anger. "I haven't spoken to my father except for an occasional polite *hello* in passing for years. I have a great deal of anger directed at him, and little affection for him."

Helryn settled back slightly.

Ty continued. "I truly knew nothing of this current debate, and I was thinking of this more from a resource allocation standpoint—that you were asking me about centralization against branching out. If a noble wanted to fund an expedition to recover his lands and assume his previous title, while simultaneously assuming the risk of doing so, I think that's a fine idea."

"And do you think that, on their own lands, elves should be forbidden to own non-elves?"

Ty knew what the politic answer was, but due to his own parents' history and his captivity to the orcs, he had very strong feelings on the matter. "From personal experience, I know slavery is wrong, and I would want King Leo's decree against the practice propagated to all lands."

"*Fool*," Count Grayshore muttered.

Helryn's face reddened again, and Ty feared another outburst. He mentally prepared to summon his dungeon monster.

"Can you not see," Helryn ground out, "that elves are far superior to others? There were *four million* people in the lands that house tens of thousands now. There were more human and beast-kin slaves in these lands than there are people remaining, put together, since the elves fell. Enslaving them was for their own benefit, as well as ours. I understand you're only half-elven, but clearly, your elven side dominates. Surely, you can see that enslaving the humans is for their own benefit? Without us, they're barely better than beasts."

Ty was normally polite and phlegmatic, but his personal reasons to be angry about this issue were too much to overcome. "Slavery is *evil*, Helryn, and I don't understand what you've done that makes you believe the elves are superior."

Ivy gasped, and Helryn slammed the table so hard, his end *shattered*, proving his strength was supernatural—as if more proof were needed. The strength of his blow propelled him to standing, as if he were unused to his own power, and he almost fell.

Everyone flew back from the table, and Count Grayshore and Dalryn both drew blades.

"*Miserable half-breed!*" Helryn screamed, spittle landing on Ty's face. "It's not what *I've* done, it's what *they've* done. In their jealousy over our wealth and prestige, the human beasts who claim to be mortal races threw a riot when the elven refugees arrived in Lakusi. They *killed my wife* while I watched, unable to prevent it with all my power, the mob too numerous! I butchered them by the hundreds that day, and the Noble Square in Lakusi ran with their foul blood! But it didn't bring her back! Nothing will—because humans only destroy and occupy the ruins of their betters, barely different than goblins!"

He drew his sword, his eye mad, but Dalryn threw himself in the way. "Dad! Ty's all right, even though he's a halfie! He's actually a really good man who's getting both your kids, two elves I might add, a ton of levels! He doesn't even work with any humans! Our whole group is elves and dryads, the races of old Averia."

Helryn trembled, visibly on the edge of a killing rage, but then he sheathed his sword.

Dalryn relaxed, putting his own blade down.

Helryn backhanded his son so hard that Ty heard something break. Dalryn slammed into the wall and slid down, unmoving.

"I'll not stand for my own spawn to raise his blade against me."

"No!" Ivy screamed, rushing at her father.

Helryn held his hand up. "This is over. Take your brother and go, you whorish piece of filth. I'll not stand for those who defend the humans, or those who pleasure them, to be under this roof."

Tears spilled down Ivy's face, but after a moment, she nodded.

Helryn turned and strode from the room as everyone else stared in shocked silence.

Except Dalryn, who lay in an awkward puddle on the floor, as still as a corpse.

Chapter Twenty-Two

JUST SO MUCH FAMILY

Ten minutes later, in the chill, night air of the Green Apple district of Star Port, among the shadows cast by the trees of the various orchards intercepting moonlight, Dalryn stood, rubbing his jaw. Ty and Ivy were close, watching as he managed to heave himself upright, and Forli was a bit back.

"You're fully healed, right, Dalryn?" Ivy asked for the third time.

He nodded but worked his jaw anyway. "Yeah, sorry. What happened?"

"You stood up for me against your dad," Ty said, smiling at Dalryn. "Thanks, genuinely. You're a bit of an ass—okay, a colossal ass and a criminal who once tried to murder me—but for all that, you're kinda a good guy."

Dalryn muttered, "I didn't try to murder you," but Ty could tell his heart wasn't in the argument.

"You okay?" Ty asked.

Dalryn slowly nodded. "Yeah. I just can't remember anything about what you guys are talking about. Last I remember, you and Dad were getting along, talking about how *your* dad was a bad person, and then I woke up here, in agony for a few seconds, till my face finished healing."

Ty had heard some soldiers from the Founding War complain after head blows of losing a few minutes of time, but he was surprised that the effect held after healing.

"Well, you did a good thing, so I appreciate it," Ty reiterated. "I'm glad."

There was a pause.

Ivy put her foot back and lightly toe-kicked the marble road. "So, Dad said we're not welcome back in the house."

Dalryn frowned. "Great. Feel like lending me some coin to stay at the Emerald Bee?"

"Why not stay with Cuwylla?" Ty asked.

Dalryn frowned again. "Eh... apparently, Thea talked to someone, and word about me attacking you got around. I kinda think I'm gonna be in trouble when the king gets back. Cuwylla told me I'd 'betrayed her trust' and we needed to take a break."

Dalryn frowned at Ty. "I've gotten in a lot of trouble over you, you onion. I hope you appreciate it."

For a moment, Ty almost lost his proverbial feces, at the injustice of Dalryn telling him that it was *Ty's* fault. Dalryn was in trouble for trying to bandit him on the road. But Ty restrained himself—Dalryn had been trying hard to make right with his new group.

It took Ty a moment, though, and Ivy came over and slipped her hand around his waist, then kissed his ear, whispering, "Thank you for being nice to Dalryn, Ty," in a barely audible whisper. "I already promised I'd make it up to you, and I will. So much."

Ty finished calming himself and nodded brusquely to Dalryn. "Thank you. Would you rather stay at my place? You can use my sister's room, which is quite far from mine, if you wish. I'll get some furniture for one of our guest rooms tomorrow."

Dalryn shrugged, furrowing his eyes again. "Yeah, that works."

"Um, can I stay as well?" Forli asked. "I don't actually need to sleep much, and I can do it on a wooden floor easily enough."

Ty looked sideways at Ivy, and she smiled, nodding.

"We'll get you some furniture tomorrow as well, I guess," he said.

***

Ty's steamy dream, which had involved Ivy and Forli both, suddenly involved his sister yelling.

A sudden jolt next to him caused him to sit upright in his bed, and he could hear people yelling. Ivy was sitting up next to Ty in the bed, deliciously naked in the moonlight, her hand clutched to her chest, where she still wore her medallion to Cerivae Nerithin but nothing else.

Ty's brief musings were shattered by the continued yelling. He couldn't quite make out the words, but he recognized the voices—his sister and Dalryn.

Of course this was the day she got back with the king, Ty thought to himself disgustedly.

"I'll be back," Ty said to Ivy, although she was already climbing from bed, gloriously beautiful. Ty grabbed his blue robe and slipped into it before rushing from the room.

He raced to his sister's room—halfway across his house. As he got close, he heard his sister say, "And put some pants on, you hobo!"

Remembering his own naked moment with Dalryn a couple of days ago, Ty laughed to himself as he rushed into the room.

"Sorry, sorry, this is my fault," Ty cried out as he entered.

"Oh, thank Eturia, you're awake," Dalryn said, trying to step into his breeches but catching his leg and crashing to the ground, his pale buttocks poking up at Ty and his sister, Val.

Ty laughed outright as Dalryn cursed and jammed his legs into his pants while upside down.

Ty's sister turned to face him. Val—Valynrae il Belmoria, technically—was superficially similar in appearance to Ty. She had copper hair, green eyes, freckles, and human ears, even though she was technically a half-elf like himself. Once, she had been weedy, but a few levels and a harsh training regimen had made her lean and muscled, further reinforcing how human she appeared.

At the moment, she was still dressed for war, however, in her riding leathers. She carried her wolf's-head bow on her back, and her wolf's head-hilted saber at her belt. Val was Level Six, like Ty had been, but her build was a hybrid Animal Companion build—she was bonded to a ghost wolf—and Air magic archery and speed build. She was also the general for King Leo, although he relied on mercenary leaders more often than his sister to provide tactical acumen. She was barely older than Ty, still green in the ways of war despite her levels.

"You put some strange guy in my bed?" she asked, quirking an eyebrow at Ty. Then she gave Dalryn a onceover. "Not the worst-looking guy, I admit, but I can see just from the way he's adjusting to this situation that he's like all those petty House sons back home in Steelport."

"I'm not like a human!" Dalryn said indignantly.

"See?" Val said, motioning to him with her head.

Forli walked into the room, wearing only her longish dress, her green-pine hair sticking straight up. She appeared nervous as she entered but a wide smile crossed her face when she took in the situation.

Ty half-smiled himself but held his hands up apologetically. "Sorry, Val, I thought you'd be gone for a few more days with the king. It was a bit of an emergency—Dalryn here is my adventuring group guardian, but his dad kicked him out. I'll get the rest of the guest rooms set up tomorrow morning, swear."

Val gave another glance at Dalryn, who was lacing his pants up as they talked, technically decent. "So he really *is* a hobo?"

"Hey!"

Ty's smile went full at the sight of someone else taking the wind out of Dalryn's sails.

His sister smiled back at him. "Well, it could be worse than a hot hobo in my bed, I guess. But all of you need to get your ass in gear. King Leo came back with another thousand rescued elf slaves—all either from our hometown of Steelport, or recent additions from the various slaves our enemies had picked up in the orc lands. Even though you're a dungeon lord, you haven't resigned your minister-at-large position—we need you to help get everyone fed, into temporary quarters, and assigned to farm plots in the area. That's something you're good at, remember?"

Ty nodded. "All right, I'm on it. Ivy, you stay here, please."

Val motioned to Dalryn. "Since this dude is your adventuring companion and owes me coin for using my bed, he's coming even if your girlfriend is staying."

"What? How is that fair?" Dalryn asked.

"Well, have any coin for the bed?"

"No."

"Then you can choose between lending your aid or getting your ass kicked in front of everyone. I'd give it some careful thought. Trust me. I'm Level Six—it won't go well for you."

Dalryn frowned but nodded and reached for his shirt while Val looked on.

***

Ty was exhausted but trying to do his best by everyone as he coordinated from an outdoor table lit only by torchlight. Forli had joined him, her own part in food preparation done for the night, and she stood off to the side and behind him. She was quite cute, dressed in a white shift, and her spiky, pine-needle hair had somehow gotten messed up, with a third of it pressed in a different direction than the rest and slightly discolored. He couldn't even imagine what had caused it. Weirdest stew spill ever?

Ty tore his mind from Forli and stared at the next group walking up, eight elves already sorted to be sent to an assignment, since they were a group that could get along with itself. "All right, we've got the eight of you in the old Leafrain warehouse on South Dock Street. Vyneal, can you take them please?"

The eight elves, all thin and weathered and wearing rags, gave various nods or grunts of affirmation. Vyneal, a one-handed soldier-turned-farmer who still adventured—Sunday only—in the ruins of old Calasti and Ty's dungeon both, gave the 'hand over heart' gesture with his one hand, then called, "All right, newbies, please follow me. It's a half-mile-walk to your temporary quarters, and I'm *so* late to see my wife."

As the group headed off, the next one came to the front. The one at the front was a young female elf who would have been pretty if she didn't appear half-starved. Long, bronze hair, crystal-green eyes...

Ty could feel his own eyes going wide. "Yenrael?"

That's the last girl who rejected me before I went adventuring!

Yen stared up at him, her own eyes going wide. "Ty?"

"Yeah, it's me."

She stared at him for a moment, then sagged. Ty caught a muttered, "Of course it is, by the fall."

There were a few other elves around, and Yen looked around, her cheeks flushing so red that Ty could see it even in the bare torchlight. She stepped forward and leaned over so she was bare inches from Ty. "Ty, look, I'm really sorry about before... Please don't send me away or... something, okay? Please? I'll... I'll be with you if you want..."

Ty was disgusted with himself, disgusted because his first thought had been to use his position to take advantage of her. She had spurned him before, when she'd been a slave and he just a poor seamstress's son, but now that he had power, she was willing to sleep with him? It made him angry. Angry, but also disgusted with himself for the shameful temptation to 'get revenge' for her rejection. Ty sometimes hated the darkness within him. But, as he constantly reminded himself, he wasn't his thoughts—only his actions.

He did a quick search of the options in front of him—he saw that the Emerald Bee had some rooms free for refugees, and he knew those would be the best places anyone could stay. As a way to make up for his own dark thoughts, he decided to be extra kind.

Ty shook his head slightly, and Yen's eyes widened—in fear, Ty thought. He hastily clarified. "I appreciate that you want to take up old relations," he said loudly. "But I'm currently seeing a duke's daughter—I'm not sure she would be okay with it. However, in light of our past friendship, I do have a few rooms at the local inn I can hand out—it's about as good as it gets at the moment."

Yen nodded, relief written all over her face, although upon hearing that he was dating a duke's daughter, her eyes focused on him more clearly, appraisingly, Ty thought. After a moment, she asked, "What happened to your skin?"

"Manifestation of one of my level abilities," Ty said—a lie, technically, but basically true.

Yen nodded, seeming to accept it. "Thank you, Ty. I'm sorry about before. I—"

"It's fine, Yen. Just go get some sleep. If you really want to talk, we can some other day, but I bear you no ill will."

She nodded, and another soldier took the group away.

Ty glanced up for the next group, only to see that there wasn't one. He slumped in his chair, exhausted beyond words. He was stiff from all the day's tension and fear, and now from sitting as well.

Forli came up and began kneading his shoulders with her wood-grain hands, her fingers delicate for all that she was a dryad. Ty had gotten used to suppressing his sexual attraction to Forli, but with her working the knots from his muscles, it came back in full force. But he didn't push—there were a lot of dangers down that road, especially since he was with Ivy.

After a bit, Forli asked, "So you think Ivy will be mad if you're with other women? Like you told that Yenrael girl?"

"I—ah, that feels good—don't know, Forli. We've been together about seventy-two hours at this point. She does seem very okay with me checking out other women, but I have no idea if it goes any further than that. I wasn't going to bring it up in our first week."

"But it's extremely important that we make more dryads!" Forli said, quietly but forcefully. "Plus, every day since you became a dungeon lord, instead of imagining my tree, or how to improve nature, or anything, I imagine you inside me, rutting me like an animal. I want it! I can tell you want it as well."

Ty sighed. "I... I do want it, Forli. But that's the price of being with one girl—you can't be with more."

Forli's hands briefly tightened. "I went to the library, and I checked. That's not completely true. Some places practice polygamy, or just keep a harem."

Ty grimaced at the sudden pain, then relaxed as she went back to massaging him a touch more gently. "Not the Kingdom of Averia. It's been a monogamous society since the first elves began speaking Middle Averian."

"I read about how most of the nobles kept mistresses—or in one queen's case, a whole bevy of men in high positions who would have sex with her. Even our current king, King Evans, is only king because he was a bastard who got sent away by the previous ruler. All the old king's legitimate children died in the dragon attack on Old Calasti. I've been studying all about sex stuff now that I'm attracted to you."

Forli sounded proud of her research, although the fact that she was researching sexual mores as a complete outsider almost made Ty want to laugh. He could only imagine how the librarians were handling this.

But it was a path that couldn't be. Not yet, at the very least. From where he was slouched, enjoying her attentions, he tried to explain. "Forli—I would love, I mean absolutely *love*, to have a harem. Very nearly every guy's dream, right? But I'm not asking Ivy on day three to do so. Period. I'm really, really sorry, and I promise I want you, as you said. But this sounds crazy. If you'd grown up with desires for intimacy and thought about it all the time, instead of suddenly getting sexual urges a few days ago, I think you would understand how *very* crazy it sounds."

"You won't even *ask* Ivy?"

"Even asking will cause all kinds of problems."

"Ty!" Ty's dad, George, called from the darkness. Ty heard the slow *tink* of his cane on the marble path as he walked up.

Ah, crap, I really didn't want to deal with him—or anyone really—right now. I should quit being a minister—I'm already making more as a dungeon lord, and I won't have incredibly late nights helping the kingdom.

Although, in his heart of hearts, Ty knew that he did, in fact, want to help the kingdom—to win everyone's approval, if nothing else.

Ty's musings were interrupted when Forli stopped massaging his shoulders and stood up straight. "Well, *I'm* going to go ask Ivy, then, if you won't!"

Chapter Twenty-Three

JUST ONE MORE THING IN THE LONGEST DAY EVER

Ty tried to come out of the chair, but his new dryad stats betrayed him, and he tripped, hitting the ground hard.

Forli giggled as she rushed out into the darkness in the direction of Ty's home.

Ty's father loomed over him briefly as Ty struggled to his feet.

George Orsini had been born a prodigal child in many ways—talented, driven, handsome, and with all the arrogance that came with that. Now, however, he was old, almost seventy. His hair was white and wispy, his hands spotted and trembling. Remarkably, he'd kept his eyesight and most of his teeth, somehow, but his back was nearly completely gone, and he walked with a hunch and a cane.

"I need to—" Ty began.

"Minister-at-Large Tywyndyll il Belmoria, I would have a word with you," Ty's dad said.

Ty hesitated, his attention almost wholly focused on the disaster that he was sure was being created *right now* by Forli. But his father had addressed him formally, meaning that it was, to some degree, a formal meeting.

"Quickly, please," Ty said, turning back to his father.

"I see that you finished—how did it go?" Ty's father asked.

Ty recited it all from memory. "I sent out runners to everyone I knew who had extra space, as well as sent out feelers for others. I allocated only fourteen copper of the ten gold you gave me to purchase space, as every elf here was freed less than a year ago and wanted to return the favor to the next elf—a positive cornucopia of volunteerism."

George smiled at that. "We're building something special here."

Ty didn't respond, just continuing his report. "In a lot of cases, the people who took one of the freed slaves in made a caveat that if the situation goes on for too long, they'll want some compensation. I have those people, and their dates of payment requested, listed on the papers there. It's organized so that the ones requesting payment are at the top so that we can get farms, shops, and homes for those elves first. I also have the prepaid spaces you arranged sorted here, and I only used one—the Emerald Bee. Technically, I did that to resolve a personal situation, even though it wasn't my fault, so I'll pay the king back tomorrow morning."

"Where did most of them get placed?"

"Apple Grove and the First District—we're going to need to expand the farming settlements along the west bank of the Blue River, between here and Wheat Town, soon. As well as resettle the old orchard towns in the Forest of Averia."

George frowned. "The king won't like that—the forest outside the ruins walls is still dangerous, with goblin tribes and corrupted magical beasts both. We need champions willing to act as strong points in order to do that."

Ty shrugged. The city itself was still dangerous, something Ty had learned roughly eighteen hours ago. Plus, Ty needed to go after Forli, not sit here and make small talk.

"What happened to your skin, by the way?" Ty's dad asked, peering at him in the torchlight. "Your mom mentioned that it had changed—tell me about it."

It still flabbergasts me that Mom and Dad get along well enough to talk. "I don't think my formal duties extend to talking about this, Seneschal Orsini."

George shifted uncomfortably where he leaned on his cane. "Well, I have other news, semi-official, to talk to you about."

"*Quickly*, please."

"King Leo conquered our house, House Orsini."

Ty envisioned all his cousins. The cousins who had called him "slavey," had refused to admit he was related, had given him rancid food rather than coin when he'd been hungry, and had just generally conducted themselves like horse droppings.

"Oh, no, I'm heartbroken," Ty said, his voice so dry, he almost expected dust to settle between him and his father.

Although his sarcasm masked real anger. *That's the House that bought Mom and then refused to support us through some very hard years once Dad had freed her.*

George gave a phlegmy chuckle. "I'm sure. But it's not like you think—the king did it nearly bloodlessly, with only two people in the whole House dying. And then he appointed me head of the family."

Ty grimaced.

His dad continued. "To keep the House financially afloat—since most of these ex-slaves were taken from the family—he gave it special trading rights here in the city. So you'll be seeing your aunts, uncles, and cousins quite a bit more. I'll be establishing a branch of the family here, in fact, under Aunt Velma."

"Joy," Ty said, quirking one eyebrow. He didn't want to sound like a child, and he could read between the lines—it was this or everyone in the House would end up on the street if King Leo had removed that much money from the House in the form of its slaves. Ty's dad was doing this for everyone's benefit.

At least that explains why Yen showed up. I'm sure that there'll be more people around I knew back in Steelport. Again—joy.

"How's the dungeon doing?" Ty's dad asked. "What level is it, and how's it been interacting with the town?"

Ty hesitated, but that felt like a formal enough question that he needed to answer. "It's Level Two, and four people died the second day it was in operation, a group of nearly new residents. We lost two rabbit-kin—both distantly related to Captain Whitewater—a human who was visiting on a trade mission from the Havi Imperium, and a local elf named Rarnyll Olthandea who was without family. Last I checked, Kadrath said that eighteen people have made Level Two. No one else has died or been seriously injured—Kadrath keeps two healers on staff to make sure that anyone who makes it out of the dungeon at all will be totally fine."

Ty guffawed. "He joked that he wouldn't have adventurers leaving pieces behind."

George nodded but must have taken the extra information that Ty had provided as an opening. "And how have you been?"

"Dad... I'm sorry, I don't want to talk about that. I take it our official business is done?"

George reached over and gathered the papers that Ty had indicated earlier. "I guess it is. You're welcome at my house anytime, you know. Your sister visits. You could—"

"Dad... look, I've had some conversations lately about my relationship with you. Including with my dungeon boss, the Crone of Averia."

George raised an eyebrow at that, but Ty waved away further explanation before continuing.

"A lot of people are urging I get over... everything you did. They're saying that you coming to the recognition that slavery was wrong on your own and freeing Mom makes up for the fact that you'd bought her and had us with her just to breed her magic line into House Orsini in the first place."

"I didn't know better then, and I regret that with my—"

Ty held a hand up. "Those same people said that sending me to live with Mom was the right decision. Even though I was dirt poor to the point I remember going hungry a lot. Maybe it was the right decision. A lot of people I respect think so. So, intellectually, I forgive you. But it's still a bit awkward at times. I've had a lot of awkwardness lately."

George sagged, appearing as old as Ty had ever seen him. He stood there for a moment, his face working.

Finally, he glanced up at Ty. "I have the wasting disease—King Leo calls it 'cancer.'"

Ty was shocked speechless for a moment. The wasting disease was a part of a person's body, somehow, that had gone wrong—which meant that the ones who got it couldn't be healed by magical means, as it wasn't an 'injury' or 'disease' in the traditional sense. It was one of the main ways rich people died, since most other wounds and diseases could be cured by magic—if you could afford it.

In Ty's silence, George continued to talk. "So, I don't have a lot of time."

Ty remained quiet.

George sighed heavily. "I'll go now, Ty. If you do decide to have any relationship with me, however... do so soon."

Ty felt defeated—he would be an ass if he didn't go see his dad when the man was *dying*. But he hated that his past, the past he didn't like, was coming here in every way and form. He wanted to get on with being a dungeon lord, with being rich, with being important and desirable.

He didn't want to deal with all this, the dark past when he'd been weak gutter trash—a past that haunted him because he worried it was secretly the real him.

But if Dad's dying... "I'm sorry, Dad. I'll arrange a dinner. But it'll have to be soon—in a few days, I'll be heading out to grab things for my dungeon in Zadrid's Hallow. I just need to make a few levels for my team first."

George quirked his bushy, white eyebrow again. "I didn't know dungeons needed 'things.'"

"Sapient dungeons do, apparently. I'll tell you about it over supper, apparently—whatever flaws you may possess, Dad, I'll concede that a loose tongue isn't one of them. And your advice would be most welcome in truth. But for now, I really do need to go see to a personal matter, desperately. Then I need to sleep—this has been the longest day of my life that wasn't one of captivity by the orcs."

George reached out to wrist-clasp his son, and Ty obliged briefly. Then he grabbed a lantern, turned, and rushed into the darkness after Forli.

***

Ty didn't find Forli, and eventually, he headed to his own room, praying to Iluvin Eturia in her capacity as goddess of elves and to Cerivae Nerithin in her capacity as goddess of small favors that he wouldn't find the two of them together there.

There was a light flickering beneath the door, and Ty opened it quietly.

Ivy was sitting up in bed. A candle, barely melted, was on the end table, providing light. Ty briefly forgot all of his irritations, fears, and even why he was here as he drank in the sight of Ivy. He could feel himself getting tight in his breeches.

She smiled at him playfully. "Forli came to see me."

Suddenly, he had lots of room in his breeches. "I told her not to, I swear! I didn't put her—"

She giggled, putting one hand in front of her mouth and held her other hand up, palm facing him. "It's okay, Ty. I asked her, and she told me it was her idea."

"So you're not mad at me?" Ty asked.

"Of course not," she said, smiling at him. "You saved me from my dad, helped me make levels, gave me a place to live, even gave my brother, who tried to beat you up, a place to stay and helped *him* make levels as well. I would never be mad at you, Ty. You've been so good to me, Cerivae Nerithin knows—it's only right that I be good to you."

"Um, okay, well... still. Sorry it—"

"Forli also told me that the reason she's attracted to you, even though she's a dryad and normally has no sexual interest at all, is that you can, well, seed her. As in, make a dryad seed by having sex with her. Is that correct?"

Ty nodded. "I don't exactly know how it works, but that does seem to be the crux of it. I'm really sorry, Ivy, but she's very... *insistent* that she be personally responsible for growing the dryads. She was the weakest, most scorned dryad before. She wants the respect of her sisters like I want the respect of all the elves. Apparently, the big crisis in the dryad community is that the Crone was dying and there would be no more dryads."

Ivy nodded, her mouth pursed, and her brow lightly furrowed. "That *is* a major crisis."

Ty would have given a lot to know what she was thinking beyond that quip.

After a moment, she smiled at him again, a glowing thing. "Well, I don't know what I want to do about all that, but for now, you must be tired. Come to bed."

Ty shrugged out of his robes and breeches, then climbed into bed with her, pulling the woolen blanket over them.

Ivy reached out, her hands lascivious on him. "To prove that I'm not mad, I'm going to make you forget everything that worries you—and every other girl you find attractive as well."

She began stroking and playing with all of him.

Ty relaxed as she got started, the whole, long day—much of it incredibly stressful—fading away.

Chapter Twenty-Four

A WEEK OF BLISS AND POWER LEVELING

Ty woke in the sunlight, his mouth cotton, his wrist covered in his own drool where his hand stuck out from under the pillow. The sunlight was clearly dawn, half-light, half-dark. Although it seemed too reddish to him, somehow.

His last memory was of laying himself down and Ivy starting to touch him. *Did I forget having sex? Did I fall asleep for an hour?*

Ty groggily glanced around and didn't see Ivy anywhere. *Weird. Although I'm not going to panic like last time.*

Ty got up and put his robes on, then opened the door.

Immediately, the smell of spices hit him. Someone was cooking.

Ty walked to his kitchen, following his nose. When he entered, he found Dalryn and his sister, Val, sitting at the table on a bench next to each other, eating a pile of sad grapes. They were talking to each other, with Dalryn gesturing wildly and his sister looking amused.

A quick around glance showed Ivy at the fire, teaching Forli how to fry potatoes and make sugar-coated apples as well. They couldn't look more different—the thin, almost boyish Ivy with her pale skin and long, metallic-copper hair next to the short, curvy, spiked-needle hair and pine-wood skin Forli. But Ty enjoyed the sight of both of them—especially since they were smiling and laughing together.

"Potatoes for breakfast?" Ty asked.

His sister exploded into laughter. "Breakfast? You slept for *twelve hours*, Ty. It's easily suppertime."

Ty glanced over at Ivy, who nodded her head in confirmation. "We, um, started to—"

"Hey!" Dalryn barked out.

Ivy blushed. "You fell asleep immediately. Must've been a day, huh?"

"Well, yesterday I did a dungeon run, almost got murdered by wolves, met your dad, who threw us all from the house, was woken by my sister finding a hobo in her bed—"

"Hey!" Dalryn barked again, and everyone laughed.

"—and then I had to coordinate a significant portion of a thousand new citizens arriving. I earned some rest."

Ivy smiled. "Well, I got our dungeon time switched—Kadrath was hesitant to allow it since I'm not the group leader, but he knows we're together, and I found a group willing to trade times in return for an extra silver. So eat up—we're due for a run in about three hours. Also, I'm teaching Forli to cook, since she'll be staying with us from now on—you need to go buy two sets of furniture for the empty guest rooms. Forli agreed that instead of rent, she'll pay with cooking, cleaning, and other chores."

Wow... I suppose it's a good thing that I've suddenly got a girl taking care of everything for me, and she can't be too upset if Forli is going to continue to stay with us... but I feel a bit cut out of the loop of my own life.

Some of his thoughts must have shown on his face, because his sister threw a grape at him. "The response here, brother mine, is 'Thank you, my wonderful dear, for taking care of me so well.'"

"Thank you, my wonderful dear, for taking care of me so well," Ty mimicked as he sat at the head of the small table, next to his sister.

"Dad said you'll have supper with him sometime, by the way."

When does everyone find the time to see each other? Ty thought exasperatedly.

"Yeah, but it'll need to fit the schedule. I've done the math—I want us to make Level Four before we head to Zadrid's Hallow."

"Zadrid's Hallow?" Val asked, eyes wide. "Why Zadrid's Hallow?"

"I'll go over it all when we have supper with Dad. I already promised him an explanation."

Ivy and Forli brought a huge pile of slightly burned and lightly spiced potatoes and sugar-coated apple slices and placed them on the table, then sat down, Ivy closest to him. She rested one hand on his leg while she ate with the other.

Ty moved some of the food to his plate with his fork, then resumed.

"I want all of us to be Level Four before we go. It takes three on-level kills to make a level. There are four of us, so that would be twelve. But we need twice as many to make Level Three, and four times as many to make Level Four. So seventy-two dead Level Two rats. With me?"

"I'm already Level Three," Ivy said. "I thought you were as well."

"Yes, you and I and Forli will be a bit ahead, but we need to get Dalryn caught up as well."

Everyone nodded as most had mouths too full to make verbal agreement, although Dalryn added a grunt.

"All right, the dungeon has Level One monsters, thirteen each time in its current configuration, which are worth half as much experience as Level Two ones, and the equivalent of four Level Two monsters. So the equivalent of ten and a half Level Two kills."

Dalryn swallowed and pointed his fork at Ty. "How do you do that? With the math, I mean."

"You get used to him," Val said with a smile as she clapped Dalryn on the back. "Just eat your food."

Dalryn stuffed another potato slice into his mouth and Ty took it as acceptance of his sister's answer. He continued. "All right, the point is, we need seven runs if we do the whole dungeon. Then the four of us will be Level Four and have a decent shot at getting Zadrid's Hallow completed safely. That's one week for us to do all the runs, and everyone here can close up whatever affairs they have, as we'll be gone for a month or two, maybe an entire season, after that. Zadrid's Hallow is almost five hundred miles away—farther, by the route we'll have to take. It'll be a week by boat, and then a couple of weeks by land, each way."

Dalryn grimaced. "Can't you just pick a normal room for your dungeon, you onion? Do you have to drag us all away for months to go find a slightly better room?"

Ty folded his arms across his chest, but before he could launch into Dalryn's various inadequacies, Ivy squeezed his leg. *Be nice to Dalryn, right.*

Val turned and punched Ty in the shoulder but spoke to Ivy's brother. "Oh, Dalryn, you're about to get him started. He's going to be all 'best possible long-term,' and 'it's the course with the highest return,' and a lot of similar things. Just give in now and accept that you're going on a trip. You can't fight him when he gets like this, whether he's right or wrong."

Ty, irritated with the round of laughter that followed that comment, was about to start in on *Val's* inadequacies but stopped. "Wait a minute! You're free now, Val, right? So you can come with us to Zadrid's Hallow!"

Everyone stared at him with wide eyes, then Val slapped her forehead. "You were asleep, right. No can do, brother. King Leo triggered Ygg'drasil."

Ty gasped involuntarily, glad he didn't have food in his mouth at the moment.

His sister continued. "Yeah. We're officially an inter-planar city now. King Leo wants us to establish a beachhead in the new dimension, a thing of ice and cold and chill. I suspect he wants you to do it, actually, given how well you've handled the bureaucratic portions of most of his long-distance projects since he saved you from the orcs. For the dungeon, he'll likely make an exception. Still... I can't join you, no chance. I'm not a minister-at-large, I'm his *general*. Also, I'm going to be trying to get a Sun Eagle to bond with me. I don't want to just have a ghost wolf as my only bonded creature forever, no matter how much I like Helwo."

Ty was completely stunned. The thought *They let me sleep through a dimensional gate being formed?* warred with *I can't wait to go look for a new dungeon core!* and *If it connected to a node, I can plant another dungeon 'inside the city,' so to speak.*

"What's the new world like?"

"Frozen, like I just said," Val commented, standing. "However, speaking of, I should go see what the king wants to do. Keep Dalryn out of trouble."

"Unlikely," Ty managed as his only feeble comeback.

⁂

Forli froze the ground around the baby rats as they charged, and Dalryn kept them busy with wide sword swipes and his new tower shield.

Ty kept hitting the Momma Rat—the floor sub-boss—where she was on the small hill in the center of the boss room.

Every eighteen seconds, she spawned another rat, to a maximum of ten. The adventurers' guild had tested it every which way, and that was the rule. But if you could get her down before the time passed, she obviously wasn't spawning while dead—and she was easy to kill. Decent health, but no real defenses.

As she died, Ty received a welcome notification—he had made Level Four. The week had been well spent.

The boss creature dissipated, and a small chest dropped.

Dalryn slapped his sword against his huge shield with a metallic *bong*. "Level Four! I am *such* a champion!"

"Keep it in your pants, champion," Ivy said, quirking a half-smile at him as she said it.

He smirked at her. "You should say that to Ty more often."

The group climbed the hill to reach the chest, and Dalryn held his shield out, half-reached around it, and flipped the lid up. So far, they hadn't ever encountered a trap—and the trap rating of the dungeon was zero—but Ty wanted them to practice good habits.

Inside, they found four silver and a well-designed dagger with a rawhide hilt—and the now-ubiquitous 'Wyld faerie' fork.

There was a chuckle in the group. Apparently, one of the people who had died in that first group had accidentally—everyone assumed, as it wasn't worth much—taken one of the forks from the Emerald Bee with them into the dungeon, and now the dungeon dropped the magically carved wooden forks fairly often, about once a day. Mirafol had designed new, fancier forks, but so far, about forty of the things had entered circulation. Ty wondered if, once the dungeon grew and the forks dropped almost never, they would become collector items.

"Well, shall we head to the Bee for lunch?" Ty asked.

Forli turned, swaying and brushing her curvy hip against Ty as she did so. It sent an electric thrill down him. He turned to see her smiling at him wide, her eyes slightly glassy. He quickly glanced up to see Ivy smiling indulgently.

Ty was fairly sure he was gonna get to sex a dryad soon—maybe even a dryad and an elf together.

As Ty fantasized, Ivy's gaze drifted downward. Her eyes widened and she laughed, hand in front of her mouth.

She declined to explain when everyone looked up at her, and neither Dalryn nor Forli caught Ty blushing furiously.

"Sure, I'd love to go to the Bee," Ivy said. "One last day of luxury before we head out. Have you decided between the overland trip or the shorter trip through the West Forest or the Lakusi riverboat?"

They had to head nearly five hundred miles north up the Blue River regardless, but at the end, the path diverged. One path was an easy path through a lake and up another river, but through a country that was *very* anti-elven. The second path was a long, arduous overland slog through a forest.

"Forest," Ty said with a sigh. "I simply don't trust that human empire, or its king, enough to risk us against it. We'll start by heading to see Thea, to make sure she'll give us the first part of the heart once we head back... and then we'll head to Zadrid's Hallow. But we'll skip the Havi Imperium entirely."

Ivy sagged with relief—The Havi Imperium was where she was from. Her father, Helryn, had fled there after the fall of the first Kingdom of Averia, and she had been raised there before coming to Star Port six months ago. But the Havi Imperium was also the country that had imprisoned elves, and one whose riots had killed her mom.

Ty knew that Averia had treated the Imperium poorly in the past. Still, being an elf there wasn't easy. It was, in fact, frequently fatal, and the reason the Mosstone family was currently so very racist against humans.

Ty shook away his thoughts. "Tomorrow morning, we'll all go purchase potions, and then we'll head out, assuming I can find a riverboat captain tonight. I'm going to be using all the gold I've gotten as my share over the last week from the dungeon and borrowing a bit as well. But tonight is for relaxation. I'll spring for the good stuff and get the magical honey—as you said, one last night with all the comforts of civilization."

Chapter Twenty-Five

THEA AGAIN

Ty had been having déjà vu for the last couple of days as he'd traveled the marble road, but he had finally reached his destination—they had come out into the smaller grove that Thea used as her home.

It was only a couple of days north of town, and Ty was glad—his party wasn't exactly made for long travels, especially Ivy. Even in the cool, winter air of the temperate forest they were in, sweat beaded on her forehead and they had to stop every couple of hours. She was obviously ashamed of holding everyone up and had broken into tears once—tears that Dalryn had claimed were Ty's fault, along with referring to him as no less than three separate vegetables.

Ty promised himself that he would get her some amazing steed or magical carriage soon, but he hadn't thought to do so at this point.

Ty stopped his musing as they stepped from the trees into the grove proper. It was similar to Saelenia's grove, but smaller. Maybe fifty feet across, with a stream running through and a pond—almost more of a widening of the stream—occupying about a fourth of it. On the banks was a huge willow that made the entire grove shaded. Beautiful flowers occupied the entire field of grass, even in winter, and even under the tree.

As Ty stepped into the grove, Thea rose gracefully from where she had been sitting, cross-legged, in the middle of the flowers, and turned to stare at them. As she did so, Ty felt the familiar, although now more manageable, sexual attraction to dryads. It almost took a moment for her green vine hair and pine-wood-grain skin to register to Ty, she was so elfin and feminine both.

Ty could see that Thea was affected as well, licking her lips as her eyes roamed over him, blatantly hungry and slightly glassy both.

Forli was fun and cute both, with her spiky, green hair and short and curvy body, easy smile and laughs. She was also a friend of Ty's.

But Thea was the dryad equivalent of sex personified.

Thea stopped her examination. "Ty.... Forli. What has brought you back to see me mere weeks after you made Mother into a dungeon?"

"Rotten fish, I am," Dalryn muttered.

Ivy gently took his arm but also shushed him.

Ty took a few steps into the grove, which smelled of spring—new growth and flowers. "I was told to tell you that 'The six and the twenty-nine have passed, but the forest perseveres.'"

Thea's eyes widened, but after a brief second, she smiled at him. It showed a ton of teeth, and Ty was pretty sure she was still being affected by his dryad status.

After a moment of longer staring at him, Thea spoke. "I doubt that's exactly what the Crone told you—that phrase is supposed to be used *after* a request, but I get why you might say it first. However, I need to know what you—and purportedly my mother—want before I can decide if it warrants being listened to."

"Zadrid's heart," Ty said, simply.

One of Thea's perfect, leaf-green eyebrows rose toward her equally leafy hairline, and she seemed to shake the last of the attraction to Ty from herself at those words. "Zadrid's heart, hmm? Why could you possibly need that? It seems more likely that you got those words from my Mother through your control of the dungeon."

Ty let out an involuntary explosion of laughter at that one, and a single bird fluttered from the trees at the noise. "Yeah, I have, like, *zero* control over your mother. Most back-talking boss of any dungeon, I'd be willing to bet, and she had the gall to accuse *me* of sass as well."

It was Thea's turn to chuckle, a laugh that Forli joined in.

"That makes a lot of sense," Thea said. "Still, I need a lot more explanation of what's going on before I'll trust you."

Forli started in, taking a step forward as she spoke. "Ty is totally trustworthy and totally—"

"I have this," Ty said, holding up a hand. Forli stopped.

"Are you aware that dungeons have secret routes to power? The ones Sae—the Crone mentioned when we first talked?"

Thea nodded, and her second eyebrow raised at Ty's almost slip of the tongue on Saelenia's name.

"Well, apparently, she has two sort of... clustered routes to power. One is called the 'legacy of the forest' and involves getting the pieces that are magically significant remnants of her life. Remnants like the first progenitor she ever killed. I need to gather the entire heart, including your portion, and take it back to the dungeon in order to gain a super-special, super-rare room for the dungeon. The Crone believes Zadrid's ability to regenerate will be forever lost by using his heart in the dungeon."

Thea considered, simply standing still. Ty had seen this behavior in dryads before. Many of them went completely still when thinking, the opposite of the tics a lot of mortal species displayed.

After a moment, she turned to face Ty. "I just have to believe you on this?"

"I can't take anyone else in to see the Crone. I'm not sure how I would prove it. But the Crone trusted me, and Forli trusts me."

Thea went still for a few seconds again, then nodded. "Very well, I will do as you wish."

Yes!

She turned and walked to the tree, then reached *into* it and pulled out a small chunk of black heart. It still pulsed slightly, and black liquid—blood, Ty thought, but he wasn't sure—dripped from it.

"Can you store anything in your tree?" Ty asked.

She nodded. "When I became Level Twenty, I got a dryad-unique power that made my tree an extra-dimensional storage space—and also made it damage-resistant as a powerful magic item. It would be very hard to recover anything from the tree without killing me, and given my level, well... I may not be the safest vault in existence, but I'm not that far off."

Ty nodded.

"But enough about how wonderful I am. Are you aware of the dangers inherent to this ventricle of darkness?"

Ty nodded again but then hesitated. "I think so? I can't leave it close to the other pieces for very long or they'll reform into a cheap, broken version of Zadrid. Is there something else?"

"It radiates dark magic—magic that calls the undead, empowers the undead, and makes undead. You mustn't be around the dead too long. Zadrid's Hallow is what happens when three pieces are allowed to reassemble skeletons and such that have been destroyed thousands of times. But if you take this through a graveyard or something... a lot worse can happen. So just... be careful."

Ty nodded a third time.

Thea stepped closer and held the heart out to Ty. "Here... take it."

Ty gingerly reached his hand out. Even as he got close, he could feel the malevolent darkness of the thing, a powerful hatred of the living, a coldness of existence that fed on fear and wanted to remake everything in that dark image. It was horrid; he pulled his hand back.

"Actually, I think it'll be safer if we just leave this piece here, and I bring the other three back. Then the full heart will only be together for a few days before I get it to the dungeon. That's what your mother advised, anyway. But I agree with her."

Thea smiled. "That makes more sense and makes me think well of you. And I can see you hate having it near you, which convinces me more than anything else that you are, in fact, on a mission from Mother and not simply seeking power."

Ty nodded slowly to her words. "Well, full disclosure, I *am* seeking power. But I want riches and, um, society's approval, not some kind of homicidal item that'll make me the villain of every history book for the next thousand years."

"You onion," Dalryn muttered. "Never admit stuff like that out loud. Iluvin Eturia, you need to learn not to give people handles on you."

Ty ignored that bit of wisdom from Dalryn.

Thea returned the heart piece to the tree, then came back. She smiled, reached down, and picked a fallen flower off the ground. "I want to ask you something else."

Ty was pretty sure he knew what she was going to say but politely motioned for her to continue.

"Why..." Thea paused, as if to find the words. "Why am I attracted to you... like a male animal to a female in rut? I have a powerful urge to mate with you, and dryads don't... mate."

"So, long story, but the short of it is I got changed into a master dryad and can breed with dryads to make more dryad seeds. Something about that magical power also causes female dryads to find me very attractive."

"Distractingly so," Forli muttered.

"You're a dryad?!" Dalryn exploded. "Seriously? You're not a half-human, half-elf?"

Oh, right, I haven't told him yet.

"Yeah, so, that's a thing," Ty muttered.

Thea held up her hand. "Wait, elf. Yell at him later. I need to make sure I understand this."

Dalryn's face was mutinous, and he crossed his arms—tower shield and all, which looked faintly ridiculous as it covered him from feet to neck—over his chest, but he didn't say anything else.

"You can... make more dryad seeds?" Thea asked.

Ty nodded, and Ivy came up and put her hands in his.

"By putting your penis inside a dryad?"

Well, that isn't awkward or anything. "Yes."

Thea thought for a moment. "Do you know how often? Does it take magic? What are the restrictions?"

Ty pursed his lips. "Well I'm with Ivy, so I haven't been having sex with any dryads... so I don't really know yet. No, well... no field tests yet."

Thea crossed her arms over her chest in an unconscious mimicry of Dalryn and stared daggers at Ivy. "You know that new dryads can't come into existence at the moment, right?"

Ivy shrank back, but Ty didn't let go of her hand.

He did glare at Thea. "Hey. I like Ivy very, very much. Please don't be mean to her in any way."

"Yeah, ya branch!" Dalryn added.

There was a brief pause, and Ivy stepped forward again. "Look, I... I already think I'll be okay sharing Ty with the dryads. I've let Forli live with us, and I've been getting used to the idea through that. I really like Forli. I also worship Cerivae Nerithin and want to make everyone happy, truly."

"So, you'll—" Thea started.

Ivy just kept talking. "But, not just yet, okay? I think it's fair to be with him for a while before I start sharing. Especially since, if this goes the way you want it to, he'll be having a lot of children and moving to a whole different life. I think it's fair I get to be with him without that first."

"What?!" Dalryn exploded again, uncrossing his arms and moving forward. "What nonsense is this?! My sister is going to be part of a weird tree harem? This is crap! I know Dad is awful, but you don't have to do this!"

Ivy shrank back. "I... I want to stay with Ty, no matter what. I... I love him, Dalryn."

Ty felt his cheeks heating. Ivy had never said that to him, formally, even though he had kinda known. He squeezed her hand tighter, then pulled her into his embrace.

Ivy kept talking to Dalryn. "And it would be wrong to stop new dryads from coming into the world. But also, Dalryn, I'm sorry, but I kinda wanna... also maybe try to be with a woman."

"What?! You've never told me you like girls!"

"Well, I like... a lot. And we didn't talk about me liking men much, either."

"I can't believe we're talking about this at all," Dalryn muttered, obviously absolutely flabbergasted.

Ivy was so red, Ty was worried she might spontaneously combust. "Well, you keep butting in on my sex life, lately. Ever since I got with Ty."

Dalryn opened his mouth, hesitated, pointed his finger at Ivy, hesitated again, then spoke. "Well, no offense, but I just heard my sister tell another woman that she planned to let some halfie—no, sorry, some tree guy—start a freaking tree harem and have kids with other people while she stays with him. I didn't ask for that information, but it feels like something I should address, you know?"

Forli walked up to Dalryn. "I'll do everything to make it worth Ivy's while. I'll cook, I'll clean, I'll raise children, I'll do whatever sex st—"

"Nope. No, no, no. We're not discussing the details of my sister's sex life," Dalryn said, waving his hand at Forli.

Forli tilted her head to the side slightly. "Why not?"

"What? Are ya daft, you twig? I don't want to know about whom, or by all the gods, *how*, my sister is rutting. Sheesh."

Ty laughed, absurdly pleased to see Dalryn being the one on the side of a 'dryads have no idea about sex' situation.

Ivy turned to Thea again. "Please. I make no promises, but I do, genuinely, believe I'll reach a point where it's okay to me. Just, again... Please give me time."

Thea nodded. "I don't understand at all, since mortal males can have sex nearly at will, I heard. But I can tell that every mortal here thinks you're being incredibly nice and generous, so I'll assume that's true and I respect your decision."

"Thank you."

Dalryn ground out, "I cannot believe that we're sitting here, having just gotten permission to take a piece of a dark god's heart, discussing whether my sister's paramour will be having sex with other girls. Not even elven girls...no, it'll be tree girls."

Thea nodded seriously. "Well, brother of Ty's paramour, you can think it over as you go to get the remaining three pieces of Zadrid's heart, but don't be too distracted. If you're heading straight there, you're going to be heading through a hundred miles or so of Blood Tribes territory. It's not their heart territory, and there are almost no orcs... but there are tens of thousands of goblins throughout the territory."

"Joy," Dalryn muttered, an unconscious mimicry of Ty. "'Brother of Ty's paramour.' I've fallen so far. And nothing like tens of thousands of goblins to really take my irritation off."

Ty chuckled. "Well... I guess it depends on how you feel about stabbing enemies of Averia."

Dalryn perked up. "Yeah, that might be a relief, actually. Let's go find some goblins to stab. I mean, at this point, fighting for my life will be a welcome distraction."

So much drama with this one, Ty thought, laughing.

Chapter Twenty-Seven

ZADRID'S HALLOW

Somehow, despite all the warning and concerns, they made it to Zadrid's Hallow without running into a single goblin. They had passed through the Forest of Averia, hired a passing trading ship to take them from one side of the river to another, and then traveled through the western Averian forest and finally into the Blue Lands, which were rainy plains and flooded forest lands, mostly—but they had climbed, finally, through the mountains on the southern side to reach their target. *Not,* Ty thought to himself, *that the Hallow is some kind of relief.*

Ty, flanked by Ivy, Forli, and Dalryn, looked down on a hellish forest in a small valley that looked more crater than true valley. One side of the crater appeared almost melted, and Ty could see a few rivulets with aspiration to creek-hood that dropped over the side and down the mountain.

The trees were all skeletal, with only a few leaves, a sharp contrast to the rest of the forest Ty had traveled through, where trees had been flush with vibrant life. And in between them were the ruins of a small village.

Three of the trees were clearly larger than the rest, towering hundreds of feet into the sky, their topmost branches pointed upward like spears. The tree had huge, horizontal branches. Those, in turn, had numerous vines with corpses hanging from them in turn like so much rotting fruit.

And Ty could *feel* the dark magic of the place, and malevolence that wouldn't be contained, which felt like insects worming their way into his wooden skin, trying to make him a dark mockery of his former self.

"What... What is this place?" Forli asked, shuddering. Ty assumed she could feel the Entropic magic throughout the skeletal forest.

Ty shrugged, even though he felt uneasy as well. "This is our goal, Zadrid's Hallow. I assume all this Entropic magic we feel is the result of the god's presence."

Ty's backpack twitched.

"We should go collect the other pieces soon, if we can."

"Well, it's going to be a challenge," Dalryn said, pointing. Even as they stood on the edge of the caldera that made up the ruin's edge, skeletons were stirring among the trees. Most of them were unarmed, although Ty could see black energy on their hands.

Entropic powers are the deadliest of all the magics, at least the twelve that mortals can use. Entropy has almost no benefit to a civilization, no auras of life, no crafting, nothing like that. It's the end. It can dispose of waste, sometimes purge negative things... but everything it does is killing. The magic does that very, very well.

I wonder what abilities, specifically, those skeletons are using?

"Well, it's been weeks of traveling," Ty said, trying to sound confident and certain. "Let's go. We need to work our way to each piece and capture it, adding it to the main heart. Once reformed, its abilities will be neutralized for a bit as it turns its powers to regenerating Zadrid instead of making undead, from what the Crone told me."

Everyone nodded.

"Potion check," Ty said.

Forli spoke—she had been becoming the group's logistics expert, as well as handling a lot of the cooking and cleaning and such. As if she were extending the deal she had made with

Ivy to stay in the house to the adventuring group as well. "All accounted for. We have twelve potions, three each, assuming yours are still intact, for healing, and a rare glintberry potion for essence restoration as well—again, assuming yours is intact."

Ty did a quick check of his belt and then gave the three-fingers symbol for 'okay' that the Averians used.

Forli looked briefly confused then smiled for a second, until her eyes drifted back to the dead forest below them, and the skeletons that moved among the trees.

Ty motioned to the trees below. "Shall we?"

Everyone headed down, Dalryn in front. It was hard going, and Ty fell not once, but twice thanks to his new, clumsier body. Forli tripped once, yelping as she face-planted and slid a bit. But in both cases, their armored skin and higher Toughness protected them from any real damage.

When they reached the bottom, the group dusted itself off and stared at the treeline, such as it was. A few skeletons moved among the trees.

"How much are skeletons affected by lightning?" Ty asked.

No one answered. *I have a feeling this might be... challenging.*

Ty had picked his two leveling powers—he had replaced his shock shield and taken dungeon passage, the super-rare ability that made him a conduit to add magic to the world from his dungeon. He was hoping for significantly increased powers from it, but at the moment, he was only very slightly stronger than he had been at Level Two. And since he was almost positive skeletons took less damage from lightning energy attacks...

He knew that Dalryn had gotten *a lot* stronger from Strength and Toughness increases in Wyld, and rocklike skin from Earth. But at the end of the day, he wouldn't be enough by himself.

Forli had Ice, and Ivy her healing—but no familiar yet, even though she had taken the abilities.

Maybe we really should have waited to come here, Ty thought.

On the other hand, if they were extremely careful, they could level and take more abilities while here. The only real trick was to not die.

"All right, if we're fighting Level Six enemies, we can theoretically level by killing eight of them—all four of us. So, let's move forward, carefully, and try to keep Dalryn alive. See what we can do. At this point, leveling and keeping safe is a bigger deal than necessarily getting the chunks of Zadrid."

Everyone nodded, and Dalryn put his shield down in front of him, taking his sword in hand, and slowly stalked forward, his stance wide and planted for stability, the opposite of most fighting styles but appropriate for a guardian.

As he reached the treeline, three skeletons rushed him at once. None had black energy on them, and none carried weapons or wore armor.

Ty thrust his hand out and called his lightning, which arced over and blasted one of the undead. Scorch marks appeared across it, and part of its arm exploded, but little else happened.

Ty frowned at the notification that popped up.

> Ty hits Zadrid Skeletal minion with lightning. Does 2 total damage (3 x1.28 magic stat of 17, x1.18 occult score of 9, x1.1 Air affinity of 1, halved against skeletal undead.)

This is going to be a challenge.

Dalryn swept the first one to attack him into a pile of bones and caught the damaged one on his tower shield. The last reached him and scratched along his armor.

Forli hit the damaged one with ice, avoiding Dalryn. Ty ran over and slammed the one scratching Dalryn's armor with his staff, doing slight physical and lightning damage both. Dalryn finished it off with his sword.

"Well, those were easy," Dalryn commented. "Jokes for Level Six, really. I expected more from the moldy, old undead."

Ty dismissed his experience notification. "Look at your notification, idiot. Apparently, the outer ring was merely Level One. And they *are* resistant to my lightning."

"And my ice abilities," Forli said.

Dalryn waved his arms around. "Why are you guys such a pack of onions? Cry me a freaking pond, why don't ya? If you suck that bad, let's just move forward and do exactly what you said, Ty—make more levels. Sheesh."

Ty frowned. *Why did that become a huge thing? Because I called him an 'idiot'? That might have been my bad.*

"A good point, Dalryn. Let's keep going."

The next few minutes involved a lot of dead Level One and Level Two skeletons, but they weren't even close to enough to make Ty—or anyone else—a level. But Dalryn handled all of them with aplomb.

But the next group they came to looked... different. They were still mortal skeletons, but these had black energy in eyes, teeth, and on the ends of their fingerbones. And there were four of them.

"So... still going forward?" Dalryn asked.

"Yes."

Dalryn started to walk forward, and the skeletons rushed. But the outer two circled, left and right. Dalryn shifted, blocking the left one, and Ty hit the right with lightning. As the three attacked Dalryn, the last rushed at Forli.

Ty rushed into the way as it swung its skeletal hands, the ends of each covered in a dark miasma. The fingerbones were sharpened, and they raked over his skin like claws, although not the most effective ones. But they did do damage, and Ty hissed in pain. He and Forli hit the skeleton with lightning and ice, and it fell back a step, one arm popping off and a tibia exploding. But it came forward again. Ty batted it away with his staff, and another blast from Forli dropped it.

He looked back to see that Dalryn had finished one, but his armor was hanging in tatters, somehow, and his shield had *broken*.

"Little help?" Dalryn called, backing up and swinging his sword, knocking one charging him. But the other managed to claw his arm.

Ty hit that one with lightning, as fast as he could, and it went down after a moment. Dalryn finished smashing the other, accounting for the last one.

Ty dismissed the experience notification. It hadn't been that much.

Ivy came up and pushed regenerate into him. Ty felt the magic, the power of health, youth, and renewal, and his scratches healed a bit, but not fully.

> All remaining damage on Tywyndyll il Belmoria is entropic aggravated damage and cannot be healed by your level of regeneration. One additional point may be healed tomorrow, and each day after. Regeneration remains ongoing but is having no effect.

Ah, shit. I'm starting to hate Entropy magic. Not that I didn't before. Still.

Ty turned to the group. "So apparently, these things inflict entropic wounds that can't be fully healed at our level. It says I can heal another point tomorrow. I've read about this—hits are magically infected and resist healing."

Dalryn walked up, shieldless, with huge rents in his armor. "I also have some fun news. It turns out that one of those guys had a... wrecking effect, where whatever objects it scratched took vastly increased damage. I just lost my shield, and the armor won't be far behind."

Ty met the eyes of his teammates and felt he saw fear in all of them.

But Forli was the worst, shaking notably. "Our energy powers both do half damage as well."

There was a long pause.

"Should we, um, head back?" Forli asked.

Ty shook his head. "We've committed months to this. We need to see it through. We can still level and increase our powers."

"How?"

"We set up camp. We move forward until we're out of essence, then rest. We'll keep going, as much as we need, till we're strong enough to push into the heart of this realm and seize... the heart. Sorry, that was awkwardly stated," Ty finished with a grimace.

Dalryn laughed, and even Ivy calmed enough to giggle, hand in front of her mouth.

Ty also gave a slight chuckle. "Yeah, that sounded dumb. But still, that's the plan. We can make a level, again, on eight Level Four, or sixteen Level Three, enemies. Then we can take the second rank of Lightning and Ice powers. And Dalryn can increase his rocklike skin so that he's tough even without armor."

"And for a shield?" Dalryn asked.

Ty winced. "I have no idea."

"You absolute tuber."

"How is this my fault?" Ty asked, glaring at Dalryn. "Unless I can afford a magic shield—wake-up knock, that would have required giving up *all* the potions to get—then we were pretty much doomed from the start on that. Let's make levels and *quit complaining*, huh?"

Dalryn heaved a sigh. "Fine. Although if they claw my sword, I'm going to be *really* useless."

Ty felt his eyes widen. "That... would be bad."

Dalryn nodded. "Very bad."

"All right... Let's try to get a few more Level Three kills in, maybe one or two Level Four creatures, and then we'll fall back to the ridge and establish camp. I have a feeling we'll be here for a while."

Chapter Twenty-Seven

ALL LEVELED UP

Ty dodged back, the claws scraping across his flesh and leaving small entropic wounds.

He hissed and smacked the skeleton away with his staff, a sweeping motion more than a strike, per se. They had learned that the skeletons were fast and had devastating Entropic magic, but they were also very light and weak both.

The skeleton stumbled away and collapsed to the ground. They were clumsy as well.

Ty took the moment to turn and smash another in the back of the knee as it reached for Forli. It collapsed backward, and Dalryn stomp-kicked it in the face. He was up to an eighteen Strength stat, with workout bonuses, and he crushed the skull with the single blow.

"Level Six," Ty said.

"I need one more," Dalryn said, then he turned and smashed his sword into the one getting to its feet. "And level," he added.

"Great!" Ivy called out. "Me too!"

Forli didn't say anything. Ty stared at her with concern—he felt that he didn't really have the word for what was wrong with her, but she was obviously suffering, the fear and pain eating at her over time, building up the longer they went. He was really concerned that she wasn't cut out to be an adventurer and thought he might at least talk to her about giving up the lifestyle when they got back.

Forli was Level Six, after all—she could easily make a huge amount of money doing all kinds of things. She was higher level than everyone in town except the very upper tier—which was composed of the king and his chosen companions, Helryn and maybe one or two of his chosen companions, and a few of the people who had come in with Kadrath to run the Adventurers' Guild.

She didn't need this anymore if she didn't want the lifestyle, and she had helped Ty a great deal with his mission in life. He liked adventuring with her, but compared to Ty, Ivy, and Dalryn, she brought little to the table. She was, easily, the weakest member. And that could mean that she was the one most likely to die. Something Ty didn't want to see.

Although Ty also had to admit that Ivy was still a bit useless except for her one role as the extremely important healer. But Ty knew that was from her constant delay in getting a familiar. Once she did, he suspected she would be truly amazing. Far, far stronger than the usually joyful Forli.

And Dalryn was very good at his job. Although less so without a shield.

"So, what powers are you taking?" Ivy asked, interrupting Ty's thoughts.

"Well... I had a few ideas. One moment. Let me just check my status sheet to be sure."

Tywyndyll il Belmoria							
Level Six	Air, Soul, Wyld						
Health	28	Stamina	17	Essence	21		
Level Stats							
Strength	12	180 base pound-lifting capacity, +10% melee damage, +6% running speed.					
Agility	8	+10% enemy hit chance, -10% hit chance with all weapons, -4% running speed					
Dexterity	8	-10% base success for crafting and physical skill success rate, 20% chance to lower base weapon damage roll by one step					
Endurance	12	+2 base Stamina, +20% Stamina Recovery Rate, +20% base Health Recovery Rate					
Toughness	19	+9 base Health, +45% base Health, +45% base Stamina, +4 to resist poison, disease, and physical status effects					
Perception	10						
Connection	10	+00% Essence recovery rate (17/day)					
Capacity	16	+6 Base essence, +30% essence					
Appearance	12	Slightly good-looking					
Non-Level Stats							
Intelligence	16	+60% skill acquisition rate.					
Magic	17	+28% Magic Effects, +1 Maximum affinity					
Charisma	10	+00% perceived social skills					
Luck	10	The Fates neither dislike nor care for you					
Secondary Stats							
Air Affinity		2	-20% essence cost to all Air abilities, +20% effect for all Air abilities and/or +2 to the difficulty to resist				
Armor		1	-1 from all physical damage				

Birth Perks	
Race: Master Dryad	Unique
	+2 to Strength and Endurance. +4 to Toughness. -2 to Agility and Dexterity. +1 armor.
	+4 to Magic stat base
	Tireless (Needs only 2 hours of sleep per 24-hour period.)
	Gain an additional Wyld ability at Levels 2, 10, and every multiple of 10 thereafter.
	Immortal.
	Access to the 'branching path.' One pick per 10 levels of the bonded dungeon.
	May breed with female dryads, producing dryad seeds. Female dryads will feel attraction to you.
Rank: Natural	May obtain Level 80 without ascension. Access to a significant number of rare or upgraded magical abilities.
Remnants of the Storm	The levels and power were altered and assisted by the magic that came down the dungeon to you. The Belmoria magic line, and 5 gained levels as a lightning mage, have been combined to this perk. Gain 1 extra Air ability at Level 5 and every 10 levels thereafter. Gain Air auras 15 levels early. Gain +1 actual and +1 maximum Air affinity.
Dungeon Lord	You may become a dungeon lord
Smart	+6 intelligence
Acquired Perks	
Bonded Dungeon Lord of the Dungeon of the Dryad's Grove	No powers of the dungeon lord are gained. Instead, powers taken through the 'branching path' may synergize with the dungeon.
Polite	Naturally inoffensive. -10% chance for someone to take offense to your position on a matter.

Skills	Level	Effect
Academics	5	Moderate understanding of history, culture, geography, and important people throughout the world
Architecture	3	+3% to final building quality, may build basic buildings
Administration	9	-5% to realm administration costs, -18% to business costs
Athletics	3	+9% to run speed, +3 to check to climb or avoid obstacles
Business	3	+15% to expected income, and -3% to expected costs, for operating any business
Cooking	5	+25% quality to cooking
Dodge	6	+18% to dodge incoming attacks
Farming	4	+16% to base farming output
Imbuing	7	May use advanced lesser rituals in magics possessed to create items
Leadership	5	People consider you to have 10% more status than you do, and if they are followers, are willing to accept conditions 2% worse than baseline without complaint
Natural Sciences	4	You have a solid grasp of basic concepts
Occult	12	You can sense magic that is not concealed that is connected to you, whose area of effect you are in, or that is within 9 feet of you. Your magic powers have 24% greater effect. You can sense the purpose of simple magic and vaguely discern more complicated magical purposes. +24% to accuracy with magic attacks. Lightning Mastery: +10% damage, +10% range, and +1 difficulty to resist lightning attacks

Seduction	2	People find your attempts to seduce them 4% more favorable than baseline, compared to what they are looking for
Staff	2	+8% damage with staffs, +4% to hit with staves, 8% chance of knockout on critical.
Survival	4	+12% hunting and foraging
Sword	3	+12% damage with swords, +12% to hit with swords

Abilities	Effect
Air	
Lightning, Rank II	2 essence. Do 2-5 base lightning damage, with +100% to accuracy, as a ranged occult attack. (5-11 final (x1.28 Magic, x1.1 Affinity, x1.24 occult, x1.1 occult specialty x1.1 Eldritch power, rank I)).
Shocking Shield, Rank I	1 essence per 6 seconds. Anyone attacking takes 1 base (2 total) lightning damage and must make a Toughness check at +2, -1 per Air Affinity, to resist shock (lose 6 seconds of actions and take -40% to dodge)
Soul	
*Eldritch Power, Rank I	+10% damage to all energy attacks, as well as all shields and barriers
+Dungeon Passage, Rank I	+100% magic benefit to region and world from all dungeons tied directly or indirectly (through sub-dungeon lords) to the dungeon lord
Wyld	
+Thicken Root to the Dryad's Grove	The dungeon lord enhances his connection to the Dryad Grove Dungeon. His stat gain becomes +3 Magic and +3 Toughness, and the dungeon gains +1 magic effect and +.1 loot rating.

Air	
N/A	
Soul	
N/A	
Wyld	
N/A	

The Branching Path (1 available)	
Abilities	Effect
Roots of the Dungeon Tree	Your power slowly stretches between numerous dungeons, multiplying and increasing all future powers.
	You *may* become dungeon lord for multiple dungeons. When you do this, you pick a subordinate dungeon lord, regardless of whether they have the dungeon lord perk. When a dungeon lord dies, you choose the next one, breaking the normal dungeon lord cycle. The dungeons will become a loosely interconnected, single mega-dungeon with separate segments. Each dungeon so gained will provide additional benefits for all remaining 'branching paths' abilities chosen, as well as a small static bonus. Additionally, each dungeon will provide a small bonus to your primary dungeon.
	If not taken at Level 1 this path is forever lost. Dungeon of the Dryad's Grove*: +3 Toughness, +3 Magic

At Level Five, Ty had chosen lightning, rank II and eldritch power, rank I, raising his lightning damage considerably. He had also been dumping points into Capacity, expanding his essence so that he could fight longer. Although, somehow, his Toughness had also gone through the roof. He had twenty-eight health, about four times what the average elf did, and about three times what the average human thug back in his hometown of Steelport did.

But he had also taken some very random abilities that he had *hoped* would lead to unusual combination powers. So far, they hadn't really opened up anything super unusual, although the next step of the thicken power, web of the grove, was about one and a half times as strong as the benefit from normal stat gain a second time.

Still, Ty was hopeful. Most exciting new abilities were revealed at Level Two, Level Ten, and every ten thereafter.

He pulled up his leveling options, looking over his list again.

Air	
Airborne Reflexes, Rank I	+4 Agility
Strike of the Wind, Rank I	Spend 2 essence. You move with blinding speed, gaining +50% accuracy and a 50% chance to land an extra blow against an equal speed target every 6 seconds
Wind Parry	Spend 1 essence, +50% to dodge incoming ranged physical attacks and +20% to dodge all normal attacks
Master Parry, Rank I	+20% dodge as a static buff
Sky Archer	+50% to rate of fire and damage with archery weapons
#Lightning, Rank III	1 essence. Do 3-8 base lightning damage, with +100% to accuracy, as a ranged occult attack. Need to be Level Ten.
Agonizing	Anyone hit by your lightning that takes at least one damage must make a Toughness check at -1 per rank of lightning or suffer shock (lose offensive actions for 6 seconds, -40% to dodge)
Whispered Words	1 essence. You can speak and have it carried by the wind to only your chosen target, up to 200 feet away
Wind-Boosted Leap	Jump +10 feet, modified by all air-magic-modifying abilities

Shocking Shield, Rank II	2 essence per 6 seconds. Anyone attacking takes 2 base lightning damage and must make a Toughness check at +0, -1 per Air Affinity, to resist shock (lose 6 seconds of actions and take -40% to dodge)
Air Affinity, Rank II	+2 Air Affinity
Soul	
Soul of Magic, Rank I	+2 Magic
Natural Leader, Rank I	+2 Charisma
Improved Connection, Rank I	+4 Connection
Improved Capacity, Rank I	+4 Capacity
Shield, Rank I	May spend 1 essence and gain a 4-hit-point shield that lasts for 6 seconds.
Barrier, Rank I	May spend 1 essence and gain a 2-hit-point shield that lasts for 1 minute. Damage is taken off from the barrier before any critical multiplier is applied.
Talk Down	The wielder may spend 2 essence and make a contested Charisma check against the target's highest Intelligence, Magic, or Charisma score, with the defender getting any bonuses against mind-affecting powers. Success will calm the target so that they won't initiate or continue aggression, unless harmed or witnessing others they care for being harmed
Soul Affinity, Rank I	+1 Soul affinity
*Eldritch Power, Rank II	+20% damage to all energy attacks, as well as all damage reduced by shields and barriers.

*Magic Wellspring, Rank I	+10% to Capacity and Connection Score
+Dungeon Passage, Rank II	+200% magic benefit to region and world from all dungeons tied directly or indirectly (through sub-dungeon lords) to the dungeon lord. Will create a small effect in the world related to the dungeon in the same node
Wyld	
Bestial Strength, Rank I	+4 Strength
Bestial Agility, Rank I	+4 Agility
Bestial Endurance, Rank I	+4 Endurance
Bestial Toughness, Rank I	+4 Toughness
Bestial Senses, Rank I	+4 Perception
Were Form, Rank I	May spend 1 essence, and 1 essence per every 6 seconds, to assume a partial were form. Gain +4 to Strength, Agility, Endurance, and Toughness for the duration of the ability.
Resilient, Rank I	Gain back 1 Health per 10 minutes at no cost.
Regeneration, Rank I	Spend 2 essence. Gain 1 health until max per 6 seconds for 1 minute.
True Grit	Wound penalties to accuracy, dodge, and Stamina recovery are halved
Wyld Affinity, Rank I	+1 Wyld affinity

Animal Companion, Rank I	Gain an animal companion. That animal gains +2 to all physical stats. "Animals" includes any magical beast less than Level 6 for this power.
Soul/Wyld	
Familiar, Rank I	May bond with a single familiar. This familiar gains half the level of its master and is a sapient magical beast.
+Web of the Grove's Power, Rank I	The dungeon lord enhances his connection to the Dryad Grove Dungeon. His stat gain becomes +5 Magic and +5 Toughness, and the dungeon gains an additional +1 magic effect and +.1 loot rating.

Ty was very tempted to take the Web of the Grove's power for the extra survivability and the damage... and he would for sure at some point. But for now, he had a different build in mind.

He selected barrier. It was empowered by nearly every modifier he had and would already operate at an additional hundred percent, roughly.

Ty wasn't really working his Agility or dodge—he needed something else. He had not one, but *two*, powerful barrier-type abilities, barrier itself and shocking shield. If he maintained those at close to level and added a few other abilities, he would be a *very* tough nut to crack. When that was added to his now hideously high Health total... Well, he didn't doubt for his survivability.

And for this fight... It didn't matter if Ty was hit with the permanent entropic attacks if they only did damage to his barrier. Given his low agility, he would also be susceptible to critical hits, but barrier would weaken those as well. His real limitation was very powerful monsters and his own essence pool at this point. And he had raised his Capacity by a total of six stat points, out of the last ten he had gained.

He thought he might focus almost exclusively on it from here on out, as well as take some of the other essence-increasing powers. An 'unlimited pool' for his powers would be very, very valuable, since he planned to be running multiple abilities at the same time.

"Every single time you make a level, you tune us out completely for about ten minutes," Ivy said before licking his ear.

Ty jumped, blushing.

Dalryn barked, "Hey!" and made gagging motions.

Forli just looked at them.

"What did you take, Forli?" Ty asked gently.

Forli clasped her hands together. "I, um, I haven't looked, Ty. I'm... I'm gonna figure it out tonight, okay?"

Ty sighed. *Two weeks and she's worn down.*

Not that Ty blamed her much. It had rained most of the time, and the fights had been frustrating, since wounds took far longer to heal and they couldn't rely on the healing of Ivy. Still, though...

"I don't think we can wait till tonight. Those skeletons were stronger than the ones usually here. I'm not sure what's happening. I wanted to try for a heart piece—maybe all three—today. We're at the same level as the strongest creatures here now, so even though three of us aren't very effective against the skeletons, I'm hopeful we can complete this."

Forli broke into a smile. "We can leave today?"

"Assuming we get the heart pieces."

She sighed. "Okay, then, yeah. I'll look at my abilities."

Forli's green eyes unfocused out. She stayed frozen in position, eyes flickering but also dilated oddly, for a couple of minutes, then she blinked and focused on Ty again.

"Okay, I took my second-rank ice ability last rank, and I took deep cold this rank. It adds a decent amount to the chance I inflict slow on people. I know it's not, um, very useful now because skeletons are resistant to stuff. I'm not sure what else I would take, though."

Ty nodded to her words. "It'll work for now, and far more later." He looked around at his team. "Are the rest of you ready for the real push? To take the heart pieces?"

Dalryn directed a cocky grin at Ty. "I'm geared and ready. As the one doing most of the work, that seems to be the key point."

Ivy slapped Dalryn on the arm—Ty doubted her brother felt it through his still somewhat-intact plate armor. "I'm ready. Full essence and ready to heal."

Forli sighed but nodded.

Ty gestured ahead. "Then let's go."

Chapter Twenty-Eight

I WAS AN ADVENTURER UNTIL I TOOK AN ARROW TO THE KNEE

Dalryn strode forward. They had already cleared the lower-end skeletons, and there was just a small group around the first heart piece, which Ty could clearly see—it was attached to the trunk of a large, skeletal tree. The tree had corpses hanging from the branches on ropes that didn't decay, for some reason.

But it was the group of four skeletons around the trunk that Ty was most interested in.

Each had eyes with black energy in them, and each had a *weapon* made of what appeared to be the same magic that they had in their eyes. Two had swords, one an axe, and the last skeleton, who just had to be himself, Ty guessed, had a flanged mace. The four otherwise appeared as the normal skeletons for Zadrid's Hallow: yellow-white bones that looked as if they ought to be falling to pieces rather than animated and carrying dark power.

"Same tactic?" Ty asked.

Everyone nodded, and Forli moved into place to the side, prepared to spray the whole group with ice before she retreated.

Ty picked Flanged Mace—*this is what you get for standing out*, Ty snickered to himself—and hit it with a bolt of lightning.

Scorch marks appeared across the bones, but Ty did a base ten damage, modified down to five, and the skeletons usually had twelve to fifteen—quite low for a fifth-level creature, but speed and a lot of unusual resistances seemed to be the skeletons' forte, not health.

As they came in, Dalryn showed his worth. He shield-bashed one, knocking the lightweight thing off its feet and onto the ground. He sword-swept another, breaking a forearm bone and sweeping it back as well.

Forli unleashed her ice. It wasn't very damaging to the skeletons, and the slow effect almost never worked on them, but it hit all four, probably doing more total damage than Ty even if it was spread out.

But four was too many for Dalryn to handle. Two too many.

Forli screamed, a piteous noise, as an axe slashed through her forearm, cleaving it entirely from her body. She fell back, a viscous blood coming from the wound, slower than the blood loss a fully mortal creature would have experienced in the same situation.

Ty activated his barrier and shocking shield. The skeleton facing him took minor damage and smashed his barrier from existence with the flanged mace, but the remaining damage didn't pierce Ty's armored skin.

Ty made a choice, grimacing, knowing he would take a hit. He expended essence to damage the one facing Forli, even though he hadn't reestablished his barrier.

Ivy rushed forward, touching Forli, and the wound where her hand had been closed—but the hand didn't regrow.

Forli was used to the damaged and now-healed pattern and must not have figured out what had happened because she hit the skeleton with a blast of cold. At the same time, Dalryn turned—and took a stab to the back for doing so from the still-standing skeleton—and slashed the one near Forli. It collapsed.

Ty grunted in pain as the flanged mace one fighting him smashed him again, on the shoulder. But Ty had a huge amount of health now, and it didn't hurt as much as it should have, merely bruising him.

But his notification box informed him that it was an entropic wound and could only be healed magically at the rate of one per day.

Crap, no wonder her arm is still missing.

Dalryn was engaged in a protracted fight with the two skeletons, the Level Six guardian a match for the two Level Five warriors, apparently.

Ty reactivated his barrier as the skeleton smashed him again. The barrier broke again, but it did its job. Ty only took mild damage from the remaining force of the blow.

The skeleton was also still slowly frying from the shock shield. Very slowly.

Ivy rushed over and smashed her sword—which she almost never used—onto the back of the skeleton fighting Ty. It turned, and Ty took the opportunity to hit it with lightning. Flanged Mace finally went down.

Dalryn was cut a couple of times, and a huge chunk of his armor finally just fell off completely.

Object decay and chaotic wounds? Seems harsh.

Ty started rapidly hitting the skeletons with bolt after bolt. It wasn't as effective as it could have been, but unmolested, he could just turn essence into pain for his enemies.

The other two fell rapidly.

Forli was staring at the stump of her left hand, her mouth agape, brown eyes so wide, they threatened to annex the rest of her face.

Ty rushed over. "Check the notifications, Forli! It isn't permanent—it'll just heal slowly! It's okay!" He knelt down and threw his arms around her.

She shuddered and started bawling. "I don't—I don't have my *hand*, Ty!"

"It'll be back in a couple of days, Forli. Truly. It'll be fine!"

Ivy knelt as well, hugging Forli from the other side.

Slowly, Forli calmed, the shaking slowing and stopping. "Okay, okay, I'm okay. Did we win?"

Ty stood and pointed over at the tree, where the quarter of Zadrid's heart pulsed, like it was still trying to beat. "We did. The way is clear."

"That wasn't hard at all!" Dalryn declared.

Ivy turned and smacked the back of his head. "Forli will be going *days* without a hand, you jackanapes! Please don't be your usual colossal ass self."

Dalryn frowned. "You didn't call me either of those things before you started dating Ty."

Ivy rolled her eyes. "Before I got out of the house and had more than just Dad to compare you to. You need to improve your ways, brother."

"Hmph."

Ty judged Forli to be all right. Well, all right enough. As the siblings argued, he stood from her and walked over to the tree.

No one had been able to permanently take the pieces before, because they would dissolve and reform. Saelenia had told him that he just needed to combine it with the first piece once he got back to make it stable. Ty grabbed the piece and ripped it from the tree.

For a few seconds, Ty thought everything was okay, but then he felt the Entropy magic spewing from the heart, heading downward into the ground.

"Trouble!" Ty yelled, running back as the ground heaved.

The other three stopped their discussions and glanced over. They were all pointing and yelling, and Ty glanced back.

The ground exploded and a massive skeleton surged out. It took a moment for Ty to recognize what kind of creature it was from, but he blanched when he did.

Dragon.

It was about twelve feet long, with dark energy running across the whole thing where a normal creature would have muscles and tendons. It stretched its skeletal wings out and *roared*, despite a complete lack of lungs or mouth.

Ty leapt to the side, somehow avoiding being eviscerated despite his clumsy body as the thing charged.

Dalryn rushed forward. Ivy's brother had few redeeming features, but Ty forgave nearly everything because of his guardian skills and general protectiveness. The dragon's charge met Dalryn's shield bash and almost had its head knocked off, but Dalryn exploded back from the hit—apparently, a skeleton had about the same weight as something an eighth of its size, give or take, but it was the one charging.

The dragon's jawbone cracked and broke, which Ty figured might be the thing that had saved all their lives. But Dalryn was thrown and slammed to the ground, then trampled by the creature, its claws raking him where his armor was missing. He screamed once and stabbed up as the thing passed, losing his weapon for his trouble.

Forli rushed to the side, throwing ice even as Ty started his lightning strikes over and over. He wasn't sure he would have enough essence, so he grabbed an essence potion from his belt and downed it.

"Use your potion, Forli!" Ty screamed as the beast scrabbled to a stop and reached out, catching her with a claw and throwing her to the ground in front of its body to land with a breathless grunt.

Forli fought and tried to escape, grabbing a regeneration potion and downing it. The creature tried to bite her, barely scratching her as its teeth raked across her hardened skin.

But Ty knew what was next. He picked himself into a run, putting barrier up, and leapt over Forli as the claw came down.

White-hot agony flashed through his back and he collapsed onto Forli. For a moment, he couldn't understand what was happening, but then he realized she was screaming again.

Ty saw that the claw hit had penetrated his shield, armor, and health enough to pass through his body but had still slid off and slammed into Forli's legs, somehow hitting both. Ty tried to roll over but couldn't, his legs not working right, although he couldn't figure that out, either.

But he put his hand back and unleashed lightning into the beast over and over. At the same time, lying on Forli, he took a regeneration potion himself.

Dalryn slammed his shield into the beast's face again, and its already scorched and broken jaw fell off completely. His sword swing scratched it in the claw, and when Ty added another lightning bolt, that broke as well.

Ivy was healing both Forli and Ty, and Ty quickly realized he'd had his spine severed when feeling, as well as a prickly and painful sensation, suddenly returned to everything.

But only one point restored—thank the good gods it was enough to reattach the spine. Or fix it—it didn't seem literally severed.

Able to use his legs again, Ty painfully rolled over, stuck his hand into the roof of the dragon's mouth, now exposed, and blasted lightning right into where its brain would have been. A black cloud inside the skull pulsed, and the dragon stumbled back.

He hit it again, and then again.

Finally, it dropped, collapsing to the side.

Forli lay on the ground, blood slowly weeping from her wounds. Ivy was bandaging them as opposed to using healing as Forli cried and tried not to scream.

I got too sure of myself again, Ty thought helplessly, looking at Forli. *We've only got the one piece and we'll need a fortnight to heal her—and she'll be in absolute agony for the first couple of days.*

Dalryn stepped close. "Plan?"

Ty shuddered. "I'm... not sure. We have to do something, but I honestly have no idea at this point. I don't want to go back without the heart pieces, but we're too weak at the moment. And Forli is messed up, bad. If we try to fight a second piece, and it's stronger as well, we'll be utterly doomed."

Dalryn nodded, but he was still watching Ty.

Ty needed something, some plan... but he wasn't sure what. He thought about his team, where the weaknesses were... and how to make them better at fighting undead.

At the moment, he had no idea.

But he knew one thing. "We need to get her out of the area before the skeletons come back."

Chapter Twenty-Nine

LOSSES...

Forli lay in a makeshift bed, composed of all their sleeping rolls, inside the tent. It had been a harrowing experience, moving her when every slight jostle could make her scream. The three of them—Ty, Ivy, and Dalryn—were kneeling around the bed.

Forli was crying as she spoke to them. "I can't, Ty. I'm sorry. I'm *really, really* sorry. But I'm done."

"I know I'm asking a lot, but do you think you can handle helping us for just a bit longer?" Ty asked.

She shook her head carefully, tears still falling down the side of her face. "No. No, I can't. I'll freeze, I'll run, something. This... This is agony, Ty. I know I got a few rat bites before, and I thought I could handle that. I can't handle this. I'm simply not cut out for the lifestyle. I'm nearly Level Seven, and maybe if you guys do a few lower-level runs in the dungeon, where I know it's safe and easy, I'll join just to make the last level. But beyond that, I'm out. I hate it. The pain. The fear. The exhaustion. It's flaying my soul, Ty. Level Seven is farther than I thought I'd ever go, farther than most people *do* ever go. It's enough for me."

Ty sighed. He had known that Forli had been on edge, but the massive damage and near-death experience hadn't so much pushed her over the cliff edge as thrown her bodily over it. He felt like a complete ass for even suggesting she continue, but he also didn't have any idea how else to complete his goal.

"Can... Can I still live with you?" Forli asked, hiccupping.

Ty turned to Ivy, whose lip was trembling.

She nodded. "Of course." Ivy reached down and checked Forli's bandages. "Everything else okay?"

Forli nodded. "As okay as it can be. Thanks for letting me stay, and for being so kind to me."

Tears leaked down Ivy's face. "It's my fault, Forli. I wanted to wait to see what familiars we could find in the dungeon, but if I'd had my familiars already, that dragon fight would almost certainly have gone differently."

Ty had a sudden flash of hope, followed by frustration. If they tried to find familiars now, they would almost certainly either fail or, more likely, find mediocre ones. Which would make the waiting and agony Forli was going through extra pointless. But without Forli, Ty had no chance to complete Zadrid's Hallow and get the heart. Given he had started combining pieces, it might even resurrect Zadrid. But with two familiars who hopefully wouldn't be weak to undead like Ty and Forli were... maybe they could still do it.

Ty turned to his paramour. "Ivy, I *really* hate to ask this, given that we've been waiting, but is there any chance we could at least check for a familiar nearby? I mean, if we get one or two, we might still be able to complete everything. And since I've started it, I think it's really bad to leave the heart partially assembled and not take it back to the dungeon."

Ivy bit her lip. "Could you use just part of the heart for the dungeon?"

Ty wasn't actually sure. "Maybe? I don't know. I'd rather not, however. My history of half-arseing things has come back to bite me in the ass more than I care to admit. And each level of the dungeon that has amazing rooms will increase the dungeon disproportionately."

Ivy pursed her lips. "What? I'm sorry, Ty, you're not explaining that well."

Dalryn nodded. "Seconded. Speak like an elf, ya onion."

Ty rolled his eyes at Dalryn but continued. "The dungeon needs the adventurers it attracts to be high level in order for the dungeon itself to level."

"Everyone knows that," Dalryn said haughtily.

"So, when I pick a room, it adds *something* to the dungeon capacity. If I get a room that adds monster levels and loot both, for example, it's worth way more than one that adds only half that. Number of rooms multiplied by quality of the rooms is the maximum attraction. My dungeon always gets one room per level. So, if at Level Ten, all my rooms have been crappy ones, making Level Eleven will be really hard. Few adventurers will come, or they'll be low level, etc. But if it has Level Twelve monsters, a huge loot rating, bosses with improved loot drop odds for the rooms, etc., it'll attract over-leveled adventurers. But that can only happen if I have the absolute best rooms."

Ivy's brow was slightly furrowed as she listened. "That... makes sense."

"The whole point of getting the Crone to be my boss was the special advancement options and unusual power. I really don't want to fail now, by the fall."

Ivy sighed. "All right, let's go find a familiar."

Ty glanced at Forli. "Will you be okay for a few days here in the tent?"

She nodded. "Yeah. Nothing has bothered this campsite the whole time we've been here."

"Then we'll be back, hopefully soon."

***

Ty reached out his hand, blasting one goblin in its green head with lightning. It dropped to the ground twitching, while Ty dodged to the side and tried to kick another goblin but missed.

234

That one stabbed at him with a spear but missed in turn, goring the tree behind Ty.

There was an entire horde of goblins around them, a good fifty or sixty. They had ambushed—if you could call a horde running screaming from down a forest path 'ambushing'—Ty and his team in the early morning hours, before they had finished picking up their smaller makeshift camp.

Another goblin from the horde around them bonked a rock off of Ty's shoulder.

Ty made a fist and brought his hand down on the spear-wielding goblin's head, doing only a single damage but knocking the overextended thing onto the nearly empty forest floor beneath them.

A dart hit Ty. It bounced off his slightly hardened skin, but Ty saw the tip coated in something viscous and green. He hoped Ivy wouldn't get hit.

Fortunately, Dalryn was pretty much able to focus totally on protecting Ivy—Ty had slightly armored skin and a whole load of health, and these goblins weren't very damaging.

He looked into the mess of goblins fighting them and spotted the dart thrower, standing on a log about thirty feet away. Lightning crackled from his fingertips, briefly connecting Ty to the goblin, which screamed, twitched, and roasted. Ty dismissed the '1 experience' notification.

I'm going to run out of essence before they run out of goblins, Ty thought. He hadn't put up his shocking shield. It was hugely effective against masses of enemies like this, but it drained a lot of power. And his skin was preventing a decent amount of the damage.

"Fall back!" Ty called out. "Find some kind of defensive emplacement where Dalryn can do most of the work!"

Everyone took a quick glance around, although Ivy let out a bit-off scream as her lack of attention caused her to take a spear-stab to her side. She touched herself and the wound started to heal.

"Over there!" she cried, pointing to four trees very close together with thick berry bushes clogging two of the four approaches.

"Thanks, you carrot. I just love being the only one doing work," Dalryn huffed at Ty.

Their guardian pushed his shield forward—not even a full bash, just a lumbering movement—and knocked a goblin from its feet, even as he slashed another, which ran howling deeper into the woods. As the first goblin Dalryn had knocked over scrambled to its feet, their guardian kicked it in its head, and it dropped, out like a snuffed candle.

Everyone pulled back into the small glade that Ivy had pointed out. Dalryn held one side, and Ty and Ivy held another.

Ty grunted as another stone bounced off his shoulder, but it did no actual damage, his skin protecting him again. A goblin with a stone knife tried to cut Ivy, but she swept his blade aside with her sword and kicked him in the face. The goblin stumbled back.

Seven goblins decided to charge the two of them at the same time, and Ty triggered his shocking shield ability. Four went down to that and another to a bolt he flung at it, and Ivy stabbed a sixth. The last one took a single look and fled back to its lines.

Dalryn left one knocked out and another bleeding to death on the ground as the goblins pulled back from his side as well.

A small horde, still thirty-five or forty strong, quite a few wounded, was outside the defensive position that the adventuring group had established. A few desultory rock throws and a dart sailed into the group ineffectually before the goblins wound down fully.

Dalryn hamstrung the knocked-out one on a single leg. While Ty agreed they couldn't leave the goblin to recover and threaten them again, Ty wasn't sure if that was Dalryn being a nice guy—or a foolish one. Most people with a ruined leg had terrible lives, and Ty was pretty sure that goblins made everything far more horrible. A one-legged goblin probably led a short, horrid life.

It would have been better to end the tiny green bandit's life while it was still blissfully unconscious.

One of the goblins walked forward a bit. It appeared about the same as every other goblin, at least to Ty's eyes, but it carried a couple of elf skulls on strings around its waist—which couldn't have been comfortable, given the size difference.

It stopped about halfway from the milling goblin horde and Ty's defensive position. It spoke in heavily accented Middle Averian. "You put down sharps now, I, Gragtu Bonecaster, not kill. Slave. Some work, some bed. Not die. Just work and bed. Like other elf."

Ty simply raised his hands and hit the goblin with one of his last lightning blasts. The gross thing went down, twitching. The goblin didn't die, however, surprising Ty.

The skull-wearing goblin rolled over and pushed its hands out. Black energy flew at Ty, surprising him a second time. The goblin was still shocked, however, and it missed, even though Ty hadn't had the presence of mind to dodge.

Ty used the last of his essence to hit it again, hoping that this was a leader and the goblins would be demoralized. His enemy spasmed and released its bowels audibly as it died.

"Gross," Dalryn muttered, and Ty heard gagging noises from Ivy behind him.

The other goblins threw a few more rocks, yelled at him, and muttered among themselves. But it did appear as if they didn't have a leader or other coordinating force.

Ty raised his hand again, yelling, "Get out of here!" and the goblins scattered, running back into the forest from where they had come.

Dalryn spit into the berry bushes. "How did we go the entire trip here and not meet a single goblin band, and now—inside dragon territory, I might add, even if we're on the edge—we've hit a goblin group? It seems like the gods themselves are cursing us."

"Did you hear that?" Ty asked, ignoring Dalryn's complaints.

"The goblin shitting itself?" Dalryn asked, wiping his blade and putting it back in its sheath. "Yeah. It was crazy gross, especially when you consider we could hear it all the way over here. Goblins are just the worst."

"You're such a child, Dalryn. I was talking about the fact that they have elf slaves."

Dalryn's eyes widened. "Oh, yeah! He did say something about that!"

"We have to save them," Ivy said, reaching up and clutching her amulet. "Cerivae Nerithin demands that we remove their suffering."

Ty smacked one fist into the palm of his other hand. "Perfect! We're in agreement. Also, we could recruit them once we rescue them, have multiple elves to help us fight the undead instead."

Dalryn mimicked Ty, smacking one fist into another. "Or perhaps the goblins will have familiars!"

Ty gave it some thought. *Maybe.* "Goblins are insular, but it's not impossible. If the goblins found familiars out here, that would work with them, even if the familiars couldn't level up without a bond practitioner."

"How do we find the goblins' camp?" Ivy asked.

Dalryn laughed. "Roughly thirty of the buggers went and ran off in one direction, like the cowardly parsley sprigs they are. It shouldn't be hard to track them, even for amateurs like us."

Ty raised a finger. "Well, we need a day before we go after the 'parsley.' I'm essentially out of essence. Tomorrow morning, we see what their certainly squalid village has to offer. Or, perhaps, just after morning. Goblins don't do well in bright sunlight."

"Let's hope for a cloudless day," Dalryn quipped.

Chapter Thirty

...AND GAINS

The goblin camp had been ridiculously easy to find. They made little effort to hide anything about themselves, from their location to their hunting parties, and even their stench. As Ty watched from the bushes they were hiding in, bright sunlight filtering through the trees, he came to the conclusion that it was a camp of about four hundred, more than he could kill.

The camp also had about fifty elf slaves, mostly female. They were obviously worn down. They almost universally appeared either sick or crippled or both, and abused to boot in most cases. They cooked and cleaned and were very obviously being used as bed partners, although Ty wondered about how the four-and-a-half feet goblins got the elves to do what they wanted. *Threats of over-the-top violence, I assume.*

The camp was decently built, a huge surprise to Ty. It had a palisade around the outside with a gate and a small tower. The gate was unmanned, however.

The camp had multiple log cabins, although each had filth visible at various points on it.

But not wear and tear. They all appeared either new, or very well maintained, which surprised Ty, given the general lack of giving a hoot apparent to every other aspect of the goblins' conduct, from gear to personal hygiene.

It was an incongruity that Ty doubted he would have a chance to delve into, since he was just here on a raid. The one thing the goblins did seem to spend some time on was the pen where they were keeping most of the elves. It was a huge fenced enclosure, but the fence was ten feet tall, and two goblins patrolled it, mostly looking inward. A few of the elves were maintained elsewhere, but forty or so were in the cage.

Those were the ones whom Ty hoped to rescue.

Goblins had low-light vision, allowing them to work well in caves. But outdoors, they worked best in the early morning or at twilight. At noon, which was the rough current time, they functioned barely better than they would have in complete darkness.

Goblins also had penalties to almost all stats and were in the absolute bottom tier of mortal species, except they had an absurdly high resistance to poison and disease and an equally absurdly high birthrate. They were just about the single-most ubiquitous 'evil' mortal race, although there were a few members on the side of good, and quite a few who were merely selfish from what Ty had read back in Steelport as a child.

But right now, they were tired, half-blind from the light, and individually weak, even if numerous. It was as good an opportunity as Ty was likely to get.

"Here's the plan," Ty said quietly, turning where he squatted to speak to the Mosstone siblings. "They've got *no* guards except the two watching the slaves, and they're mostly watching inward. We're going to sneak over there, rush through the gate to the first set of buildings, and then sneak along till we reach the edge of that"—Ty pointed to one of the log cabin buildings—"one there. Once that's done, will wait for the guard to pass by, and then I'll lightning one goblin and you, Dalryn, jump out and stab the other."

"That's your plan, you tuber?" Dalryn asked. "Get 'em? This is a big risk."

"Well, we don't have an Eclipse user, or anything else like that…" Ty said, raising an eyebrow.

Dalryn grimaced. "Doesn't mean that this is a good plan. Or that you're not a tuber. But I *do* have your back, and I *don't* have a better idea. So I guess 'get 'em' will be our plan."

Ty chuckled quietly, reached out, and put his hand on Dalryn's shoulder. "Never change."

"Stop that."

Ty turned, did a quick check, then harshly whispered, "Now!" and rushed the gate, his body hunched slightly, trying to move softly across the ground.

The others followed, and while Ty was pretty sure their group's sneaking skills were barely worthy of the name, no goblin noticed them. He reached the gate, zipped through, and dashed across to the first building.

"See? No big deal."

Ivy's eyes were wide, and Ty could see sweat at Dalryn's armpits, but both gave him the three-finger gesture that meant 'okay' or perhaps 'good job' to the elves of Averia.

Ty turned around and rushed around the corner... and came face to carapace with a dog-sized spider. He skidded to a halt so hard, he fell on his butt, and he scrabbled backward, trying to pull his staff off his back and raising his hand for lightning simultaneously.

Dalryn followed him and tripped over Ty with a muted yelp, then whipped his sword out as well while face-down on the ground.

But Ty didn't fire the lightning that sparked on his fingertips as he stared at the spider. It had huge, comically oversized eyes even for a spider, and its eight legs ended in small human hands. It also had a normal human mouth under its eight eyes, although that mouth still had large fangs.

The spider spoke in a ridiculously cute young child's voice. "*Thaj ik ro? Elevesti bahk do Sahur ith kevelto ik gyo.*"

Ivy came around the corner, managing to not trip. The thing stared up at her, all eight of its eyes widening. Ivy stared down at it in turn.

It scrunched its face up for a moment, then cutely said, "Hi! I'm Shreve. You're a familiar bond practitioner! Can I bond to you? I don't want to work for the goblins anymore."

"A... A spider?" Ivy asked. "I always imagined myself with something, well, more... like a bird of paradise. Or a unicorn."

"An amazing spider familiar!" the spider said. "I'm the best, seriously. You won't believe what I can make. Well, my siblings, Welwyn and Boring, are also the best."

"What... What do you—" Ivy began.

Dalryn cut Ivy off as he stood and sheathed his sword. "Sis, look, I don't want to be 'that guy'—"

"You always are," Ty quipped while nervously glancing around and getting to his own feet.

"But we need to get going. Every second we wait here is a potential disaster." Dalryn gave Ty the stink eye as he finished up his little speech.

Ivy bit her lip. "Right, yeah, saving people. Okay, Shreve, let's do this."

She held her hand out, and Shreve walked up and brushed against her. Ty felt a faint hint of magic, and then Shreve sighed. "That's the good stuff, right there. Great soul, seriously."

"Let's go!" Dalryn hissed.

"Wait, wait, wait," Shreve said. "I can sense that she has another bond spot! Can I get my sister, Welwyn?"

Ivy bit her lip again. "I don't know..."

All of Shreve's eyes got comically big, and they watered. "Please?"

Ivy dropped to the ground on her knees and *hugged* Shreve. "Yes, okay, I'm sorry, I'll bond with your sister."

"Yay! I'll be right back!"

Shreve scuttled off deeper into the small goblin encampment.

"You just got played by a spider," Dalryn said disgustedly. "Do you have any idea what it does?"

"Makes stuff?" Ivy asked.

Dalryn shook his head sadly, *tsked*, and then pointed in the direction of the pens. "Let's just go rescue the stupid slaves."

"Make sure to grab the smart ones as well," Ty quipped, and Dalryn frowned at him then rolled his eyes.

The three of them moved forward again, rushed across the small, open space to another log cabin, then looked around the corner.

One of the guards was missing, and the other was pushing a small, just-over-four-foot-tall goblin woman—girl?—up against the bars of the pens. He was trying to pull her dirty shift, which appeared to be her only clothing, over her head. She was trying to push off the bars and keep her shift down, giving little grunts of effort, obviously trying to avoid the 'attentions' of the guard. The elves right on the other side ignored her plight, probably just happy it wasn't them.

That guard has a bunch of slaves right there, and this is still how it treats a fellow goblin?

Ty rushed forward rapidly, hearing Dalryn's muted curse as their guardian followed. Ty slammed his lightning staff into the back of the guard's head and dropped him to the ground, out cold. He dismissed the notification of the knockout and stared at the goblin girl, who pulled her shift down and picked up a leather bag with a strap, which Ty hadn't noticed, off the ground, putting it on. She stared up at Ty with huge, wide eyes.

She's seen us...

Dalryn rushed up and swung his sword at her. She rolled to the side while Ty pushed his staff out, intercepting the blow.

"What are you doing?!" Dalryn said, then hissed out, "She's seen us!"

"I... I can't just kill her," Ty said lamely. "Or let you kill her."

The goblin girl didn't hang around for them to figure it out, instead scuttling away and running.

Ty glanced up and saw that all the elves were staring at him, and a few were standing.

Dalryn brought his attention back. "You're going to get Ivy and me *killed* with your pathetic weakness! She's gonna raise the whole camp!"

As Ivy ran up, Ty wedged his staff—a nearly invulnerable magic item—into the locked pen door, which was made of wood.

He turned to Dalryn. "Then shut up and help me!"

The three of them slammed into the stick, wedging the door apart, then did it a couple more times.

"Let's go!" Ty called to the elves inside. "We have almost no time!"

Half the elves didn't move, but about fifteen to twenty raced to the door of the pen, wedging themselves out from where they were holding it open.

"What are you guys doing?" Ty hissed to the elves inside. "Let's go!"

"We're just going to get caught and punished," a woman with a missing hand and ratty, bronze hair muttered. "I can't handle being beaten again."

"My daughter is in the main house, and I'll not leave her," said a man with a twisted knee and metallic-leaf-green hair, a color Ty hadn't seen on an elf before.

Ty stared at the man who had spoken about his daughter. Somehow, even while straining to hold the break in the cage, Ty could feel magic from the man. Something in the man's demeanor, or magic, called to Ty.

Ty called out to him. "Which one is the main house? They all look exactly the same!"

"That one," the man said, pointing.

"Dalryn, finish this, figure out from the slaves which one is the armory, and then raid it," Ty said, picking up a knife from one of the goblins and tossing it to a lean-appearing elf. "Then arm the elves and head to the glade we stopped at last before we got here."

"What're you doing?" Dalryn asked.

Ty spoke louder. "I'm going to rescue the man's daughter. If he goes *now*."

The man hesitated, then stood and dashed over. When he went, nine more followed, leaving only ten.

Ty dashed off in the direction of the house. *I can't believe no one has raised an alarm on us yet, even though we have all the stealth of a cow parade. These goblins are utterly incompetent.*

Ty reached the edge of the building and duck-walked along the bottom until he got to a window, then popped his head up and looked in. About thirty goblins were sleeping in the thirty-by-thirty space, each on a tiny cot with blankets. At the far end of the room, there was a larger cot, and in it was a slightly larger goblin and an elf girl wearing nothing but bruises. She had the same metallic-green hair as the man from before, and Ty assumed this was his daughter.

How in all the dark dimensions am I going to get her out?

As Ty watched, something poked him in the leg.

He whirled, pulling his staff. The goblin girl from before was standing before him, nervously clutching her hands together around a steel knife. Her satchel now bulged, but she otherwise appeared the same.

"Take with," she said in extremely broken Middle Averian.

Ty stared at her, completely baffled by the rapid switch in situations. *She wants to leave her own kind?*

Ty glanced around at the camp, then contemplated the fact that he had interrupted what had clearly been her rape. *Okay, it makes some sense, I'll not deny.*

"Okay, but I need to rescue the elf woman," he whispered.

She looked confused, and he dredged up his memory of the tiny bit of Blood Cant he knew. Ty pointed into the window. "Elvesti. Elvesti."

Her eyes widened, and she nodded. "I get Elvesti. You take with."

Ty grinned wildly. *Yes!*

The goblin pointed to the gate. "You go. I meet there."

Yes, yes, yes! "All right."

Ty hustled away as the goblin girl went to the door of the log cabin and pulled it open. He couldn't guarantee that she would rescue the elf inside, but it was by far the best option.

But as Ty walked back among the buildings, a high-pitched scream ran out, then shouting in the Blood Cant.

Chapter Thirty-One

THE FALLEN

By the fall, I knew this was going too well!

Ty rushed through the encampment, over the smelly dirt and between the weirdly pristine log cabins. He found Dalryn and Ivy rapidly passing out weapons to the elves—all smaller, made for goblins, and most of extremely poor quality. But weapons nonetheless. There were now *three* of the weird spiders near them. One was Shreve, and the second one appeared to be a slightly bigger version of him. The last was smaller, and the top of that spider's carapace, both abdomen and thorax, was covered in moss and small flowers.

Just as Ty reached his team and their charges, goblins began pouring into the streets.

"Get to the gate!" Ty yelled. A goblin, more awake or aware than the rest, brandished a spear at a slave, blinking in the harsh light. Ty hit him with lightning and he went down.

"Someone, get his spear!" Ty called.

He pointed to the man with the green hair. "Get out of here, and take the elves with you!"

"My daughter's not here!" the man cried, anguish plain in the cast of the crow's feet around his pale-green eyes.

"I have a plan for that! But I need you to save these people. Get into the forest—we'll find you!"

"What are you going to do?" the man asked.

"Hold the gate to give you a slight head start," Ty said.

"They have a back gate!" the man cried, but he was already running and calling for people to move.

Of course they do. But they'll try to charge through the three weak-looking elves holding the gate first. It'll buy ten to fifteen minutes to get going.

Ty cast his eye to the nearest tree, whose top he could see over the gate. "Iluvin Eturia, please aid me now."

Dalryn rushed up. "The weapons are in the hands of the elves. What now?"

"The gate," Ty said simply.

"I can't explain to you how *little* I wanted to be a hero before you met me," Dalryn said as they started backing toward the gate, out front a bit to let the elves get out before they tried to block it.

"Well, I've heard the prettiest flowers admire heroes," Ty replied, one eyebrow lifted. The appreciation of a pretty woman was a notable motivator to him, certainly.

"That something your sister told you?" Dalryn asked.

Ty didn't answer, instead blasting one goblin that seemed to be rallying some of the buggers for a charge. It hit the ground, smoking and still.

Dalryn continued complaining. "Seriously though, my mom warned me about bad company. I remember her talking about it. 'You don't want to fall in with the wrong sort,' she said. Now look at me, going on dangerous-ass camping trips to grab illicit dark substances with some tree who's rutting my sister. Lo, how I have fallen."

Ty snorted, and from behind them, Ivy giggled as well.

"Did you really just say 'Lo'?" Ivy asked.

"Eh. It was funny."

Ty appreciated the weird morale boost that was coming with Dalryn's complaining, but even as the elves streamed back, the few goblins that had poured into the dirt paths between the various log cabins tried to rush them, no leader apparent to shock as a discouragement.

Ty summoned his essence and formed it into his two defensive abilities: shocking shield and barrier. He swung his staff into one goblin, knocking it prone, and two others shocked themselves on his defenses.

Dalryn slashed one, dodged a spear thrust, and kicked another in the face so hard, it almost flipped, hitting the ground with its jaw clearly broken. Then Dalryn threw back his head and *howled.*

The howl sounded nothing like Dalryn. Instead, it felt like the hunting call of a primal wolf, an alpha from a particularly powerful magical pack, the most dangerous thing in the room.

Most of the goblins briefly hesitated, either afraid or changing directions to stab at Dalryn.

The spiders took advantage, charging en masse at a small group of distracted goblins. The biggest spider got a bite in. The goblin he bit dropped his weapon and screamed wildly, but when the spider retreated, the bite looked small to Ty. And the goblin stopped screaming shortly after, touching the wound and wincing but getting back up and running.

I don't think the spiders are poisonous, or terribly effective in combat. Hopefully, they get a lot stronger as they level.

The goblin rush fell apart and said goblins fell back as Ty and his team reached the gate. Ivy fell back a bit, along with the spiders, to the outside of the gate. Ty dropped his shields again.

Two more waves at my current essence expenditure and I turn into just a high-Health guy with a staff.

Dalryn and Ty stood in the gate, next to each other.

"New ability?" Ty asked.

"Older ability, I took it back at Level Four. But it doesn't work on the undead. Figures, right?" Dalryn eyed the milling goblins and adjusted his stance.

Ty chuckled, bravado in the face of bad odds. "So your leveling ability was 'scream of attention,' huh? Seems in character."

Dalryn gave him a slight sneer. "You're such a tuber. It's called 'primal howl,' which is much more elite."

The two of them were Level Seven—and tough. Dalryn had a huge amount of Health and armored skin. Ty had similar Health, defensive abilities, and slight resistance to damage.

But Dalryn had no armor or shield, and Ty was dependent on a finite essence pool. They had a limited amount of time—although in the tight confines, he hoped they could trade Ivy's essence for staying power in the form of heals.

No pain, no gain. Here, quite literally. The two of us, with one healer for backup, need to hold this gate against, like, fifty goblins. With more coming.

Ty felt weirdly close to Dalryn in that moment.

The goblins were milling about. After a moment, the creatures rushed them again, about twice as numerous as before.

Ty turned his shields on again. "Let's do this."

***

Ten minutes, and two waves, later, Ty and Dalryn had managed to pile about twenty goblin bodies around them in a tiny makeshift palisade. The dirt was now bloody mud, and the whole place had a coppery-shit stink about it.

Ivy had only used about a third of her essence, and Ty was clean out. And over a hundred goblins now faced him, occasionally firing darts or slinging rocks. His own skin prevented a lot of the harassing chip damage, but not all of it, and he had quite the collection of small cuts and bruises. It would go away once enough damage was done to warrant another regenerate, but they weren't there yet.

"Seriously *loving* my decision to be your guardian," Dalryn whined for the thirteenth or maybe thirtieth time—it all kinda blurred together into one long '*who cares?*' in Ty's mind.

"You're starting to get a bit repetitive, Dal. We were having a cool moment of comrades in arms before you got utterly whiny again."

"Don't call me 'Dal,' you tuber."

Ty rolled his eyes.

"Guys!" Ivy shouted, pointing to the other side of the gate. Ty stepped back and looked where she was pointing. A good twenty goblins were jogging along the outside of the palisade, weapons out. If they got to Ty's group, the three would be surrounded and under attack with no way to protect Ivy. It was time to go.

"Run!" Ty yelled. "We've got longer legs. Hit the forest edge and then follow me!"

The three of them started running, but they quickly left the two smaller spiders behind.

"Help me!" Shreve called.

Ty stopped, ran back, and grabbed the thing, shuddering as he did. Dalryn briefly watched Ty wide-eyed, then ran and grabbed the moss-covered one.

"Gross," the copper-haired elf muttered as he lifted the spider, his thin arms bulging with enough muscle to appear human.

An actual arrow hit Ty in his back, piercing him but not deeply. Spurred on with the extra incentive, Ty belted his way out to the forest's edge, weighed down by the spider but still ahead of the goblins. Once in the forest, he figured the spider would have an advantage of terrain.

"Keep up with us," Ty grunted, dropping Shreve. The spider hit the ground, somehow tripped even with all his legs, and then got up and ran after Ty. With the ability to go over and under logs and through rough terrain easily, he did keep up better than he had on the open space around the encampment.

The cries of the goblins, and one tinny-sounding horn, followed them into the forest.

A few minutes later, Ty found the footprints he had been looking for, and switched directions a touch. He slowed to a jog, and Dalryn easily pulled beside him. Ivy managed to keep up, but she was sucking wind, sweating, and barely able to talk.

The three spiders weren't much better.

Eventually, however, Ty, Dalryn, Ivy, and her companions caught up to the elves.

As they reached the elves, Ty slowed to a walk, raising his hand in a three-fingered salute, wondering how many would remember the gesture.

A few smiled a tiny bit at him, but most maintained their slack-faced, dead-eyed stares.

Ty shuddered, knowing he wouldn't have been much different if he had suffered for fifty years at the hands of the orcs that had captured him a mere year ago, before he had been freed. The worst month of his life by a wide, wide margin, had been his time as a captive of the orcs.

Still, he needed to try to motivate these people.

Before he could say anything, the older male elf with the metallic-green hair rushed up and grabbed him by the shoulders. "Where's my daughter?!"

Dalryn rushed forward, drawing his blade, but Ty waved him back.

Praying to Iluvin Eturia that he would be right, he said, "I told you, I had a plan for that. She'll be here."

"She better be, or I'll, I'll..." The man's speech trailed off, and his eyes widened as he glanced over Ty's shoulder.

Ty whirled, prepared to fight, but he saw the tiny female goblin leading the metallic-green-haired elf girl he had been tasked to rescue. The goblin still had her knife and leather bag and shift but had added a small belt and pouch.

The man rushed past Ty and flung his arms around his daughter. "Leu, Leu, you're okay! And we're free. It'll never happen again!"

As they hugged it out, Ty faced the small goblin.

"Thank you."

She pointed to herself. "I Belika. You take with."

Ty nodded. "Of course."

Dalryn groaned. "Now we're rescuing a *goblin*? Are you crazy?"

The man let go of his daughter. He turned to Ty. "I'm Jeryl, Jeryl Flowerpot. I swear I'll make this up to you—I'm your sworn man from now on, no matter what."

Before Ty could respond to Jeryl, the goblin stepped forward again, pointing at herself again. "I... fight. I make fight with you."

"You want to fight me?" Ty asked, very confused. He didn't think that was what she wanted, but...

Dalryn, Ivy, and even Jeryl were all staring at her curiously as well.

She frowned, her hands grasping at nothing. Then she walked over and put herself in front of Ty, holding her knife out. "You. Me. Fight... Not you, not me."

She wants to be my companion? Adventure with us?

"Um..."

"Don't you dare, Ty," Dalryn muttered.

At the same time, Ivy said, "Oh my god, we're going to have a little goblin mascot!"

"I... I guess you can hang with us, for a bit at least. I'll get your status chart when we get back, and we can see for sure."

Dalryn sneered at the goblin before turning to Ty, his nose wrinkled. "You absolute tuber."

Chapter Thirty-Two

HOW THE DRYAD GOT HIS GROVE BACK

"And how did it end?" Saelenia asked from her throne of flowers, a month later. "I mean, I can see you were successful, youngling, but it leaves a lot of questions."

Ty was sitting on the ground of the cavern, the now-complete Heart of Zadrid resting on the rock floor just in front of him. His position made Saelenia even more impressive. He would have looked up at her regardless, since her twelve-foot, fertility-goddess frame towered over him even when she was sitting and he was standing. But when Ty sat, he felt more cat than child in comparison.

Despite having rested in his own bed the previous night, Ty was bone-tired—the months spent on the mission had worn on him. He gave a long sigh before answering. "It ended with a mobbing of the last two heart sites. We lost no fewer than five of the elves, but the rest made Level Two or, in a couple of cases, Level Three. It turns out that Jeryl is a wood elf with a high elf mother, and a great gardener with levels and magical abilities. He agreed to work for me."

"Hmm."

"Forli is still living with us. Once we had an entire mob—or maybe just because we gave her a week of rest, effectively—she changed her mind and agreed to adventure with us for the last part of Zadrid's Hallow. We all made Level Seven, including her, and the rest of us are very nearly Level Eight."

"And you'll seed her soon?" Saelenia asked, leaning forward.

Ty pursed his lips. "It's weird how... direct you dryads are about this. I mean, I rarely walk up to someone and ask them, 'Do you plan to rut her?'"

"We're different, it's true, but answer the question."

Ty sighed. "I think so? I haven't really had much chance to make love to anyone while we were out, just a few very furtive hookups with Ivy—I mean, her brother was camping with us. But things seem to be moving in that direction."

Saelenia leaned back in the chair again and crossed her legs. "I know your special ability is an unexpected bonus, but I joined your dungeon partially to keep bringing dryads into the world. I hope you'll work to make that happen."

I'm not sure if I should be excited or concerned that a pro-to-god is telling me I need to bed women, but I'm certainly flabbergasted.

Ty coughed. "So, how did the dungeon do while I was out?"

Saelenia waved her hand, and the plinth and tablet rose from the ground, showing the dungeon's information. "I—the dungeon part of 'me'—made two levels during your extended absence. Very nearly three. It's become fairly routine now, over the three months."

"Wow..." Ty said, his mind immediately going to dark places. "A lot of death, I take it?"

"Ten died," Saelenia said, frowning. "In turn, almost four hundred made Level Two and unlocked their magic, youngling. In most cases, that means for the rest of their lives, they'll make over twice what they would have, be able to support a dream, or a hobby, or numerous children well instead of a few on the edge of starvation."

"Still—" Ty began.

Saelenia just talked over him. "Would you deny them that life? Make all those children go hungry, or not exist? All of that just to get back the ten who died, youngling?"

"Well, no, but—"

"Many of those who leveled became farmers who can grow twice the food, many multiples of that higher in terms of excess past what they need to feed their family. Food that'll be cheaper for everyone else now, including poor families that *also* have starving children. Would you have those children go hungry, just so you don't feel bad? How selfish, youngling."

"Now wait a damned minute," Ty said, getting angry.

Saelenia didn't wait. "But a great deal of them are now true adventurers, and ninety or so made Level Three, and twenty made Level Four. Those are people who can defend this realm, and its inhabitants, from the orcs, goblins, and other things that oppose it. People and beings who will kill far more than ten if good men do nothing or haven't the ability to do anything."

Ty let his breath out and held his hands up. "All right, I get it. Fine. It nets to a better world, and everyone made their own choices. Sorry I cared. How about you just tell me what else happened here while I was gone? I know that Ygg'drasil has a portal open. I also saw a few new faces around town. How'd that all come about?"

Saelenia, a smug smile that somehow reminded Ty of his mom plastered to her face, nodded. "King Stardew went through and had a brief war to protect some new subspecies of elves in a snow dimension. A new proto-god has joined the forest triad: Zurika, Sky Lynx Progenitor."

"Wow."

"But, most importantly—although for later—it's a new dimension with even stronger magic than this one, including new magical trees. So you'll be able to look for more dungeon cores and create new and hopefully even stronger dryads."

Ty rubbed his hands together. "Excellent. I have hope that my planned build will pay off in the long run, then."

Saelenia sighed. "You can learn far more about all that from others who didn't themselves learn from listening in to cross-talk in the dungeon. How about we build said dungeon, instead?"

Ty nodded.

"Leave Zadrid's Heart on the floor, exit the dungeon, then return. Be sure to declare you're returning as dungeon lord again. When you get back, I'll have absorbed the heart and the new options should have hopefully populated."

Ty nodded, climbed to his feet far more awkwardly than his stats would normally suggest due to his fatigue, and walked upstairs.

He saw that a crowd was waiting for him. His father, Kadrath, Ivy, and Belika were all outside. Not Dalryn, though— Ty figured he was at the Bee, trying to woo some elf woman. Or perhaps trying to make things right with Cuwylla. Forli was also absent, back at their shared home. Ty suspected that Forli was afraid to show herself to the other members of the Adventurers' Guild since she was abandoning the profession, even though at Level Seven, she was considerably stronger than most of them.

And, to his surprise, Val was absent as well.

He gave a quick wave, quipped, "It's still under construction, please form an orderly queue," and then walked back in.

When he came back downstairs, he found things as they'd been before, except that now, a series of flowering vines descended from the ceiling near the Crone's throne, and the heart of Zadrid was held in the middle of their mass, easy to view from one side and completely surrounded on the others. A few of the vines connected to the now-beating black heart, and he could see them faintly pulsing in time to it.

It was faintly disturbing.

Ty walked over to the plinth in the center of the cavern and touched it, bringing the dungeon's status chart to his mind.

The Dungeon of the Dryad's Grove		
Air, Soul, Wyld	Level Four Dungeon (two picks remaining)	Score 11 (12-1) Dungeon
Category	Score	Effect
Monster Level	2	The dungeon has a maximum of Level 2 monsters. [1/10th of Base Dungeon Score, rounded up. Monster Levels may not normally exceed dungeon Level +2]
Maximum Monsters	17	The dungeon can have 17 monsters (cost 16 recovery), spread out roughly equally between its possible levels. [Base Dungeon Score + Nest(x1)]

Monster	Number	Total Recovery Cost
Special		
Boss	0	0
Sub-Boss	1	2
Monster	12	12
Baby Monster/ Minion	4	2

Category	Score	Effect
Recovery Rate	3.2	The dungeon recovers 3.2 monsters per hour. [.1 x Base Dungeon Score + Nest(x1)
Magic Effects	5	5 small magical effects or 2 slightly bigger ones. [Base Dungeon Score, rounded up, + Ty, + Zadrid's Heart]
Traps	0	
Loot Rate	1	If they find any monster that drops loot, they'll count themselves lucky. [Always 1 base]
Loot Quality	1.2	Oh, joy, a rusty knife! Mom can stop working the fields! [Always 1 base, +.1 Ty, +.1 Zadrid's Heart]

Magic Output	30	The dungeon adds to the magic of the world, and in its local area. At current level, it adds 30% to the base magic level and node effects and .03% to the rest of the world's base magic level. (Base score plus Dungeon Level and same over 1000 percent. Doubled from 'Dungeon Passage' dungeon lord ability.)
Special Categories		
Rooms		
Category	Number	Effect
Floor One		
Nest	1	+1 Sub-Boss. +4 Baby Monsters. +2 Recovery. This is a breeding space for monsters.
Heart of the Grove	1	+1 Magic effects Level. May accept pieces of progenitors to increase power and gain new rooms. Each one adds a small direct amount of power as well as new room options.
		Zadrid's Heart: +1 Magic effect, will be Entropy. +.1 loot Quality.

"So, months of pain and losing Forli as an adventuring partner bought me... one magic effect and a tenth of a point increase in the loot level?" Ty asked. "Be still, my beating heart."

Saelenia rose from her throne in all her twelve-foot-tall, naked-fertility-goddess glory and strode over to the plinth. As she did so, Ty noticed a tattoo of a black wolf on her flat, muscled stomach.

"Don't sass me, youngling," Saelenia said as she towered over him and stared down at the chart. "You know dang well that the true power of the object is in the rooms it opens up. Pull up the room chart and we can talk the picks. I can sense rare and powerful rooms awaiting us."

Dryad Dungeon

Ty rolled his eyes, even though he was also excited to see the options. "Sure."

Room	Effect
Basic Rooms [Available to all dungeons, no specialty requirements]	
Lair	+8 Maximum Monsters. This will look like an inhabited space for monsters, and encounters in this room will seem like it is, in fact, a lair.
Nest	+1 Sub-Boss. +4 Baby Monsters. +2 Recovery. This is a breeding space for monsters.
Spark	+1 Magic Effects Level. +1% Local Magic Level. +.1 Loot Quality.
Treasure Room	+.5 Loot Rate, +1 additional Loot Rate for the floor it's on.
Advanced Rooms [Available because of combinations of Basic rooms]	
N/A	
Specialty Rooms [Available because of the Dungeon's Magics or Boss]	
Air Spark (Max 1 per floor)	+2 Magic Effects Level, shifts the magic toward Air. +3% Local Magic Level. +.2 Loot Quality.
Fae Grove (Max 1 per floor)	+2 Monster Level. +4 Max Monsters. The monsters on this floor are shifted toward Fae and Fae subtypes.
Beast Woods (Max 1 per floor)	+1 Monster Level. +6 Max Monsters. The monsters on this floor are shifted toward beasts and magical beasts.
Living Forest (Max 1 per floor)	+1 Monster Level. +4 Max Monsters. +.2 loot rate. The monsters on this floor are shifted toward plant monsters and the loot toward rare plants.
Shrine to Lost Glory	+.1 Loot rate and loot quality both. May accept the regalia of lost heroes still venerated enough to have faith. Each set adds a tiny amount of direct power and will generate a special encounter. May add more room options, but it's unlikely.

The Forest Temple	+1 Monster Level. May accept attuned Temple Stones to gods associated with the Crone or the Forest faction. Each adds a decent amount of power and may add new room options.
Master Rooms [Available because of combinations of Basic rooms and advanced, specialty rooms, or Eldritch rooms, always number limited]	
N/A	
Eldritch Rooms [Available from fulfilling conditions of the Shrine of the Forest, or fulfilling the conditions and having prerequisite other rooms.]	
The Dark Heart of the Forest	Beast Woods double their benefits on this floor. The floor this is placed on can gain Entropy magic effects and rooms. All entropy magic effects gained on this floor are doubled. The "Endless Undead" room and "Zadrid, Lost Progenitor" rooms can be discovered through other room combinations. +1 Magic effect, +25% experience gain in the dungeon for Entropy users. +1 Sub-boss. May pick Beast Woods for this floor an additional time.

Ty stared at the room. It was strong, but still... "It takes a room to add a beast woods. It's only a bit stronger than if I just took two beast woods, in fact."

Saelenia furrowed her brow. "Would that I could swat you. It gives an entire new magic option to the floor as well, youngling—which means more items, more possibilities. And gaining experience faster is *huge*, and it applies to the entire dungeon, not just the floor it's placed on. This will be a huge, permanent draw to adventurers. It's stronger by a lot."

"I also don't really like Entropy as a magic," Ty said.

"Just pick the room and come back to see what populated, and then we can make a decision about what you should pick next."

Ty sighed, nodded, and picked the room.

Then he left the dungeon, waved to everyone sheepishly, and went back in, calling out his entry.

He looked at the list. There was a single new room.

Specialty Rooms [Available because of the Dungeon's Magics or Boss]	
Entropy Spark (Max 1 per floor)	+2 Magic Effects Level, shifts the magic toward Entropy. +3% Local Magic Level. +.2 Loot Quality.

Ty sighed again. He was pretty sure if he picked the Entropy Spark, he would get amazing new rooms. But his dungeon was Level Four, and his current monster maximum was only Level Two.

"So, Beast Woods?"

"For now," Saelenia said. "I think if you get those and the Entropy Spark, you'll get a lot more options. I mean, Zadrid *was* an entropic beast. It makes sense."

Ty nodded—it mirrored his own thoughts. "A double Beast Woods will also give me an *insane* amount of monsters—truly absurd for my dungeon's level. But the recovery rate is the same... I need to up that. Right now, I'm not sure how much this benefits me."

"Such a complainer. You need monsters as well."

Ty laughed and picked the Beast Woods room. Then he opened his chart one more time.

The Dungeon of the Dryad's Grove		
Air, Soul, Wyld	Level Four Dungeon	Score 11 (12-1) Dungeon

Category	Score	Effect
Monster Level	4	The dungeon has a maximum of Level 2 monsters. [1/10th of Base Dungeon Score, rounded up + Beast Woods w/ doubled effect(x1). Monster Levels may not normally exceed dungeon Level +2]

Maximum Monsters	30	The dungeon can have 30 monsters (cost 30 recovery), spread out roughly equally between its possible levels. [Base Dungeon Score + Nest(x1) + Beast Woods doubled effect(x1)]		
		Monster	Number	Total Recovery Cost
		Special		
		Boss	0	0
		Sub-Boss	2	4
		Monster	24	24
		Baby Monster/ Minion	4	2
Recovery Rate	3.2	The dungeon recovers 3.2 monsters per hour. [.1 x Base Dungeon Score + Nest(x1)]		
Magic Effects	5	5 small magical effects or 2 slightly bigger ones or 1 great effect. [Base Dungeon Score, rounded up + Zadrid's Heart + Dark Heart of the Forest]		
Traps	0			
Loot Rate	1	If they find any monster that drops loot, they'll count themselves lucky. [Always 1 base]		
Loot Quality	1.2	Oh, joy, a knife! Mom can stop working the fields! [Always 1 base +.1 Ty, +.1 Zadrid's Heart]		
Magic Output	30	The dungeon adds to the magic of the world, and in its local area. At current level, it adds 15% to the base magic level and node effects and .03% to the rest of the world's base magic level. (Base score plus Dungeon Level and same over 1000 percent. Doubled for 'Dungeon Passage' dungeon lord ability.)		

Special Categories		
Entropy Experience Gain	25%	25% faster experience gain for anyone with Entropy as a magic. [Dark Heart of the Forest.]
Rooms		
Category	Number	Effect
Floor One		
Nest	1	+1 Sub-Boss. +4 Baby Monsters. +2 Recovery. This is a breeding space for monsters.
Heart of the Grove	1	+1 Magic effects Level. May accept pieces of progenitors to increase power and gain new rooms. Each one adds a small direct amount of power as well as new room options.
		Zadrid's Heart: +1 Magic effect, will be entropy. +.1 loot Quality.
Dark Heart of the Forest	1	Beast Woods double their benefits on this floor and provide 1 recovery each. The floor this is placed on can gain Entropy magic effects and rooms. All entropy magics effects gained on this floor are doubled. The "Endless Undead" room and "Zadrid, Lost Progenitor" rooms can be discovered through other room combinations. +1 Magic effect, +25% experience gain in the dungeon for Entropy users. +1 Sub-boss.
Beast Woods	1	[effect doubled from Dark heart of the Forest] +2 Maximum Monster Levels. +12 Monsters. Floor is beast-themed.

Ty stared at the chart. "Hmm... up to Level Four monsters, but I'm slightly below three runs a day now, down from the five before."

Saelenia frowned. "But for those who don't complete it, like your morning Level One group, you'll recover at the same rate, youngling. I'll admit you've always been a bit of a whiner, but why the sudden complete wet blanket attack? You were always a go-getter before."

Ty nodded to her words. "Sorry, you're right. This is probably actually amazing, and this floor will likely be amazing as well. I'm just tired and worn out. I need to go talk to the Adventurers' Guild, but then I'm going to go see about sleeping for a week straight in my big, soft bed. I'll be better after, I'm sure."

"Well, hurry up. I prefer quippy, excited you to this dour, whiny copy."

"I suppose I can't argue with being told to hurry up and get some sleep."

Chapter Thirty-Three

IT'S GOOD TO BE THE DUNGEON LORD

Ty emerged from the darkness of the cavern and into the interior of the Marble Gazebo a third time. As he exited, he saw that one pillar was now carved with an indistinct impression of a diseased wolf.

Well, isn't that just peachy? I wonder if people will ever figure out where the various pillar markings are coming from.

Ivy dropped down into the central garden portion of the odd gazebo that was the entrance to Ty's Dungeon of the Dryad's Grove. *Although it really doesn't feel terribly 'dryad' anymore. The next floor, though, for sure. No more beast and undead stuff. I'll just treat it as getting through the dark forest to the good stuff.*

Ty could see the bags under Ivy's eyes as well, and her copper hair was covered in grime, but she gave a huge smile as Ty came out from the dungeon entrance. "How'd it go, my love?"

Belika waited on the gazebo's inner edge, watching. She had fought with them in Zadrid's Hallow, and her shadow seemed to shift and shimmer around her.

Ty smiled at Ivy in turn. "Well enough. I'll explain it to the guild, and I'm sure we'll talk about it in bed, but significant improvements were made. Although the loot rating and quality are both still really bad—I need to work on that soon."

She leaned in and whispered into his ear. "Shall we go celebrate, then? Celebrate for an entire day, most of it in your bed?"

Ty's mouth went dry. *By all the gods, yes!*

Before Ty could voice his enthusiastic acceptance of Ivy's proposal, Kadrath jumped down the few feet into the center of the gazebo next to Ty with a crash of metal. The fully armored dworc put his arms around Ty. "Ty, my boy. Sorry. Dungeon Lord—"

"My boy," Ivy muttered and laughed.

"—Tywyndyll il Belmoria. It's good to see you again. I wish to give my report and turn your earnings over to you, if you've time."

Ivy smiled at him. "We'll talk—and other things—later."

"Oh, ho ho," Kadrath said, his green face split into a grin. He slapped Ty on his back. Even through his armored skin, he felt that one—since Kadrath was, as he freakishly always was, in plate armor, including his gauntlets.

"Heh," Ty responded halfheartedly, trying to rub the spot between his shoulder blades that Kadrath had smacked.

Kadrath kept smiling down at him. "Well, before you go die in her lap, a few moments of your time, Dungeon Lord."

Gross.

"Of course, Guildmaster," Ty muttered. "Let's go talk—never again about that."

Kadrath laughed, a hearty, deep, bellowing laugh that somehow seemed to declare Kadrath's thorough lack of giving a rat's behind about people's opinion of him.

"—and then I'll have need of your facilities if you don't mind."

"This way."

In a near-perfect replay of the time that Ty had first created his dungeon, Kadrath put his armored arm around Ty's shoulders and guided him to the guildhall. As he did so, Ty could see his father's shoulders slump the tiniest bit.

Ty mouthed, "I'll talk to you later, tomorrow, dinner," to his dad.

Then he was pulled, almost tripping, into the guildhall. Ivy and Belika followed him.

It appeared similar to how it had the time Ty had visited before, but not the same. It had been extended a bit, and now, there was a second door with the "Ty Belmoria Leveling Program" across the top in Middle Averian, and a badly done portrait of Ty, smiling down cornily at everyone.

Ty rolled his eyes. He was very glad the Guildmaster had followed his requests, but still a bit iffy on the specific implementation.

However, as he came in, a lot of people smiled at him, a few called good-natured greetings, and about half of them just gave the three-fingers sign that Averian elves used to signal approval.

Kadrath guided Ty through the same door as he had last time, and then into the same meeting room. But this time, the room came equipped with more than just the meeting table. Now, it had a metal safe, a huge luxury, and a couple of paintings of heroic adventurers. Also a young elf, male but a bit on the stringy side with silver hair, in a nice, white robe.

"Guy, get Ty here our best honeyed wine, and get me a mug of lager, please."

The elf nodded very precisely and left.

"Gygyll is the best," Kadrath said, smiling at the elf as he exited. Then he motioned to Ty to take a seat at the room's sole table, which Ty did.

Ty also giggled slightly at the weird wordplay of the name but waved off an explanation when Kadrath quirked an eyebrow.

"Right, so, what did you want to see me about?" Ty asked.

"Well, mostly about this. In the two months you've been gone, we've had one hundred and ninety-three dungeon runs, not counting your free morning ones. We charged differently based on a variety of factors, as well as taking a flat twenty percent of the loot acquired, and here is your ninety percent of the total acquired."

Kadrath walked over to the metal safe and twirled it before yanking it open and taking out a large bag and a sheath of papers.

He walked back over to Ty. "Here you go, Dungeon Lord. Your share is one hundred and three gold, seven silver, and fourteen copper coins."

He plunked the bag down in front of Ty and then held the sheath of papers. "Here's the proof of receipts and amounts paid. You can check with the people listed to confirm accuracy."

Ty barely paid attention, just staring at the bag. He was vaguely aware that his eyes were so wide, they kinda hurt, but he couldn't help it. *A hundred gold.* It was a staggering sum, not really *real* to Ty in any sense. *My house costs a couple of gold. A magic item of least quality costs two gold and change. What would I possibly* do *with all this money?*

Kadrath gave another bellowing laugh and slapped Ty on the back so hard, he hit the table's edge. "Ha ha. Never even considered you'd be this rich, I take it? Not knowing what you'll do with all your money is a problem worth having, though, you have to admit."

Ty rotated his shoulders, trying to remove the sting. *I swear to all the gods if he smacks me again, I'm going to hit him with lightning.*

"This is… crazy. That's so much money. I assume you made a ton of coin as well?"

Kadrath frowned. "Our share was just shy of eleven gold. At the cost of about twenty silver per adventurer, we've equipped over a hundred people. The trainers were cheaper, but not that much cheaper. We're actually down about fifteen gold."

Kadrath showed Ty another sheet, and Ty's quick eyeballing of the accounting, amounts paid to blacksmiths and such, convinced him it was true.

Kadrath smiled again. "Not to worry, though. Now that you've upped the dungeon, I'm sure we'll start making some real money for the guild. We did agree that I'd probably lose money for a bit. And there are a lot of Level Two and Three adventurers in town now. Since you've leveled the dungeon, I suspect it'll be totally fine."

Ty hesitated. The idea of what he was about to do was a bit absurd, but he would still have *so much* money... and he wanted this partnership to last.

He poured the gold onto the table carefully, holding his hand out to make sure none of it rolled away. Kadrath watched with a raised eyebrow as Ty counted out fifteen coins.

Ty pushed the coins across the table to Kadrath. "About the dungeon... the loot rating *barely* went up at all. It has a ton more monsters and magic effects, and max Level Four on the monsters. It also has a twenty-five percent higher gain for experience on Entropy users of all things. But that's not like to help much here, given that very few elves gain Entropy magic. I think the dungeon will level again quickly, so I can add to its loot rating. You can charge a lot more for higher-level people to enter, I assume. But still... I'm just going to increase your share for this portion to 'didn't lose money.' I'm not sure if you'll make money in the next couple of months regardless."

Kadrath squinted at the coins. "Are you sure, Dungeon Lord? I mean, I knew the deal when I made it, and I'm still pretty sure it'll pay off in spades given a bit more time."

Ty nodded. "You basically just handled everything I wanted perfectly and made me an obscene amount of money while I was away. Consider it a bonus to the Adventurers' Guild for work well done."

"You're a good man, Ty, a good man!" Kadrath boomed, a smile splitting his face.

He also slapped Ty on the back a third time. Ty took a step forward off his chair, his back screaming in agony, and lightning played across his fingers.

"You might even get a bonus next season as well, provided you never slap my back again," Ty ground out, and Kadrath laughed like it had been a joke.

Guy saved them from any further awkward conversation by opening the door, carrying drinks.

***

After a brief drinking session and meaningless pleasantries, Ty left the meeting room, leaving Kadrath, who stayed to deal with the new coin the guild had received—a not insubstantial sum.

Slightly fearful of being mugged, despite his own Level Seven status, Ty walked out into the common hall. There were adventurers all around, far more obvious adventurers than they'd been when Ty had been here a few months before. Most had decent gear, and some even had magical gear. Occasionally, one of the adventurers had abilities that manifested physically, like Belika's sentient shadow line that gave her shadow substance, or the rocklike skin of Earth mages that gave an alabaster sheen to the ones that picked that ability line.

And there were *a lot* more elves with adventuring abilities around as well. They fell pretty heavily into three categories: healers using Body or Wyld magic, archers using Air magic or simply enhanced stats, and swordsmen using energy attacks from magics like Fire and Ty's own Air Lightning. There were others, of course, but those three were very common.

A few dwarves were in the guild as well, most obviously guardians in heavy armor, and frequently with giant shields, as tall as they were. But there were people of nearly every race, from wood elves to rabbitkin to an orc, the sight of which curdled Ty's blood.

But he was looking for a goblin.

"Belika?" he called out, hoping she was around.

The little goblin, barely over four feet, appeared from behind a mass of other adventurers. She stared at him with her red eyes, twirling her knife on her fingers.

"You want?"

She had been learning Middle Averian extremely quickly but still spoke it in a broken cadence most of the time.

"Yes. May we go get your adventurer sheet now please?"

Fortunately, he had explained what that was to her some time ago, during their travels. It had taken over an hour.

"Yes, Ty."

Chapter Thirty-Four

ENTER BELIKA... AND ONE MORE, ITSY-BITSY, TINY THING

Ty walked to the counter where the gnome worked. There were numerous people clamoring for her attention, and Ty got in line, waiting his turn.

However, when the gnome saw him, she called out, "Ho, Dungeon Lord! You need me?"

"Yes, sorry. I can wait, though."

Most of the people ahead of him stepped aside. He saw that Ulivarae, her glowing-green bracelets a dead giveaway, and her ox-kin, whose name Ty couldn't remember, was there as well.

But one elf didn't move, a thin kid with metallic-black hair. Only the second person whom Ty had ever seen with that color of hair.

Ulivarae called out, "No need to wait, Dungeon Lord. I'll happily make room for you. Everyone here will, with all you've done for us."

Ty was touched. He moved to the near-front of the line.

The elf in front turned, sneering at the line. He glanced at Ty, and his lip turned up like he'd smelled bad fish. With a sniff, he said, "My apologies, Dungeon Lord, but I'll be finishing my business first. You can wait your turn."

Ty couldn't fault him for keeping his place in line, but everything about the black-haired elf's demeanor said they weren't going to get along.

There's at least four thousand people in this city, Ty. No need to get along with all of them.

Ulivarae rolled her eyes. "C'mon, Jacinth, give it a rest. You just look like a jackass."

Jacinth narrowed his eyes. "And you look like a lowborn piece of wolf droppings. We all have our problems, but I'll certainly not give in to the pressures of those I deem lesser."

"What did you say, elf?" the ox-kin said, walking up to tower over Jacinth.

Who didn't back down, staring up at the giant guardian.

Ulivarae joined the cluster at the front and put her hand on the ox-kin's forearm. "Let it go, Rathcorb. The little *ex*-noble twit isn't worth the price of brawling."

Right, Rathcorb, Ty thought. *That's his name.*

For a moment, Rathcorb stared downward, then, with a snort that blew a few strands of Jacinth's hair around, he stepped back. "Yeah, little man isn't worth the trouble."

Jacinth's sneer deepened to the point that Ty thought his upper lip might try to escape his face, but after a moment, he turned back to the counter.

Ulivarae came up and very lightly punched Ty in the shoulder. "Sorry about him, Dungeon Lord. You've got a great name here. Half the adventurers in the guild got their start on your dime, apparently, and I know you did decent by me. Heck, our healer, Blossom, got her start on your dime, so you've kinda done triply right by us."

Ty felt warm in his stomach and cheeks to have all this said about him. It beat his previous life as a nobody all to heck and gone.

Ulivarae continued. "But there're a few jackass noble hold-outs who are all butt-hurt they aren't just getting all their coin back. That Grayshore bastard is still sore that his family aren't counts anymore."

"'Butt-hurt'?" Ty asked, raising an eyebrow and chuckling at the absurd phrase.

"Something King Leo says, and it's caught on. Pretty funny though, right, Dungeon Lord?"

"Yeah."

Ty knew all about the old nobles. Deeply, from his relationship with Ivy and her family. And *of course* Jacinth was related to Count Grayshore, the only other elf Ty had ever seen with metallic-black hair. Ty was irritated with himself it hadn't immediately occurred to him, although he *was* very tired.

All Ty offered in reply to that, however, was, "Call me 'Ty.' And don't worry about Jacinth."

A moment later, Jacinth left, pushing his way out, and Ty was admitted to the front.

The gnome woman smiled down at him. "So, after all that discussion, what did you need me for?"

"I was hoping to get a reading on a potential adventuring partner."

She pursed her lips. "A reading? You mean the status sheet?"

"Yes." Ty fished a gold coin out, passing it to the lady.

She raised an eyebrow and called a runner over. "I'll have him get your change. In the meantime, shall we head to the back?"

Ty nodded and went around to the side door. Ivy and Belika, both of whom had remained entirely silent during the little tiff with Jacinth, followed behind. The gnome woman hopped off her stool, briefly disappearing, then pulled open the wooden, and now decorated, door. The three of them followed her into the back.

It was about the same as Ty remembered it being from a few months ago. A small room off the room the gnome had been working in. There was a large table with a strange device on it—a metal tube, about three feet long and about six inches in diameter on the interior. Medium-sized, gray crystals were all along the inside, and a flat, metal table stuck out to the side.

There was a chair right in front of the device, and a stool next to the chair.

The lady hopped up onto the stool and placed a piece of paper next to the black tube. "All right, whoever is getting their status sheet, please sit on the chair and put your arm in the device."

Belika awkwardly climbed onto what, to her, was a huge chair. She stood on it and put her arm into the device.

There was a brief sense of Mind magic, inquisitive, probing, and curious, and then words appeared on the page.

Having done this before, neither Ty nor Ivy tried to look at the page. Instead, they waited as the gnome handed it to Belika. She stared at it for a moment, then passed it to Ty with a muttered, "Here. You take."

Ty put it on the table and they all leaned over, even Belika, whom Ty was almost positive couldn't read.

Belika					
Level Three	Eclipse, Body				
Health	10	Stamina	12	Essence	12
Level Stats					
Strength	11	165 base pound-lifting capacity, +3% melee damage, +3% running speed.			
Agility	13	-15% enemy hit chance, +15% hit chance with all weapons, +6% running speed			
Dexterity	13	+15% base success for crafting and physical skill success rate, 30% chance to increase base weapon damage roll by one step			
Endurance	11	+1 base Stamina, +10% Stamina Recovery Rate, +10% base Health Recovery Rate			
Toughness	11	+1 base Health, +5% base Health, +5% base Stamina, +0 to resist poison, disease, and physical status effects			

Perception	11	+3% hit, +3% critical chance with ranged weapons. +5% chance to notice stealthed individuals. General small increase in discovery rate.
Connection	11	+10% Essence recovery (26/day)
Capacity	11	+1 base Essence, +5% base essence
Appearance	11	Average
Non-Level Stats		
Intelligence	11	+10% skill acquisition rate, may gain rare and difficult skills.
Magic	11	+4% Magic Effects. +1 Maximum affinity.
Charisma	11	+10% perceived importance
Luck	10	The Fates neither dislike nor care for you
Secondary Stats		
Eclipse Affinity	1	-10% essence cost to all Eclipse abilities, +10% effect for all Eclipse abilities or +1 to the difficulty to resist.
Birth Perks		
Race: Forest Goblin		-2 to all stats except Agility, Dexterity, and Luck. -20% Health. +6 on Toughness checks against poison and disease, +4 on Toughness checks against environmental damage. Senescence around age 40.
Magical Rank: Remarkable		May obtain Level 70 without ascension. Access to some rare and unusual abilities in her magics.
Goblin Paragon		+3 to all stats, Level and Non-Level, except Luck.
Blood of Shadows		Gain 1 Health for every armor provided by sentient shadow. This is modified by all other factors affecting Health. Considered a rank higher of magical quality for purposes of obtaining rare Eclipse abilities. +1 To actual and maximum Eclipse affinity. +1 Eclipse ability at Level Two.
Open-Minded		+30% skill learn rate
Acquired Perks		
Timid		-2 to resist all intimidation attempts

Skills	Level	Effect
Athletics	3	+9% to run speed, +3 to check to climb or avoid obstacles
Cooking	3	+15% quality to cooking
Dodge	6	+18% to dodge incoming attacks
Occult	2	You can sense magic that is not concealed, and that is connected to you, whose area of effect you are in, or that is within 2 feet of you. Your magic powers have 4% greater effect. You can vaguely sense the purpose of simple magic. +4% to accuracy with magic attacks.
Search	3	+9% to effective Perception when looking for things.
Small Blades	4	+16% Accuracy and +8% to damage and critical rate with small blades
Stealth	6	-30% enemy chance to detect
Survival	4	+12% hunting and foraging
Tinkering	2	Can increase average value of found items of average or lower quality by 20%
Traps	3	+15% to disarm or craft traps. +6% to notice them. This is considered a craft skill and modified accordingly.

Abilities	Effect
Eclipse	
Sentient Shadow, Rank I	+1 armor, +3% dodge as the user's shadow gains a semblance of physical form and can slightly push attacks away. Always in effect. Once this power is taken, no familiar may ever bond to user.
Shadowed Weapon, Rank I	Spend 1 essence. For 6 seconds, shadows cover all the user's weapons, adding length without weight and making the weapons more damaging. +1 base damage and +5% accuracy.

Body	
Brutal Reaction, Rank I	Spend 2 essence and 2 stamina. Gain brief speed, doubling physical movement rates, including attack, for 6 seconds. +1 attack, +1 damage, +10% accuracy, and deal 1 damage to yourself. If used for movement, +5' base jump distance in a single leap.

Ty stared at the sheet, surprised by the natural talent that Belika possessed.

Ty met Ivy's eyes over Belika's head.

She giggled, putting her hand in front of her mouth. "Dalryn's gonna be so pissed."

Ty raised an eyebrow at her.

She fingered her amulet to Cerivae Nerithin, goddess of families and kindness. "Because Belika should *definitely* join our party. She provides trap skills, detection, stealth, and melee damage dealing, all of which we lack, Ty. And she needs us as well. She has no home, no family to call her own. That's our fault."

Ty nodded soberly. *Dalryn probably is gonna pitch a fit. Getting 'butt-hurt' over nothing is practically his own unique, special magic.*

Although he's got nothing on his dad.

And Belika damn near hijacked me, not the other way around. Still, that's a solid status sheet. On anything other than a goblin, it would be an amazing status sheet, but those racial penalties—oof.

"You do have the talent, Belika, I'll not deny. Feel like joining the Dungeon Lord's Own formally?"

Belika frowned at him. "Use smaller words. Please."

"Do you want to join us for fighting?"

She smiled. "I'm already with you. You my new tribe. We one."

Didn't know that's what we were doing, but I guess it's formal now.

"We should get some more furniture on the way home," Ivy said.

Very formal now, Ty thought, amending his last opinion.

***

That evening, Ty returned to his house, the one he owned with his sister. He had an extra room's worth of furniture—all small girls' furniture, which made him laugh every time he stared at it—for Belika.

He'd had multiple porters to carry all the stuff, and Ivy and Belika were both with him, going to what was now all of their home—that of his entire adventuring party, as well as Forli and, of course, his sister.

Ty opened the door to the house first, entering the room.

He heard a slap of flesh on flesh, and his sister screamed, "I'll never spread for you!"

Ty's mind broke for half a second at the complete non-sequitur to everything that had been happening to him this day. *Is someone raping Val? Who's Level Six? At least?*

Ty raced toward the back of the house, where the scream had come from. His sister's room. Praying to Iluvin Eturia that he would be early enough, he slammed into the door and threw it open.

His sister yelled and threw herself off the side of her bed, where she had been kneeling, naked. He heard the thump of his sister hitting the floor, but his attention was almost entirely on the man at the foot of the bed. A man dressed in an orc mask, with a belt around his waist that had a whip and a knife in a sheath, but who was wearing nothing else.

Ty stared in horror at the orc mask as the man turned to him and whipped it off.

Dalryn stared back at Ty with clenched teeth and a brow so furrowed, it threatened to split his face in twain.

"By the fall, why are you here, you onion?!"

280

Chapter Thirty-Five

TIT FOR TAT AND THEN TIT AGAIN

Dalryn and Val sat on one side of the table in their kitchen, while Ivy sat on the other, obviously trying not to giggle and occasionally failing. It wasn't helping Ty's mood that Ivy obviously considered this whole thing silly.

Ty, whose mood was 'semi-enraged,' paced back and forth. Belika, ever quiet, watched from the shadows near the cooking fire.

At least Dalryn and Ty's sister were dressed now, although Val had a handprint bruise on her cheek.

"Val... how could you?"

"Have sex with someone?" she asked. "I mean, technically, I'm older than you. Also, a general. Of a mostly male army. This wasn't the first time."

"What? It was too!" Dalryn exclaimed.

Val smacked the back of his head. "Not my first time having sex, Dalryn. It was just my first time with you."

Dalryn frowned. "Oh."

Ty pinched the bridge of his nose. "No, no, no. How could you have sex with *Dalryn*, of all people?"

"Hey! Pot kettle, you tuber. You're rutting *my* sister!"

"I didn't try to kill you, Dalryn—it happened the other way around! Remember?"

Val quirked her lips to the side. "Wait, I thought you guys were totally over that and he saved your life a bunch."

Ty stopped his ranting. That was very true.

Instead, he pointed at her bruised face. "Fine. Then explain… that."

Val's pale-white cheeks went a deep red, making her freckles stand out even more, and she twirled her fingers in her bronze-colored hair. "Well, I'm a general. Who just came off a campaign in another dimension. People died. It was on me, all the time. Every moment, every day, for most of the time you were away. A crushing amount of responsibility."

Ty softened. He understood, and for him, it was just the responsibility of an adventuring party, far less. "I'm sorry. I still don't get it, though. Are you punishing yourself for letting people die?"

Val frowned at him. "This feels like a huge helping of 'not your business.'"

Ty sighed and nodded—she was right. "Fair."

Ivy reached over and touched Val, and Ty felt the magic of her healing. The bruise disappeared.

Everyone was quiet for a moment, but then Val continued despite Ty acknowledging it wasn't his concern. "I guess… I guess I just wanted one blissful hour where I had absolutely no power or control, and, at some level, enough verisimilitude to buy into the illusion. Where the outcome of the encounter, and how much the man enjoyed it, was all on him and not me. *Absolutely* no responsibility. But an encounter that I would still probably enjoy. Dalryn here feels just cocky and… unaware enough to not feel awkward doing what I wanted and physically talented enough that I had a decent chance of enjoying it, I guess."

Dalryn, expression smug, commented, "Damn right you would've had a decent chance of enjoying it."

Ivy, Val, and Ty all lost it at that, laughing long and hard, dispelling a lot of the more somber mood. Ivy kept giggling non-stop even when the others calmed down a bit.

It was Dalryn's turn to blush. "You know what I meant."

Val gave him a smile. "Cuwylla said you were pretty good."

Dalryn flushed even redder. "What? Just 'pretty good'? Is she telling other people?"

Val just shrugged, and Ivy laughed harder, slapping the table once.

Ty sighed. He already knew that he was gonna be stuck with Dalryn as a 'sister's boyfriend', and he supposed he might become his brother-in-law twice over now. But at the end of the day, Ty had mellowed on Dalryn. He was an ass, but a weirdly loyal and brave ass whose heart was in the right place, even if his brain was usually out to lunch. Ty could tolerate him.

But he was still getting something out of this. Dalryn had gotten seven levels, a dungeon lord buddy, and now Ty's sister out of Ty having sex with Ivy.

"I hired Belika," Ty said.

"What?!" Dalryn said, coming off the table. Val started giggling, and Ivy laughed even harder.

Ty grinned evilly. "It's trading time, Dalryn. You never get to complain about that, and I'll drop this."

"I think your sister would stop you from mentioning it all the time," Dalryn said, frowning.

Val twirled her finger in her hair again, looking comically wide-eyed innocent, and stared off to the side. "I don't know, Dalryn. I kinda think it's a good deal."

Ivy was now crying with laughter and leaning over the table.

Dalryn frowned harder and muttered, "All right, gods damn it. You win, ya tuber."

Then it was Dalryn's turn to smile evilly. He held his hand out to Val. "Well, shall we get back to it, then, my little kidnapped elf?"

Ivy finally gave it up completely, laughing so hard, she was breathing weird, and she slid off the chair onto the floor, gasping and crying with her non-stop hilarity, even banging the floor with one hand.

Val put her head down and stared up at Dalryn with upward-facing eyes. "Actually, hon, can we wait till tonight? I'm kinda out of the mood after talking about everything."

Dalryn stood, obviously frustrated with no outlet for it. He stared down at his sister.

"Stop that!"

Her howls were his only answer.

⁂

"This is all mine?" Belika asked again. "For reals? No trick?"

Ty motioned to the room. "Yes, it's all yours, Belika. For real."

"You are good chieftain." Belika stopped for a moment. "You are *a* good chieftain. Sorry."

"It's fine. Do you like the room?"

"I like it much," Belika said fervently. "I am thanking you."

"Just 'Thank you,'" Ty said.

"Thank you."

Ty felt a bit uncomfortable. "You know, this isn't all that much for me. I get a lot of money for just having a Dungeon Core, really. You don't need to thank me."

"Do. How many just let guard hurt me? How many take me with them?"

"I got something out of helping you," Ty said, rubbing the back of his head.

"You got help other person. Is not same. The same. Is not the same. You know what I am saying. You fool, Ty, but nice fool. I like you."

Ty was pretty sure if he had still been a high elf, he would have had red cheeks now. "Thanks."

"Hmm."

They sat looking at a room that, to Ty's eyes, still appeared to be a room that was made for a well-to-do family's youngest daughter. There was a lot of pink.

Belika turned to him. "Thank you for making me a part of your tribe."

"Sure."

Ty thought to the antics he had just been through. "It's a weird one."

"Yes."

There was a brief, awkward silence.

"So, why run away, Belika? At first, I thought it was because of the abuse, that you just wanted to be safe and unmolested. But you've gladly walked into danger, multiple times, and fought by my side recklessly in Zadrid's Hallow. Against things way above your level and horrible to boot. So why?"

She turned to stare him in the eye, her red ones to his green. "You nice, Ty. I like you. But you talk too much. All the time move lips. I want to sleep now."

Ty frowned, then laughed at himself. It had been that kind of day. "Very well. I'll head to bed myself."

***

Ty returned to his room after his brief and weirdly monosyllabic discussion with Belika, opening the door. He was dead tired. It had been a very long day, after a *very* long two months. He wanted to sleep for an entire century.

As he opened the door, he was presented with a sight to wake the dead, never mind Ty.

Ivy was kneeling on the bed, completely naked. She had obviously bathed and was utterly gorgeous. Her long, copper hair fell wildly around her and down to her waist, her otherwise entirely hairless body, lean with both leveling and all the exercise they had been doing, lewdly on display. Her indigo eyes stared into his with what Ty felt was somehow mirth, kindness, and deep love all.

But what drove him to the highest of heights of excitement was that *Forli* was there as well, right next to Ivy on the bed, holding her hand as he entered. He could feel the attraction to the green-needle-haired dryad, her pine-board body bared to him in all its curvy glory.

They both seemed smaller than he remembered, for some reason, but that made them even more feminine to him.

Ty walked in, closing the door behind him, feeling detached from what his body was doing as his whole focus was on the two women in front of him.

"It's time, Ty," Ivy said, smiling at him. "Time to do your duty to the dryad race, and to Forli. I'll be here with you, the whole time, enjoying as well and letting you know it's okay."

"Mu," was the only sound that came from Ty's mouth, a nothing noise as he felt himself sinking blissfully into his most base nature.

Ivy smiled and leaned back on the bed, pulling Forli down with her. "Come, my wonderful love. Come to us."

Ty had never been more willing to follow an instruction in his entire life.

Chapter Thirty-Six

PLANNING DOMESTIC BLISS

Ty woke from the slumber of the dead, glancing out his glass window. It was clearly high noon outside, a bright and sunny springtime day. His sheets had a slight smell of pine needles to them, a welcome and wonderful reminder of sleep well lost last night.

Ty felt *good*. Even though he had slept more than twelve hours, he felt loose and limber, not at all stiff or sore. But more so, he felt rejuvenated.

He gave himself a sniff. He'd already known, but the sniff reminded him that being a master dryad didn't remove his sweating, apparently. *He* didn't smell like pine needles.

Ty got up, used the pot, and then headed to the bathroom, where he had a 'shower,' a new invention that King Leo had introduced to the world. The cold water raining down on him washed away his smell, and also much of his lassitude—by the end, he felt invigorated and ready to work.

He left the bathroom in his house robe, a slightly ratty blue robe with the Belmoria family symbol—a cloud on blue—on the back. It only went down to his shins, and he wondered if it had shrunk while he'd been away. His nose told him that someone was cooking, and he followed it to reach the kitchen.

Everyone Ty had expected was already gathered around the table: Ivy, Val, Dalryn, and Belika, with Forli handing out plates of sautéed onions and spiced potatoes. Everyone already had earthenware cups of what, to judge by the bottle, was a very lightly alcoholic apple cider. Val was leaning into Dalryn, so Ty assumed he wasn't the only one who had had a great evening.

"Hey!" Ivy said, glancing over and smiling up at him, her movements languid.

Ty figured there was no point in trying to hide his new status, so he walked over to Forli, took her in his arms, and kissed her.

She stiffened slightly for a moment, and when she kissed back, there wasn't any real enthusiasm. In general, she didn't seem at all like the Forli he knew from last night—a veritable animal in bed that couldn't get enough of him. She seemed, in fact, like the Forli he had once known—the dryad uninterested in sex.

"Morning, Ty," she said cheerfully. "Thanks again for last night."

"Yeah, just brag about it." Dalryn huffed. "No need to advertise. Ivy already explained everything—not that this isn't the fourth or fifth time I've been dragged into a conversation about my sister's rutting life I didn't want to be involved in."

Ty ignored Dalryn—somedays, his irritations felt like background noises. And Dalryn just grabbed his cup and started downing the light cider anyway. Ty was pretty sure he didn't want a response.

Forli's obviously 'happy' that we did stuff and is being friendly... So why does she seem... off?

Something of his confusion must have shown on his face, because Forli smiled up at him. "I, um, don't really feel the sexual attraction I did before. I think it's because of my new temporary perk."

"New perk?" Ty asked.

"It's called 'germinating,'" Forli said.

Ty blinked, completely floored, but Dalryn coughed and sprayed cider all across Val, who held her hands up too late.

Val glared at him. "By the fall, Dalryn, you're lucky you were, in fact, a 'decent chance of enjoyment' last night."

"*Don't* call it that."

"Oh, hon… that's what I'm going to say about your prowess as long as we're together."

Ty ignored their byplay entirely. "You're… germinating? Does that mean… with child?"

Germinating is when a seed turns into a plant—if she's generating a seed, why that term?

Forli pursed her lips. "The perk says that I'm creating a dryad seed now. So, um, kinda? She won't turn into a dryad until she gets her third parent—a tree—so… kinda, yeah?"

Then she smiled. "But I think that's why I don't feel an attraction to you right now. I mean sexually. I still feel really close to you, Ty, very close. You're my favorite person. And I know men are weird and always want to touch women, and so you can—"

"No!" Dalryn said. "It's already crazy, like absolutely, *cataclysm come again* crazy, how much I hear about Ty's sex life. No more. Talk about it later."

Dalryn mopped up his cider and then poured himself more. "Sheesh."

Ty laughed at him, but it was a perfunctory sound, laughter because he knew, at some level, it was expected of him. Most of his mind was on the concept of "I'm going to be a father."

Although not really. Dryads were born fully grown, so long as their trees were mature. He would never 'raise' a dryad in any real way. Just provide a part of the magical material that made up the dryad. Still, though… It was weirdly wonderful.

He turned to Ivy, and she was smiling up at him, her eyes alight. She fingered her amulet to Cerivae Nerithin, goddess of family and kindness.

Ty was excited for Forli and his new 'daughter,' but right now, what he really wanted was to have a true child, one he raised from infancy. More so, he wanted Ivy to be the one who had his child. Ivy was what he wanted—kind, caring, gorgeous, joyful, soft, and feminine. Someone with a beautiful soul whom he could protect and provide for.

Ivy must have sensed what he was thinking because her smile widened even further, and she blushed ever-so-slightly. She stood from the chair and gathered both Ty and Forli into her embrace, kissing Ty deeply.

Dalryn made gagging sounds.

Ty looked over at him, just in time to catch Val smacking him in the back of the head again.

As Ty cuddled Ivy and Forli and watched Dalryn rubbing the back of his head and glaring at Val, all he could think was—*life is good.*

But after a moment, his usual intellectual, slightly detached attitude reasserted itself. "I think that I want to move."

Val looked shocked, her eyes widening. "You don't want to live together anymore? I mean, I thought it was working out fairly well, and I'm not really in the mood to establish my own household yet."

"Not what I meant Val, sorry. I was thinking that the six of us—you, Dalryn, gods help us, me, Ivy, Forli, and Belika should all move. It's a big house, but I would want to get a larger one, on a far larger plot of land. I want to be able to plant a ton of magical trees, and I want to have a huge amount of land to build on, gardens, bonus houses... things like that."

"Bonus houses, huh?" Val asked, smiling at him.

"You know what I mean."

"Why all this?" Val asked.

Ty disentangled himself from his woman—a feat that required a bit of willpower—and took a seat at the table. Everyone else joined him as well.

"Ever since I became a master dryad, I've had this urge to own a huge tract of land. But more than that, I think we'll need it. If I'm going to be 'propagating the dryad species,' then we'll need a lot of trees—and room for the dryads in houses."

"Never say 'propagating' again," Dalryn contributed.

"And, well, I'd like an actual family someday. And we do pick up a lot of guests. Things like that. But it needs to be close enough that we can make it to the dungeon easily and regularly. So we should move fast—we're about a mile from the dungeon right now. Five miles is pretty much the absolute limit, and that makes for a long trek every day. Maybe a house in the city and back to the main lands a couple of days a month. Something. But that land I want, the land just outside the ruins, will be bought fast."

"So grab while the grabbing is good," Val mused. She smacked her fist into the palm of her hand. "I like it!" Then she gave a smug smile to Ty. "Also, we'll need an aerie."

"What?"

"I bonded to my second—and third—animal companion, a pair of sister sun eagles. I can actually fly on them now, and it'll make the trek to town ten minutes once Aster and Freya are regularly available."

Ty shoved a potato into his mouth, chewed, and swallowed. "Well, let's head into town and see Dad about some land grants. I think he'll probably pass it up to King Leo since my move would be an expansion into more dangerous territory. But if anyone in Star Port can form the kind of strongpoint needed to base an expansion around, it's probably our adventuring group. I think they'll say *yes*. Additionally, it's time to up our level in another way. We need to pick up magical items, so I want to visit the Forges of Stonehaven and perhaps peruse any new magic item shops that have appeared. We need to gear out Belika, and we need to gear up the rest of us."

Ivy nodded seriously. "I think that would be good."

Forli sighed. "You're still okay if I don't adventure?"

Ty nodded. "Yes. But would you be willing to take over the domestic duties? Coordinate the move, get lists of what we'll need, and prepare to hire the people we'll need as well? I want a home that will be impressive to everyone."

Val rolled her eyes. "You and your need to be seen to be as wealthy and important."

Ty frowned, although he felt so good today that his heart wasn't really in it. "Hey, you know how we grew up. It's not unreasonable that I *don't* want people looking down on us like they used to."

"I get it. I just feel like you could give it a rest from time to time—but I'll not deny it seems to be driving you to do great things for me, so what do I care?" Val smiled at him, saccharine sweet.

Ty rolled his eyes and chuckled a little. "Well, for that eminently selfish yet practical approach, I thank you."

"No prob, little brother."

Ivy drummed her fingers on the table. "Actually, I have sort of good news, bad news, related to the move. My familiars have leveled a couple of times, and both are Level Six now. But they're only hybrid combatants—they're also builders. Shreve is a building builder and architect, and Welwyn, the other one I bonded to, is a gardener and garden-builder. So, we'll not need architects—just materials."

"Are they good?"

"Level Six familiar good—so probably equivalent to a Level Three focused elf with the same skills. We aren't going to find a lot better."

Ty nodded. "Okay, Forli, take that into account. The rest of us haven't changed our missions. We need to go shopping for combat items, since tomorrow, we'll run my new Level Four dungeon for the first time."

"Mind if I join you?" Val asked.

Ty smiled. "Not at all. Given we're all, except Belika, Level Seven, it should be an easy run."

"*Should be* and *are* sometimes don't get close where you're concerned, little brother."

Chapter Thirty-Seven

A NEW LOOK

Ty, with Dalryn, Ivy, and Belika near him, stared at the Forges of Stonehaven. Technically, Ty had seen it when he had first come back, as the store was on one side of the Grand Plaza, and his dungeon entrance was on another. But Ty hadn't really *looked* at it.

Since he had first been here, it had grown considerably. It had clearly absorbed the building nearby, and Ty could see smoke pouring from multiple chimneys in the sides.

Ty considered it a good sign that they'd been so successful in such a short time. The sound of metal on metal filled the air as he approached, and the front door had a 'Come in—we can't hear you' sign, with the lettering scorched into a large piece of wood. It felt like a nice, aesthetic touch for a forge to Ty.

He stepped in, and the sound intensified immensely. The front area was a mere bubble out from the forges. At the forges, numerous dwarves and humans, and a lone elf, worked tirelessly. Ty could see markings in the floor that clearly showed a plan to add a wall, likely to create a room where the terrible banging was at least a bit muted.

Belika put her hands over her ears, and Ivy faked turning and walking out for a moment before curving back, her own hands over her ears. Ty could sympathize. Successful the forge might well have been, but acoustically pleasing it certainly was not.

One dwarf set down some etching tools and the sword he was working on and ambled over. The dwarf had a bushy, black beard and close-cropped black hair, with intelligent brown eyes. It took a moment, but Ty recognized Andul, the king's personal bodyguard, fixer, and adventuring companion.

"Wha' can I do fer ya, Minister-at-Large Belmoria?" he said, holding his hand out in the dwarven clasp.

Ty yelled to Andul. "It's just 'Ty,' Andul, you knew me back when. Mind if we step outside to talk, though?"

"Sure," Andul said, and they all moved, leaving the banging behind.

Andul continued. "Ya saved my liege that one time, back when, even if ya were kinda a pansy the rest of tha time. So, ya get my respect. But I ken call ya 'Ty' if that's yer wish. But back to my question: What can I get'ya?"

"I need gear—a lot of it magical."

Andul's eyes widened and he smiled at that. Ty knew it was the smile of a creator. Andul played the good, loyal soldier dwarf, and meant it, but his true passion was in the making of magical items.

Although he had a bit of an overenthusiastic bent sometimes. Ty rolled his eyes. "Just the simple stuff, please. None of your crazy inventions, Andul. I need magical knives for Belika here, good, solid armor for Ivy now that she has a bit more stats in Strength, and Dalryn needs—everything. Magical plate armor, a magical sword, and a magical great shield all."

"Least tier?" Andul asked.

Ty hesitated. Least-Tier magical items were, by far, the most common. They cost about two and a half gold each. Lesser Tier, which required the person creating them to be Level Six, have two feats, and have a great deal of schooling besides, tended to cost about six gold each.

People could have one magic item, and one additional magic item per magic they could wield. So Ty, who had three magics, could use four. Dalryn, Belika, and Ivy all had two magics and could use three items.

So, thirteen items. At six gold each, that was seventy-eight gold—and he only had eighty-eight to his name.

He would have done it if he didn't also want the house and lands, but he would need a lot of money for that as well.

"One Lesser per person, and the rest Least. They can figure the specifics out."

Andul rubbed his hands together. The cost to make a magical item was about two gold, twenty silver, so about thirty silver per item profit. He would make roughly four *gold* profit today, a huge sum even for a high-level individual like Andul. Enough to pay for most of the workers here for the entire year.

Andul quickly got down to business, however. "I've got tha ability to make Lesser items in Metal magic, Earth magic, and Fire magic. I can probably get tha king's woman to make them in Mind and Wyld. For everything else, however, it's Least at the most. So keep that in mind."

"I will."

Andul stroked his black beard, staring off into nothing. "An' doan' forget it takes time, as well. Probably need the day for all the Least ones, and depending on what you're ordering, how much overlap in the magic choices, I'll probably need a couple of days for the lesser items."

"Sure. Now, let's figure out what everyone needs to be the best they can be."

***

The next morning, Ty stared at his team in the watery light of the Grand Plaza. Around them, merchants were setting up stalls or trying to attract their first customers, and sailors walked around, yawning. Star Port wasn't at the level where the main market would be busy all the time, but it was still a major trade port, and the market got up early.

Ty also saw *blue* elves walking around, a kind he had never seen before, most dressed in only strips of fur over their chests and privates. He knew that his liege had opened a portal with Ygg'drasil to another dimension, one of ice, tundra, and a few boreal forests. One populated by these elves—the 'ice flower' elves who were running about now. His sister, Val, had just run a military campaign on the other side, and Ty had already learned a decent amount. Despite that, Ty hadn't seen one of the ice flower elves until today.

Although he had access to his sister's knowledge, Ty would have to make a point of talking to some of them soon—he knew that most dimensions had more magic inherent to them than his own dimension of Toth, and he desperately wanted to get more dungeon cores, for a lot of reasons—but mostly because his own 'branching paths' pick nearly required it to be very useful. Any his sister learned about would likely be royal knowledge. Ty needed something else to work with.

Ty let that go for a moment and focused in on his own team. Despite Andul's warnings, the Dungeon Lord's Own had managed to get everything they had ordered ready to go in a single day, although Ty had needed to go to a different shop for a few items for himself.

Ty himself had a new robe, green and brown now. On the back was a sewn pattern of two dryads framing a large tree, which Ty felt was 'him' more than his old Belmoria house robes. The new robes had been enchanted with two pink Soul crystals and now added two to his Capacity and Connectivity stats both. He needed the increase to his essence and essence recovery since he relied almost entirely on magic.

The best part, however, was that the robe was quite damage resistant and wouldn't decay naturally. Ty was tired of losing all his nice robes while adventuring.

His staff was still an electrical staff, to shock opponents in an emergency, but Ty had added two more items to his ensemble. An amulet, fashioned to look like an amulet of Iluvin Eturia but enchanted with Soul magic added to his barrier. When he used it, he would get an extra two protection so long as he had the item. On his left wrist, he wore a bracelet of smooth, beautifully grained pine wood with an Earth crystal—which looked like a topaz—embedded in it. That one added two points to his Toughness.

Ivy had gotten a breastplate, helm, gorget, and metal-pleated skirt over leather breeches. She also had leather-with-metal-insert bracers. The metal armor had a crystal of gold embedded in the front, making it more damage resistant. Heavy armor interfered with a great deal of magic, but neither healing nor familiars were affected, for reasons only scholars far deeper enmeshed in the lore of magic than Ty was knew. To that, she added a shield of her own, similarly reinforced, and one of her bracers had an Earth crystal in it that added to her Health. Overall, her protection and survivability had gone *way* up. Something Ty was deeply glad for.

Although it looked absurd on her relatively small frame, frankly. Magic was odd—no way someone who appeared as lithe as her could move in her armor without magical enhancements.

Beside her were her two familiars, Shreve and Welwyn. They were both spiders, now the size of a person. But each had eight comically oversized human-appearing eyes and a human mouth, and they had human hands where their legs ended. Although they did have the fangs of spiders coming from their mouths. Each was a Level Six creature, the result of Ivy's powers, but each was also hybrid, half-combat and half-builder. Still, they added some power to her build overall. Although not as much as they could have.

Belika was dressed in light leather armor, chest, pleated skirt, breeches, and a leather cap with a leather gorget to protect her neck. But her shadow still played across her. She carried a pair of knives, both with a gold crystal in the hilt. Each was a 'metalline' weapon—a metal magic power that made them lighter, harder, and sharper. They ignored a bit of armor, did a touch more damage, and had a slightly higher critical rating. Perfect for a rogue hit-and-fade build. Her last item was also Metal, but it wasn't a weapon. It was a trap kit that enhanced how effectively she removed traps. Ty didn't really plan on building his dungeon into a 'trap' dungeon, but he was sure that at some point, it would get some trap score at least, so that was still ideal.

But of all of them, Dalryn took the cake. He had been taking an absolutely *absurd* amount of physical-stat-enhancing abilities in addition to his level-gained stats. Ty knew that he was now in the supernatural range for both Strength and Toughness, although just barely. He was able to wear and walk around in plate mail, the same way Kadrath the Guildmaster did.

His stats had also increased his size, and Dalryn very much appeared more human than elven now, being over six feet tall and muscled. With the plate armor, it was more six-and-a-half, and he added a bastard sword and a tower shield to his ensemble. His armor was reinforced by the magic of a gold and a topaz crystal, both Earth and Metal magic, a dual-magic item that had cost another ten gold.

But now, Dalryn had armor that provided six points of protection from physical damage, and his own rocklike skin, rank II, ability provided another three. Nine armor was at a level such that if Dalryn sat still and let a normal human smack him with a warhammer, the blow would bounce off.

Although he had *zero* resistance to magical damage. But for the dungeon they were entering, Ty was pretty sure Dalryn would be nearly invulnerable. 'Beast' monsters used mostly physical damage.

Ty only had a one armor score, but Belika had three and Ivy four, and Belika's would go up to five as soon as she hit Level Five and took the next level of the sentient shadow ability. And Ty was sitting on a huge pile of Health to compensate.

Their team had *a lot* of survivability now, all of them.

Dalryn frowned at him. "You done checking me out, ya tuber, or are you going to buy me dinner?"

"Dinner."

Ivy giggled, putting her hand in front of her mouth.

Dalryn narrowed his eyes. "You're not as funny as you think you are."

Ty rolled his eyes. "We're waiting for Val anyway. Why do you care if I'm checking out the gear that *I* bought everyone? Plus, I always buy everyone's dinner."

Dalryn smirked. "You're being creepy."

Any further discussion was brought to a halt when a deafening screech filled the air. Ty stared upward as an eagle, glowing with a soft but warm light, forty feet from wingtip to wingtip, descended to the ground, landing with a massive blast of air in the plaza next to them.

Belika was blown off her feet, hitting the ground and trying to roll back to standing, only to need three more rotations to pull it off. Ty, Ivy in her armor, and Dalryn stayed standing. Merchants yelled and sailors shook fists as stalls blew over and people were knocked from their feet around Ty's adventuring team.

With another, smaller blast of air, Val leapt down from the eagle's back and alighted in the center of the ground. She glanced around a bit sheepishly and waved. When the people saw it was their beloved general, they stopped complaining and went about their business.

Val turned to the giant bird and put her hand on it. "This is Aster, my first sun eagle. Amazing, isn't she?"

Ty nodded. "Very. Although we definitely need a roost here in town, as the center of the plaza isn't really an ideal landing spot."

Ty turned and stared at his dungeon entrance. The large, marble gazebo had an outer walkway with stairs to get to it, with an ornate, marble lattice around the outside as a fence. Numerous large pillars held the top up. One was clearly a carving of Saelenia in her current, fertility-goddess form, although only Ty knew that. The other was the vaguest shape of a wolf.

Inside the gazebo wasn't a floor, just a huge garden. Numerous plants, including a tiny few that now looked black and threatening, abounded. In the center of all of it was a stairway leading down into a natural-looking tunnel that was anything but—it was the entrance to the dungeon.

Ty motioned to it. "Shall we?"

Chapter Thirty-Eight

THIS IS MORE LIKE IT

Ty took the entrance down, the natural-seeming tunnel in offset by the stone stairs carved in it. He had just walked this way yesterday as dungeon lord, but this was the first time he had entered the dungeon proper in over two months, and the first time he had been in since he had made alterations.

Ty knew he was being a tiny bit foolish, but he hadn't checked with Kadrath to see to the changes. He knew the dungeon's monsters would be a maximum of Level Four and beast types, so he decided to just experience it clean, since he and his party—without Val—had already beaten a Level Six collection of monsters with resistances to his party's abilities. Monsters that used Entropy magic.

This ought to be a cakewalk. Hopefully.

Ty walked out into the cavern in the bottom. He was still half-expecting what he had seen before: a mostly bare cavern with a few bioluminescent mushrooms to light the place up.

Instead, he was confronted with a veritable riot of a forest. The ceiling was shrouded almost entirely, covered by a forest canopy. The forest appeared old, primeval. Great oaks, draped in hanging, flowering vines and moss, were the predominate tree. There was a small creek that wandered through with cattails inside, its banks covered in sticker-filled wild berry bushes. The hoots of owls filled the place. The floor had enough bioluminescent mushrooms to see by, but the shadows were extremely unusual and moved slightly as numerous glowing moths flitted through the trees.

"Wow," Ivy said, staring around. "Remember when I said your dungeon was underwhelming? And you said it would get better?"

Ty nodded. "Yeah."

Ivy sighed wistfully. "It really did—I mean, I know we have to fight through this, but this would be a great place to come and make love."

Dalryn slapped his forehead. "Sis, please, I'm begging you—stop that."

Ivy glanced over at Dalryn. "Wow, you're not threatening me or berating me. You must really be tired of it."

Dalryn pulled out his huge bastard sword from its sheath on his back, its hilt providing light from the tiny, glowing gold gem set in it. "Can we just go murder whatever beasts are here, please?"

Ty motioned to the forest, where a path was clearly visible beside the tiny creek. "Lead on, guardian."

Dalryn did so, moving out onto the path, sword out and shield ready. Belika kept near his heels, and Ty and Ivy followed shortly after. Val came next, and the two spiders, Shreve and Welwyn, brought up the rear.

A high-pitched yipping-giggling sound came from the trees—the clear sound of fox calls. Almost immediately, three of them raced down the path toward the adventuring party. Each fox appeared normal except for the far larger teeth and claws they had.

None of them made it. Dalryn slashed one, cutting it in half. Belika trisected another with double slashes from her magically sharp knives. And the last leapt through the air, only to be hit with an arrow that blew clear through it, sending it spinning through the air backward.

Ty dismissed the '3 experience' notification, surprised he had even gotten credit for the fight.

"I would need about two hundred more fights like that to level," Dalryn said.

Val chuckled. "Well, they would take about as much effort as a training session in the yard, so that seems fair. You would whine *about* free wine, Dalryn. Not your most manly trait."

"I'm gonna make you pay for that tonight," Dalryn said.

"Pot, kettle, brother?" Ivy asked.

Before he could respond, the three foxes dissolved into light. One left behind a couple of nice oak planks.

Ivy laughed. "Ah, there's that treasure I remembered and loved. I know you're working on some super-secret, amazing dungeon build, Ty, but you gotta get that loot rating up."

He grimaced. Ivy was, of course, completely correct. "Well, Sae... I mean, the Crone said she's—well, the dungeon is— almost Level Five. I'll try to fix the loot score then. Although I would want higher-level monsters as well, so it's a bit of a hard call. How do dungeons without secret paths even stay viable with their room choices?"

No one answered, probably assuming it was a rhetorical question. They moved forward on the path. It really was gorgeous—a magically lit nighttime forest, beautiful and mysterious. After a bit, however, Ty started to feel evil in the air, magic with malicious intent.

He called out to his group. "Beware, everyone. I can feel Entropy magic. The dungeon has a decent number of magical effects, and on this floor, they can be Entropy-based. Watch for undead, chaotic wounds that can't be healed normally, as well as pollution effects that stat drain in particular."

"But it'll still be basically Level One?" Dalryn asked.

"I mean... it should be."

"I'm sure we'll be fine," Dalryn said, his voice such that Ty could easily imagine the eyeroll.

Ty didn't say anything else, even though he wanted to castigate his guardian. But either Dalryn would be fine, in which case it wouldn't do any good to castigate, or Ty could bring it up after he got wounded.

The group walked into a small grove. Most of it was as beautiful as the rest of the forest that the dungeon had created, but in the center there was a mushroom from which spores leaked into the air, a slight, black haze throughout the glade.

Two paths led off into the underbrush.

"Anyone have anti-gas effects?" Ty asked.

"Forli did," Ivy said.

"Lovely," Ty muttered. "Let's just try going through the underbrush instead of the glade."

The group moved from the path, pushing into the brambles and bushes around the edge. It quickly became apparent that after a few feet of vegetation, it was immobile and invulnerable, no different than the dungeon cavern walls from before.

They had to pass through the glade.

"All right, everyone, run through," Ty said.

The group did, covering their mouths. As Ty entered, he got a notification.

> Ty makes his resistance check (Toughness +4) against entropic pollution. No further effects.

Ty hadn't said where to go, but Dalryn curved to the right path and ran down it. A few feet past the glade, he stopped, and everyone else did as well.

"See? No problem at all. A plus four check is easy—I literally couldn't fail with my Toughness score."

Toughness added one to the check for each two points above ten, and a plus ten or higher total modifier made one immune. Dalryn had basically just bragged that he had a twenty-two or higher Toughness stat.

Ty glanced around. "Everyone else fine?"

Belika shook her head. "I lost one Toughness. It won't come back for one hour or until I get healing but not healing."

"Curing?" Ivy asked, referring to the Body effect that could cure ailments depending on its level. Wyld mages got regenerate and Body mages heal, both of which could restore Health, but only Body mages could cure ailments and stat drain.

Belika nodded. "That."

Ty glanced over at Dalryn, one eyebrow raised.

"Stop whining," he muttered, to Val's laugh.

"I lost a stat as well," Welwyn, the moss-covered spider of Ivy's pair, said. "Also, can I harvest that mushroom?"

Dalryn stared back at her. "I forgot you guys were even here. You stop whining as well. Also, no, you can't get the mushroom that is actively spewing stat loss effects."

All eight of Welwyn's eyes narrowed in anger, almost comically.

Before anything crazy could happen, Ty motioned the group forward. "C'mon, let's keep going. Despite that, it's been pretty easy so far. And we need to make Belika a level."

***

Almost a full hour later, they had toured most of the beautiful forest. Ty's team had fought twelve foxes of Levels One and Two, as well as seven oversized and over-muscled Level Three wolves. They had also run across a glade filled with vines that grabbed and bound adventurers to make them easier for the foxes to fight, and another grove that let the wolves run through the air. Still—he had to admit he was loving his primeval forest level. It felt like a real dungeon to him, somehow, unlike what he had possessed before. And at their level, it was scary, but kind of fun scary, not *really* scary.

Also, Belika had made Level Four.

But somehow, they hadn't run into either sub-boss yet. Until, probably, now.

Ty stared at the large glade in front of them. In the center was a two-headed wolf, and around it were two-headed pups. Orthrus, Ty was pretty sure they were called.

They had clearly found the 'nest' room. Ty thought it much… nicer… than the rat birthing room it had been before. Wolves were just more amazing than rats, end of discussion.

"So, these are likely Level Three or Four?" Dalryn asked.

Ty nodded almost unconsciously, even though Dalryn was in front of him and looking away. "Very likely, given where we found them. The dungeon's floors usually have the stronger monsters farther from the entrance. No monster can be higher than Level Four, anyway."

"Let's do this then." With his pronouncement, Dalryn moved into the room, covered head to toe in armor, his shield out in front.

Immediately, the orthrus got to its feet, both heads howling. Each of the pups was surrounded by a slight, green energy. *Wyld has some minor pack- or group-related buffs. It must have one of those.*

The babies began frothing at the mouth, barking wildly, and charged.

Or the rage buffs. Rage buffs were dangerous, giving huge stat bonuses but forcing things to fight recklessly and foolishly.

But for a disposable dungeon mob, it seemed perfect.

Dalryn swept the first one aside with his shield, *hurling* the puppy into the undergrowth on the side of the glade, then stabbed another. But for once, his near-instinctual guardian abilities failed him, as the giant one hit him just after, bearing him to the ground and snapping and biting at him.

Ty electrocuted a pup with a blast of lightning, and Belika stabbed another to death.

Dalryn's armor *didn't* fail him as the giant, two-headed wolf bit and clawed at him. A moment later, an arrow buried itself fletching-deep into the side of the wolf, and Belika ran around and cut the back legs off the wolf.

When the fourth puppy crawled from the undergrowth, Ty hit it with lightning.

"Get this fat onion off me!" Dalryn yelled, abandoning his sword to start punching the giant dog in its left head. He was strong enough that even while prone, he managed to do a bit of damage, splitting the wolf's lip and busting a tooth, but it was Val's second arrow burying itself in the right throat that did real damage.

The orthrus howled with its left head, then tried to bite at the arrow, but it wasn't fighting Dalryn anymore. Belika cut it a bit more, and the two spiders rushed it, biting its side as well. Finally, it collapsed.

Dalryn pushed it off with a huge shout and shove, then climbed to his feet, his plate armor covered nearly head-to-toe in orthrus blood.

"I find your blood-and-steel ensemble to be *so* last season," Ty said, to the general titter of the group.

"Laugh it up, Tree Boy. I find your everything to be so last year."

Ty mimed taking a sword blow. "Cut to the quick. Such stinging insults. Such *wit*."

Ivy lightly ran her hand over Ty's forearm. "C'mon, you're getting a bit mean."

Before anyone else could respond, the orthrus dissolved, leaving behind two very finely stitched leather bracers and twenty well-made wooden arrows with stone tips.

Dalryn stared at it. "That was treasure for a Level Four sub-boss, Ty. That's pathetic. I mean, sure, you could get a few silver for this, but even a Level One peasant with no magic at all could make this in two weeks without risking death. You've *got* to up the treasure rating."

"The rest of the dungeon is pretty amazing," Val said.

"People come here for levels and treasure," Dalryn said. "Ty's dungeon only has half of it."

"Yeah, I've heard it," Ty muttered. "C'mon, let's go find the last sub-boss."

Chapter Thirty-Nine

A GREAT SPOT TO RAISE A FAMILY

"I can't believe the dungeon had an undead bear," Dalryn said again as they climbed out of the pit. "Good thing that was only Level Four—it was doing chaotic wound damage, by the fall. That would have been absolutely terrible to deal with on level. Guardian needs his sweet, *sweet* heals."

Ty nodded. "Yeah. The magical arms and armor we have, as well as our levels, makes this pretty much child's play. On the other side, as you pointed out, the experience is bad. We'll have to run it every single day for a month in order for most of us to make a level. That cuts into my income about ten gold, based on the last two months' receipts. Probably more now that the dungeon is higher level and can do fewer runs a day."

Val laughed from behind him. "You have *way* more than enough money, Ty."

He shook his head. "No. I have way too *much* money for one person. But if I want to start building a company, or a town, or something of that scale, I have vastly too little money."

"Building a town?" Ivy asked.

Ty nodded. "Yeah. I mean, the old Averian Kingdom had a whole ton of super prosperous orchard villages that traded through Star Port—well, it was Calasti then, but you know what I mean. Our town here. The Calasti Tree Node adds to tree growth and productivity, as the name suggests. The orchards made a lot of money, like they do in Green Apple Grove. And all the magically hardened marble roads are still there, needing only a little repair. It would be easy to build secondary towns."

"But still, a town?" Ivy asked.

"It's all part of the 'get it while it's cheap' plan, just a larger extension of it. I thought that in addition to our tract of land, we could start some serious fruit businesses."

"Dungeon lord isn't enough, huh?" Val asked.

Ty shrugged, frowning a bit. "Why let anything be 'enough'? Why not build everything we can and make all the things we can? It's better for everyone, and we'll get respect for doing it as well. Something we've been sorely lacking."

Dalryn pointed at Ty. "Well, I repeat myself, you onion, but hurry up and add to the loot rate and quality for your dungeon so that I can get in on this. I mean, I'm almost Level Eight. I could be earning way more doing other things than adventuring with you right now."

Ty nodded. "Yeah, yeah, you've been making your position *really* clear. Let me go see about the land tracts, and we can work on building our new home for a couple of days while the dungeon hopefully makes Level Five."

Val nodded. "I think you would best be served if I came with you. I'm the general, and I'm in pretty good light with King Stardew at the moment, thanks to the successful campaign to save the ice flower elves in the other dimension. If I support your plan, even as your sister, I think the king will give it a bit more of an ear."

"I mean, technically, we've adventured together," Ty said. "Me and the king, I mean. You don't think he'll listen to just me?"

"Maybe," Val said. "Want to risk it, or do you want your argument to be as high level as possible?"

"You make a good point," Ty said, frowning. "Fine. Ivy, Dalryn, please help Forli with the purchases and organization for a move. It'll probably only be a two-hour move by caravan, but we'll likely need *a lot* of caravans to make the move in one go."

"What I do?" Belika asked, then she furrowed her brow. "What *should* I do?"

Ty stopped. She was going to live with them and he had been barely paying attention to her. "Well—how about you help them start packing, and then, once I have a land tract, you can explore it for me?"

She held a knife out. "I will not fail you."

Ty nodded his head to Val, who followed him. Ty left the Grand Plaza, with its statue of the first Averian king, the Adventurers' Guild, his dungeon entrance, the Forges of Stonehaven, and numerous other peoples and businesses. He headed west. He walked down the main road half a mile to the docks, chatting with Val about all the people back in their home city of Steelport that would be impressed to see them now. Then he took the east bridge, traveling west of the mouth of the Blue River where it emptied into the Inner Sea, until he reached Elgin Isle. From there, he walked to the old admiralty building, which was still—despite numerous plans for the government to move into the old palace next to the heart of the node and Ygg'drasil—the seat of the government of the new Kingdom of Averia.

He went into the offices of the seneschal, his father, George Orsini.

It was a modest affair for the seneschal of a kingdom that had about six thousand people directly under its control, and another four thousand or so in outlying dukedoms. Just a secretary's room and the room where his father worked.

A pretty elf woman with metallic-brass hair that went to her shoulders and blue-purple eyes manned the lonely front desk. *Cuwylla.* His dad's secretary. She wore a stitched, white dress like she did almost every day that Ty had ever seen her.

When he came in, her eyes widened and her lips trembled.

"Dungeon lord!" she exclaimed. "I'm so, so sorry. I heard about what Dalryn, that blackheart, did. But it was my fault. I... I don't know how I'll ever make it up to you!"

Ty had completely forgotten that it was Cuwylla who had told Dalryn about his trip to see the Crone all those months ago. It had also worked out pretty well, and he was honestly over it. In fact, he had forgotten about it completely.

His eyes slid sideways to his sister. She usually got the better of the games siblings played...

"Oh, don't worry about it at all, Cuwylla," Ty said. "Seriously. I have become absolute fast friends with Dalryn, and if you hadn't accidentally spilled the wine about my trip, that probably wouldn't have happened. Surely, you've heard that we adventure together?"

Val smiled at him—no doubt appreciating him not trying to throw her current paramour in the dungeon—the not-leveling-you-up version of a dungeon.

She nodded, her face lighting up. "I had heard that, but I wasn't sure..."

"Yeah. Dalryn is the best guy ever. Ever. A close friend to myself, the dungeon lord. Also, he's Level Eight now, one of the strongest in the kingdom."

Val was giving him a quirked eye—she knew he didn't exactly love Dalryn.

"But he's sad, and I really want him to be as happy as I am. He talks about you constantly—how much he misses you, how much you meant to him. How much he wishes he could take back everything he ever did to hurt you. Why, just the other day, he was showing me a sonnet he had com—"

Ty felt a sharp kick to his fortunately damage-resistant ankle and hopped sideways.

Cuwylla evidently didn't notice the pursed lips of Val and clasped her hands to her chest. "Really, he said all that?"

"Oh, ye—ouch!"

Cuwylla was smiling from ear to ear. "Wow… Well, if you can forgive him for trying to rob you, maybe I can as well! Thank you so much, Ty!"

"Oh, you're most welcome."

"I'll get your dad!"

Cuwylla rushed from the room in a swirl of her white dress.

Val turned to him and punched him in the shoulder hard enough that he yelped for real, although she wrung her hand out afterward.

"When you least expect it, Ty…"

Ty laughed. "C'mon, think of it as a small test of your man. Or maybe Dalryn can have a harem like me."

"Or *I* can have a harem like you."

Before Ty could explore that crazy line of thought—he had never had any sense whatsoever that his sister liked women and wasn't sure what she was trying to tell him—Cuwylla came back into the room, still smiling from ear to ear. "Your dad will see you now!"

Ty headed into the room. He had mostly made up with his dad, even had dinner with him a few times. Everything had turned out all right for Ty, even if his dad still had some very bad calls to his name. Plus, his dad was dying. But Ty still didn't feel comfortable around his father at all. He had left House Orsini—his father's House—when he'd been very young, and he had spent near forty years seeing his father maybe twice a year.

But the man had incredible talent, and now, in his old age and infirmity, he had somehow nabbed an important position again.

"Hey, Dad," Ty said.

"You wanted to see me?" George asked, his face alight.

"Yeah, I wanted to talk to you about a couple of things. I was wondering about possible expansion. I wanted to grab a land grant to the north of the city, just outside it."

George coughed. "Why? Something wrong with your current house? It's a lot larger and nicer than most of the houses the other elves around here have."

Ty shifted on his feet, still awkward. "I wanted to start a fruit-cultivating business, as well as have a lot of land to help the dryads. Between dryad trees and making money off of fruit, I think I'll need a considerable amount of money to do that."

"Hmm... you know that the king has been pretty strongly opposed to letting people expand away from our protections, for the most part, right?"

Ty nodded. "I know. But I'm nearly Level Eight—"

His father beamed at him. "Congratulations, Ty, that's amazing!"

"—and so I figured he might make an exception."

Ty's dad coughed again, dabbing at his mouth with a little scrap of fabric. "Well, there's something else as well, although I'll talk to him. We've convinced him to take the risk of opening up the Temple District, district two of old Calasti. It'll have a ton of corrupted spells and monsters, ones that are considerably stronger than you're used to dealing with from this district. As a second issue, the old elf nobles—Mosstone, Grayshore, Greenlily, and all the rest—have been pushing for permission to expand. Between the two, I think it'll make it harder to convince him to approve that. But he likes you to some degree, and Val more, so perhaps he'll okay it."

Val poked Ty in the ribs and whispered, "Told ya."

Ty glared at her but didn't respond directly. "Well, Dad, if you could get this win for me, I'd really appreciate it."

His dad frowned. "I'll try, I promise. I've been trying to convince the king that the rewards of expansion are worth the risks. But he knows everything I do. This isn't a 'he's wrong' situation—it's more a matter of how much he values 'people not dying' as compared to how much I value 'citizens making levels and expanding our holdings with knowledge of the risks.'"

Ty could sympathize with the king's position—he didn't like people who depended on him dying, either. On the other hand, Ty knew *he* could handle it, so...

Ty's dad gave a long sigh. "Any chance I can convince you to join me for dinner again tonight? I already agree with you, but you can try arguments out on me, maybe I'll use some with the king."

"Yeah," Ty said. Then a thought occurred to him. "Hey, can you invite Cuwylla for me as well? I want to have her meet—"

Ty felt a pain in his ankle and laughed, even as his dad gave him a strange look and a muttered, "Sure."

Chapter Forty

A BRIEF IDYLLIC INTERLUDE

A few days later, newly Level Eight, Ty glanced around the land that he had secured. It was everything he had hoped for, at least in terms of a starting plot. It had a few marble ruins on it, for either starting houses or, more likely, raw building material. Most of it was overgrown orchards, which, with decent effort, could be returned to a productive state. A small stream meandered through on its way to the Blue River. And it was a full square mile of territory, purchased for ten gold from the king.

It was also *very* ideally located. His plot's center was about a mile north of the ruins of the old elven capital of Calasti. The city of Star Port was built in the southernmost portion of the ruins, so he was a good five miles and change from Star Port, but even that wasn't as bad as it sounded. His plot was close to the old riverfront road and the Great Marble way both, and he could make a trip to town of about five miles without ever leaving a major road *or* entering the actual ruins—the riverfront road led directly to the First District, what was now Star Port proper.

Val slightly smacked him in the head. "C'mon, Ty, tell us what to do and stop mooning over your land."

Ty turned, staring at his team, although Val was only kind of a member—she ran the dungeon with them a bit more than half the time but was very clearly the king's general first. But everyone was here—Ivy, Forli, Dalryn, Belika, and Ivy's two spiders.

Behind them were about a hundred people who had come out to assist Ty with a free day of labor, basically. They were all Level Two—they were people whom his training and gear program had gotten through a dungeon run. A few were still adventurers, but most had become farmers, carpenters, blacksmiths, fishermen—things of that nature. And most had abilities useful to what he was doing today.

"Well, we need to clear a large area for the garden, and we need to build the main house," Ty said. He pulled out two large pieces of parchment, on which he had diagrammed—with the help of Shreve and Welwyn—a house pattern and a garden layout respectively.

He set them down and everyone crowded around, although Ty doubted most people could see over their friends' and countrymen's shoulders.

"I want everyone with any kind of boosted strength, plant-based ability, or anything similar, to clear this area. Once that's done, work with Welwyn—that's the spider—and Jeryl, our metallic-green-haired gardener here, to start the gardens and orchards. It'll be five acres, so it'll take some time, to put it mildly. Those with advanced cooking abilities, fire starting abilities, and similar things, please place yourself at Forli's disposal—she'll be in charge of victualling this group. If you get too many, Forli, just send the extras to the garden portion until you need them."

Forli nodded enthusiastically, clearly proud to be in charge of something.

"For the rest of you, you'll be in two groups. If you have stone meld or hardening abilities—or familiars that are architects—you'll be helping Shreve and me to build the main house. For everyone else—I'm sorry, you've drawn rock-moving detail. We have carts that I want you to load with marble chunks from the various ruins and move them to the house site. Start with the two ruins inside the garden area."

A few good-natured *boo*s answered that proclamation.

Ty held his hands up. "To everyone—thank you. It means the world. May the gods see your kindness and smile upon you."

Everyone broke up and headed to their designated spots.

Ty enjoyed his work on the house. In truth, he mostly provided direction, but he also helped move things, working his body. He had recently acquired the 'athletic, rank I' perk, and his physical stats were decent despite him barely focusing on them. Working in the sun, building a home for his burgeoning family, was actually quite rewarding, even if physically demanding. He also came to appreciate the familiars of Ivy for the first time. Shreve was strong and coordinated and could move things with ease, use stone melding and strengthening magics, and was a natural architect. He was worth as much as the whole rest of the team building the house. Welwyn could grow plants magically, and she had the same strength and skills as Shreve. She was worth almost her whole team in building the garden.

Ty worked through to lunch, joking and talking with the people who were his fellow countrymen and sometimes neighbors. No one called him a "halfie." No one called him a "slavey." No one except Dalryn called him a "tree boy."

Instead, they obviously cared for him and looked up to him. Most of them valued what he had done for them and wanted to return the favor, and many wanted to hear his stories. He told them of saving the king, of rescuing the elves from the goblins, of his dungeon delves. But never the stories of him being captured by the orcs or the similar. He tried to make the stories funny and self-deprecating. Ty could tell that was what most people wanted to hear.

He knew that he didn't always fit in with everyone, but these people had already been helped by him and were willing to give him the credit if he told off jokes or slipped up in the social norms, and he valued them greatly for it.

Lunch was a huge vegetable stew, with chilled—courtesy of Forli and her ice powers—wine, a lighter salad for those who wanted it, and lightly seared, spiced deer for those who cared for meat, which included some of the few humans and other non-elves who had shown up, as well as a very few elves.

Dalryn, probably due to his massive physical stat increase, had undergone a change in his diet. He now ate at least a decent amount of meat, and he joined in the consumption of venison.

After lunch, Ty worked until sundown, which was coming fairly late now that they were well into spring. Magic joined with muscle, and the sixty-ish people managed to do a truly heroic job. They cleared all of the five acres, planted the portions of the garden nearest the house, and got the lowest foundations of the house and most of the basement built, as well as the outer walls of the first floor. The helpful mob also removed all the ruins and loose stone from the outlined areas and made nice piles near the house for later building.

Forli pulled out all the stops for dinner, cooking very thin fish strips for most of the elves with numerous spices and a huge salad, more and more-varied chilled wines and hot spiced cider both, and spiced potatoes for heartier fare. Toward the end, she also produced a ton of candied and compote apples for dessert.

As evening fell, everyone pulled out tents, which they set up on the floors of the partially built house they had been working on. He and Ivy made love extremely quietly and slowly before falling asleep.

Despite nothing of any real significance happening, it had been one of the best days of Ty's entire life.

***

The next morning, Ty woke to the smell of cooking pancakes and syrup as Ivy entered his tent with a plate of the same.

Ty sat up, still naked, grabbed the wooden fork, and started shoveling them into his mouth. They were wonderful, far more than normal. Ty had learned that food just tasted better to him after a major bout of physical effort.

After a few mouthfuls, Ty glanced up at Ivy, who was staring at him with kind eyes as he ate. "Is everyone ready to for us to head back?"

"Almost. They're working on getting the last of the tools and such stowed in the caravan and ready to head back. It's going well, though. You can take a few minutes to savor the pancakes, I promise."

Ty smiled. "Thanks, Ivy. For everything."

She leaned over and kissed his head. "No, thank you, Ty. Not the other way around. You've made every dream, or near enough, that I had come true. I'm safe and away from my father. A healer. High level. And with a great guy."

Ty put the pancakes down and gave her hand a squeeze.

She gave him a half-smile that called for him to join in a joke. "Heck, you even took care of my brother."

Ty laughed and mimed an over-the-top look of horror. "Now *that*, I feel you owe me something *really* kinky for."

She chuckled. "Later. For now, eat your pancakes, and let's go face your admirers. You have to give a speech thanking them, you know."

Ty grimaced. He wasn't really the 'speech' type.

A sudden commotion outside, a couple of calls and a sound of clattering wooden wheels, brought Ty's ruminations up short.

"What the...?"

Ivy shrugged, but Ty was already grabbing his breeches and pulling them on and lacing them up in the front. "Can you find my shirt please, hon?"

She rooted around for a second and then handed it to him. A few moments later, Ty, barefoot and without his usual robe, stepped out into the morning light.

A whole second caravan was making its way into his land across the marble road.

Chapter Forty-One

REDEMPTION?

The caravan coming down the road was even larger than the one that Ty had brought, and Ty could see that most of the wagons carried additional marble and tools, and one had barrels marked with food and water symbols. Numerous people walked alongside the wagons, with a very few riding ghost wolves.

At the head of the procession walked the one person Ty least wanted to see—Helryn Mosstone, Ivy and Dalryn's dad. He was dressed in plate armor that was colored a sinister red, with almost organic swirls around it. His diamond eye glowed. His remaining eye, pale blue, wandered across the setup that Ty had going, and all of the people.

When his eye alighted on Ty and Ivy standing next to each other, Helryn broke into a jog, reaching them before the rest of the caravan came to a stop.

There was a brief, awkward moment as the three looked at each other. Their last meeting had ended with Helryn denouncing Ty and everything he stood for and calling his daughter a whore. Ty had honestly, albeit perhaps foolishly, thought he would never see Helryn again.

Finally, Helryn broke the silence, dropping to one knee and bowing to Ty and then his daughter. He briefly spoke in High

Averian, and Ty saw tears, of happiness he thought, come to Ivy's face. Then Helryn faced Ty, still on his knees.

"I would beg your forgiveness, Tywyndyll il Belmoria. I have acted abominably to you, treated you terribly without reason. Shamed myself in failing as a host, and far more by striking my son in front of you and by saying all the horrible, terrible things I did. I know that I have deserved every hurt, every loneliness, but I have spent months regretting everything that happened that day. I am, truly, sorry."

Ty wasn't sure what to do, and even though he didn't *really* mean it, his automatic politeness kicked in and he muttered a half-hearted "forgiven."

Helryn must have sensed the insincerity, for he remained kneeling. "I offer not as excuse, but merely explanation, the fact that I lost my own father to orcs, my land and people to a dragon, and my wife to humans that had promised to protect us. My rage at these injustices blinded me and caused me to perpetuate injustice against you and my children. I would, again, beg of you your forgiveness."

Ty hesitated, torn. He could genuinely understand what Helryn was going through, even empathize. His own bitterness over past wrongs haunted Ty as well. The racism of the humans in Steelport toward him, who had called him a slavey. The disdain of his fellow elves, who, even when slaves themselves, had treated him terribly and called him a halfie. Ty's own human family casting him from their ranks to live in poverty on the streets.

Ty wanted to hate everyone as well, sometimes. He could remember his brief, shameful and visceral desire to 'punish' Yenrael by forcing her to be *his* slave. But far more than he wanted to hate people or hurt them back, Ty wanted to prove them all wrong. To prove that he wasn't what they said.

He truly believed that he had taken the pain of the rejections and jeers, and fueled himself to do amazing things, for himself and others.

Helryn seemed to have gone the other route. To have wallowed in his own hatred like a poison, turning himself bitter until he lashed out at everyone, even the ones he should love. His own children.

But Ty could empathize. Ty could feel how easy it might have been for him to go down that path instead of his own. What if his father hadn't cared enough to convince King Leo to rescue Ty from the orcs? What if King Leo had stolen Ty's dungeon core when he'd had the chance? What if Dalryn had successfully stolen it on the road?

He might have fallen to the same bitterness. Ty was man enough to admit he wasn't sure how he would have held up.

And maybe, just maybe, Helryn could be turned back to a tree-side path. To raise himself up in a way that helped others as well, instead of hurting them. Ty wasn't dumb—he knew the odds were low that Helryn would truly change.

But they weren't zero.

Ty breathed out, letting his festering anger at Helryn go as well. Meaning it fully this time, at least provisionally, Ty held his hand out to Helryn. "I understand, Helryn, truly. I have my own bones to pick with the humans of Steelport like you do the humans of the Havi Imperium. And the orcs hurt me as well. I know the pain, helplessness, and anger that breeds. I forgive you."

Helryn nodded, and Ty was shocked to see a bit of water around his one good eye, although no tear fell. He pulled himself to his feet on Ty's hand.

Ivy threw herself into her father's arms, despite his evil-appearing plate armor, balling her eyes out and hugging him. "I've missed you, Dad. Even with everything, I've missed you. Thank you. I know that took everything you had, and I love you for doing it for me."

Helryn hugged his daughter, and finally, a tear did run down his face. He buried his face in her hair as he practically crushed her to his armored chest. "I'm so, so sorry, buttercup. Thank you as well, for believing in me and forgiving me."

He hugged her for a few more seconds, then turned back to Ty.

As he did, Ty noticed that Forli had come over, staying off to the side but close enough to hear what was happening. He *didn't* see Belika, but figured there was a decent chance she was around, hidden.

Helryn gave him a smile filled with the confidence and arrogance that Ty had expected from Helryn, but one that somehow reached his eyes—it didn't feel quite as predatory to Ty, or as dismissive.

He hooked a finger back at the caravan. "I didn't think for a moment that words would be proof, Ty. But hopefully, to some degree, this will help as well. I've got all the materials you could want, including some rare magical trees from the new dimension—Ice Pines. I've also got a ton of paid workers, and—"

Helryn raised his voice. "I'll pay anyone here that wants to stay an extra day and help build Ty's home a week's wages of what they'd make based on their level working for the government!"

There were cheers at that, and Ty raised his eyebrow. That was probably about two gold Helryn had just promised, since he'd offered a week's wages to fifty Level Two and up people.

Although, at some weird level, Ty wished Helryn *hadn't* done all this. A sincere, truly felt apology would have meant more to Ty, and Ty felt to Helryn as well, than Helryn trying to buy his way out of his cruelty. It was hard to explain, but Ty felt that Helryn was still trading things to be in the right, instead of just doing good.

Still, it was a nice gesture. Certainly better than nothing at all.

A lot of people cheered, and most agreed to stay. Overseers working for Helryn stepped in, and the whole thing began running at a breakneck pace as Ty, Helryn, and Ivy watched.

After a moment, Ty turned to Helryn, who still had one arm around Ivy. "So, how'd you get the armor?"

Helryn smiled sheepishly, an expression that didn't sit easily on his face. "It does look like I'm trying to play into some weird villain fantasy, doesn't it? I found it adventuring in the under-city, like most of my stuff. Made Level Thirteen as well, although I hear you and my children have been leveling even faster. It's good armor though. It's extremely resistant to damage and gives me a huge boost in health. Worth the villain look."

Ty chuckled. He had to admit for the right item he would happily look like a rat, so he guessed he could understand it.

Helryn's face fell. "Well, I have one more apology, the largest. Do you know where my son is?"

"He's in a tent around here... with my sister. They might not be... paying attention to the situation going on around us."

Helryn raised an eyebrow. "I see. I guess in this new age of the Averian Empire, the dukedoms of Belmoria and Mosstone will become one house."

Well, I mean, maybe, although no one is talking marriage yet.

"Well, from your mouth to Iluvin Eturia's ears," Ty said, and Ivy smiled.

"Or Cerivae Nerithin's," she added. "She is the goddess of family, after all."

Ty nodded.

Helryn let his arm drop from Ivy. "Well, I'm off to see your brother. I brought some magical tree seeds for you, so feel free to look and add any to your land that you wish. We have an expert here to help with that."

"Thank you."

Helryn nodded, opened his mouth and then closed it, and strode off to presumably see Dalryn. Ty hoped they would have a good time of their reunion.

Ivy turned and kissed him hard, then buried her head in his shoulder. "Thank you, Ty. Thank you so much! I know Dad doesn't deserve a second chance, I really do. I'm still really, *really* glad you gave him one anyway."

Ty stroked her green-tinged copper hair. "Sure, hon, anything for you. Although you know he might, well... *revert*."

Ivy gave a small laugh. "I know. He probably *will* revert. He's done things like this before to try and make up for his anger, only to fall to it again later. But still, he might *not* revert. Then things will be wonderful and perfect."

Ty smiled to hear his own thoughts on the matter parroted back to him.

Chapter Forty-Two

DISTRICT TWO (BUT ALSO FIVE)

The meeting of the royal government was being held in the Emerald Bee, of all places. While Ty had been out getting Zadrid's Heart, King Leo had rescued a bunch more dragons which had occupied all of Elgin Isle—so they had decided to shut down the temporary admiralty headquarters. At the same time, Ygg'drasil, the tree, had grown so much its roots threatened the old palace, so the government was planning on building an entirely new palace. But they hadn't done it yet.

So, instead, they had rented out the Bee for the evening and closed it off to everyone else, and King Leo had sworn Mirafol to secrecy, since she was serving everyone food while they talked, a map of the old city of Calasti on one half of the table's center, and a map of the current Star Port on the other.

A separate table had a huge, blown up map of the ruins of district two of old Calasti. It was the old Temple District, where the great temples had all had their temple stones, and a huge number of lesser faiths had kept their smaller, non-magical shrines. As well as the Reliquary of the Kings, where each old king had been entombed along with their favorite non-magical items. Also the Auditorium of the High, the place meant for most religious ceremonies.

King Leo was pacing back and forth with his hands clasped behind his back as he spoke. His metallic-golden hair had been cut close to his head, and he was dressed far too casually for a king in Ty's private thoughts.

His entire council sat and listened. At this point that was a lot of individuals. His inner council, the ministers, only numbered four, but when he called every minister-at-large, representative of an outlying territory, and leaders of certain parts of the community, a lot of people showed.

There was Ty's dad, George. The King's magic advisor and significant other, the beautiful Lily, a silver-haired high elf illusionist. Molly, a brown-skinned, sexy wood elf priestess of Iluvin Eturia. Hugh, a giant, twelve-foot-long bronze dragon and the king's best friend. Kadrath as the representative of the adventuring guild. Laurel Whitewater, a rabbit-kin captain and representative of the merchants. Val, their general. They also had 'district' representatives from each district—all elves—and now representatives of the various dukes, including one from the new dimension, Ice Pines. Four local districts and three dukedoms made for another seven individuals. Then, there were the ministers-at-large like Ty, for odd jobs. Almost twenty people in total, mostly elves, clustered around the tables. Even then it was elves of five varieties—high, wood, deep, half, and ice flower. Between that, the human, the rabbit-kin, and the dragon, it was an extremely eclectic council.

Helryn, who was representative of Green Apple Grove since the districts had gotten formal representation, glanced around with a sneer at the various races, but cleared his face quickly.

"So, that's the plan," King Leo was concluding. "I intend for us to sweep the Temple District clear. We have hundreds of Level Two and Level Three adventurers, and tens of Level Four, thanks in no small part to our own minister-at-large, Ty, and his generosity with his dungeon."

There were a few perfunctory claps at that.

"So, we'll let them handle the surface. What I need from the stronger members of our society is to explore the undercity wherever an entrance to it is discovered. The undercity usually has the stronger corrupted beasts. Ty, since your adventuring group is mostly around Level Seven, I'll designate you the first team. You'll be stationed in a central location, and when someone finds an area that needs exploring, please do it. Since my group is closer to Level Fifteen, we'll be there for anything truly unusual—come get us if you run into something you can't handle."

Helryn spoke up from his carved-fairy chair, surprising Ty. "Should we even be exploring the undercity yet? That just seems like a way to end up with dead elves—my son and daughter, and their lovers, among them. Perhaps we should just seal everything from the top?"

Leo looked at Helryn, an eyebrow raised. "That's an odd position for you, Helryn, but I can appreciate not wanting family to die. But if we're going to expand—something you pushed for—I want to know what's there. I don't want some giant monster popping up and murdering everyone at Sunday Mass."

At the blank looks of almost everyone around the table, Leo clarified, "At some major religious service."

Helryn narrowed both his eyes, although the normal blue eye narrowed faster than the diamond one.

There was a brief pause, and Kadrath spoke into the silence. "When are we doing this?"

"Two days," King Leo said. "Take the rest of today and tomorrow to get everyone organized into teams and give them their spots. The district is about a square mile, so it's six hundred and forty acres, give or take, of ruins. We can have about eighty competent teams of five made, leaders picked, and each assigned a six-or-so acre area to clear in that time I think."

Everyone nodded.

Val spoke. "We can also get some of the dragons to help. Most of our storm dragons are teenagers, and about Level Five equivalent. If we kept a reaction team flying above, and made some kind of signal, that would aid us greatly as well."

"Right," Leo said. "Anything else?"

No one had anything.

"Dismissed."

A couple people stayed to clean up or grab a last bite of food, but most everyone headed out. Ty wondered why they had even needed to bar people from what was about to immediately become public knowledge.

As Ty mused about the government, Kadrath clanked up, his massive armor giving a bit of warning before he put his arm around Ty's shoulder.

Ty glanced sideways at him. "Yes?"

"Didn't get a chance to talk to you before the meeting," the dworc said, a slight smile on his green face. "Your dungeon made its level. A Level Five adventurer from out of town got *really* cocky against that undead bear sub-boss at the end of the dungeon. Critical hit to the neck from a chaotic wounds bite after he uppercut the thing for some inane reason. Nasty, but at least it was pretty fast from what his buddies said. But he pushed the dungeon to Level Five."

Ty grimaced—he knew the arguments and had hashed them out with everyone, but he did wish his wealth wasn't tied to something that killed people. "Alright, I'll jump into the dungeon and add the treasury. As much as I have a bunch of amazing stuff to add, I know that's what everyone wants right now, and what I need to start really attracting people."

"You're a good man, Ty."

***

"So, how have you been?" Saelenia asked as Ty entered the room.

Ty walked across to the podium with the dungeon information. "Pretty decent. You'll be happy, I think, to know that Forli is with seed."

"With seed, youngling? A dryad seed?" Saelenia asked, coming off her throne to stand in all her majestic, twelve-foot glory. "She didn't just produce one, she's making it inside her?"

Ty nodded. "Yes. At least that's what the perk is indicating."

Saelenia moved forward, towering over him as she did. "Weird. But still excellent. When can you 'seed' the next dryad?"

"Um, maybe after I buy her dinner first?" Ty said, half-bemused, but half-inured, to this type of questioning.

"Buy her dinner?" Saelenia said, then smiled slightly as Ty rolled his eyes. "Ah, a jest, youngling. Which tells me I need to find a way around the restrictions so I can smack the back of your head. But nevermind all that—when can you make another seed?"

Ty shrugged. "I don't know, truthfully. It might be now with a new dryad, but I can't with Forli at least till she, well, births the seed."

"Well, you need to find—" Saelenia began, but Ty held his hands up.

He pushed them at her a bit. "Hold your wolves, progenitor. I'm all for sex with tons of dryads, I promise, but I can handle it without constant exhortations from you. I'm here to change the dungeon, since Kadrath said it leveled. But I need to do it fast because we're all headed into the undercity in two days, and I need to help coordinate that. I don't have time to listen to another 'I should sleep with every single dryad right now' speech."

Saelenia tapped her leg with one finger. "Where in the undercity?"

Ty blinked at the question. "Under the temple district? What they're calling district two, even though it's really our fifth district. Why?"

Saelenia sighed. "Ah, youngling, it feels like the fates are just pressing for everything at once. Remember the second set of progenitor parts that I told you that you could get?"

"The claws of Foriveltain, the Primeval Bear," Ty said. He wouldn't forget something like that; it had too much potential for power for him.

She nodded. "Yes. I told you it's located in the undercity. The temple to the elder god Xalkri that I spoke of is located beneath the temple district. I will show you."

She reached down and touched the ground, and crystals with the same bioluminescence as the mushrooms sprang up, showing maps. Multiple maps, each of a floor, with directions down to the next level on each, till the last showed the temple itself.

"If you're going down to clear it all out, you should stop by the temple. It has numerous treasures you might use, but the two most important—and ones I locked myself, with means different than every other treasure there—are the claws and gear of the Ancient One hero Zar'Kre'Rusth."

"How do I open it?" Ty asked.

Saelenia smiled, her eyes crinkling with mirth. "That's the best part. You just have to will it—it's locked to my power. Which flows through your soul, now."

Ty pursed his lips. "Even though I barely have any of it, and your power is different now?"

"Well, you could also use artifact-level anti-magic or perhaps Eclipse or Mind magic to fool the spell of protection. But I'd be willing to bet that you'll be fine."

This seems way too easy. Especially since... "Why didn't you tell me about this for the first god piece? Why send me after Zadrid's heart? This seems... vastly easier."

It was Saelenia's turn to parse her lips. "The undercity is corrupted with dark energies, and has many powerful, magical beasts. Not to mention quite a few traps."

"I handled Zadrid's Hallow..." Ty started.

But Saelenia kept talking. "There are also numerous dark presences beneath the city, the fragments of the gods of the Ancient Ones that are left after their fall... and their servants. Those powers are corrupting and might turn you to evil. Many are still quite powerful, even if but a shadowy fragment of their past glory. So, I very, very seriously doubt it'll be easy. In fact, I wouldn't recommend this at all... but since you're apparently going anyway..."

Ty grimaced. *Got it.* "Well, can we just pick the room, then?"

"Treasure Room?" Saelenia asked.

Ty grimaced. He had told everyone that he would get the treasury. But the more he thought about it, the more he wanted to push the Entropy Spark room to get what he thought would be the next huge room. It would also add an additional almost half point of loot quality, since its effects would be doubled. But the treasury would add loot rate, more than doubling his current loot drop rate on the floor he was currently on. He didn't really understand loot quality against loot rate, just that he wanted more of both. But would increasing the quality of items be worth more than increasing the quantity?

He also *knew* that a spark and a nest—which he already had— would add up to a boss room. That gave loot increases as well.

He just wasn't sure.

Finally, he reached down and hit Entropy Spark. He would deal with the disappointment. He wanted to get a boss room next, and he wanted every room to be as powerful as possible.

And I can always make sure my personal powers add to the dungeon as well, unlike every other dungeon lord I've ever read about.

"A bold choice," Saelenia said. "I hope it isn't foolishness. But, for now, go forth and claim the remainder of my legacy that is here beneath the city."

Chapter Forty-Three

THE UNDERCITY OF THE ANCIENT ONES, PART 1

Ty had left the dungeon, gotten a ton of paper—which cost quite a bit—gone back, and then carefully gotten every map he could of the undercity from Saelenia. She didn't know most of it, but she knew the main route to the temple and a bit more—although it was very out of date information. Almost a thousand years out of date, and Ty had trouble imagining how accurate it could still be. Saelenia assured him that a lot of the undercity was magical, and immune to the decay of time.

He was still very skeptical of its value. But not *so* skeptical as to not get the maps.

As he waited in the base camp just inside the temple district's walls, Ty was being fed a couple grapes by Forli—who had joined them only to run said base camp—and drinking some *very* watered-down wine. He was inside a tent dedicated to just his team, to keep the sun off, with his feet kicked up on a cheap wooden table.

Ty knew he would be called out again soon to earn his keep, and was enjoying the break.

The temple district had once contained numerous grand temples to multiple deities, and those temples had possessed a ton of magical rituals. Which meant a ton of now *corrupted* magical rituals. Which, in turn, meant a ton of corrupted magical beasts.

There had already been *three* deaths. Even though Ty had been scheduled to only be used for the undercity, they had barely even made it to the undercity at this point. Instead, The Dungeon Lord's Own adventuring party had gone to a couple temples—an Ancient One to Iluvin Eturia, one to Kellen the god of justice, and a last to Livesti the goddess of luck—to put down huge 'boss' versions of Level Six and Seven monsters. They had done so with very heavy support, but still.

Dalryn groaned out loud. "I'm honestly not sure how I keep getting paid nearly nothing for almost dying. I'm almost Level Eight for crying out loud. I'd make more just joining the king's army."

"We're a team, Dalryn," Ivy said. "Stop being selfish."

"I'm not being selfish!" Dalryn said, brow furrowed, as he grabbed a cup of pure water and poured it over his sweat-plastered copper hair, then shook his head, spraying droplets. "I've stayed with you guys from damn near the beginning. But I still feel as if I should be making more than just room and board, here. Literally boards in this dungeon's case quite a few times. That's a reasonable request."

"The dungeon gave us magically hardened lumber yesterday," Ivy said.

Belika, who was cleaning her daggers, commented, "You get more than just place. You are consort for Val, Dalryn."

"I hate that phrase," Dalryn muttered, and Ty snickered. Belika hadn't even been there when Thea had said that, but everyone used 'Val's consort' and 'a decent chance of a good time' with Dalryn to his constant frustration. "Also, I love how *my* girl isn't here to feed me grapes, but Forli's here."

Belika laughed and stabbed a thin slice of meat with her dagger. "If Val were, you feed *her* grapes."

Ty joined the laughter outright this time—Belika wasn't wrong.

Armored boots on stone outside alerted Ty that someone was coming, and a familiar voice that Ty couldn't quite place called out, "Dungeon Lord's Own, you're needed."

Ty dropped his feet down from the table and stood as Forli backed up a bit, grapes held in her hand.

"Come in!" Ty called.

The tent flap pushed open and Keltren Orsini walked in. Ty grimaced as the young, copper-haired man—a mirror of Ty in many ways but for Ty's new skin—entered. Keltren was one of the new members of House Orsini that had come to Star Port—and Ty's cousin. While he had never been *directly* mean or hurtful to Ty, he had certainly never helped him, either. Or so much as invited Ty to lunch.

Keltren was a decent combatant, although not Ty's level. He ran a Body magic build, a combat build combining self-healing and magically increased physical stats. Ty had to admit that the scion of House Orsini had been doing good work in the ruins around town today, and House Orsini was funding *two* separate adventuring groups into Ty's dungeon, putting a lot of coin in his pocket. Ty sighed and did his best to let his annoyance go.

Keltren started right in. "Dungeon Lord Belmoria, we have a situation. After you so ably cleared the old temple of Livesti, we discovered an entire basement level to it. A segment is broken in, with direct access to the undercity. It also had an entire swarm of the stupid Averian Demon-rats, the cold-based ones made from corrupted icebox rituals."

"Joy," Ty muttered.

"We took them out, but it cost a lot of essence to handle all those rats, and the decision was made by your sister to send you down and make sure the undercity is clear beneath us."

It sounded like the opportunity they were waiting for. Ty knew it wasn't really kosher, but they had already decided to do a deep exploration. He glanced over and caught Dalryn's eye. Ivy's brother gave a subtle nod. A quick glance around showed him no one openly disagreeing.

Keltren must have caught the byplay and misinterpreted it, as he reached a hand out and put it on Ty's shoulder. "Hey, don't worry. It'll be verdant. You guys are amazing."

'Verdant' had recently become slang among the Averian elves to mean 'good' or 'neat.' It didn't surprise Ty that Keltren was already using it. Nor did it surprise him that his cousin was misinterpreting the looks among them as worry for their safety.

But Ty would work with what he was given. "Thanks, cousin," he said. "You give me courage."

Ivy coughed, but no one else said anything, and Keltren seemed to accept it.

"I'll let the men there know you're on your way."

Once Keltren had left, everyone began gathering their new gear and equipping themselves. Ty was done nearly instantly, with just a robe and a few magic bracers, as was

Belika with her leather armor. But Ivy and Dalryn used the heavy stuff, and it took a decent amount of time to get suited.

Quick reaction troops they weren't.

Eventually, however, the four pushed their way out of the tent, fully ready. Ty in his green and brown robes. Ivy in her gleaming, magical breastplate and helm. Belika in leather, knives out and in hand already. Leading them was Dalryn, dressed in six-and-a-half feet of magically enhanced steel and carrying a towershield nearly as tall.

They picked up Shreve and Welwyn—Ivy's two familiars—from nearby, where the two were helping with the construction of a temporary guards' outpost.

The group of six then headed to the giant central square of district two, where the largest faiths of old Averia had their temples. While not nearly as important as Iluvin Eturia, Livesti, goddess of luck, had her temple on that square as well. She had been popular with a large segment of the old empire, although she had precious few dedicated followers in the city now.

None of the ex-slaves of the Averian Kigndom felt that luck had really been on their side.

Ty walked down the ruined path, overgrown with vines, that had once been a statue-filled walkway and entered the front. An elf guard with long brass hair tied in a ponytail and reddish-brown eyes was stationed just inside, in the first foyer. He smiled at them as they entered.

The guard motioned to the left of the entrance with one leather-bracer clad arm. "This way, Dungeon Lord. The entrance to the basement is just to the side here, and you can enter the undercity from there."

Ty entered the room through a doorway with rusted hinges hanging into a smaller marble room with spiral stairs heading into the floor. Dalryn took the lead, clanking down the stairs, and everyone followed him. They entered into a wide but shallow room, a mere six feet from floor to ceiling. It had numerous pillars to hold the upper temple from collapsing into it, with the result that it felt notably claustrophobic. Ty brushed the ceiling, and Dalryn had to out and out duck to walk anywhere.

The rusted remains of iron hoops, for holding barrels, were everywhere, but little else remained beyond the bare room. Someone had put two torches down recently, and they burned on the floor, giving enough light to see but making the room smokey and even more claustrophobic somehow.

"Of course it's small," Dalryn muttered as he walked forward in a crouch, his bastard sword held warily in front of him. The others followed. As they did, they saw the markings of a cold-generating ritual on the floor, recently hacked apart. It had almost certainly been the reason that the Averian demon rats had developed—once the ritual became corrupted, that was what it spawned every time.

Ivy brought out her glowstone lantern, fiddled with it for a second, and a powerful and smokeless light filled the room.

They followed Dalryn to the back, where they found the wall that was broken down—surrounded by a veritable slaughterhouse of dead Averian demon rats and sticky, drying blood. Averian demon rats were a hairless rat with rotting flesh and, when alive, frost across their bodies. They stank in life and were far worse in death. Ivy made gagging noises as they walked through the battlefield.

As they walked past the corpses and through the collapsed wall into a huge tunnel. Ty couldn't help but notice he hadn't seen a hive mother rat in the pile of the dead.

Ty had seen pictures of the undercity of the ancient ones before, but he had never been there. The ancient ones—which had become the lizard folk after a cataclysm tens of thousands of years ago—had a very *organic* feel to their architecture. The tunnel curved in odd manners, twisting away in both directions for no reason Ty could fathom. The tunnel was almost circular, with the path at the bottom narrower than it needed to be. And the walls had striations and patterns that had survived millennia somehow that added to the 'living tunnel' feel.

He ran his hands along the side of the tunnel. It was just stone. *So why the organic look?*

Ty shrugged—he needed to find one of a couple places that he could use as starting points to follow the maps he had, not wonder about the architectural choices of a nearly dead race.

He stepped to the side as far as the odd temple would allow so he could address his entire team. "Alright, guys. Let's search the immediate area, clear any monsters from it, so that we complete our duty. Then, if everyone is okay, we'll try and find something that clearly matches one of the maps we have and then follow them where we need to go."

Dalryn and Ivy nodded, and Belika crossed her arms over her chest. The two spiders just stood in place, vibrating a bit. Creepily.

Ty interpreted the lack of response from the three as agreement. "Alright, let's move out. We have a lot to do quickly. Keep an eye out specifically for the Averian Demon rat queen—every time a larger group is found, they have a queen somewhere. We have to eliminate that as an absolute minimum for the safety of those above before we take care of our own business."

Everyone nodded.

"Let's pray an Amalgarat hasn't developed," Dalryn muttered.

Chapter Forty-Four

THE UNDERCITY OF THE ANCIENT ONES, PART 11

Ty stepped away from the corpse of the hive queen demon rat as it fell along his shield. It had been a big one, almost six feet from snout to the tip of its tail, and there had been another twelve rats in the nest. But nothing here had been able to pierce the armor of the team—or, in Ty's case, his Barrier. Shreve and Welwyn had stayed back, and everyone else had simply gotten to the butchery. The fight had used a touch of Ty's essence, but no other resource had been expended.

"Well, that's that," Dalryn said. "And no Amalgarat, thank all the good gods. Back to that five-way intersection that you swore is the same one on your map and downward, now?"

Ty nodded—although the map had them going sideways more than downward. But the first step was to go lower. He honestly wasn't sure how or why the temple to Xalkri had ended up lower than random passages—maybe sunk faster over time—but it had. But only about three levels lower.

The group left the nest room—Ty thought it had once been a living space, but so little was left he wasn't sure—and headed back down a couple tunnels to the five-way intersection.

The intersection was a fairly normal four-way one with a tunnel slanting down. Carefully examining his map, Ty began following it.

If it goes down for a couple hundred feet—I think we're on the right one.

Ty studied the map and counted steps as he walked.

"Watch out!" Dalryn screamed, slamming into Ty's back and knocking him forward into the wall. There was a brief screech of something on metal, and Ty turned back to see a massive, reverse-pallet black widow spider the size of a wolf scrabbling on the top of Dalryn. Dalryn tried to stab it or bring his shield to bear but couldn't manage either in the confusion.

He screamed as the spider bit down, its fangs the perfect weapon to pierce armor.

"Kill it!" their guardian yelled hoarsely, now trying to fling the spider away—but its legs were locked into the armor, tiny little jagged pieces letting it cling.

Ty pushed his hand forward and blasted the spider with lightning. It twitched but didn't let go—until Belika appeared and slashed one of the hook legs off. Dalryn managed to throw it down, and when it leaped back, he shield-bashed it into the wall. Ivy healed Dalryn as their guardian slashed at the spider. Ty knew it would go down now, and held back to preserve essence as Belika joined Dalryn in stabbing it to death.

He was both pleased and horrified when he got a '17 experience' notification. Doing quick math in his head, he came to a dark conclusion.

"That was a Level Six enemy," he informed the group.

Dalryn wiped his sword off on the spider's body, but held it loosely in his hand rather than sheathing it. "So? We're Level Eight. Piece of cake."

Ty gave him the stink eye. "You were screaming like a baby sixty seconds ago, and got injected with spider venom. Don't get cocky."

"I'm fine—I made my Toughness check so it just did a bit more damage than the bite." Dalryn pointed his sword at the ceiling. "Plus, you walked under a fairly obvious enemy without paying attention—this situation was on you. I'm verdant."

Ty was starting to hate that word and everyone's use of it. "Point is, it's just a random enemy, not even one around a ritual or anything. I'm sure it's going to get a lot tougher as we move forward."

"So we'll get experience," Dalryn scoffed. "That's a good thing."

Ty wanted to strangle their guardian for his pigheadedness, but Ivy laid her hand on his forearm and he stilled. He sighed and admonished Dalryn gently. "Just be careful, please."

"Pot Kettle, you potato, but I'll try and be careful."

They continued down into darkness.

***

"Just admit, you're lost," Ivy said, fatigue in her voice. "It's okay. We can retrace our steps and try again."

Ty was a touch fatigued himself, although not as much as Ivy. They had been walking for hours. Along the way, they had faced mutated spiders, rats, centipedes, and bats—all of which had blood-based diseases or powers.

Before Ty could answer, a stone flew from the dark outside Ivy's light radius and smacked into Ty's temple. His mild armor and high Toughness mitigated what would have been a knock-out or possibly fatal blow to an unleveled mortal into a merely stunning blow.

"Son of a—" Ty cried, staggering as blood poured down the side of his face.

Relief came immediately as Ivy touched him and the wound healed. Ty turned and fired lightning into the darkness, about where the stone had come from, but he hit nothing.

A small fusillade of stones came his way, but he put his barrier up. The first couple that hit bounced off the shield, but the damage eventually broke it and a couple hit him. None hit with the power of the one to his temple, however, and despite the hits, Ty merely grunted in mild pain and irritation.

Ivy healed him up regardless.

Belika dropped into the shadows and shifted across the ground into the darkness. Ty surreptitiously moved behind Dalryn and waited. There was a scream from the darkness, choked off, and then a brief sound of scuffling. A naked goblin with a sling in its hand came running into their light, stopping part way. It looked at them with eyes wide as dinner plates, glanced back, and then tried to run along the side of the tunnel past them.

"Don't kill him," Ty said.

Dalryn nodded and stepped sideways, swinging his shield into the goblin. It failed to dodge and hit the wall, crumpling to the ground, one limb splayed awkwardly.

Iluvin that thing was weak.

Ivy stepped forward and healed the goblin, and Dalryn grabbed it and held it as it squealed and thrashed.

And peed itself.

With a sneer of his upper lip so strong that it threatened to break his face in half, Dalryn held it out away from him. "Real winner we have here."

Belika walked back into the light, blood dripping from both her daggers as she carried them at her side. She appeared a proper demented little demon in the dim light of the tunnel as she came forward.

She stopped in front of them and wiped her daggers down using the goblin, who thrashed even harder, but she hadn't cut the gross creature, just left blood on him. "You not even finish one?"

"I wanted to question him," Ty said. "I actually hoped you knew his language."

Belika half shrugged and sheathed her daggers. "Maybe. Maybe no. Fifty years ago goblins come to forest of Averia. Is short time for elf, less than one child. For goblin, is maybe five, maybe six child."

She scrunched her face up. "Not six child. Have child, child have child, child child have child…"

"Generations," Ty said.

"Yes."

"I see. Can you try?"

Belika babbled at the goblin. The goblin just thrashed and squealed, and Belika slapped him.

The goblin stilled and she tried talking to him again. After a back and forth that lasted a couple minutes, and sounded very repetitive to Ty, she turned back to face Ty. "Their language is bad, but I think I know the answer. This goblin thought we were with the elves that come down here a lot, and tried to ambush us to stop them from hurting them. There was some kind of civil war, and most of the goblins are slaves to the elves now, except for a few that help them keep slaves."

Everyone glanced at one another.

"It doesn't… have to be Dad," Ivy said after a moment.

"Asnandi damn him to the worst dimension ever, *of course* it's Dad," Dalryn said disgustedly. "He couldn't get slaves up there so he's building a little empire down here. King Leo is gonna go *ballistic* and arrest him, and Dad'll probably fight till he's killed. Shit shit *shit.*"

Dalryn slammed his shield into the wall on the last repetition, the goblin he still held in his other hand swinging wildly.

"Belika, ask him if he knows where the elves are, please."

Belika spoke the guttural language again, and the goblin nodded vigorously and began talking. After a few minutes, Belika held her hand up.

"He says he does, and he says how to get there. But his words are no good. Would have to show. There is not enough words—language, sorry—between us to make work without him coming."

"What's his name?" Ty asked reflexively, just buying himself time to think.

Her eyes widened briefly and she talked to the goblin.

She chortled and slapped her knee after a moment. "He say—says—his name is 'coward stone thrower.' I not have word, but I think he means like, good thrower. Like hit head all the time."

Ty chuckled as well—the goblin was certainly a coward.

Should I go get help or just go see Helryn, if that is who this is? I mean, I feel like we had a breakthrough the other day, maybe I can get him to stop keeping slaves and we can make this right...

Ty turned to Ivy and raised his eyebrow. She shrugged and turned to Dalryn, who sighed.

Yeah, no one knows the best course. "Alright," Ty said, his voice heavy. "Let's go give Helryn another chance. I feel like an idiot, but he did try really hard to make nice with us and do the right thing a couple days ago. Maybe he'll listen."

"What we do—what *do* we do—with this one?" Belika asked, lightly slapping the captured goblin on the upper arm.

"I don't suppose you have spare breeches or something, Belika?" he asked.

"I do."

Ty gave a half-hearted flick of his wrist toward the goblin. "Well, can this guy borrow them? We'll give him a spare steel dagger or something to lead us there, but I don't think I wanna watch his tiny flag flying in the wind the whole time."

Belika gave a sniff. "He can have. I not want them back, I am thinking."

Ty nodded. "Well, shall we go find daddy dearest then?"

Expressions grim, Ivy and Dalryn both nodded.

Chapter Forty-Five

THE UNDERCITY OF THE ANCIENT ONES, PART III

Ty ran to the side, the bulky, seven-foot-tall bronze golem following him across the metal-riddled stone floor. The thing glowed with an unhealthy red light, reminiscent of blood.

"Someone *block* the thing!" Ty yelled. "I'm the only one that can hit it but it'll run through me in no time!"

"Coming!" Dalryn screamed, lurching from where Ivy had been healing him, behind the statue of an ancient one.

Dalryn ran forward and *plowed* into the golem shield-first. He caught the golem off balance and it fell back onto the ground, a long, thin piece of metal underneath it. Dalryn yelled triumphantly and slammed his sword down. It bounced off the golem, leaving only a tiny scratch, and Dalryn cussed. Then he screamed as the golem grabbed his leg from the ground and began to squeeze. First Dalryn's armored sabaton was crushed, but blood showed it was slicing into his lower leg.

In an insane moment, Ty reached down and grabbed the metal that ran across the ground and discharged his lightning into that. It raced across and into the golem, which melted slightly—far more damage than Ty had expected.

He turned his shock shield on, and the power from it ran continuously into the golem. The damage was *far* greater than expected, and the golem twitched and shook, its limbs flailing wildly.

Dalryn yanked his leg free and crawled back, half crying, half yelling. Belika reached him and pried the metal from his leg as Ivy ran up and healed Dalryn.

Ty, bemused, just held his shock shield on and let it feed lightning to the golem through the ritual. *Is it empowering it?*

Dalryn grabbed a huge stone and carried it in both hands to the golem, then smashed it down on the golem's head as hard as he could. It only moderately dented the golem, and Dalryn went back for more stone among the rubble of the area.

It was unnecessary—the golem finally collapsed into half-melted slag.

Ty released his magic.

The experience gain was *huge*. The golem had been a Level Eleven enemy, and it gave eighteen hundred and eighty-four experience, divided four ways—which was still four hundred and seventy-one. Ty leveled up.

"This is so verdant!" Dalryn exclaimed. "I made another level! That was awesome!"

Chuckling at Dalryn's exuberance—which apparently overcame his 'crushed foot' trauma—Ty quickly gave himself another two stats of Capacity and then took the second level of shocking shield. He had been directly attacked far too often, and the second rank of the shield would raise his net defensive damage to six and also increase the shocking effect. He had other, more advanced plans for his leveling after ten, but he wanted to be sure he would survive this little adventure.

That golem was Level Eleven—no wonder Saelenia wanted me to wait to do this mission.

The huge plaza they were in was oddly quiet after the fight. The rubble and statues were common, the twisting, semi-organic hallways ubiquitous. But the metal across the floor was new.

Dalryn glanced over at Ty. "First time I think I've seen you make your bookish ways work for you. How'd you know to do that?"

"I didn't. I knew that lightning will pass through metal—the descriptor talks about ignoring metal armor. I had hoped I could get the lightning to hit the golem without hitting you, because you were in the way. This other effect is interesting, though."

Ty glanced at the odd geometric shapes across the floor, all filled with metal. He couldn't identify the ritual—or even see the magic crystals, which he assumed were under the floor—but it obviously empowered something. Perhaps the golem? Said golem had started standing in the center.

"What effect?" Dalryn asked.

"It seemed to multiply the damage," Ty said, kneeling down and examining the ritual. "I'm hardly an expert, but I think it's empowering all magic that passes through it. This shouldn't be possible—it's Meta magic."

"Unless a god made it," Ivy said with a shudder.

Belika marched into the patch of light around Ivy carrying the slinger they had conscripted.

She held the goblin forward. "This smelly rat say the place with the elves is very near. Through the hallway past the golem."

The goblin squirmed in her grasp, but nodded enthusiastically and spoke rapidly. She listened for a bit. "He say, says, it safe, about a thousand feet—I think, he just used how long to walk through I try and make better description. You come out on ledge over great evil place. The bad elves are there."

Ty pulled the maps he had drawn with Saelenia and put them onto the ground, smoothing them out. He traced the path they had taken, and the most likely path they would take when they followed cowardly slinger's directions.

He glanced up. "I know Helryn openly admitted that they had been to the temple of Xalkri, but this confirms it. We're headed directly into the ruins of the temple where the Crone claimed that both the claws of Foriveltain and the hero's regalia are. I suspect that this is also where he has been getting all his advanced gear. I think he set up his new slave society in the ruins."

Ivy put her hand on Ty's shoulder and massaged it slowly. "So... what does that mean?"

"Well, in addition to trying to convince Helryn to give up his dark ways, I think we can possibly grab the claws and the regalia—supposedly, they were in containers that would only open to my touch."

"Why your touch?" Dalryn asked. "What's so special about you, you onion?"

"My connection to the Crone. She put them away and locked them to her own magical signature, but she says I carry it now, through the dungeon."

Dalryn folded his arms, tower shield and all, across his chest, which nearly hid his helmeted face. "Some people have all the luck."

Ty rolled his eyes and tried not to laugh at the ridiculous frame that Dalryn cut as he tried to glower them all while appearing to be little more than a badly posed statue. Ivy also snickered slightly.

"We have things to do," Belika said. "You want me to cut stupid smelly guy loose or keep to make sure he told true?" She held the goblin forward again. Ty moved slightly to the side to see that she was gripping him with shadow-extended hands by his back.

That has to hurt. "We can let him go—his directions confirm what the maps were saying."

Belika released the goblin, who dropped to his knees, spoke rapidly in the pidgin blood tribes cant he spoke, and then scrabbled to his feet and disappeared into the darkness of the cavern systems.

Ty thought it likely the poor sap would die to giant spiders or the equivalent on the way out, but he wished him the best of luck... and if he had wanted a safe life, he shouldn't have thunked Ty in the head with a nearly lethal stone throw.

Dalryn started walking toward the tunnel they had been directed to, and Ty, Ivy, and Belika fell in behind them. As they went, Ty saw that the metal ran from the ritual all the way down the tunnel.

Ty wondered if they would survive encountering Helryn. He had to imagine that Dalryn's father had extremely impressive gear from adventuring down here, between the armor and his eye... and Ty knew Helryn had the wealth to have lots of other gear as well. He was also at least Level Thirteen. Not an easy opponent if it came to that.

And who was to say what happened, a hundred feet beneath the earth in the ancient ruins? Ty's death would have no witness.

The group walked down the twisting, rounded tunnel more quietly than Ty could remember them ever being. Each stepped lightly, even Dalryn in his armor, and no one spoke. Each fingered their weapons, except for Ivy, who absently petted Welwyn. Ty guessed they were all thinking the same thing—they were going to confront someone whose temper had led him to truly interesting horrors, including mass slaughter and attacking his own children with near-lethal intent.

As they got closer, the air itself filled with magic—Ty could sense numerous types, with a predominance of Body, Soul, and a type he was unfamiliar with. But all of it felt corrupted—dark and polluted, like the beasts that had once attacked him and occupied the ruins still.

The tunnel opened up into the edge of a truly huge cavern. It stretched over a thousand feet in each direction, and was about fifty feet from floor to ceiling, curving up near the outside rim. He could see a tunnel entering closer to the base floor level, and another across the way that exited, but no other egress or entrance appeared to him.

The center was occupied by a massive temple or ritual—Ty wasn't even sure what it was. It appeared to be a building shaped like a massive slug with thirty-seven tentacles coming off of its back, each one of which stretched down to touch the top of another statue. In front of the building was a massive ritual space.

On the top of the ritual space was a smaller, living version of the building—a multi-tentacled slug. The magic that Ty had felt earlier was coming from the slug, radiating away from it in waves. It was so powerful that a full five hundred feet away he could feel it. Around the ritual were five elves and hundreds of goblins. Each of the goblins was tied in chains and placed over metal imbedded in the ground that led to the ritual.

Ty recognized four of the five elves—the count and countess Grayshore, as well as their son, Jacinth Grayshore. The fourth was Helryn, and the last was a female that mostly appeared to be an elf, but with blood-red hair, an unnatural color for any race Ty knew about, and certainly for any elven subrace.

Ty could sense the magic leaving each of the five, as well as the hundreds of goblins. And each of the goblins was also slowly losing blood, which trickled sideways across the floor, slowly absorbing into the monstrosity on the ritual plinth.

"What's... what's happening?" Ivy said, her voice quavering.

"I think your dad is trying to return an Ancient One god to power, right now, in front of us. This wasn't about building a society that had slaves in the depths. He must have his sights on a greater prize—the throne."

Chapter Forty-Six

SUMMONUS INTERRUPTUS

Ivy stared at Ty with wide eyes. "Why?"

Ty's eyes flickered around, trying to find the solution. "Because he can't accept that King Leo doesn't want the old kingdom, with its privileges for elves and slave status for most non-elves, back. At least I assume that's why. I can't think of another reason."

"What... what do we do?" she asked.

Ty stared at the magical metal that ran down the tunnel and past where they were. It went toward the main ritual, but it was shattered. However, past the point it was broken, it connected to the plinth—and the hundreds of goblins that were on the ritual as well.

"We have to stop the Ancient One god from manifesting, no matter what," Ty said. "Try and get your dad to stop, but if he doesn't stop instantly, we need to try and kill him, just to disrupt the ritual, if nothing else."

Ivy and Dalryn stared at Ty for a second, but then Dalryn nodded. "Yeah. You're right, Ty. Whatever the cost is, we must stop this. He's too far gone—the father I knew, that once taught me, would never have agreed to summoning an evil god."

Ty couldn't see his face behind his helm and in the semi-darkness, but Dalryn's voice was deadly serious.

Ivy didn't speak.

"Alright, let's move. I'm going to go down there"—Ty pointed to the spot just past the break in the metal leading to the ritual—"and take a defensive position. I think I can manage to end the ritual quickly."

Dalryn just nodded, his helm making it a ponderous movement. Ty ran forward, and the soft patter of feet—and clank of Dalryn's sabatons—told him that he was being followed.

The slug swelled in size as more magic and blood flowed across the grounds, and the chained goblins writhed in pain as Ty reached his destination.

In the chaos of the summoning, and among the screams and metallic clank of the chains of the goblins, no one had heard them.

Ty reached the break point. Multiple bits of the metal were across the ground, including one rune-covered spike of metal with a medium-sized magical crystal in it—worth about ten gold. Ty's greed briefly overtook him, and he grabbed the foot-long ritual fragment.

"Really? Looting now?" Dalryn said, his voice filled with disdain.

Ty flushed in embarrassment, but it hadn't cost them any time—and it might make for an excellent research project or something to feed the dungeon.

"Be ready," Ty said, grimacing at what he was about to do. He had once bemoaned his dungeon needing to kill... Ty did what he believed he must, and triggered his ability. He brought forth his new, more powerful shock shield while standing on the metal.

Instantly, lightning poured through the entire assemblage. First the avatar went crazy, its tentacles spiking outward, stiff, as the whole thing quivered. But it couldn't contain the magnified magic. It ran throughout the entire ritual. The goblins, who had already been writhing in pain, began to scream with more intensity as lightning poured into them.

The Grayshores, all of them, screamed in agony as lightning poured into them. But Helryn merely grimaced and stepped back. The blood-haired elf also grimaced, but as the lightning hit her, something disrupted. As she stepped back, tiny horns appeared on her head, a red tail and batwings grew behind her, and an orb of blood appeared in front of her head.

The older Grayshores managed to pull back, but as Ty poured power into his shocking shield, Jacinth smoked, his skin blistering at points, and finally his metallic black hair lighting on fire. He was trapped in a silent scream as he roasted, face to the ceiling, neck muscles taut in agony. He finally fell sideways, bounced slightly off the ritual, and went limp with finality, unmoving.

None of the goblins moved, either. The smell of burnt meat filled the cavern. Ty got another three hundred and seventy experience—one for each rounded-up fraction of an experience he had gotten per goblin that died.

Well, that's done it, Ty thought with disgust, mostly at himself for the horror he had just committed. But the dead goblins were nothing compared to what an elder god would do... and the slug also slumped. It started to slowly dissolve into nothingness even as Ty watched.

Count Grayshore was staring at the horned elf—which Ty recognized as a 'demoness' from the blood abyss. He had watched his king fight one before. It was a being with magic focused on control and blood manipulation.

The denizens of the blood abyss had been behind the fall of the first Averian Empire, allies to the orcs, and Grakith elf-breaker, the leader of the horde, had been half-demon.

"You... you're allied with the Blood Abyss?" the count asked, staring at Helryn.

The countess walked to her son, slowly, across the burned field of dead goblins.

Helryn grimaced. "I did what was necessary to *win*, and restore the kingdom."

Count Grayshore kept staring at Helryn. "The denizens of the Blood Abyss are the ones that helped the orcs overthrow us in the first place—they're the reason the bastard is king now!"

Ty started to walk forward cautiously, and his team—Dalryn, Belika, and Ivy—followed.

Helryn pulled his sword, a giant murdering blade. "I did what had to be done, *Count*. Certainly what had to be done if you want that title to mean anything ever again."

Countess Grayshore reached her son, dropping to her knees, and touched him gently on his wrist. Skin flaked around her finger, and she gagged and furiously wiped her hand on her dress, her eyes watering. She pulled back a bit, and stared up to Ty where he approached. "You... you *killed* my *son*, halfbreed!"

Count Grayshore was still watching Helryn, but his wife turned to him. "Celmir, they *killed our son!*"

Count Grayshore turned to face the group, then pulled his sword. "We'll discuss this later," he said to Helryn, who grimaced and nodded.

"Dad, you're under arrest!" Dalryn called out.

Ty grimaced. *That's the wrong approach to take with him.*

"You would arrest *me*? Your father? The *duke*?"

Dalryn nodded, his own sword out and extended, the tip close to the ground, his tower shield blocking his whole left side.

Helryn sneered at him. "By what authority, whelp?"

"The authority of King Leo Stardew the first," Dalryn said. "This is treason."

"*The King does not command me!*" Helryn screamed. "He's not even the king! He's some jumped-up bastard that was never confirmed! I am still a duke of the realm, and the ranking member of this society! A society that needs to be reformed, for it is a society that accepts and promotes the human *worms* that killed your mother!"

"Maybe be a bit more... conciliatory?" Ty suggested quietly to Dalryn as the count came toward them, circling right. His wife was also now standing, and her hand was outstretched. *Although I bet I can't make it up to those two.*

Ty was feeling very nervous about the confrontation. They were equally matched in numbers, but their enemies had about five levels each and better gear both. And none of his own team were seasoned combatants—they were all new to it.

Dalryn acted as if he didn't hear Ty, raised the tip of his sword till it pointed at his father. "Father, you are a *villain*. You told me the stories, every night, of our wonderful lost land. Yeah, some of the stuff here sucks by comparison to the stories. But *you* taught me that the elder gods enslaved elves, and the blood abyss allied with orcs and goblins to break our realm. You're bringing back the villains from our storybooks!"

Helryn hesitated, and Ty turned to Ivy, gently nudging her. She had always gotten the best reactions from her father. Not good... but the best.

Before she could talk, however, Count Graywater screamed out, "It doesn't matter, Helryn! We can decide what to do later, but if any of them tell the king or his guards he'll feed us to his damnable dragon. And this miserable half-breed killed my son. Take them!"

Count Graywater put his words into actions, rushing at Ty as fast as he could across the ground, his eyes glued to Ty in his rage as he did.

Ty was amazed the count would make that mistake, given what just happened. But he wasn't about to look a gift horse in the mouth. He waited till just before his boot came down on a metal piece of the ritual and fired off his shocking shield again.

The count let out a slight scream, but Ty didn't get a chance to figure out if he would have fried the count this time because his wife unleashed a blast of fire from her own hand. Ty dodged to the side—off the metal ritual connector—and yelled as fire singed him. He mentally dismissed the notification of losing a few health as he fired a lightning bolt back at the countess, who yelped, twitched, and dropped.

Dalryn charged the count, who hadn't quite recovered, and slammed his tower shield into him, knocking him to the ground. Dalryn stabbed into the count's middle, punching through his armor but drawing very little blood—Ty assumed that the count had very high Health, but wasn't sure.

Ivy touched Ty, healing him, and he fired lightning into the downed count, who also got kicked in the head by a metal-shod boot from Dalryn, which merely knocked one tooth out and split the lip rather than shattering the count's face, confirming Ty's theory about the count's Health. But the damage was taking a toll, and Dalryn simply powered through the flame that the countess hit him with.

Belika appeared behind the count and stabbed into the side of his neck with shadow-sharpened blades, and blood started to flow down the count's neck.

But the count managed to get a healing potion out and down it, keeping himself alive—but just barely.

We might win! Ty exulted.

Then Helryn entered the fight.

Chapter Forty-Seven

THE FATHER

"Traitors!" Helryn cried as he rushed into the fight, his red plate tinted almost bloody in the dim light of the cavern. His speed was supernatural, and his leaps easily cleared the various metal protrusions that Ty might have used to stop him with magnified electrical power. He bore down on them like living doom.

He flew across the space and slammed his sword at Dalryn as hard as possible. Dalryn blocked with his tower shield, but the power of the blow knocked him back. He windmilled to keep from falling, and in the moment when he threw his shield out, Helryn kicked his son in the chest, knocking him a good five feet and onto his back. Dalryn let out a pained grunt as Helryn raised his sword above his prostrate son, his face hidden behind his helm, the glint of his diamond eye the only part visible.

Frustrated he couldn't finish an enemy off but desperate to save Dalryn, Ty turned from Count Grayshore. The count rolled away as everyone turned their attention to saving Ivy's brother, fiddling at his belt for more potion.

Ty flung lightning at Helryn. His bolt arced over, briefly connecting Ty to his paramour's father, and Helryn twitched. But he still brought his sword down on Dalryn. Ivy screamed.

The sword wobbled very slightly, likely from Ty's shock, but still came down hard on Dalryn's chest, ripping into his armor and slashing his chest open in a spray of blood. Dalryn screamed, but still rolled to the side as Helryn brought his blade back up again almost immediately.

"Save him!" Ivy screamed, and Ty tried, firing his lightning into the duke again. At the same time, Belika appeared and stabbed as hard as he could into the chink in the armor at the back of Helryn's knee. Helryn shrugged off the lightning damage and didn't go down to the stab in the knee. But he was off-balanced by the dual attacks enough that he missed Dalryn with his next swing.

The spiders rushed in, and Shreve died to a single downward thrust of the sword. Ivy staggered and screamed wordlessly as her bonded familiar died.

Belika tried to stab Helryn again, but he kicked back, using his sword and other leg to post himself. Belika took the armored boot to the center of her face, blood spewing from her nose and mouth and she went hurtling away from Helryn.

Ty started to throw lightning again, but the demoness landed in front of him, red-pink bat-wings splayed, and immediately lunged forward, her human hands outstretched with decidedly inhuman claws at the end. Ty was caught flat-footed, and she slashed him across the face. She barely drew blood, but a notification appeared in his mind's eye.

Ty fails Toughness check against drain. Leo loses 1 Strength, 1 Endurance, and 1 Toughness. Unknown Blood Abyss denizen gains the same.

Ty dismissed it as the demoness licked her lips. "Your power will be mine shortly, and all your friends and lovers shall die or serve me."

"Verdant," Ty sarcastically muttered, too distracted by his plight to engage in any further banter with his enemy.

She'll defeat me with stat drain in no time, and my team needs me, Ty thought desperately, his mind reaching for any plan he could think of.

She's physically very weak and doesn't appear to have any ar-mor, but has a ton of magical power...

He stared at the ritual—the ritual that pulled magic along it and multiplied it. An idea formed.

He began to back away, very obviously in the direction of the ritual, stepping over a broken piece of the ritual as he did.

The demoness eyed where he was walking and laughed. "Such an obvious ploy, but you'll not catch me so easily."

She leapt upward, her wings propelling her, and dropped down next to Ty, keeping him between the ritual and her, then lunged for him.

Ty ripped the spiked shard of the ritual he had pocketed ear-lier out and stepped into her attack. Her eyes widened as he al-lowed the claws to scrap him, and Ty dismissed the further stat drain notification. But Ty also stabbed her in the abdomen with the shard, as hard as he could. The sheer surprise of the attack seemed to be enough, as his shard sank six inches into her stom-ach. Her own lunge also carried her forward, and Ty stuck his foot on top of hers and allowed them to both fall back.

She landed and drove the spike another four inches into her abdomen as she landed on top of Ty, pressed against him in a parody of a lover's embrace. She screamed and reared back, still on top of Ty. He figured he had seconds to finish her, and rolled to the side, taking her down, then grabbed the loose chunk of metal, and touched one end to the spike in her abdomen and the other to the ritual, praying each piece would work even though they were broken.

Magic ripped from her and along the line that Ty had formed. Her eyes bulged and she thrashed, but Ty held her for the few seconds until he felt no more magic passing down the ritual.

Without her essence and magic, she was just a winged woman, considerably lower weight than Ty. He grabbed her and turned his shocking shield ability on. She stiffened and then twitched wildly, her face locked in a rictus as she bit down on her own tongue, spewing blood. Ty grimaced as the blood flowed across him and the demoness twitched and spasmed, locked in his embrace, a gross and terrible mockery of a loving hug. It took almost half a minute of her violently twitching and shaking before she died.

Unlike his lightning, touching her never caused his shocking shield to pass back into Ty for some reason, for which he was profoundly glad.

Experience poured into Ty as he pushed the charred body off him. The demoness had been Level Thirteen. Killing her, solo, had been worth an *insane* amount of experience. He cleared to Level Ten, and almost to Level Eleven as power poured into him. He had an insane amount of new ability options, but no time to figure them out, because he needed to change the dynamic of this fight quickly. He took the third rank of the lightning ability, and stood to see his enemies.

Dalryn had regained his footing, and he and Ivy were fighting Helryn together. But while Ivy was untouched, Dalryn was covered in numerous wounds, his armor was rent in places, and his shield was on the ground, somehow.

Belika was nowhere to be seen, and Welwyn was bisected on the ground as well, her corpse mingling with Shreve's.

Ty saw that the count and countess had reached each other, and were healed. Even as Ty watched, assuming they would reenter the fight and change the balance again, the countess fired a bolt of magical flame at Dalryn, who dodged and caught his father's sword on his both—but then was off balance when Helryn slammed his leg, metal-shod shin first, into his own son's leg. Dalryn grunted and fell to one knee, hand down to catch himself, as the metal of his armor bent inward and bled his leg.

Ty used his go-to move and hit Helryn with lightning, considerably more powerful lightning than it had been before Ty killed the demoness, even as Helryn raised his sword. This time, Helryn twitched badly, and Dalryn was able to roll back and away, and then come to his feet.

The count charged into the fray, making sure not to touch any of the metal lines of the giant ritual again. He headed toward Ivy, and Dalryn stumbled into his path, half-crippled. Ivy touched him from behind, and Dalryn began to heal.

But he was outmatched by both men, and while he had been surviving and delaying against one, with help, he couldn't handle both.

Ty hit Helryn *again* with his lightning, wondering how much health the Level Thirteen warrior had, as he was doing ten to fifteen every hit, enough to kill a normal human. But Helryn still managed to bring his blade around and slashed at Dalryn. Dalryn, now with a two-handed grip, set his own blade and prevented his father's attack.

But Count Grayshore's blade swung down onto Dalryn's exposed wrists. Dalryn screamed, followed closely by Ivy, as his hands and sword flew away from him in a spray of blood. It was too much even for their guardian, and he fell to the ground, trying to cradle his gushing wrists to his chest.

Helryn's blade rose again, but the duke hesitated, his sword in the air.

Count Graywater didn't. He stepped past the downed Dalryn and slashed his sword downward at Ivy's head. She tried to dodge, but the sword cut deep into, just beside her neck, breaking through her armor. She screamed and fell to her knees as well, hands scrabbling at her own wound.

Chapter Forty-Eight

THE LAST REMNANTS

Ty screamed as well, watching as his lover and his party all sank toward defeat and death, regretting the path he had taken, although he had no idea what other path he could have chosen when they had been summoning an Ancient One god remnant.

Fire slammed into Ty as he held his own hand out.

The count put his foot on Ivy's armored chest, braced himself, and pushed her as he pulled his sword. Ivy fell back and lay on the ground, staring up as blood pooled around the junction of her shoulder and neck. He raised his own sword high for a killing blow.

Ty had a moment of clarity, a possible path forward, based on what he knew of everyone. "You'll never get to tell her you're sorry, Helryn!"

Helryn was still, staring down.

Ty pushed lightning into the count, ignoring the massive damage he was taking, and the agony, from the countess's attacks in his bid to somehow save Ivy. He ran forward, hand outstretched, pouring essence into his attacks.

Count Graywater started to bring his own sword down toward Ivy, but it was his own chest that exploded outward, a sword sticking out through it. He half turned, staring back at Helryn. Ty would have given gold to see the expression on

Helryn's face as he skewered his strongest and oldest remaining supporter through the chest.

The count's lips silently shaped the question "Why?" before blood spilled from them, and the count collapsed to his knees, jarringly, his sword dropping from nerveless fingers before he fell forward on top of Ivy, his metallic black hair coming to land in the pool of blood forming around her neck.

The countess screamed, and turned her fire to Helryn.

Helryn turned, briefly, staring at Ty with such over-riding hatred that Ty almost stopped running forward.

But Helryn had already been damaged heavily by Ty's lightning, and couldn't just stand in the countess's fire. He turned and ran, dodging and weaving. Ty was tempted to finish him—he knew he could. But Ivy was lying on the ground, nearly dead, and Dalryn's life blood was pumping from his wrists.

He heard a choked-off scream from the countess and the fire stopped, but Ty ignored it as he rushed over and took a potion from his belt, pouring the liquid into Ivy's mouth. She swallowed involuntarily, probably not completely lost to her wounds. The blood stopped running from her neck, and her eyes flooded open.

"Did..." she coughed, blood spittle coming from her own mouth, a sign that Count Graywater had cut so deep he must have nicked a lung. She coughed a tiny bit more blood, wiped her hand across her lips, and then stared at Ty with her indigo eyes. "Did we win?"

"Heal Dalryn," Ty said, turning to glance at the countess as another experience notification hit him. He had made Level Eleven, even though the count and countess had been split four ways.

Ivy reached out, still on her back, and touched Dalryn. His wounds closed, and his arms started to freakishly regrow. *Thank the good gods those weren't entropic,* Ty thought to himself.

He glanced around, in time to catch Helryn running down a tunnel leading out from the giant room. He glanced over at the countess. She was on the ground, facedown, and Belika was standing on her and pulling her knives from the countess's back. Belika's face was a shattered mess, but she had obviously found a way to help the team again.

"Sort of. Your father got away, and I think we'll see him again. But there is no Ancient One godling running around, I slew a denizen of the Blood Abyss, and the entire Grayshore family is slain."

Ty reached out and pulled the aforementioned dead count off of Ivy, then helped her to sit up. She coughed out a bit more red-flecked spittle, obviously clearing her lungs. Ty stroked her copper-green metallic hair as he held her.

"Your father... saved you, kinda," Ty said.

"Horse apples, ya freakin' tuber," Dalryn said as he sat up as well, staring at his regrowing limbs.

Ty raised an eyebrow.

"Horse apples," Dalryn repeated, his voice bitter as he looked down at his hands. "Dad was the *source* of every wound we took, every damage inflicted. He's been the source of every bad thing that happened to me except maybe Zadrid's Hallow. But in your case, you made me a ton of levels and such. What did Dad do?"

"Dad...tries," Ivy said. "And he could have finished us off, but instead he killed the count and saved me."

"Yeah, Ivy," Dalryn repeated, standing and grabbing his sword with his newly regrown right hand. "He saved *you*. It's always you that brings him back after he hurts us, even when it's you he hurts. But he didn't change. We talked, back when we were building Ty's house. He promised to be better. But he never *is*! He just gets more and more evil. He was allied with a Blood Abyss demon and an Ancient One godling, for Iluvin's sake!"

Ivy leaned away from Dalryn, eyes wide, as he yelled.

Dalryn pulled himself together and spoke more sedately. "He's obviously been planning this for a while, Sis. Which means he was planning to overthrow the king with dark powers even while he talked to Ty and me. He was deceptive even then. I'm sure he told himself it was for you and me. But whatever he planned to accomplish, how do you think that reality would have turned out for Ty?"

Ty was shocked by how much insight Dalryn was showing. It was notably unlike him.

Ivy hesitated a moment before speaking. "Well, I mean, he spared me, so there has to be some—"

"No," Dalryn said, loudly again as he slashed his sword through the air. "No. I'm done, Ivy. Done. Done with Dad, done with being a part of this family, 'cept I'm still your brother. I renounce being a Mosstone."

Ivy's eyes widened at Dalryn's vehemence.

And he wasn't done. "Ty's right, and Dad's wrong. You know it too, whether you want to admit it or not. But *I* don't worship the god of kindness. *I'm* going where I'm wanted. I'm gonna make myself worthy of Val, and when I am, I'm gonna ask her to marry me. If she says yes, I'm gonna take the Belmoria name. I want nothing to do with Dad, not ever again."

Ty laughed. He couldn't help it. "Wow... so, my reward for saving you is you're gonna propose to my sister? Seems more like a penalty."

Dalryn glanced at him. His eyes were watering and his brow furrowed. For a moment, Ty was worried his joke hadn't landed as intended.

But something in Ty's demeanor must have gotten through because Dalryn started to chuckle as well, a sound more exhaustion than humor. "Ha ha, you onion."

Ivy's brother took a deep breath. "I thought *maybe* I was wrong about you, once upon a time... very wrong. In fact, I was *about* to tell my sister that if she had an ounce of sense, she'd beg you to marry her as well. I was going to say, unlike with me and your sister, that you were already worthy of her. That she should take your name as well, join me in switching families, and stop thinking about Dad at all... I was even going to tell her that you're probably the only one in this whole screwed-up world that is actually worthy of taking care of my idiotically self-sacrificing, too-precious-for-this-world, cinnamon roll of a sister. The only one I would trust to keep her happy, anyway."

Dalryn smirked at him. "Hell, I was even thinking of apologizing. But you'll never hear me say sorry now."

Ty was deeply touched. "Thanks, Dalryn. Seriously."

Ivy slipped her hand into Ty's.

"Bah," Dalryn said, waving his hand at Ty. "Mushy stuff is stupid and pointless. Don't go mooning over me, you tuber, no matter how verdant I am."

"It was a beautiful twenty seconds," Ty quipped.

Ivy half-laughed, then hiccupped.

"So what now?" Dalryn asked, glancing around the giant, ritual-and-corpse-filled chamber they were in.

Belika walked up next to them. "We going to loot?"

All of their eyes turned to the massive statue that was the temple, and the tentacles that came down onto the thirty-seven remaining tentacles.

Why did Saelenia store the parts here? Ty thought. *Is it because the hero she fought beside was an Ancient One himself? Was this some tribute to him, in front of his people?*

Ty walked among the statues. All of them were statues of ancient ones—scaled humanoids with long, scaled tails that replaced their legs. Almost all had hands that had once carried things, and those were gone. But a few statues still had things in them.

One had a bow. The string appeared to be sinew, and the wood was filled with entropy shards. Another carried a knife which appeared to be made of bone, but for an eye, still moving, in the handle. It blinked at Ty.

But around each, Ty could feel an indescribably powerful magic, protective and deadly. As much as the objects, made with shards and obviously artifacts, called to him, he moved past them.

Eventually, he came to a statue at the far end of the room. It featured an ancient one that appeared barely different than any of the others to Ty. But in its hand it had a feathered spear, and in its other, a small wooden shield. It wore a cape composed entirely of feathers and crystals. The objects themselves weren't artifacts... but at the feet of the hero was a pair of claws, each as big as a man's torso. Ty could feel magic radiating from them— bestial and fierce, but also protective and primeval.

These had to be the claws of Foriveltain, and the regalia of Zar'Kre'Rusth, the hero that had stood beside Saelenia in her first great fight against evil, in the form of Zadrid.

But a powerful magic was still guarding the objects, a field that Ty could sense easily with his occult. He suspected a fly that had never encountered magic in its life could have felt it.

Ivy slipped her hand into his. "We... you don't have to, Ty. I don't know what I would do if I lost you now."

Ty was hesitant himself, but he wasn't going to wait. "The Crone said I would be able to overcome this. And we need to be stronger, is what I learned from that fight. I killed a Blood Abyss demoness with tricks. I stopped the summoning of a godling. But still, in the end, if your father had stayed on his path, we would have lost."

He turned and kissed Ivy, then pulled back and held her. "I would have lost you forever. I cannot remain less than I could be."

He let go of her and reached for the claws, willing the field to fade.

And it did. No flash, no fuss, no great magic, no contest of wills. It simply disappeared like it had never been.

Dalryn laughed.

Ty did as well. "I guess I should be happy that we had one thing go anticlimactically. But still... that was a disappointment, yeah."

"Thank Cerivae Nerithin for small favors," Ivy muttered.

Ty yanked the first claw up. It had to weigh at least fifty pounds, and he staggered under the huge weight. "Get the other one, Dalryn, please."

"Seriously? My reward for helping you is to carry a bunch of shit?"

"There's the whining brother of my lover I knew and missed, back already."

Dalryn flushed. "Shut up, you tuber. I was doing it." He picked the other one up, almost effortlessly, and held it over his back. "Someone tie this to me."

"With what?" Ivy asked.

"We may need to use the chains on the goblin corpses," Ty said. "Meanwhile, Belika, can you loot the corpses of the Grayshore family and the demoness? We need to get some treasure to Dalryn, after all. I think he earned it."

"Damned right I did. We all did. The King can't complain we didn't clear the danger from the undercity—we just cleared more danger than anyone expected."

Dalryn smiled again. "We're heroes."

Chapter Forty-Nine

DÉJÀ VU, JUST A BIT

The Emerald Bee was as busy as Ty had ever seen it, despite the early morning hour. Every seat was taken; a few people were even standing. The waitresses, beautiful elves all in dresses, hurried between tables, bringing food, wine, and, in a few cases, magical honey. During the clearing of the Temple District, quite a few of the citizens of Star Port had managed to make a level. Many of those here had already decided to celebrate, even though King Leo had yet to give his formal speech and hand out accolades.

"So what's next?" Dalryn asked as he set three glasses of wine and a mug of beer down on the table with a series of light wood-on-wood clacks. He had fetched them himself to save on waiting for the waitresses.

"Next?" Forli asked, now dressed in a beautiful green dress and white sash ensemble herself, dressed much as the higher social status elves of the city did. "You guys are doing more? Why is there a next?"

Dalryn gave a snort, pushing his chair back and trying to kick his feet on the table. He started to answer, but his chair back hit a waitress, who gave a slight gasp and bumped into the table behind Dalryn.

He leaned forward again, flushing. "Sorry, sorry."

The waitress smiled. "No problem, Dalryn. I know you're the dungeon lord's sidekick. Thanks for helping him make everything better!"

Most of the table giggled, and Ty gave his own snort of laughter.

The waitress wandered off as Dalryn flushed. "I hate that."

"Is it better, or worse, than being the consort of Val?" Ivy asked through her own giggling.

"Someday, sister, when you least expect it..."

There was more laughter, but Dalryn took a sip of his wine and then addressed the original question. "*Of course* we're gonna do more. This onion"—Dalryn clapped Ty on the back—"can't ever stop doing. Usually doing crazy things. So we'll keep pushing, I assume. The question is not *if* we'll be doing something, it's *what* we'll be doing."

All eyes turned to Ty. "I don't want to stop. I want to keep growing, help everyone, become even more important. Protect everything and everyone I care about. Dalryn is right about that."

There were nods around the table.

Ty took a deep breath, smiling. "The dungeon is almost Level Six. I need to add Foriveltain's claws to it, to advance the build. I also need to continue working on my new orchard town and business. We need to make more levels. But after that..."

"Yes?" Forli asked, leaning forward.

"After that, we'll head through the portal. The lands of Ice Pines await us. My power will grow if I get more dungeon cores... and make you all dungeon lords."

"Pft. I don't have the perk, you tuber," Dalryn said. "You can't be a dungeon lord without the perk."

Ty leaned forward. "*I* have a special ability, to appoint dungeon lords under me, whether they have the perk or not. There's a whole different dimension out there, through Ygg'drasil. More magical than ours, perhaps with its own dungeon cores. The king is making this city a dimensional nexus, but *I'm* going to make it a city of dungeons."

Dalryn nodded thoughtfully. "So, Ice Pines next?"

Ty nodded. "We'll rest, level a bit, grow the dungeon... but yes, then Ice Pines. That's where our real greatness will begin."

Raised eyebrows met his pronouncement, but Ty just smiled back.

***

Ty stared up at the king as he spoke from a raised dais in the middle of the Grand Plaza. The morning light was glorious, and birds sang in the air. A crowd of elves was gathered below the dais, hundreds of them. It had been a productive couple of days clearing the temple district... the most important, by far, had been the first. But the king had waited till after the work was done, and the district declared safe, to make a speech.

To the side, he could see the marble gazebo, with one dryad and one wolf pillar. He strongly suspected that they would be joined by a bear pillar before long.

King Leo's long golden hair was a sign of his elf heritage, and once, Ty would have felt jealous that his own copper hair was the only part of him that reflected his elf heritage.

But now, he wasn't a half-elf. He was a master dryad, a dungeon lord, and, after the fight with Helryn and his cronies and a few more days of clearing the undercity, he was Level Eleven. He had embraced who he was, fully and truly.

"Thank you, again, Vyrneal Ironbranch, for service to the Kingdom of Averia above and beyond!"

There was clapping and a few laughs in the crowd as the one-handed part-time guard made his way down from the dais, waving his stump at his fellow citizens.

King Leo smiled from his platform, and his eyes sought out Ty. "But there is one last person we need to honor, more than any other. One that we honor for his actions in securing the second district, but who we should honor for far more than just that."

A few people cheered, including most of Ty's adventuring party. They knew whom the king was referring to. "Tywyndyll il Belmoria, if you'll please join me."

Ty smiled, glancing around. Gone was the indifference from last time, and also gone were the hostile stares from the last time. Everyone smiled at Ty, and clapped. He saw the adventurers in a block, near the entrance to the guild. At the front of them, *** clapped and raised her hands, both giving the three-fingered elf gesture of approval.

She shouted out, "Go, dungeon lord!"

Ty smiled and waved to her as he walked down the path that parted for him, citizens smiling and clapping his back, even among the slightly more reserved elves.

Ty's family—his father, his mother and her new husband and child, and Val all cheered him as well from the sides. He smiled and waved at them as well as he ascended the steps to the dais.

Ty glanced out at the crowds of his new home, the City of Star Port. The citizens cheered him. Elf, human, rabbit-kin, even dragon, it didn't matter. His acclaim seemed universal.

Ty almost cried with joy. He had dreamed of moments like this, but never truly believed he would have it. But this was real. He pinched himself, forgetting for a moment that anything less than a knife wouldn't hurt him through his new skin.

But his eyes sought his friends, the ones that had helped get him here. He saw Belika, face healed from Ivy's magic. She gave him a single brusque nod, but she was smiling as well.

Dalryn, who was standing tall and proud, his powerful frame nearly human, representative of the levels he had gained. Dalryn was giving him the typical elven symbol of approval, the informal three fingers everyone else did. But his grin, unusual on the disagreeable elf, threatened to split his face in half.

Forli stood among other dryads that had come, or that lived in the city. She was cheering openly and jumping up and down.

Lastly, his eyes rested on Ivy. Her indigo eyes met his as she twirled her finger in her copper-patina hair.

She mouthed, "I love you," to him.

"First and foremost, I want to give Ty royal acknowledgement. Although I've already appointed two dukes to rule over far realms, I would appoint another noble. Ty has taken land north of the city, the first person to re-establish an orchard town outside the city. I have been resistant to expanding where people can be put in danger, but Ty has shown himself resourceful and powerful both. I extend to him the title of Baron of Belmoria, ruler of the first of the orchard towns."

The King kept talking, and then there was a brief ceremony in which Ty re-swore himself to the kingdom. Ty didn't really listen or pay attention through the cheers, however. He just basked in the moment. *A formal noble title... wow. I've recovered the family name to a degree. I'm still a dungeon lord. I have good friends, lovers, and prestige. The respect of my people.*

Apparently, when it came to greatness, the third time was the best attempt.

The End: Book One

THANK YOU SO MUCH FOR READING!

If you want to read more in the series before it's officially pub-lished, several books are up on my Patreon, right now. Please go here to read:

https://www.patreon.com/Johnstovall

If you want to hear updates, please join my newsletter!!
https://john-stovall-author.com/join-john-newsletter/

If you liked this book, please check out Elf Empire, the story of King Leo, an isekai'd engineer that starts the rebuilding of the Kingdom of Averia that Ty lives in. It's an adventure novel with kingdom building and some slice of life, four books writ-ten, two already out as of the publication of this novel, and the third one coming 11/8/2023.

If you're interested in more work from me, please check out my author page for other series, or sign up for the newsletter! I have a lot of other books, both dungeon core and adventure, quite a few set in the Toth universe!

www.ingramcontent.com/pod-product-compliance
Lightning Source LLC
Chambersburg PA
CBHW051939240626
47153CB00005B/1559